P9-CDG-314

Acclaim for HARUKI MURAKAMI'S

THE ELEPHANT VANISHES

"Charming, humorous and frequently puzzling...*The Elephant Vanishes* [is] fun to read." — *The New York Times*

"These stories show us Japan as it's experienced from the inside.... [They] take place in parallel worlds not so much remote from ordinary life as hidden within its surfaces.... Even in the slipperiest of Mr. Murakami's stories, pinpoints of detail flash out...warm with life, hopelessly — and wonderfully — unstable."
— *The New York Times Book Review*

"A stunning writer at work in an era of international literature."
— *Newsday*

"Murakami is one of the great Japanese masters, and his style is sexy, funny, mysterious, and always coolly deadpan."
— *Details*

"Enchanting...intriguing...all of these tales have a wonderfully surreal quality and a hip, witty tone. Mr. Murakami has pulled off a tricky feat, writing stories about people who are bored but never boring. He left me lying awake at night, hungry for more."
— *Wall Street Journal*

"What's unique to Murakami's stories is that they manage to kindle up all sorts of feelings at once.... Reading *The Elephant Vanishes* leaves you wanting more." — *Philadelphia Inquirer*

"*The Elephant Vanishes*, through [its] bold originality and charming surrealism, should win the author new readers in this country." — *Detroit Free Press*

ALSO BY HARUKI MURAKAMI

Dance, Dance, Dance

Hard-Boiled Wonderland and the End of the World

A Wild Sheep Chase

HARUKI MURAKAMI

THE

ELEPHANT

VANISHES

Haruki Murakami was born in Kyoto in 1949 and grew up in Kobe. He is the author of *A Wild Sheep Chase; Hard-Boiled Wonderland and the End of the World;* and *Dance, Dance, Dance.* He lives with his wife in Cambridge, Massachusetts.

VINTAGE

INTERNATIONAL

THE ELEPHANT VANISHES

STORIES BY

HARUKI MURAKAMI

TRANSLATED FROM THE JAPANESE
BY ALFRED BIRNBAUM AND
JAY RUBIN

VINTAGE INTERNATIONAL
VINTAGE BOOKS
A DIVISION OF RANDOM HOUSE, INC.
NEW YORK

FIRST VINTAGE INTERNATIONAL EDITION, JULY 1994

Copyright © 1993 by Haruki Murakami

All rights reserved under International and Pan-American Copyright Conventions. Published in the United States by Vintage Books, a division of Random House, Inc., New York, and simultaneously in Canada by Random House of Canada Limited, Toronto. Originally published in hardcover by Alfred A. Knopf, Inc., New York, in 1993.

Some of the stories in this collection originally appeared in the following publicatons: *The Magazine (Mobil Corp.):* "The Fall of the Roman Empire, the 1881 Indian Uprising, Hitler's Invasion of Poland, and the Realm of the Raging Winds" (in a previous translation; translated in this volume by Alfred Birnbaum), *The New Yorker:* "TV People" and "The Wind-up Bird and Tuesday's Women" (translated by Alfred Birnbaum), "The Elephant Vanishes" and "Sleep" (translated by Jay Rubin), and "Barn Burning" (in a previous translation; translated in this volume by Alfred Birnbaum) *Playboy:* "The Second Bakery Attack" (translated by Jay Rubin, January 1992).

Library of Congress Cataloging-in-Publication Data
Murakami, Haruki, 1949–
    The elephant vanishes / stories by Haruki Murakami; translated
    from the Japanese by Alfred Birnbaum and Jay Rubin. — 1st Vintage
    International ed.
      p.   cm.
    ISBN 0-679-75053-3
    I. Title.
    PL856.U673E44   1993   93-43493
    895.6'35—dc20   CIP

Book design by Iris Weinstein

Author photograph © Jerry Bauer

Manufactured in the United States of America
10 9 8 7 6 5 4

cont**EN T**s

THE WIND—UP BIRD AND
TUESDAY'S WOMEN   3

THE SECOND BAKERY ATTACK   3 5

THE KANGAROO COMMUNIQUÉ   5 1

ON SEEING THE 100% PERFECT GIRL
ONE BEAUTIFUL APRIL MORNING   6 7

SLEEP   7 3

THE FALL OF THE ROMAN EMPIRE,
THE 1881 INDIAN UPRISING, HITLER'S
INVASION OF POLAND, AND THE REALM
OF RAGING WINDS   1 1 1

LEDERHOSEN   1 1 9

BARN BURNING   1 3 1

CONTENTS

THE LITTLE GREEN MONSTER   151

FAMILY AFFAIR   157

A WINDOW   187

TV PEOPLE   195

A SLOW BOAT TO CHINA   217

THE DANCING DWARF   241

THE LAST LAWN OF THE AFTERNOON   267

THE SILENCE   291

THE ELEPHANT VANISHES   307

THE ELEPHANT VANISHES

THE
WIND-UP BIRD AND
TUESDAY'S
WOMEN

I'M IN THE KITCHEN cooking spaghetti when the woman calls. Another moment until the spaghetti is done; there I am, whistling the prelude to Rossini's *La Gazza Ladra* along with the FM radio. Perfect spaghetti-cooking music.

I hear the telephone ring but tell myself, Ignore it. Let the spaghetti finish cooking. It's almost done, and besides, Claudio Abbado and the London Symphony Orchestra are coming to a crescendo. Still, on second thought, I figure I might as well turn down the flame and head into the living room, cooking chopsticks in hand, to pick up the receiver. It might be a friend, it occurs to me, possibly with word of a new job.

"I want ten minutes of your time," comes a woman's voice out of the blue.

"Excuse me?" I blurt back in surprise. "How's that again?"

"I said, just ten minutes of your time, that's all I want," the woman repeats.

I have absolutely no recollection of ever hearing this woman's voice before. And I pride myself on a near-perfect ear for voices, so I'm sure there's no mistake. This is the voice of a woman I don't know. A soft, low, nondescript voice.

"Pardon me, but what number might you have been calling?" I put on my most polite language.

"What difference does that make? All I want is ten minutes of your time. Ten minutes to come to an understanding." She cinches the matter quick and neat.

"Come to an understanding?"

"Of our feelings," says the woman succinctly.

I crane my neck back through the door I've left open to peer into the kitchen. A plume of white steam rising cheerfully from the spaghetti pot, and Abbado is still conducting his *Gazza*.

"If you don't mind, I've got spaghetti on right now. It's almost done, and it'll be ruined if I talk with you for ten minutes. So I'm going to hang up, all right?"

"Spaghetti?" the woman sputters in disbelief. "It's only ten-thirty in the morning. What are you doing cooking spaghetti at ten-thirty in the morning? Kind of strange, don't you think?"

"Strange or not, what's it to you?" I say. "I hardly had any breakfast, so I was getting hungry right about now. And as long as I do the cooking, when and what I eat is my own business, is it not?"

"Well, whatever you say. Hang up, then," says the woman in a slow, sappy trickle of a voice. A peculiar voice. The slightest emotional shift and her tone switches to another frequency. "I'll call back later."

"Now, wait just one minute," I stammer. "If you're selling something, you can forget right now about calling back. I'm unemployed at present and can't afford to buy anything."

"I know that, so don't give it another thought," says the woman.

"You know that? You know what?"

"That you're unemployed, of course. That much I knew. So cook your spaghetti and let's get on with it, okay?"

"Hey, who the—" I launch forth, when suddenly the phone

goes dead. Cut me off. Too abruptly to have set down the receiver; she must have pressed the button with her finger.

I'm left hanging. I stare blankly at the receiver in my hand and only then remember the spaghetti. I put down the receiver and return to the kitchen. Turn off the gas, empty the spaghetti into a colander, top it with tomato sauce I've heated in a saucepan, then eat. It's overcooked, thanks to that pointless telephone call. No matter of life-and-death, nor am I in any mood to fuss over the subtleties of cooking spaghetti—I'm too hungry. I simply listen to the radio playing send-off music for two hundred fifty grams of spaghetti as I eagerly dispatch every last strand to my stomach.

I wash up plate and pans while boiling a kettle of water, then pour a cup for a tea bag. As I drink my tea, I think about that phone call.

So we could come to an understanding?

What on earth did that woman mean, calling me up like that? And who on earth was she?

The whole thing is a mystery. I can't recall any woman ever telephoning me before without identifying herself, nor do I have the slightest clue what she could have wanted to talk about.

What the hell, I tell myself, what do I care about understanding some strange woman's *feelings,* anyway? What possible good could come of it? What matters now is that I find a job. Then I can settle into a new life cycle.

Yet even as I return to the sofa to resume the Len Deighton novel I took out of the library, the mere glimpse out of the corner of my eye of the telephone sets my mind going. Just what were those *feelings* that would take ten minutes to come to an understanding about? I mean, really, *ten minutes to come to an understanding of our feelings?*

Come to think of it, the woman specified precisely ten minutes right from the start. Seems she was quite certain about that exact amount of time. As if nine minutes would have been too short, eleven minutes maybe too long. Just like for spaghetti al dente.

What with these thoughts running through my head, I lose track of the plot of the novel. So I decide to do a few quick exercises, perhaps iron a shirt or two. Whenever things get in a muddle, I always iron shirts. A habit of long standing with me.

I divide the shirt-ironing process into twelve steps total: from (1) Collar <Front>, to (12) Cuff <Left Sleeve>. Absolutely no deviation from that order. One by one, I count off the steps. The ironing doesn't go right if I don't.

So there I am, ironing my third shirt, enjoying the hiss of the steam iron and the distinctive smell of hot cotton, checking for wrinkles before hanging up each shirt in the wardrobe. I switch off the iron and put it away in the closet with the ironing board.

I'm getting thirsty by now and am heading to the kitchen for some water when once more the telephone rings. Here we go again, I think. And for a moment I wonder whether I shouldn't just ignore it and keep on going into the kitchen. But you never know, so I retrace my steps back to the living room and pick up the receiver. If it's that woman again, I'll say I'm in the middle of ironing and hang up.

The call, however, is from my wife. By the clock atop the TV, it's eleven-thirty.

"How're things?" she asks.

"Fine," I answer, relieved.

"What've you been up to?"

"Ironing."

"Is anything wrong?" my wife asks. A slight tension invades her voice. She knows all about my ironing when I'm unsettled.

"Nothing at all. I just felt like ironing some shirts. No particular reason," I say, switching the receiver from right hand to left as I sit down on a chair. "So, is there something you wanted to tell me about?"

"Yes, it's about work. There's the possibility of a job."

"Uh-huh," I say.

"Can you write poetry?"

"Poetry?" I shoot back in surprise. What's this about poetry?

"A magazine company where someone I know works puts out this popular fiction monthly for young girls and they're looking for someone to select and brush up poetry submissions. Then they want one leadoff poem each month for the section. The work's easy and the pay's not bad. Of course it's only part-time, but if things go well they might string you on for editorial work and—"

"Easy?" I say. "Now hold on just one minute. I've been looking for a position with a law firm. Just where do you come up with this brushing up of poetry?"

"Well, didn't you say you used to do some writing in high school?"

"In a newspaper. The high-school newspaper. Such-and-such team won the soccer meet; the physics teacher fell down the stairs and had to go to the hospital. Dumb little articles like that I wrote. Not poetry. I can't write poetry."

"Not real poetry, just the kind of poems high-school girls might read. They don't even have to be that good. It's not like they're expecting you to write like Allen Ginsberg. Just whatever you can make do."

"I absolutely cannot write make-do poetry," I snap. The very idea.

"Hmph," pouts my wife. "This talk of legal work, though. Nothing seems to be materializing, does it?"

"Several prospects have come my way already. The final word'll be in sometime this week. If those fall through, maybe then I'll consider it."

"Oh? Have it your way, then. But say, what day is it today?"

"Tuesday," I tell her after a moment's thought.

"Okay, then, could you stop by the bank and pay the gas and phone bills?"

"Sure thing. I was going out to shop for dinner soon, anyway. I can take care of it at the same time."

"And what are we having for dinner?"

"Hmm, let's see," I say. "Haven't made up my mind yet. I thought I'd decide when I go shopping."

"You know," my wife starts in with a new tone of voice, "I've been thinking. Maybe you don't really need to be looking for work."

"And why not?" I spit out. Yet more surprises? Is every woman in the world out to shake me up over the phone? "Why don't I have to be looking for work? Another three months and my unemployment compensation is due to run out. No time for idle hands."

"My salary's gone up, and my side job is going well, not to mention we have plenty in savings. So if we don't go overboard on luxuries, we should be able to keep food on the table."

"And I'd do the housework?"

"Is that so bad?"

"I don't know," I say in all honesty. I really don't know. "I'll have to think it over."

"Do think it over," reiterates my wife. "Oh, and by the way, has the cat come back?"

"The cat?" I'm caught off guard, then I realize I'd completely forgotten about the cat all morning. "No, doesn't seem so."

"Could you scout around the neighborhood a bit? He's been gone four days now."

I give some spur-of-the-moment reply, switching the receiver back to my right hand.

"My guess is that the cat's probably in the yard of that vacant house at the end of the passage. The yard with the stone bird figurine. I've seen him there often enough. You know where I'm talking about?"

"No, I'm afraid I don't," I say. "And since when have you been snooping around in the passage on your own? Never once have you mentioned—"

"You'll have to forgive me, but I've got to hang up. Have to be getting back to work. Don't forget about the cat, now."

And the telephone cuts off.

I sit there looking dumbly at the receiver a second before setting it down.

Now why would my wife know so much about the passage? I can't figure it out. She'd have to climb over a high cinder-block wall to get there from our yard, and what possible reason was there to go to all that trouble to begin with?

I go to the kitchen for that drink of water, turn on the FM radio, and trim my nails. They're doing a feature on Robert Plant's new album. I listen to two songs before my ears start to hurt and I switch the thing off. I go out to the porch to check the cat's food dish; the dried fish I put in the previous night hasn't been touched. Guess the cat really hasn't come back.

Standing there on the porch, I look at the bright spring sun slicing down into our tiny yard. Hardly the sort of yard that lingers fondly in the mind. The sun hits here only the briefest part of the day, so the soil is always dark and damp. Not much growing: just a couple of unremarkable hydrangeas. And I'm not terribly crazy about hydrangeas in the first place.

From a nearby stand of trees comes the periodic scree-ee-eech of a bird, sharp as a tightening spring. The "wind-up bird," we call it. My wife's name for it. I have no idea what it's really called. Nor even what it looks like. Nonetheless, this wind-up bird is there every morning in the trees of the neighborhood to wind things up. Us, our quiet little world, everything.

As I listen to the wind-up bird, I'm thinking, Why on earth is it up to me to go searching after that cat? And more to the point, even if I do chance to find it, what am I supposed to do then? Drag the cat home and lecture it? Plead with it—Listen, you've had everyone worried sick, so why don't you come home?

Great, I think. Just great. What's wrong with letting a cat go where it wants to go and do what it wants to do? Here I am, thirty years old, and what am I doing? Washing clothes, planning dinner menus, chasing after cats.

Not so long ago, I'm thinking, I was your regular sort of guy. Fired up with ambition. In high school, I read Clarence Darrow's autobiography and decided to become a lawyer. My grades weren't bad. And in my senior year I was voted by my classmates runner-up "Most Likely to Succeed." I even got accepted into the law department of a comparatively reputable university. So where had I screwed up?

I plant my elbows on the kitchen table, prop up my chin, and think: When the hell did the compass needle get out of whack and lead my life astray? It's more than I can figure. There's nothing I can really put my finger on. No setbacks from student politics, no disillusionment with university, never really had much girl trouble. As near as I can tell, I've had a perfectly normal existence. Yet one day, when it came time for me to be graduating, I suddenly realized I wasn't the same guy I used to be.

Probably, the seed of a schism had been there all along, however microscopic. But in time the gap widened, eventually taking me out of sight of who I was supposed to be. In terms of the solar system, if you will, I should by now have reached somewhere between Saturn and Uranus. A little bit farther and I ought to be seeing Pluto. And beyond that—let's see—was there anything after that?

At the beginning of February, I quit my longtime job at the law firm. And for no particular reason. It wasn't that I was fed up with the work. Granted, it wasn't what you could call an especially thrilling job, but the pay wasn't bad and the atmosphere around the office was friendly enough.

My role at the firm was, in a word, that of full-time office boy.

Although I still believe I did a good job of it, by my standards. Strange as it may sound coming from my own mouth, I find I'm really very capable when it comes to carrying out immediate tasks around the office like that. I catch on quickly, operate methodically, think practically, don't complain. That's why, when I told the senior partner I wanted to quit, the old man—the father half of this "—— and Son, Attorneys at Law"—even offered to raise my salary if I'd just stay on.

But stay on I didn't. I don't exactly know why I up and quit. Didn't even have any clear goals or prospects of what to do after quitting. The idea of holing up somewhere and cramming for one more shot at the bar exam was too intimidating. And besides, I didn't even especially want to become a lawyer at that point.

When I came out and told my wife over dinner I was thinking of quitting my job, all she said was "Fair enough." Just what that "Fair enough" was supposed to mean, I couldn't tell. But that was the extent of it; she didn't volunteer a word more.

When I then said nothing, she spoke up. "If you feel like quitting, why don't you quit? It's your life, you should do with it as you like." She'd said her piece and was straightaway deboning the fish on her plate with her chopsticks.

My wife does office work at a design school and really doesn't do badly, salarywise. Sometimes she gets illustration assignments from editor friends, and not for unreasonable pay, either. I, on my part, was eligible for six months' unemployment compensation. So if I stayed home and did the housework regularly every day, we could even swing a few expenses like eating out and dry cleaning, and our life-style wouldn't change all that much from when I was working and getting a salary.

So it was I quit my job.

AT TWELVE-THIRTY I go out shopping as usual, a large canvas carryall slung over my shoulder. First I stop by the bank to pay the gas and telephone bills, then I shop for dinner at the supermarket, then I have a cheeseburger and coffee at McDonald's.

I return home and am putting the groceries away in the refrigerator when the telephone rings. It sounds positively irritated, the way it rings. I leave a half-opened plastic tub of tofu on the table, head into the living room, and pick up the receiver.

"Finished with your spaghetti?" It's that woman again.

"Yeah, I'm done," I say. "But now I have to go out looking for the cat."

"Can't that wait ten minutes? Looking for the cat!"

"Well, ten minutes, maybe."

What the hell am I doing?, I think. Why am I obliged to

spend ten minutes passing the time of day with some strange woman?

"Now, then, perhaps we can come to an understanding," says the woman, nice and quiet. From the sound of it, this woman—whoever she is—is settling back into a chair there on the other end of the line, crossing her legs.

"Hmm, I don't know about that," I say. "Some people, ten years together and they still can't understand each other."

"Care to try?" the woman teases.

I undo my wristwatch and switch on the stopwatch mode, then press the timer's start button.

"Why me?" I ask. "Why not ring up somebody else?"

"I have my reasons," the woman enunciates slowly, as if measuredly masticating a morsel of food. "I've heard all about you."

"When? Where?"

"Sometime, somewhere," the woman says. "But what does that matter? The important thing is *now*. Right? What's more, talking about it only loses us time. *It's not as if I had all the time in the world, you know*."

"Give me some proof, then. Proof that you know me."

"For instance."

"How about my age?"

"Thirty," the woman answers on the spot. "Thirty and two months. Good enough?"

That shuts me up. The woman really *does* know me. Yet no matter how I rack my brains, I can't place her voice. I simply couldn't have forgotten or confused someone's voice. Faces, names—maybe—but voices, never.

"Well, now, it's your turn to see what you can tell about me," she says suggestively. "What do you imagine from my voice? What kind of woman am I? Can you picture me? This sort of thing's your forte, isn't it?"

"You got me," I say.

"Go ahead, try," the woman insists.

I glance at my watch. Not quite a minute and a half so far. I heave a sigh of resignation. Seems I've already taken her up, and once the challenge is on, there's no turning back. I used to have a knack for guessing games.

"Late twenties, university graduate, native Tokyoite, upper-middle-class upbringing," I fire away.

"Amazing," says the woman, flicking a cigarette lighter by the receiver. A Cartier, by the sound of it. "Keep going."

"Fairly good-looking. At least, you yourself think so. But you've got a complex. You're too short or your breasts are too small or something like that."

"Pretty close," the woman giggles.

"You're married. But all's not as smooth as it could be. There are problems. No woman without her share of problems would call up a man and not give her name. Yet I don't know you. At least I've never talked with you before. This much imagined, I still can't picture you."

"Oh, really?" says the woman in a hush calculated to drive a soft wedge into my skull. "How can you be so sure of yourself? Mightn't you have a fatal blind spot somewhere? If not, don't you think you'd have pulled yourself a little more together by now? Someone with your brains and talent."

"You put great stock in me," I say. "I don't know who you are, but I should tell you I'm not the wonderful human being you make me out to be. I don't seem to be able to get things done. All I do is head off down detour after detour."

"Still, I used to have a thing for you. A long time ago, that is."

"A long time ago, you say," I prompt.

Two minutes fifty-three seconds.

"Not so very long ago. We're not talking history."

"Yes, we *are* talking history," I say.

Blind spot, eh? Well, perhaps the woman does have a point. Somewhere, in my head, in my body, in my very existence, it's as if there were some long-lost subterranean element that's been skewing my life ever so slightly off.

No, not even that. Not *slightly* off—*way* off. Irretrievably.

"I'm in bed right now," the woman says. "I just took a shower and have nothing on."

That does it, I think. *Nothing on?* A regular porno tape this is getting to be.

"Or would you rather I put on panties? How about stockings? Do they turn you on?"

"Anything's fine. Do what you like," I say. "But if you don't mind, I'm not that kind of a guy, not for this sort of stuff over the telephone."

"Ten minutes, that's all. A mere ten minutes. That's not such a fatal loss, is it? I'm not asking for anything more. That much is plain goodwill. But whatever, just answer the question. Do you want me naked? Or should I put something on? I've got all kinds of things, you know. Garter belts and . . ."

Garter belts? I must be going crazy. What woman has garter belts in this day and age? Models for *Penthouse,* maybe.

"Naked is fine. And you don't have to move," I say.

Four minutes down.

"My pubic hair is still wet," the woman says. "I didn't towel it dry. So it's still wet. Warm and oh so wet."

"Listen, if you don't mind—"

"And down below that, it's a whole lot warmer. Just like hot buttercream. Oh so very hot. Honest. And what position do you think I'm in right now? I have my knee up and my left leg spread out to the side. It'd be around 10:05 if I were a clock."

I could tell from the way she said it that she wasn't making this up. She really did have her legs spread to 10:05, her vagina warm and moistened.

"Caress the lips. Gently, slowly. Then open them. Slowly, like that. Now caress them gently with the sides of your fingers. Oh, yes, slowly . . . slowly. Now let one hand fondle my left breast, from underneath, lifting gently, tweaking the nipple just so. Again and again. Until I'm about to come—"

I hang up without a word. Then I roll over on the sofa, smoke a cigarette, and gaze up at the ceiling, stopwatch clicked at five minutes twenty-three seconds.

I close my eyes and darkness descends, a darkness painted blind with colors.

What is it? Why can't everyone just leave me in peace?

Not ten minutes later, the telephone rings again, but this time I don't pick up. Fifteen rings and it stops. I let it die, and all gravity is displaced by a profound silence. The stone-chill silence of boulders frozen deep into a glacier fifty thousand years ago. Fifteen rings of the telephone have utterly transformed the quality of the air around me.

A LITTLE BEFORE two o'clock, I climb from my back-yard over the cinder-block wall into the passage. Actually, it's not the corridor you'd expect a passage to be; that's only what we call it for lack of a better name. Strictly speaking, it isn't a corridor at all. A corridor has an entrance and an exit, forming a route from one place to another.

But this passage has neither entrance nor exit, and leads smack into a cinder-block wall at one end and a chain link fence at the other. It's not even an alleyway. For starters, an alley has to at least have an entrance. The neighbors all call it "the passage" for convenience sake.

The passage meanders between everyone's backyards for about six hundred feet. Three-foot-something in width for the most part, but what with all the junk lying around and the occasional hedge cropping in, there are places you can barely squeeze through sideways.

From what I've heard—this is from a kindly uncle of mine who rents us our house ridiculously cheap—the passage used to have an entrance and an exit, offering a shortcut across the block, street-to-street. But then, with the postwar boom years, new homes were built in any available space, hemming in the common ground to a narrow path. Which ushered in the none-too-inviting prospect of having strangers walking through backyards, practically under the eaves, so the residents surreptitiously covered the entrance. At first an innocent little bush barely disguised the opening, but eventually one resident expanded his yard and extended his cinder-block wall to completely seal it over. While the corresponding other aperture was screened off with a chain link fence to keep the dogs out. It hadn't been the residents who made use of the passage to begin with, so no one complained about its being closed at both ends. And anyway, closing it wouldn't hurt as a crime-prevention measure. Thus, the path went neglected and untrafficked, like some abandoned canal, merely serving as a kind of buffer zone between the houses, the ground overgrown with weeds, sticky spiderwebs strung everywhere a bug could possibly alight.

Now, why should my wife frequent such a place? It was beyond me. Me, I'd only set foot in the passage one time before. And she can't even stand spiders.

Yet when I try to think, my head's filled to bursting with some gaseous substance. I didn't sleep well last night, plus the weather's too hot for the beginning of May, plus there was that unnerving telephone call.

Oh, well, I think, might as well look for that cat. Leave later developments for later. Anyway, it's a damn sight better to be out and about than to be cooped up indoors waiting for the telephone to ring.

The spring sun cuts clean and crisp through the ceiling of overhanging branches, scattering patches of shadow across the ground. With no wind, the shadows stay glued in place like fateful stains. Telltale stains sure to cling to the earth as it goes around and around the sun for millennia to come.

Shadows flit over my shirt as I pass under the branches, then return to the ground. All is still. You can almost hear each blade of grass respiring in the sunlight. A few small clouds float in the sky, vivid and well formed, straight out of a medieval engraving. Everything stands out with such clarity that I feel buoyant, as if somehow my body went on forever. That, and it's terribly hot.

I'm in a T-shirt, thin cotton slacks, and tennis shoes, but already, just walking around, my armpits and the cleft of my chest are drenched with sweat. I'd only just this morning pulled the T-shirt and slacks out of storage, so every time I take a deep breath there's this sharp mothball smell, as if some tiny bug had flown up my nose.

I keep an eye peeled to both sides and walk at a slow, even pace, stopping from time to time to call the cat's name in a stage whisper.

The homes that sandwich the passage are of two distinct types and blend together as well as liquids of two different specific gravities. First there are the houses dating from way back, with big backyards; then there are the comparatively newer ones. None of the new houses has any yard to speak of; some don't have a single speck of yard space. Scarcely enough room between the eaves and the passage to hang out two lines of laundry. In some places, clothes actually hang out over the passage, forcing me to inch past rows of still-dripping towels and shirts. I'm so close I can hear televisions playing and toilets flushing inside. I even smell curry cooking in one kitchen.

The old homes, by contrast, hardly betray a breath of life. Judiciously placed hedges of cypress and other shrubbery guard against inquisitive eyes, although here and there you catch a glimpse of a well-manicured spread. The houses themselves are of all different architectural styles: traditional Japanese houses with long hallways, tarnished copper-roofed early Western villas, recently remodeled "modern" homes. Common to all, however, is the absence of any visible occupants. Not a sound, not a hint of life. No noticeable laundry, either.

It's the first time I've taken in the sights of the passage at leisure, so everything is new to my eyes. Propped up in a corner of one backyard is a lone, withered, brown Christmas tree. In another yard lies several childhoods' worth of every plaything imaginable—a virtual scrap heap of tricycle parts, a ringtoss set, plastic samurai swords, rubber balls, a toy turtle, wooden trucks. One yard sports a basketball hoop, another a fine set of garden chairs and a rattan table. By the look of them, the chairs haven't been sat on in months (maybe years), they're so covered with dirt; the tabletop is rain-plastered with lavender magnolia petals.

One house presents a clear view into its living room through large glass sliding doors. There I see a kidney-shaped sofa with matching lounge furniture, a sizable television, a cellarette topped with a tank of tropical fish and two trophies of some sort, and a decorator floor lamp. It all looks as unreal as a set for a TV sitcom.

In another yard, there's a massive doghouse penned in with wire screening. No dog inside that I can see, though. Just a wide-open hole. I also notice that the screening is stretched shapeless, bulging out as if someone or something had been leaning into it for months.

The vacant house my wife told me about is only a little farther along, past the one with the doghouse. Right away, I can see it's vacant. One look tells you that this is not your scant two- or three-months' absence. The place is a fairly new two-story affair, yet the tight shutters look positively weather-beaten and the rusted railings around the upstairs windows seem about ready to fall off. The smallish yard hosts a stone figurine of a bird with wings outstretched atop a chest-high pedestal surrounded by a thicket of weeds, the taller stalks of goldenrod reaching clear to the bird's feet. The bird—beats me what kind—finds this encroachment most distressing and flaps its wings to take flight at any second.

Besides this stone figurine, the yard has little in the way of decoration. Two beat-up old vinyl chaises are parked neatly under the eaves, right next to an azalea blazing with ethereally crimson blossoms. Otherwise, weeds are about all that meets the eye.

I lean against the chest-high chain link fence and make a brief survey of the yard. Just the sort of yard a cat would love, but hope as I might, nothing catty puts in an appearance. On the rooftop TV aerial, a pigeon perches, its monotone carrying everywhere. The shadow of the stone bird falls across the tangle of weeds, their blades cutting it into fragments of different shapes.

I take a cigarette out of my pocket, light up, and smoke it, leaning against the fence the whole while. The pigeon doesn't budge from the aerial as it goes on cooing nonstop.

Cigarette finished and stamped out on the ground, I still don't move for the longest time. Just how long, I don't know. Half asleep, I stare dumbly at the shadow of the bird, hardly even thinking.

Or maybe I am thinking, somewhere out of range of my conscious mind. Phenomenologically speaking, however, I'm simply staring at the shadow of the bird falling over stalks of grass.

Gradually I become aware of something—a voice?—filtering into the bird's shadow. Whose voice? Someone seems to be calling me.

I turn around to look behind me, and there, in the yard opposite, stands a girl of maybe fifteen or sixteen. Petite, with short, straight hair, she's wearing dark sunglasses with amber frames and a light-blue Adidas T-shirt with the sleeves snipped off at the shoulders. The slender arms protruding from the openings are exceedingly well tanned for only May. One hand in her shorts, the other on a low bamboo gate, she props herself up precariously.

"Hot, huh?" the girl greets me.

"Hot all right," I echo.

Here we go again, I think—again. All day long it's going to be females striking up conversations with me, is it?

"Say, you got a cigarette?" the girl asks.

I pull a pack of Hope regulars from my pocket and offer it to her. She withdraws her hand from her shorts, extracts a cigarette, and examines it a second before putting it to her mouth. Her mouth is small, with the slightest hint of a curl to her upper lip. I strike a match and give her a light. She leans forward, revealing an ear: a freshly formed, soap-smooth, pretty ear, its delicate outline glistening with a tracery of fine hairs.

She parts her lips in the center with an accomplished air and lets out a satisfied puff of smoke, then looks up at me as if she's suddenly remembered something. I see my face split into two reflections in her sunglasses. The lenses are so hideously dark, and even mirror-coated, that there's no way to make out her eyes.

"You from the neighborhood?" the girl asks.

"Yeah," I reply, and am about to point toward the house, only I can't tell if it's really the right direction or not. What with all these odd turns getting here. So—what's the difference, anyway?—I simply point any which way.

"What you been up to over there so long?"

"I'm looking for a cat. It's been missing three or four days now," I explain, wiping a sweaty palm on my slacks. "Someone said they saw the cat around here."

"What kind of cat?"

"A big tom. Brown stripes, a slight kink at the end of its tail."

"Name?"

"Name . . . ?"

"The cat's. It has a name, no?" she says, peering into my eyes from behind her sunglasses—at least, I guess she is.

"Noboru," I reply. "Noboru Watanabe."

"Fancy name for a cat."

"It's my brother-in-law's name. My wife's little joke. Says it somehow reminds her of him."

"Like how?"

"The way it moves. Its walk, the sleepy look in its eyes. Little things."

Only then does the girl smile. And as she lets down her façade, I can see she's much more of a child than I thought on first impression. The quirky curl of her upper lip shoots out at a strange angle.

Caress, I can swear I hear someone say. The voice of that telephone woman. Not the girl's voice. I wipe the sweat from my brow with the back of my hand.

"A brown-striped cat with a kink in the end of its tail, huh?" the girl reconfirms. "Wearing a collar?"

"A black flea collar."

The girl gives it a cool ten-, fifteen-second think, hand still resting on the gate. Whereupon she flicks the stub of her cigarette to the ground by my feet.

"Stamp that out for me? I got bare feet."

I conscientiously grind it out under the sole of my tennis shoe.

"That cat, I think I just may have seen it," she phrases guardedly. "I didn't get as far as noticing the tip of its tail, but yes, there was a brown tom. Big, probably wearing a collar."

"When did you see it?"

"Yeah, when was that? I'm sure I must've seen it lots of times. I'm out here in the yard nearly every day sunbathing, so one day just blends into the rest. But anyway, it'd have to be within the last three or four days. The yard's a cat shortcut, all kinds of cats scooting through all the time. They come out of the Suzukis' hedge there, cut across our yard, and head into the Miyawakis' yard."

So saying, she points over at the vacant house. Same as ever, there's the stone bird with outspread wings, goldenrod basking in the spring rays, pigeon cooing away on the TV aerial.

"Thanks for the tip," I tell her.

"Hey, I've got it, why not come into the yard here and wait? All the cats pass this way anyhow. And besides, if you keep snooping around over there, somebody's going to mistake you for a burglar and call the cops. Wouldn't be the first time."

"But I can't just hang around waiting for a cat in somebody else's yard."

"Sure you can, like, it's no big deal. Nobody's home and it's dead boring without someone to talk to. Why don't we just get some sun, the two of us, until the cat shows up? I've got sharp eyes, I'd be a real help."

I look at my watch. Two thirty-six. All I've got left to do today is take in the laundry and fix dinner.

"Well, okay, I'll stay until three o'clock," I say, still not really grasping the situation.

I open the gate and step in, following the girl across the grass, and only then do I notice that she's dragging her left leg slightly. Her tiny shoulders sway with the periodic rhythm of a crank grinding mechanically to the left. She stops a few steps ahead of me and signals for me to walk alongside her.

"Had an accident last month," the girl says simply. "Was riding on the back of someone's bike and got thrown off. No luck."

Two canvas deck chairs are set out in the middle of the grass. A big blue towel is draped over the back of one chair, and the other is occupied by a red Marlboro box, an ashtray, and a lighter tossed together with a large radio-cassette player and some magazines. The volume is on low, but some unidentifiable hard-rock group is playing.

She removes the clutter to the grass and asks me to sit down, switching off the music. No sooner am I seated than I get a clear view of the passage and the vacant house beyond. I can even see the white stone bird figurine and the goldenrod and the chain link fence. I bet she's been watching me from here the whole time.

The yard is large and unpretentious. The grass sweeps down a gentle slope, graced here and there with plants. To the left of the deck chairs is a sizable concrete pond, which obviously hasn't seen much use of late. Drained of water, it presents a greenish, discolored bottom to the sun, like some overturned aquatic creature. The elegant beveled façade of an old Western-style house, neither particularly large nor all that luxurious, poses behind a stand of trees to the rear. Only the yard is of any scale or shows any real upkeep.

"Once, I used to part-time for a lawn-mowing service," I say.

"Oh yeah?" says the girl without much interest.

"Must be hard work maintaining a yard this big," I comment, looking around me.

"Don't you have a yard?"

"Just a little yard. Two, three hydrangeas, that's about the size of it," I say. "You alone here all the time?"

"Yeah, you said it. Daytime, I'm always alone. Mornings and evenings, a maid comes around, though otherwise I'm alone. Say, how about a cold drink? There's even beer."

"No, I'm fine."

"Really? Like, it's no big deal."

"I'm not thirsty," I say. "Don't you go to school?"

"Don't you go to work?"

"No work to go to," I admit.

"Unemployed?"

"Kind of. I quit."

"What sort of work were you doing?"

"Lawyer's gofer," I equivocate, taking a slow, deep breath to cut the talk. "Collecting papers from city-hall and government offices, filing materials, checking case precedents, taking care of court procedures, busywork like that."

"But you quit?"

"Correct."

"Your wife work?"

"She does," I say.

I take out a cigarette and put it to my mouth, strike a match, and light up. The wind-up bird screeches from a nearby tree. A good twelve or thirteen turns of the watch spring, then it flits off to another tree.

"Cats are always going past there," the girl remarks apropos of nothing, pointing over at the edge of the grass in front. "See that incinerator behind the Suzukis' hedge? Well, they come out from right next to it, run all the way across, duck under the gate, and make for the yard over there. Always the same route. Say, you know Mr. Suzuki? College professor, on TV half the time?"

"Mr. Suzuki?"

She goes on in some detail, but it turns out that I don't know our Mr. Suzuki.

"I hardly ever watch TV," I say.

"Horrible family," the girl sneers. "Stuck-up, the whole lot of them. TV people are all a bunch of phonies."

"Oh?"

The girl picks up her Marlboros, takes one out, and rolls it around unlit between her fingers.

"Well, I suppose there's decent folk among them, but they're not my type. Now, the Miyawakis, they were okay people. Mrs. Miyawaki was nice. And Mr. Miyawaki, he ran two or three family restaurants."

"What happened to them?"

"Don't know," said the girl, flicking the end of her cigarette. "Probably owed money. There was a real commotion when they left. Been gone two years now, I guess. Dropped everything and just left. The cats just keep multiplying, no consideration. Mom's always complaining."

"Are there that many cats?"

She puts the cigarette to her lips and lights up with her lighter. Then nods.

"All kinds of cats. Some losing their fur, even a one-eyed cat . . . big lump of flesh where the eye was. Gross, huh?"

"Gross," I concur.

"I've got a cousin with six fingers. A girl, little older than me, has this baby pinkie right beside her little finger. Always keeps it neatly folded under, so you can barely tell. A real pretty girl."

"Hmm," I say.

"You think stuff like that's hereditary? Like, you know . . . runs in the blood?"

"I couldn't tell you," I say.

The girl says nothing for the moment. I smoke my cigarette and train my eyes on the cat path. Not a single cat has shown the whole time.

"Hey, you sure you won't drink something? I'm going to have a cola," says the girl.

"No thanks," I tell her.

The girl gets up from her deck chair and disappears into the shade, dragging her leg; meanwhile, I pick up one of the magazines lying by my feet and flip through the pages. Contrary to what I'd expected, it's a men's monthly. The center spread has a woman sitting in an unnatural pose, legs wide apart, so that you can see her genitals and pubic hair through a sheer body stocking. Never a dull moment, I think, and put the magazine back where I found it, then redirect my gaze toward the cat path, arms folded across my chest.

After what seems like ages, the girl returns, glass of cola in hand. She's shed her Adidas T-shirt for a bikini top with her shorts. It's a small bra that shows off the full shape of her breasts, with tie-strings in back.

For sure, it's one hot afternoon. Just lying there in the sun on the deck chair, my gray T-shirt is blotched dark with sweat.

"Tell me," the girl picks up where she left off, "suppose you found out the girl you liked had a sixth finger, what would you do?"

"I'd sell her to the circus," I say.

"Really?"

"Just kidding," I come back, startled. "I probably wouldn't mind."

"Even if there's the possibility of passing it on to your kids?"

I give it some thought.

"I don't think I'd mind. One finger too many's no great harm."

"What about if she had four breasts?"

I think it over a while.

"I don't know," I say.

Four breasts? This conversation's going nowhere fast, so I decide to change the subject.

"How old are you?"

"Sixteen," the girl answers. "Just turned sixteen. Freshman in high school."

"But you're taking time off from school."

"Can't walk too much before my leg starts to hurt. Got a gash right by my eye, too. It's a pretty straight school, no telling

what kind of trouble I'd be in if they found out I hurt myself
falling off a bike . . . which is why I'm out sick. I can take a
whole year off if I want. I'm in no big hurry to graduate from
high school."

"Hmm" is all I can say.

"But anyway, back to what we were talking about, you said
you thought it was okay to marry a girl with six fingers, but
four breasts turned you off."

"I didn't say it turned me off, I just said I didn't know."

"Why don't you know?"

"I can't quite picture it."

"But you can picture a sixth finger."

"Sort of."

"What's the difference? Six fingers or four breasts?"

Once again, I give the matter some thought, but can't begin
to think of how to explain.

"Tell me, do I ask too many questions?" the girl asks, peering into my eyes from behind her sunglasses.

"You been told that?" I ask back.

"Sometimes."

"Nothing wrong with asking questions. Makes the other
person think."

"Most people, though, don't give me much thought," she
says, looking at the tips of her toes. "Everyone just gives the
usual nothing-doing answers."

I shake my head vaguely and to realign my gaze onto the cat
path. What the hell am I doing here? *There hasn't been one lousy
cat come past here yet.*

I shut my eyes for twenty or thirty seconds, arms folded
across my chest. Lying there, eyes closed, I can feel the sweat
bead up over different parts of my body. On my forehead, under
my nose, around my neck, the slightest sensations, as if tiny
moistened feathers had been floated into place here and there.
My T-shirt clings to my chest like a drooping flag on a doldrum
day. The sunlight has a curious weight as it seeps into me. I can
hear the tinkling of ice as the girl jiggles her glass.

"Go to sleep if you want. I'll wake you if I see your cat," the girl whispers.

I nod silently with eyes closed.

For the time being, there isn't a sound. That pigeon and the wind-up bird must have gone off somewhere. Not a breeze, not even a car starting. The whole while I'm thinking about that voice on the telephone. *What if I really did know the woman?*

Yet I can't recall any such woman. She's just not there; she's long departed from my consciousness. Only her long, long shadow trailing across my path, a vision from Chirico. An endless ringing in my ears.

"Hey, you asleep?" comes the girl's voice, so faint it's almost no voice at all.

"No, I'm awake," I answer.

"Can I get closer? It's easier for me to talk in a whisper."

"Go right ahead," I say, eyes still closed.

I listen as the girl slides her deck chair alongside mine, hear the dry clack of wooden frames touching.

Strange, I think, the girl's voice with my eyes closed sounds completely different from her voice with my eyes open. What's come over me? This has never happened to me before.

"Can I talk some?" the girl asks. "I'll be real quiet. You don't have to answer, you can even fall right asleep at any time."

"Sure," I say.

"Death. People dying. It's all so fascinating," the girl begins.

She's whispering right by my ear, so the words enter my body in a warm, moist stream of breath.

"How's that?" I ask.

The girl places a one-finger seal over my lips.

"No questions," she says. "I don't want to be asked anything just now. And don't open your eyes, either. Got it?"

I give a nod as indistinct as her voice.

She removes her finger from my lips, and the same finger now travels to my wrist.

"I think about what it would be like to cut the thing open

with a scalpel. Not the corpse. That lump of death itself. There's got to be something like that in there somewhere, I just know it. Dull like a softball—and pliable—a paralyzed tangle of nerves. I'd like to remove it from the dead body and cut it open. I'm always thinking about it. Imagining what it'd be like inside. It'd probably be all gummy, like toothpaste that cakes up inside the tube, don't you think? That's okay, you don't have to answer. All gooey around the outside, getting tougher the further in. That's why the first thing I'd do once I cut through the outer skin is scoop out all the glop, and there inside where it starts to firm up would be this teeny little core. Like a superhard ball bearing, don't you think?"

The girl gives a couple of short coughs.

"Lately, it's all I think about. Probably 'cause I've got so much free time every day. But really, I do think so. If I've got nothing to do, my thoughts just wander off far away. I get so far off in my thoughts, it's hard to find my way back."

At this, the girl takes her finger away from my wrist to drink the rest of her cola. I can tell from the empty-glass sound of the ice.

"It's okay, I'm keeping an eye out for the cat. Don't worry. As soon as I see Noboru Watanabe, I'll let you know. So you can keep your eyes closed. Noboru Watanabe's bound to come walking through here any minute now. I mean, all the cats take the same route, so he's got to show up. Let's just imagine while we wait. Like, Noboru Watanabe's getting closer, closer. He's coming through the grass, sneaking under a wall, stopping and sniffing the flowers, getting closer every minute. Try and picture him."

I play along and try to see the cat in my mind's eye, but it's all I can do to conjure up even the blurriest backlit snapshot of a cat. The bright sun burns through my eyelids, dispersing any dark areas of the image; on top of which, no matter how I try I just can't recall the little fur face with any accuracy. My Noboru Watanabe is a failed portrait, somehow distorted and unnatural.

Only the quirks are there; the basics are missing. I can't even remember how he walked.

The girl places her finger on my wrist once more and this time draws a pattern. An odd diagram of indeterminate configuration. While she diagrams my wrist, as if in unison I feel a wholly other variety of darkness infiltrating my mind. I must be falling asleep, I think. Not that I'm particularly sleepy, but something tells me I can't hold out against the inevitable. My body feels unseemingly heavy in the soft canvas curve of the deck chair.

Amid the gathering darkness, a clear image of Noboru Watanabe's four feet comes into my head. Four quiet brown paws with rubbery pads on the soles. Without a sound, they go traipsing over the terrain.

What terrain? Where?

I have no idea.

Mightn't you have a fatal blind spot somewhere? says the woman softly.

I AWAKE TO FIND I'm alone. Gone is the girl from the deck chair nestled next to mine. The towel and cigarettes and magazines remain, but the cola and radio-cassette player have disappeared.

The sun is slanting westward and I'm up to my ankles in the shade of the pine trees. The hands of my watch point to 3:40. I shake my head a few times as if rattling an empty can, get up from the chair, and take a look around. Everything looks the same as when I first saw it. Big lawn, dried-up pond, hedge, stone bird, goldenrod, TV aerial, no cat. No girl, either.

I plunk myself down on a shady patch of grass and run my palm over the green turf, one eye on the cat path, while I wait for the girl to return. Ten minutes later, there's still no sign of cat or girl. Not even a whiff of anything moving about. I'm stumped for what to do now. I feel like I must have aged something awful in my sleep.

I stand up again and glance over at the house. But there's no hint of anyone about. Only the western sun glaring off the bay window. There's nothing to do but cut across the grass into the passage and beat a path home. So I didn't find the cat. Well, at least I tried.

B ACK H O M E , I take in the dry laundry and throw together the makings of a simple meal. Then I collapse onto the living-room floor, my back against the wall, to read the evening paper. At 5:30, the telephone rings twelve times, but I don't pick up the receiver. After the ringing has died away, a lingering hollowness hovers about the dark room like drifting dust. The clock atop the TV strikes an invisible panel of space with its brittle claws. A regular wind-up toy world this is, I think. Once a day the wind-up bird has to come and wind the springs of this world. Alone in this fun house, only I grow old, a pale softball of death swelling inside me. Yet even as I sleep somewhere between Saturn and Uranus, wind-up birds everywhere are busy at work fulfilling their appointed rounds.

I consider writing a poem about the wind-up bird. But no first lines come. Besides, I find it hard to believe that high-school girls would be terribly thrilled to read a poem about the wind-up bird. They don't even know that any such thing as a wind-up bird exists.

I T ' S S E V E N - T H I R T Y when my wife comes home.

"Sorry, I had to work late," she apologizes. "I had the darnedest time tracking down one pupil's tuition record. The part-time girl is so lame, it all falls to me."

"Never mind," I say. Then I step into the kitchen, panfry a piece of fish in butter, and prepare a salad and miso soup. Meanwhile, my wife reads the evening paper at the kitchen table.

"Say, weren't you home at five-thirty?" she asks. "I tried calling to tell you I'd be a little late."

"I ran out of butter and went out to buy some," I lie.

"Did you remember to go to the bank?"

"Natch," I reply.

"How about the cat?"

"Not a trace."

"Oh," says my wife.

I EMERGE from an after-dinner bath to find my wife sitting all alone in the darkened living room. I throw on a gray shirt and fumble through the dark to reach where she's been dumped like a piece of luggage. She looks so utterly forsaken. If only they'd left her in another spot, she might have seemed a little happier.

Drying my hair with a bath towel, I take a seat on the sofa opposite her.

"What's the matter?" I ask.

"The cat's dead, I just know it," my wife says.

"Oh c'mon," I protest. "He's just off exploring. Soon enough he'll get hungry and head on back. The same thing happened once before, remember? That time when we were still living in Koenji—"

"This time it's different. I can feel it. The cat's dead and rotting away in the weeds. Did you search the grass in the yard of the vacant house?"

"Hey now, stop it. It may be a vacant house, but it's somebody else's house. I'm not about to go trespassing."

"You killed it!" my wife accuses.

I heave a sigh and give my head another once-over with the towel.

"You killed it with that look of yours!" she repeats from the darkness.

"How does that follow?" I say. "The cat disappeared of its own doing. It's not my fault. That much you've got to see."

"You! You never liked that cat, anyway!"

"Okay, maybe so," I admit. "At least I wasn't as crazy about the cat as you were. Still, I never mistreated it. I fed it every day. Just because I wasn't enthralled with the little bugger doesn't mean I killed it. Start saying things like that and I end up having killed half the people on earth."

"Well, that's you all over," my wife delivers her verdict. "That's just so you. Always, always that way. You kill everything without ever playing a hand."

I'm about to counter when she bursts into tears. I can the speech and toss the towel into the bathroom basket, go to the kitchen, take a beer out of the refrigerator, and chug. What an impossible day it's been! One impossible day, of an impossible month, of an impossible year.

Noboru Watanabe, where have you gone?, I think. Didn't the wind-up bird wind your spring?

A regular poem that is:

> Noboru Watanabe
> Where have you gone?
> Didn't the wind-up bird
> Wind your spring?

I've not finished half my beer when the telephone begins to ring.

"Get that, will you?" I shout into the living-room darkness.

"No way! You get it yourself," says my wife.

"I don't want to get it," I say.

No one answers it, and the telephone keeps on ringing. The ringing stirs up the loose dust floating in the dark. Neither my wife nor I venture one word. Me drinking my beer, my wife sobbing away. Twenty rings before I lose count and just let the thing ring. You can't keep counting forever.

—*translated by Alfred Birnbaum*

THE

SECOND

BAKERY

ATTACK

I'M STILL NOT SURE I made the right choice when I told my wife about the bakery attack. But then, it might not have been a question of right and wrong. Which is to say that wrong choices can produce right results, and vice versa. I myself have adopted the position that, in fact, *we never choose anything at all.* Things happen. Or not.

If you look at it this way, *it just so happens* that I told my wife about the bakery attack. I hadn't been planning to bring it up— I had forgotten all about it—but it wasn't one of those now-that-you-mention-it kind of things, either.

What reminded me of the bakery attack was an unbearable hunger. It hit just before two o'clock in the morning. We had eaten a light supper at six, crawled into bed at nine-thirty, and gone to sleep. For some reason, we woke up at exactly the same moment. A few minutes later, the pangs struck with the force of the tornado in *The Wizard of Oz.* These were tremendous, overpowering hunger pangs.

Our refrigerator contained not a single item that could be technically categorized as food. We had a bottle of French dressing, six cans of beer, two shriveled onions, a stick of butter, and a box of refrigerator deodorizer. With only two weeks of married life behind us, we had yet to establish a precise conjugal understanding with regard to the rules of dietary behavior. Let alone anything else.

I had a job in a law firm at the time, and she was doing secretarial work at a design school. I was either twenty-eight or twenty-nine—why can't I remember the exact year we married?—and she was two years and eight months younger. Groceries were the last things on our minds.

We both felt too hungry to go back to sleep, but it hurt just to lie there. On the other hand, we were also too hungry to do anything useful. We got out of bed and drifted into the kitchen, ending up across the table from each other. What could have caused such violent hunger pangs?

We took turns opening the refrigerator door and hoping, but no matter how many times we looked inside, the contents never changed. Beer and onions and butter and dressing and deodorizer. It might have been possible to sauté the onions in the butter, but there was no chance those two shriveled onions could fill our empty stomachs. Onions are meant to be eaten with other things. They are not the kind of food you use to satisfy an appetite.

"Would madame care for some French dressing sautéed in deodorizer?"

I expected her to ignore my attempt at humor, and she did. "Let's get in the car and look for an all-night restaurant," I said. "There must be one on the highway."

She rejected that suggestion. "We can't. You're not supposed to go out to eat after midnight." She was old-fashioned that way.

I breathed once and said, "I guess not."

Whenever my wife expressed such an opinion (or thesis) back then, it reverberated in my ears with the authority of a revelation. Maybe that's what happens with newlyweds, I don't know. But when she said this to me, I began to think that this was a special hunger, not one that could be satisfied through the mere expedient of taking it to an all-night restaurant on the highway.

A special kind of hunger. And what might that be?

I can present it here in the form of a cinematic image.

One, I am in a little boat, floating on a quiet sea. *Two,* I look down, and in the water I see the peak of a volcano thrusting up from the ocean floor. *Three,* the peak seems pretty close to the water's surface, but just how close I cannot tell. *Four,* this is because the hypertransparency of the water interferes with the perception of distance.

This is a fairly accurate description of the image that arose in my mind during the two or three seconds between the time my wife said she refused to go to an all-night restaurant and I agreed with my "I guess not." Not being Sigmund Freud, I was, of course, unable to analyze with any precision what this image signified, but I knew intuitively that it was a revelation. Which is why—the almost grotesque intensity of my hunger notwithstanding—I all but automatically agreed with her thesis (or declaration).

We did the only thing we could do: opened the beer. It was a lot better than eating those onions. She didn't like beer much, so we divided the cans, two for her, four for me. While I was drinking the first one, she searched the kitchen shelves like a squirrel in November. Eventually, she turned up a package that had four butter cookies in the bottom. They were leftovers, soft and soggy, but we each ate two, savoring every crumb.

It was no use. Upon this hunger of ours, as vast and boundless as the Sinai Peninsula, the butter cookies and beer left not a trace.

Time oozed through the dark like a lead weight in a fish's gut. I read the print on the aluminum beer cans. I stared at my watch. I looked at the refrigerator door. I turned the pages of yesterday's paper. I used the edge of a postcard to scrape together the cookie crumbs on the tabletop.

"I've never been this hungry in my whole life," she said. "I wonder if it has anything to do with being married."

"Maybe," I said. "Or maybe not."

While she hunted for more fragments of food, I leaned over the edge of my boat and looked down at the peak of the under-water volcano. The clarity of the ocean water all around the boat gave me an unsettled feeling, as if a hollow had opened some-where behind my solar plexus—a hermetically sealed cavern that had neither entrance nor exit. Something about this weird sense of absence—this sense of the existential reality of non-existence—resembled the paralyzing fear you might feel when you climb to the very top of a high steeple. This connection between hunger and acrophobia was a new discovery for me.

Which is when it occurred to me that I had once before had this same kind of experience. My stomach had been just as empty then. . . . When? . . . Oh, sure, that was—

"The time of the bakery attack," I heard myself saying.

"The bakery attack? What are you talking about?"

And so it started.

"I ONCE ATTACKED a bakery. Long time ago. Not a big bakery. Not famous. The bread was nothing special. Not bad, either. One of those ordinary little neighborhood bakeries right in the middle of a block of shops. Some old guy ran it who did everything himself. Baked in the morning, and when he sold out, he closed up for the day."

"If you were going to attack a bakery, why that one?"

"Well, there was no point in attacking a big bakery. All we wanted was bread, not money. We were attackers, not robbers."

"We? Who's we?"

"My best friend back then. Ten years ago. We were so broke we couldn't buy toothpaste. Never had enough food. We did some pretty awful things to get our hands on food. The bakery attack was one."

"I don't get it." She looked hard at me. Her eyes could have been searching for a faded star in the morning sky. "Why didn't you get a job? You could have worked after school. That would have been easier than attacking bakeries."

"We didn't want to work. We were absolutely clear on that."

"Well, you're working now, aren't you?"

I nodded and sucked some more beer. Then I rubbed my eyes. A kind of beery mud had oozed into my brain and was struggling with my hunger pangs.

"Times change. People change," I said. "Let's go back to bed. We've got to get up early."

"I'm not sleepy. I want you to tell me about the bakery attack."

"There's nothing to tell. No action. No excitement."

"Was it a success?"

I gave up on sleep and ripped open another beer. Once she gets interested in a story, she has to hear it all the way through. That's just the way she is.

"Well, it was kind of a success. And kind of not. We got what we wanted. But as a holdup, it didn't work. The baker gave us the bread before we could take it from him."

"Free?"

"Not exactly, no. That's the hard part." I shook my head. "The baker was a classical-music freak, and when we got there, he was listening to an album of Wagner overtures. So he made us a deal. If we would listen to the record all the way through, we could take as much bread as we liked. I talked it over with my buddy and we figured, Okay. It wouldn't be work in the purest sense of the word, and it wouldn't hurt anybody. So we put our knives back in our bag, pulled up a couple of chairs, and listened to the overtures to *Tannhäuser* and *The Flying Dutchman*."

"And after that, you got your bread?"

"Right. Most of what he had in the shop. Stuffed it in our bag and took it home. Kept us fed for maybe four or five days." I took another sip. Like soundless waves from an undersea earthquake, my sleepiness gave my boat a long, slow rocking.

For a while, she didn't speak. She probably sensed that I wasn't telling her the whole story. But she wasn't ready to press me on it.

"Still," she said, "that's why you two broke up, isn't it? The bakery attack was the direct cause."

"Maybe so. I guess it was more intense than either of us realized. We talked about the relationship of bread to Wagner for days after that. We kept asking ourselves if we had made the right choice. We couldn't decide. Of course, if you look at it sensibly, we *did* make the right choice. Nobody got hurt. Everybody got what he wanted. The baker—I still can't figure out why he did what he did—but anyway, he succeeded with his Wagner propaganda. And we succeeded in stuffing our faces with bread.

"But even so, we had this feeling that we had made a terrible mistake. And somehow, this mistake has just stayed there, unresolved, casting a dark shadow on our lives. That's why I used the word 'curse.' It's true. It was like a curse."

"Do you think you still have it?"

I took the six pull-tabs from the ashtray and arranged them into an aluminum ring the size of a bracelet.

"Who knows? I don't know. I bet the world is full of curses. It's hard to tell which curse makes any one thing go wrong."

"That's not true." She looked right at me. "You can tell, if you think about it. And unless you, yourself, personally break the curse, it'll stick with you like a toothache. It'll torture you till you die. And not just you. Me, too."

"You?"

"Well, I'm your best friend now, aren't I? Why do you think we're both so hungry? I never, ever, once in my life felt a hunger like this until I married you. Don't you think it's abnormal? Your curse is working on me, too."

I nodded. Then I broke up the ring of pull-tabs and put them back in the ashtray. I didn't know if she was right, but I did feel she was onto something.

"Of course, we accomplished our mission. We got the bread. But you couldn't say we had committed a crime. It was more of an exchange. We listened to Wagner with him, and in return, we got our bread. Legally speaking, it was more like a commercial transaction."

"But listening to Wagner is not work," she said.

"Oh, no, absolutely not. If the baker had insisted that we wash his dishes or clean his windows or something, we would have turned him down. But he didn't. All he wanted from us was to listen to his Wagner LP from beginning to end. Nobody could have anticipated that. I mean—Wagner? It was like the baker put a curse on us. Now that I think of it, we should have refused. We should have threatened him with our knives and taken the damn bread. Then there wouldn't have been any problem."

"You had a problem?"

I rubbed my eyes again.

"Sort of. Nothing you could put your finger on. But things started to change after that. It was kind of a turning point. Like, I went back to the university, and I graduated, and I started working for the firm and studying for the bar exam, and I met you and got married. I never did anything like that again. No more bakery attacks."

"That's it?"

"Yup, that's all there was to it." I drank the last of the beer. Now all six cans were gone. Six pull-tabs lay in the ashtray like scales from a mermaid.

Of course, it wasn't true that nothing had happened as a result of the bakery attack. There were plenty of things that you could easily have put your finger on, but I didn't want to talk about them with her.

"So, this friend of yours, what's he doing now?"

"I have no idea. Something happened, some nothing kind of thing, and we stopped hanging around together. I haven't seen him since. I don't know what he's doing."

The feeling of starvation was back, stronger than ever, and it was giving me a deep headache. Every twinge of my stomach was being transmitted to the core of my head by a clutch cable, as if my insides were equipped with all kinds of complicated machinery.

I took another look at my undersea volcano. The water was even clearer than before—much clearer. Unless you looked closely, you might not even notice it was there. It felt as though the boat were floating in midair, with absolutely nothing to support it. I could see every little pebble on the bottom. All I had to do was reach out and touch them.

"We've only been living together for two weeks," she said, "but all this time I've been feeling some kind of weird presence." She looked directly into my eyes and brought her hands together on the tabletop, her fingers interlocking. "Of course, I didn't know it was a curse until now. This explains everything. You're under a curse."

"What kind of presence?"

"Like there's this heavy, dusty curtain that hasn't been washed for years, hanging down from the ceiling."

"Maybe it's not a curse. Maybe it's just me," I said, and smiled.

She did not smile.

"No, it's not you," she said.

"Okay, suppose you're right. Suppose it is a curse. What can I do about it?"

"Attack another bakery. Right away. Now. It's the only way."

"Now?"

"Yes. Now. While you're still hungry. You have to finish what you left unfinished."

"But it's the middle of the night. Would a bakery be open now?"

"We'll find one. Tokyo's a big city. There must be at least one all-night bakery."

• • •

WE GOT INTO my old Corolla and started drifting around
the streets of Tokyo at 2:30 a.m., looking for a bakery. There
we were, me clutching the steering wheel, she in the navigator's
seat, the two of us scanning the street like hungry eagles in
search of prey. Stretched out on the backseat, long and stiff as a
dead fish, was a Remington automatic shotgun. Its shells rustled
dryly in the pocket of my wife's windbreaker. We had two black
ski masks in the glove compartment. Why my wife owned a
shotgun, I had no idea. Or ski masks. Neither of us had ever
skied. But she didn't explain and I didn't ask. Married life is
weird, I felt.

Impeccably equipped, we were nevertheless unable to find
an all-night bakery. I drove through the empty streets, from
Yoyogi to Shinjuku, on to Yotsuya and Akasaka, Aoyama,
Hiroo, Roppongi, Daikanyama, and Shibuya. Late-night Tokyo had all kinds of people and shops, but no bakeries.

Twice we encountered patrol cars. One was huddled at the
side of the road, trying to look inconspicuous. The other slowly
overtook us and crept past, finally moving off into the distance.
Both times I grew damp under the arms, but my wife's concentration never faltered. She was looking for that bakery. Every
time she shifted the angle of her body, the shotgun shells in her
pocket rustled like buckwheat husks in an old-fashioned pillow.

"Let's forget it," I said. "There aren't any bakeries open at
this time of night. You've got to plan for this kind of thing or
else—"

"Stop the car!"

I slammed on the brakes.

"This is the place," she said.

The shops along the street had their shutters rolled down,
forming dark, silent walls on either side. A barbershop sign
hung in the dark like a twisted, chilling glass eye. There was a
bright McDonald's hamburger sign some two hundred yards
ahead, but nothing else.

"I don't see any bakery," I said.

Without a word, she opened the glove compartment and pulled out a roll of cloth-backed tape. Holding this, she stepped out of the car. I got out my side. Kneeling at the front end, she tore off a length of tape and covered the numbers on the license plate. Then she went around to the back and did the same. There was a practiced efficiency to her movements. I stood on the curb staring at her.

"We're going to take that McDonald's," she said, as coolly as if she were announcing what we would have for dinner.

"McDonald's is not a bakery," I pointed out to her.

"It's *like* a bakery," she said. "Sometimes you have to compromise. Let's go."

I drove to the McDonald's and parked in the lot. She handed me the blanket-wrapped shotgun.

"I've never fired a gun in my life," I protested.

"You don't have to fire it. Just hold it. Okay? Do as I say. We walk right in, and as soon as they say 'Welcome to McDonald's,' we slip on our masks. Got that?"

"Sure, but—"

"Then you shove the gun in their faces and make all the workers and customers get together. Fast. I'll do the rest."

"But—"

"How many hamburgers do you think we'll need? Thirty?"

"I guess so." With a sigh, I took the shotgun and rolled back the blanket a little. The thing was as heavy as a sandbag and as black as a dark night.

"Do we really have to do this?" I asked, half to her and half to myself.

"Of course we do."

Wearing a McDonald's hat, the girl behind the counter flashed me a McDonald's smile and said, "Welcome to McDonald's." I hadn't thought that girls would work at McDonald's late at night, so the sight of her confused me for a second. But only for a second. I caught myself and pulled on the mask. Confronted with this suddenly masked duo, the girl gaped at us.

Obviously, the McDonald's hospitality manual said nothing about how to deal with a situation like this. She had been starting to form the phrase that comes after "Welcome to McDonald's," but her mouth seemed to stiffen and the words wouldn't come out. Even so, like a crescent moon in the dawn sky, the hint of a professional smile lingered at the edges of her lips.

As quickly as I could manage, I unwrapped the shotgun and aimed it in the direction of the tables, but the only customers there were a young couple—students, probably—and they were facedown on the plastic table, sound asleep. Their two heads and two strawberry-milk-shake cups were aligned on the table like an avant-garde sculpture. They slept the sleep of the dead. They didn't look likely to obstruct our operation, so I swung my shotgun back toward the counter.

All together, there were three McDonald's workers. The girl at the counter, the manager—a guy with a pale, egg-shaped face, probably in his late twenties—and a student type in the kitchen—a thin shadow of a guy with nothing on his face that you could read as an expression. They stood together behind the register, staring into the muzzle of my shotgun like tourists peering down an Incan well. No one screamed, and no one made a threatening move. The gun was so heavy I had to rest the barrel on top of the cash register, my finger on the trigger.

"I'll give you the money," said the manager, his voice hoarse. "They collected it at eleven, so we don't have too much, but you can have everything. We're insured."

"Lower the front shutter and turn off the sign," said my wife.

"Wait a minute," said the manager. "I can't do that. I'll be held responsible if I close up without permission."

My wife repeated her order, slowly. He seemed torn.

"You'd better do what she says," I warned him.

He looked at the muzzle of the gun atop the register, then at my wife, and then back at the gun. He finally resigned himself to the inevitable. He turned off the sign and hit a switch on an electrical panel that lowered the shutter. I kept my eye on him, worried that he might hit a burglar alarm, but apparently McDonald's don't have burglar alarms. Maybe it had never occurred to anybody to attack one.

The front shutter made a huge racket when it closed, like an empty bucket being smashed with a baseball bat, but the couple sleeping at their table was still out cold. Talk about a sound sleep: I hadn't seen anything like that in years.

"Thirty Big Macs. For takeout," said my wife.

"Let me just give you the money," pleaded the manager. "I'll give you more than you need. You can go buy food somewhere else. This is going to mess up my accounts and—"

"You'd better do what she says," I said again.

The three of them went into the kitchen area together and started making the thirty Big Macs. The student grilled the burgers, the manager put them in buns, and the girl wrapped them up. Nobody said a word.

I leaned against a big refrigerator, aiming the gun toward the griddle. The meat patties were lined up on the griddle like brown polka dots, sizzling. The sweet smell of grilling meat burrowed into every pore of my body like a swarm of microscopic bugs, dissolving into my blood and circulating to the farthest corners, then massing together inside my hermetically sealed hunger cavern, clinging to its pink walls.

A pile of white-wrapped burgers was growing nearby. I wanted to grab and tear into them, but I could not be certain that such an act would be consistent with our objective. I had to wait. In the hot kitchen area, I started sweating under my ski mask.

The McDonald's people sneaked glances at the muzzle of the shotgun. I scratched my ears with the little finger of my left hand. My ears always get itchy when I'm nervous. Jabbing my finger into an ear through the wool, I was making the gun barrel wobble up and down, which seemed to bother them. It couldn't have gone off accidentally, because I had the safety on, but they didn't know that and I wasn't about to tell them.

My wife counted the finished hamburgers and put them into two small shopping bags, fifteen burgers to a bag.

"Why do you have to do this?" the girl asked me. "Why don't you just take the money and buy something you like? What's the good of eating thirty Big Macs?"

I shook my head.

My wife explained, "We're sorry, really. But there weren't any bakeries open. If there had been, we would have attacked a bakery."

That seemed to satisfy them. At least they didn't ask any more questions. Then my wife ordered two large Cokes from the girl and paid for them.

"We're stealing bread, nothing else," she said. The girl responded with a complicated head movement, sort of like nodding and sort of like shaking. She was probably trying to do both at the same time. I thought I had some idea how she felt.

My wife then pulled a ball of twine from her pocket—she came equipped—and tied the three to a post as expertly as if she were sewing on buttons. She asked if the cord hurt, or if anyone wanted to go to the toilet, but no one said a word. I wrapped the gun in the blanket, she picked up the shopping bags, and out we went. The customers at the table were still asleep, like a couple of deep-sea fish. What would it have taken to rouse them from a sleep so deep?

We drove for a half hour, found an empty parking lot by a building, and pulled in. There we ate hamburgers and drank our Cokes. I sent six Big Macs down to the cavern of my stomach, and she ate four. That left twenty Big Macs in the back seat. Our hunger—that hunger that had felt as if it could go on forever—vanished as the dawn was breaking. The first light of the sun dyed the building's filthy walls purple and made a giant SONY BETA ad tower glow with painful intensity. Soon the whine of highway truck tires was joined by the chirping of birds. The American Armed Forces radio was playing cowboy music. We shared a cigarette. Afterward, she rested her head on my shoulder.

"Still, was it really necessary for us to do this?" I asked.

"Of course it was!" With one deep sigh, she fell asleep against me. She felt as soft and as light as a kitten.

Alone now, I leaned over the edge of my boat and looked down to the bottom of the sea. The volcano was gone. The water's calm surface reflected the blue of the sky. Little waves—like silk pajamas fluttering in a breeze—lapped against the side of the boat. There was nothing else.

I stretched out in the bottom of the boat and closed my eyes, waiting for the rising tide to carry me where I belonged.

—*translated by Jay Rubin*

Tₕₑ

ₖₐₙGₐR00

COMMᵤₙᵢₐᵤÉ

SAY HEY, how's tricks?

This morning, I paid a call on the kangaroos at the local zoo. Not your biggest zoo, but it's got the standard animals. Everything from gorillas to elephants. Although if your taste runs to llamas and anteaters, don't go out of your way. There, you'll find neither llama nor anteater. No impala or hyena, either. Not even a leopard.

Instead, there are four kangaroos.

One, an infant, born just two months ago. And a male and two females. I can't for the life of me figure out how they get along as a family.

Every time I set eyes on a kangaroo, it all seems so improbable to me: I mean, what on earth would it feel like to be a kangaroo? For what possible reason do they go hopping around in such an ungodly place as Australia? Just to get killed by some clunky stick of a boomerang?

I can't figure it out.

Though, really, that's neither here nor there. No major issue.

Anyway, looking at these kangaroos, I got the urge to send you a letter.

Maybe that strikes you as odd. You ask yourself, Why should looking at kangaroos make me want to send you a letter? And just what is the connection between these kangaroos and me? Well, you can stop thinking those thoughts right now. Makes no nevermind. Kangaroos are kangaroos, you are you.

In other words, it's like this:

Thirty-six intricate procedural steps, followed one by one in just the right order, led me from the kangaroos to you—that's it. To attempt to explain each and every one of these steps would surely try your powers of comprehension, but more than that, I doubt I can even remember them all.

There were thirty-six of them, after all!

If but one of these stages had gotten screwed up, I guess I wouldn't be sending you this letter. Who knows? I might have ended up somewhere in the Antarctic Ocean careening about on the back of a sperm whale. Or maybe I'd have torched the local cigarette stand.

Yet somehow, guided by this seemingly random convergence of thirty-six coincidences, I find myself communicating with you.

Strange, isn't it?

OKAY, THEN, allow me to introduce myself.

I AM TWENTY-SIX years old and work in the product-control section of a department store. The job—as I'm sure you can easily imagine—is terribly boring. First of all, I check the merchandise that the purchasing section has decided to stock and make sure that there aren't any problems with the products. This is supposed to prevent collusion between the purchasing section and the suppliers, but actually, it's a pretty loose operation. A few tugs at shoe buckles while chatting, a nibble or two at sample sweets—that's about it. So much for product control.

Then we come to another ask, the real heart of our work, which is responding to customer complaints. Say, for instance, two pairs of stockings just purchased developed runs one after the other, or the wind-up bear fell off the table and stopped working, or a bathrobe shrank by one fourth the first time through the machine—those kind of complaints.

Well, let me tell you, the number of complaints—the sheer number—is enough to dampen anyone's spirits. Enough to keep four staffers racing around like crazy, day in and day out. These complaints include both clear-cut cases and totally unreasonable requests. Then there are those we have to puzzle over. For convenience sake, we've classified these into three categories: A, B, and C. And in the middle of the office we've got three boxes, marked A, B, and C, respectively, where we toss the letters. An operation we call "Trilevel Rationality Evaluation." In-house joke. Forget I mentioned it.

Anyway, to explain these three categories, we have:

A. Reasonable complaints. Cases where we are obliged to assume responsibility. We visit the customers' homes bearing boxes of sweets and exchange the merchandise in question.
B. Borderline cases. When in doubt, we play safe. Even where there is no moral obligation or business precedent or legal liability, we offer some appropriate gesture so as not to compromise the image of the department store and to avoid unnecessary trouble.
C. Customer negligence. When clearly the customer's fault, we offer an explanation of the situation and leave it at that.

Now, as to your complaint of a few days back, we gave the matter serious consideration and ultimately arrived at the conclusion that your complaint was of a nature that could only be classified as belonging to category C. The reasons for this were—ready? listen carefully!—we cannot exchange (1) a record once purchased (2) one whole week later (3) without a receipt. *Nowhere in the world can you do this.*

Do you get what I'm saying?

End of explanation of the situation. Your complaint has been duly processed.

NONETHELESS, professional viewpoint aside—and actually, I leave it aside a lot—my personal reaction to your plight— having mistakenly bought Mahler, not Brahms—is one of heartfelt sympathy. I kid you not. So it is I send you not your run-of the-mill form letter but this in some sense more intimate message.

ACTUALLY, I started to write you a letter any number of times last week. "We regret to inform you that our policy prohibits the exchange of records, although your letter did in some small way move me to personally . . . blah, blah, blah." A letter like that. Nothing I wrote, however, came out right. And it's not as though I'm no good at writing letters. It's just that each time I set my mind on writing you, I drew a blank, and the words that did come were consistently off base. Strangest thing.

So I decided not to respond at all. I mean, why send out a botched attempt at a letter? Better to send nothing at all, right? At least, that's what I think: A message imperfectly communicated does about as much good as a screwed-up timetable.

As fate would have it, though, this morning, standing before the kangaroo cage, I hit upon the exact permutation of those thirty-six coincidences and came up with this inspiration. To wit, the principle we shall call the Nobility of Imperfection. Now, what is this Nobility of Imperfection?, you may ask— who wouldn't ask? Well, simply put, the Nobility of Imperfection might mean nothing so much as the proposition that someone *in effect* forgives someone else. I forgive the kangaroos, the kangaroos forgive you, you forgive me—to cite but one example.

Uh–huh.

This cycle, however, is not perpetual. At some point, the kangaroos might take it into their heads not to forgive you. Please don't get angry at the kangaroos just because of that, though. It's not the kangaroos' fault and it's not your fault. Nor, for that matter, is it my fault. The kangaroos have their own pressing circumstances. And I ask you, what kind of person is it who can blame a kangaroo?

So we seize the moment. That's all we can do. Capture the moment in a snapshot. Front and center, in a row left to right: you, the kangaroos, me.

Enough of trying to write this all down. It's going nowhere. Say I write the word "coincidence." What you read in the word "coincidence" could be utterly different—even opposite—from what the very same word means to me. This is unfair, if I may say so. Here I am, stripped to my underpants, while you've only undone three buttons of your blouse. An unfair turn of events if there ever was one.

Hence I bought myself a cassette tape, having decided to directly record my letter to you.

[*Whistling—eight bars of the "Colonel Bogey" march*]

TESTING, can you hear me?

I DON'T REALLY KNOW how you will take to receiving this letter—that is, this tape—I really can't imagine. I suppose you might even get quite upset by it all. Why? . . . Because it's highly unusual for a product-control clerk of a department store to reply to a customer complaint by cassette tape—with a personalized message, too, mind you! You could even, if you were so inclined, say the whole thing was downright bizarre. And say, were you to get so upset that you sent this tape back to my boss, my standing within the organization would be placed in a terribly delicate balance indeed.

But if that is what you want to do, please do so.

If it comes to that, I will not get mad or hold a grudge against you.

Clear enough? We are on 100% equal terms: I have the right to send you a letter and you have the right to threaten my livelihood.

Isn't that right?

We're even Stephen. Just remember that.

COME TO THINK OF IT, I forgot to mention that I'm calling this letter *The Kangaroo Communiqué*.

I mean, everything needs a name, right?

Suppose, for instance, you keep a diary. Instead of writing this long-drawn-out entry, "Department-store product-control clerk's reply re complaint arrives," you could simply write "*Kangaroo Communiqué* arrives" and be done with it. And such a catchy name, too, don't you think? *The Kangaroo Communiqué:* Makes you think of kangaroos bounding off across the vast plains, pouches stuffed full of mail, doesn't it?

[*Thump, thump, thump* (rapping on tabletop)]

Now for some knocking.

[*Knock, knock, knock*]

Stop me if you've heard this.

Don't open the door if you don't feel like it. Either way is perfectly fine. If you don't want to listen anymore, please stop the tape and throw it away. I just wanted to sit down awhile by your front door talking to myself, that's all. I have no idea whatsoever if you're listening or not, but since I don't know, it's really all the same whether you do or you don't, isn't it? Ha, ha, ha.

OKAY, WHAT THE HELL, let's give it a go.

• • •

STILL AND ALL, this imperfection business is pretty tough going. Who'd have thought talking into a microphone without any script or plan would be so hard? It's like standing in the middle of the desert sprinkling water around with a cup. No visible sign of anything, not one thing to cling to.

That's why all this time I've been talking to the VU meters. You know, the VU meters? Those gizmos with the needles that twitch to the volume? I don't know what the *V* or the *U* stand for, but whatever, they're the only things showing any reaction to my ranting.

Hey, hey.

All the same, their criteria are really quite simple.

V and *U*, well, they're like a vaudeville duo. There's no *V* without *U* and no *U* without *V*—a nice little setup. As far as they're concerned, it really doesn't matter what I babble on about. The only thing they're interested in is how much my voice makes the air vibrate. To them, the air vibrates, therefore I am.

Pretty swift, don't you think?

Watching them, I get to thinking it doesn't matter what I say so long as I keep talking.

Whoa!

Come to think of it, not too long ago I saw a movie. It was about a comedian who just couldn't make anyone laugh no matter what jokes he told. Got the picture? Not one soul would laugh.

Well, talking into this microphone, I'm reminded of that movie over and over again.

It's all very odd.

The very same lines when spoken by one person will have you dying with laughter but when spoken by another won't seem funny in the least. Curious, don't you think? And the more I think about it, that difference just seems to be one of these things you're born with. See, it's like the curvature of the semicircular canals of your ears having the edge over somebody else's, or . . . you know.

Sometimes I find myself thinking, If only I had such gifts, how happy I'd be. I'm always doubling over laughing to myself when something strikes me as funny, but try to tell someone else and it falls flat, a dud. It makes me feel like the Egyptian Sandman. Even more, it's . . .

You know about the Egyptian Sandman?

Hmm, well, you see, the Egyptian Sandman was Prince of Egypt by birth. A long time ago, back in the days of pyramids and sphinxes and all that. But because he was so ugly—I mean, truly ugly—the king had him sent off into the deepest jungle to get rid of him. Well, it so happens that the kid ends up getting raised by wolves, or monkeys, maybe. One of those stories, you know. And somehow or other, he becomes a Sandman. Now, this Sandman, everything he touches turns to sand. Breezes turn into sandstorms, babbling brooks turn into dunes, grassy plains turn into deserts. So goes the tale of the Sandman. Ever hear it before? Probably not, eh? That's because I just made it up. Ha, ha, ha.

Anyway, talking to you like this, I get the feeling I've become the Egyptian Sandman myself. And whatever I touch, it's sand sand sand.

ONCE AGAIN, I see I'm talking about myself too much. But all things considered, it's unavoidable. I mean, I don't even know one solitary thing about you. I've got your address and your name, and that's it. Your age, income bracket, the shape of your nose, whether you're slender or overweight, married or not—what do I know? Not that any of that really matters. It's almost better this way. If at all possible, I prefer to keep things simple, very simple—on the metaphysical level, if you will.

To wit, here I have your letter.

This is all I need.

Just as the zoologist collects shit samples in the jungle from which to deduce the elephant's dietary habits and patterns of activity and weight and sex life, so your one letter gives me enough to go on. I can actually sense what kind of person you are. Of course, minus your looks, the kind of perfume you wear, details like that. Nonetheless—your very essence.

Your letter was, honestly, quite fascinating. Your choice of words, the handwriting, punctuation, spacing between lines, rhetoric—everything was perfect. Superlative it was not. But perfect, yes.

Every month, I read over five hundred letters, and frankly, yours was the first letter that ever moved me. I secretly took your letter home with me and read it over and over again. Then I analyzed your letter thoroughly. Being such a short letter, it was no trouble at all.

Many things came to light through my analysis. First of all, the number of punctuation marks is overwhelming. 6.36 commas for every period. On the high side, don't you think? And that's not all: The way you punctuate is markedly irregular.

Listen, please don't think I'm putting down your writing. I'm simply moved by it.

Enthralled.

And it's not just the commas, either. Every part of your letter—down to each ink smear—everything set me off, everything shook me.

Why?

Well, the long and the short of it is that there's no *you* in the whole piece of writing. Oh, there's a story to it, all right. A girl—a woman—makes a mistake buying a record. She had the feeling the record had the wrong tunes, but still, she went ahead and bought it, and it's exactly one week before she realizes. The salesgirl won't exchange it. So she writes a letter of complaint. That's the story.

I had to reread your letter three times before I grasped the story. The reason was, your letter was completely different from all the other letters of complaint that come our way. To put it bluntly, there wasn't even any complaint in your letter. Let alone any emotion. The *only* thing that was there . . . was the story.

Really and truly, you had me wondering. Was the letter in fact intended as a complaint or a confession or a proclamation, or was it perhaps meant to put forth some thesis? I had no idea. Your letter reminded me of a news photo from the scene of a massacre. With no commentary, no article, no nothing—just a photo. A shot of dead bodies littering some roadside in some country somewhere.

Bang, bang, bang . . . there's your massacre.

No, wait, we can simplify things a little. Simplify them a lot.

That is to say, your letter excites me sexually.

There you have it.

LET US NOW address the topic of sex.

[*Thud, thud, thud*]

MORE KNOCKING.

You know, if this doesn't interest you, you can stop the tape. I'm just talking to myself, blabbering away to the VU meters. Blah, blah, blah.

Okay?

PICTURE THIS: Short forearms with five fingers, but singularly huge hind legs with four toes, the fourth of which is immensely overdeveloped, while the second and third are extra tiny and fused together . . . that's a description of the feet of a kangaroo. Ha, ha, ha.

UH, MOVING ON to the topic of sex.

Ever since I took your letter home with me, all I can seem to think about is sleeping with you. That I'll climb into bed to find you next to me, wake up in the morning and there you'd be. As I open my eyes you'll already be getting out of bed, and I'll hear you zipping up your dress. There I'd be—and you know how delicate the zipper on a dress can be—well, I'd just shut my eyes and pretend to be asleep. I wouldn't even set eyes on you.

Once you cut across the room and disappeared into the bathroom, only then would I open my eyes. Then I'd get a bite to eat and head out to work.

In the pitch-black of night—I'll install special blinds on my windows to make the place extra pitch-black—of course, I wouldn't see your face. I'd know nothing, not your age or weight. So I wouldn't lay a hand on you, either.

But, well, that's fine.

If you really want to know, it makes no difference whatsoever if I have sex with you or not. . . .

No, I take that back.

Let me think that one over.

OKAY, let's put it this way. I would like to sleep with you. But it's all right if I don't sleep with you. What I'm saying is, I'd like to be as fair as possible. I don't want to force anything on anybody, any more than I'd want anything forced on me. It's enough that I feel your presence or see your commas swirling around me.

YOU SEE, it's like this:

Sometimes, when I think about entities—like in "separate entities"—it gets mighty grim. I start thinking, and I nearly go to pieces. . . .

For instance, say you're riding on the subway. And there are dozens of people in the car. Mere "passengers" you'd have to call them, as a rule. "Passengers" being conveyed from Aoyama One-chome to Akasakamitsuke. Sometimes, though, it'll strike you that each and every one of those passengers is a distinct individual entity. Like, what does this one do? Or why on earth do you suppose that one's riding the Ginza Line? Or whatever. By then it's too late. You let it get to you and you're a goner.

Looks like that businessman's hairline is receding, or the girl over there's got such hairy legs I bet she shaves at least once a week, or why is that young guy sitting across the aisle wearing that awful tie? Little things like that. Until finally you've got the shakes and you want to jump out of the car then and there. Why, just the other day—I know you're going to laugh, but—I was on the verge of pressing the emergency-brake button by the door.

I admit it. But that doesn't mean you should go thinking I'm hypersensitive or on edge all the time. I'm really a regular sort of guy, your everyday ordinary workaday type, gainfully employed in the product-control section of a department store. And I've got nothing against the subway.

Nor do I have any problem sexually. There's a woman I'm seeing—I guess you could call her my girlfriend—been sleeping with her twice a week for maybe a year now. And she and I, we're both pretty satisfied. Only I try not to take her too seriously. I have no intention of marrying her. If I thought about getting married, I'm sure I'd begin taking her seriously, and I'd lose all confidence that I could carry on from that point. I mean, that's how it is. You live with a girl and these things start to get to you—her teeth aren't exactly straight, the shape of her fingernails—how can you expect to go on like that?

LET ME SAY a little more about myself.
No knocking this time.
If you've listened this far, you might as well hear me out.
Just a second. I need a smoke.

[Rattle, rattle]

Up to now, I've hardly said a word about myself. Like, there's really not that much to say. And even if I did, probably nobody would find it terribly interesting.

So why am I telling you all this?

I think I already told you, it's because now my sights are set on the Nobility of Imperfection.

And what touched off this Nobility of Imperfection idea?

Your letter and four kangaroos.

Yes, kangaroos.

Kangaroos are such fascinating creatures, I can look at them for hours on end. What can kangaroos possibly have to think about? The whole lot of them, jumping around in their cage all day long, digging holes now and again. And then what do they do with these holes? Nothing. They dig them and that's it. Ha, ha, ha.

Kangaroos give birth to only one baby at a time. So as soon as one baby is born, the female gets pregnant again. Otherwise the kangaroo population would never sustain itself. This means the female kangaroo spends her entire life either pregnant or nursing babies. If she's not pregnant, she's nursing babies; if she's not nursing babies, she's pregnant. You could say she exists just to ensure the continuance of the species. The kangaroo species wouldn't survive if there weren't any kangaroos, and if their purpose wasn't to go on existing, kangaroos wouldn't be around in the first place.

Funny about that.

BUT I'M GETTING ahead of myself. Excuse me.

TO TALK about myself, then.

Actually, I'm extremely dissatisfied with being who I am. It's nothing to do with my looks or abilities or status or any of that. It simply has to do with being me. The situation strikes me as grossly unfair.

Still, that doesn't mean you should write me off as someone with a lot of gripes. I have not one complaint about the place where I work or about my salary. The work is undeniably boring, but then, most jobs are boring. Money is not a major issue here.

Shall I put it on the line?

I want to be able to be in two places at once. That is my one and only wish. Other than that, there's not a thing I desire.

Yet being who and what I am, my singularity hampers this desire of mine. An unhappy lot, don't you think? My wish, if anything, is rather unassuming. I don't want to be ruler of the world, nor do I want to be an artist of genius. I merely want to exist in two places simultaneously. Got it? Not three, not four, only *two*. I want to be roller-skating while I'm listening to an orchestra at a concert hall. I want to be a McDonald's Quarter Pounder and still be a clerk in the product-control section of the department store. I want to sleep with you and be sleeping with my girlfriend all the while. I want to lead a general existence and yet be a distinct, separate entity.

ALLOW ME one more cigarette.

Whoa.

Getting a little tired.

I'm not used to this, speaking so frankly about myself.

There's just one thing I'd like to get clear, though. Which is that I do not lust after you sexually as a woman. Like I told you, I am angry at the fact that I am only myself and nothing else. Being a solitary entity is dreadfully depressing. Hence I do not seek to sleep with you, a solitary individual.

If, however, you were to divide into two, and I split into two as well, and we four all shared the same bed together, wouldn't that be something! Don't you think?

PLEASE SEND no reply. If you decide you want to write me a letter, please send it care of the company in the form of a complaint. If not a complaint, then whatever you come up with.

That's about it.

I LISTENED to the tape this far on playback just now. To be honest, I'm very dissatisfied with it. I feel like an aquarium trainer who's let a seal die out of negligence. It made me worry whether I should even send you this tape or not, blowing this thing all out of proportion even by my standards.

And now that I've decided to send it, I'm still worried.

But what the hell, I'm striving for imperfection, so I've got to live happily by my choice. It was you and the four kangaroos who got me into this imperfection, after all.

SIGNING OFF.

—translated by Alfred Birnbaum

On Seeing the 100% Perfect Girl One Beautiful April Morning

ONE BEAUTIFUL APRIL MORNING, on a narrow side street in Tokyo's fashionable Harajuku neighborhood, I walk past the 100% perfect girl.

Tell you the truth, she's not that good-looking. She doesn't stand out in any way. Her clothes are nothing special. The back of her hair is still bent out of shape from sleep. She isn't young, either—must be near thirty, not even close to a "girl," properly speaking. But still, I know from fifty yards away: She's the 100% perfect girl for me. The moment I see her, there's a rumbling in my chest, and my mouth is as dry as a desert.

Maybe you have your own particular favorite type of girl— one with slim ankles, say, or big eyes, or graceful fingers, or you're drawn for no good reason to girls who take their time with every meal. I have my own preferences, of course. Sometimes in a restaurant I'll catch myself staring at the girl at the table next to mine because I like the shape of her nose.

But no one can insist that his 100% perfect girl correspond to some preconceived type. Much as I like noses, I can't recall the shape of hers—or even if she had one. All I can remember for sure is that she was no great beauty. It's weird.

"Yesterday on the street I passed the 100% perfect girl," I tell someone.

"Yeah?" he says. "Good-looking?"

"Not really."

"Your favorite type, then?"

"I don't know. I can't seem to remember anything about her—the shape of her eyes or the size of her breasts."

"Strange."

"Yeah. Strange."

"So anyhow," he says, already bored, "what did you do? Talk to her? Follow her?"

"Nah. Just passed her on the street."

She's walking east to west, and I west to east. It's a really nice April morning.

Wish I could talk to her. Half an hour would be plenty: just ask her about herself, tell her about myself, and—what I'd really like to do—explain to her the complexities of fate that have led to our passing each other on a side street in Harajuku on a beautiful April morning in 1981. This was something sure to be crammed full of warm secrets, like an antique clock built when peace filled the world.

After talking, we'd have lunch somewhere, maybe see a Woody Allen movie, stop by a hotel bar for cocktails. With any kind of luck, we might end up in bed.

Potentiality knocks on the door of my heart.

Now the distance between us has narrowed to fifteen yards.

How can I approach her? What should I say?

"Good morning, miss. Do you think you could spare half an hour for a little conversation?"

Ridiculous. I'd sound like an insurance salesman.

"Pardon me, but would you happen to know if there is an all-night cleaners in the neighborhood?"

No, this is just as ridiculous. I'm not carrying any laundry, for one thing. Who's going to buy a line like that?

Maybe the simple truth would do. "Good morning. You are the 100% perfect girl for me."

No, she wouldn't believe it. Or even if she did, she might not want to talk to me. Sorry, she could say, I might be the 100% perfect girl for you, but you're not the 100% perfect boy for me. It could happen. And if I found myself in that situation, I'd probably go to pieces. I'd never recover from the shock. I'm thirty-two, and that's what growing older is all about.

We pass in front of a flower shop. A small, warm air mass touches my skin. The asphalt is damp, and I catch the scent of roses. I can't bring myself to speak to her. She wears a white sweater, and in her right hand she holds a crisp white envelope lacking only a stamp. So: She's written somebody a letter, maybe spent the whole night writing, to judge from the sleepy look in her eyes. The envelope could contain every secret she's ever had.

I take a few more strides and turn: She's lost in the crowd.

NOW, OF COURSE, I know exactly what I should have said to her. It would have been a long speech, though, far too long for me to have delivered it properly. The ideas I come up with are never very practical.

Oh, well. It would have started "Once upon a time" and ended "A sad story, don't you think?"

ONCE UPON A TIME, there lived a boy and a girl. The boy was eighteen and the girl sixteen. He was not unusually handsome, and she was not especially beautiful. They were just an ordinary lonely boy and an ordinary lonely girl, like all the others. But they believed with their whole hearts that somewhere in the world there lived the 100% perfect boy and the 100% perfect girl for them. Yes, they believed in a miracle. And that miracle actually happened.

One day the two came upon each other on the corner of a street.

"This is amazing," he said. "I've been looking for you all my life. You may not believe this, but you're the 100% perfect girl for me."

"And you," she said to him, "are the 100% perfect boy for me, exactly as I'd pictured you in every detail. It's like a dream."

They sat on a park bench, held hands, and told each other their stories hour after hour. They were not lonely anymore. They had found and been found by their 100% perfect other. What a wonderful thing it is to find and be found by your 100% perfect other. It's a miracle, a cosmic miracle.

As they sat and talked, however, a tiny, tiny sliver of doubt took root in their hearts: Was it really all right for one's dreams to come true so easily?

And so, when there came a momentary lull in their conversation, the boy said to the girl, "Let's test ourselves—just once. If we really are each other's 100% perfect lovers, then sometime, somewhere, we will meet again without fail. And when that happens, and we know that we are the 100% perfect ones, we'll marry then and there. What do you think?"

"Yes," she said, "that is exactly what we should do."

And so they parted, she to the east, and he to the west.

The test they had agreed upon, however, was utterly unnecessary. They should never have undertaken it, because they really and truly were each other's 100% perfect lovers, and it was a miracle that they had ever met. But it was impossible for them to know this, young as they were. The cold, indifferent waves of fate proceeded to toss them unmercifully.

One winter, both the boy and the girl came down with the season's terrible influenza, and after drifting for weeks between life and death they lost all memory of their earlier years. When they awoke, their heads were as empty as the young D. H. Lawrence's piggy bank.

They were two bright, determined young people, however,

and through their unremitting efforts they were able to acquire once again the knowledge and feeling that qualified them to return as full-fledged members of society. Heaven be praised, they became truly upstanding citizens who knew how to transfer from one subway line to another, who were fully capable of sending a special-delivery letter at the post office. Indeed, they even experienced love again, sometimes as much as 75% or even 85% love.

Time passed with shocking swiftness, and soon the boy was thirty-two, the girl thirty.

One beautiful April morning, in search of a cup of coffee to start the day, the boy was walking from west to east, while the girl, intending to send a special-delivery letter, was walking from east to west, both along the same narrow street in the Harajuku neighborhood of Tokyo. They passed each other in the very center of the street. The faintest gleam of their lost memories glimmered for the briefest moment in their hearts. Each felt a rumbling in the chest. And they knew:

She is the 100% perfect girl for me.

He is the 100% perfect boy for me.

But the glow of their memories was far too weak, and their thoughts no longer had the clarity of fourteen years earlier. Without a word, they passed each other, disappearing into the crowd. Forever.

A sad story, don't you think?

YES, THAT'S IT, that is what I should have said to her.

—translated by Jay Rubin

THIS IS MY seventeenth straight day without sleep.

I'm not talking about insomnia. I know what insomnia is. I had something like it in college—"something like it" because I'm not sure that what I had then was exactly the same as what people refer to as insomnia. I suppose a doctor could have told me. But I didn't see a doctor. I knew it wouldn't do any good. Not that I had any reason to think so. Call it woman's intuition—I just felt they couldn't help me. So I didn't see a doctor, and I didn't say anything to my parents or friends, because I knew that that was exactly what they would tell me to do.

Back then, my "something like insomnia" went on for a month. I never really got to sleep that entire time. I'd go to bed at night and say to myself, "All right now, time for some sleep." That was all it took to wake me up. It was instantaneous—like a conditioned reflex. The harder I worked at sleeping, the wider awake I became. I tried alcohol, I tried sleeping pills, but they had absolutely no effect.

Finally, as the sky began to grow light in the morning, I'd feel that I might be drifting off. But that wasn't sleep. My fingertips were just barely brushing against the outermost edge of sleep. And all the while, my mind was wide awake. I would feel a hint of drowsiness, but my mind was there, in its own room, on the other side of a transparent wall, watching me. My physical self was drifting through the feeble morning light, and all the while it could feel my mind staring, breathing, close beside it. I was both a body on the verge of sleep and a mind determined to stay awake.

This incomplete drowsiness would continue on and off all day. My head was always foggy. I couldn't get an accurate fix on the things around me—their distance or mass or texture. The drowsiness would overtake me at regular, wavelike intervals: on the subway, in the classroom, at the dinner table. My mind would slip away from my body. The world would sway soundlessly. I would drop things. My pencil or my purse or my fork would clatter to the floor. All I wanted was to throw myself down and sleep. But I couldn't. The wakefulness was always there beside me. I could feel its chilling shadow. It was the shadow of myself. Weird, I would think as the drowsiness overtook me, I'm in my own shadow. I would walk and eat and talk to people inside my drowsiness. And the strangest thing was that no one noticed. I lost fifteen pounds that month, and no one noticed. No one in my family, not one of my friends or classmates, realized that I was going through life asleep.

It was literally true: I was going through life asleep. My body had no more feeling than a drowned corpse. My very existence, my life in the world, seemed like a hallucination. A strong wind would make me think that my body was about to be blown to the end of the earth, to some land I had never seen or heard of, where my mind and body would separate forever. Hold tight, I would tell myself, but there was nothing for me to hold on to.

And then, when night came, the intense wakefulness would return. I was powerless to resist it. I was locked in its core by an enormous force. All I could do was stay awake until morning, eyes wide open in the dark. I couldn't even think. As I lay there, listening to the clock tick off the seconds, I did nothing but stare at the darkness as it slowly deepened and slowly diminished.

And then one day it ended, without warning, without any external cause. I started to lose consciousness at the breakfast table. I stood up without saying anything. I may have knocked something off the table. I think someone spoke to me. But I can't be sure. I staggered to my room, crawled into bed in my clothes, and fell fast asleep. I stayed that way for twenty-seven hours. My mother became alarmed and tried to shake me out of it. She actually slapped my cheeks. But I went on sleeping for twenty-seven hours without a break. And when I finally did awaken, I was my old self again. Probably.

I have no idea why I became an insomniac then or why the condition suddenly cured itself. It was like a thick, black cloud brought from somewhere by the wind, a cloud crammed full of ominous things I have no knowledge of. No one knows where such a thing comes from or where it goes. I can only be sure that it did descend on me for a time, and then departed.

IN ANY CASE, what I have now is nothing like that insomnia, nothing at all. I just can't sleep. Not for one second. Aside from that simple fact, I'm perfectly normal. I don't feel sleepy, and my mind is as clear as ever. Clearer, if anything. Physically, too, I'm normal: My appetite is fine; I'm not fatigued. In terms of everyday reality, there's nothing wrong with me. I just can't sleep.

Neither my husband nor my son has noticed that I'm not sleeping. And I haven't mentioned it to them. I don't want to be told to see a doctor. I know it wouldn't do any good. I just know. Like before. This is something I have to deal with myself.

So they don't suspect a thing. On the surface, our life flows on unchanged. Peaceful. Routine. After I see my husband and son off in the morning, I take my car and go marketing. My husband is a dentist. His office is a ten-minute drive from our condo. He and a dental-school friend own it as partners. That way, they can afford to hire a technician and a receptionist. One partner can take the other's overflow. Both of them are good, so for an office that has been in operation for only five years and that opened without any special connections, the place is doing very well. Almost too well. "I didn't want to work so hard," says my husband. "But I can't complain."

And I always say, "Really, you can't." It's true. We had to get an enormous bank loan to open the place. A dental office requires a huge investment in equipment. And the competition is fierce. Patients don't start pouring in the minute you open your doors. Lots of dental clinics have failed for lack of patients.

Back then, we were young and poor and we had a brand-new baby. No one could guarantee that we would survive in such a tough world. But we have survived, one way or another. Five years. No, we really can't complain. We've still got almost two thirds of our debt left to pay back, though.

"I know why you've got so many patients," I always say to him. "It's because you're such a good-looking guy."

This is our little joke. He's not good-looking at all. Actually, he's kind of strange-looking. Even now I sometimes wonder why I married such a strange-looking man. I had other boyfriends who were far more handsome.

What makes his face so strange? I can't really say. It's not a handsome face, but it's not ugly, either. Nor is it the kind that people would say has "character." Honestly, "strange" is about all that fits. Or maybe it would be more accurate to say that it has no distinguishing features. Still, there must be some element that *makes* his face have no distinguishing features, and if I could grasp whatever that is, I might be able to understand the strangeness of the whole. I once tried to draw his picture, but I couldn't do it. I couldn't remember what he looked like. I sat there holding the pencil over the paper and couldn't make a mark. I was flabbergasted. How can you live with a man so long and not be able to bring his face to mind? I knew how to recognize him, of course. I would even get mental images of him now and then. But when it came to drawing his picture, I realized that I didn't remember anything about his face. What could I do? It was like running into an invisible wall. The one thing I could remember was that his face looked strange.

The memory of that often makes me nervous.

Still, he's one of those men everybody likes. That's a big plus in his business, obviously, but I think he would have been a success at just about anything. People feel secure talking to him. I had never met anyone like that before. All my women friends like him. And I'm fond of him, of course. I think I even love him. But strictly speaking, I don't actually *like* him.

Anyhow, he smiles in this natural, innocent way, just like a child. Not many grown-up men can do that. And I guess you'd expect a dentist to have nice teeth, which he does.

"It's not my fault I'm so good-looking," he always answers when we enjoy our little joke. We're the only ones who understand what it means. It's a recognition of reality—of the fact that we have managed in one way or another to survive—and it's an important ritual for us.

HE DRIVES his Sentra out of the condo parking garage every morning at 8:15. Our son is in the seat next to him. The elementary school is on the way to the office. "Be careful," I say. "Don't worry," he answers. Always the same little dialogue. I can't help myself. I have to say it. "Be careful." And my husband has to answer, "Don't worry." He starts the engine, puts a Haydn or a Mozart tape into the car stereo, and hums along with the music. My two "men" always wave to me on the way out. Their hands move in exactly the same way. It's almost uncanny. They lean their heads at exactly the same angle and turn their palms toward me, moving them slightly from side to side in exactly the same way, as if they'd been trained by a choreographer.

I have my own car, a used Honda Civic. A girlfriend sold it to me two years ago for next to nothing. One bumper is smashed in, and the body style is old-fashioned, with rust spots showing up. The odometer has over 150,000 kilometers on it. Sometimes—once or twice a month—the car is almost impossible to start. The engine simply won't catch. Still, it's not bad enough to have the thing fixed. If you baby it and let it rest for ten minutes or so, the engine will start up with a nice, solid *vroom*. Oh, well, everything—everybody—gets out of whack once or twice a month. That's life. My husband calls my car "your donkey." I don't care. It's mine.

I drive my Civic to the supermarket. After marketing, I clean the house and do the laundry. Then I fix lunch. I make a point of performing my morning chores with brisk, efficient movements. If possible, I like to finish my dinner preparations in the morning, too. Then the afternoon is all mine.

My husband comes home for lunch. He doesn't like to eat out. He says the restaurants are too crowded, the food is no good, and the smell of tobacco smoke gets into his clothes. He prefers eating at home, even with the extra travel time involved. Still, I don't make anything fancy for lunch. I warm up leftovers in the microwave or boil a pot of noodles. So the actual time involved is minimal. And of course it's more fun to eat with my husband than all alone with no one to talk to.

Before, when the clinic was just getting started, there would often be no patient in the first afternoon slot, so the two of us would go to bed after lunch. Those were the loveliest times with him. Everything was hushed, and the soft afternoon sunshine would filter into the room. We were a lot younger then, and happier.

We're still happy, of course. I really do think so. No domestic troubles cast shadows on our home. I love him and trust him. And I'm sure he feels the same about me. But little by little, as the months and years go by, your life changes. That's just how it is. There's nothing you can do about it. Now all the afternoon slots are taken. When we finish eating, my husband brushes his teeth, hurries out to his car, and goes back to the office. He's got all those sick teeth waiting for him. But that's all right. We both know you can't have everything your own way.

After my husband goes back to the office, I take a bathing suit and towel and drive to the neighborhood athletic club. I swim for half an hour. I swim hard. I'm not that crazy about the swimming itself: I just want to keep the flab off. I've always liked my own figure. Actually, I've never liked my face. It's not bad, but I've never really liked it. My body is another matter. I like to stand naked in front of the mirror. I like to study the soft outlines I see there, the balanced vitality. I'm not sure what it is, but I get the feeling that something inside there is very important to me. Whatever it is, I don't want to lose it.

I'm thirty. When you reach thirty, you realize it's not the end of the world. I'm not especially happy about getting older, but it does make some things easier. It's a question of attitude. One thing I know for sure, though: If a thirty-year-old woman loves her body and is serious about keeping it looking the way it should, she has to put in a certain amount of effort. I learned that from my mother. She used to be a slim, lovely woman, but not anymore. I don't want the same thing to happen to me.

After I've had my swim, I use the rest of my afternoon in various ways. Sometimes I'll wander over to the station plaza and window-shop. Sometimes I'll go home, curl up on the sofa, and read a book or listen to the FM station or just rest. Eventually, my son comes home from school. I help him change into his playclothes, and give him a snack. When he's through eating, he goes out to play with his friends. He's too young to go to an afternoon cram school, and we aren't making him take piano lessons or anything. "Let him play," says my husband. "Let him grow up naturally." When my son leaves the house, I have the same little dialogue with him as I do with my husband. "Be careful," I say, and he answers, "Don't worry."

As evening approaches, I begin preparing dinner. My son is always back by six. He watches cartoons on TV. If no emergency patients show up, my husband is home before seven. He doesn't drink a drop and he's not fond of pointless socializing. He almost always comes straight home from work.

The three of us talk during dinner, mostly about what we've

done that day. My son always has the most to say. Everything that happens in his life is fresh and full of mystery. He talks, and we offer our comments. After dinner, he does what he likes—watches television or reads or plays some kind of game with my husband. When he has homework, he shuts himself up in his room and does it. He goes to bed at 8:30. I tuck him in and stroke his hair and say good night to him and turn off the light.

Then it's husband and wife together. He sits on the sofa, reading the newspaper and talking to me now and then about his patients or something in the paper. Then he listens to Haydn or Mozart. I don't mind listening to music, but I can never seem to tell the difference between those two composers. They sound the same to me. When I say that to my husband, he tells me it doesn't matter. "It's all beautiful. That's what counts."

"Just like you," I say.

"Just like me," he answers with a big smile. He seems genuinely pleased.

SO THAT'S MY LIFE—or my life before I stopped sleeping—each day pretty much a repetition of the one before. I used to keep a diary, but if I forgot for two or three days, I'd lose track of what had happened on which day. Yesterday could have been the day before yesterday, or vice versa. I'd sometimes wonder what kind of life this was. Which is not to say that I found it empty. I was—very simply—amazed. At the lack of demarcation between the days. At the fact that I was part of such a life, a life that had swallowed me up so completely. At the fact that my footprints were being blown away before I even had a chance to turn and look at them.

Whenever I felt like that, I would look at my face in the bathroom mirror—just look at it for fifteen minutes at a time, my mind a total blank. I'd stare at my face purely as a physical object, and gradually it would disconnect from the rest of me, becoming just some thing that happened to exist at the same time as myself. And a realization would come to me: This is happening here and now. It's got nothing to do with footprints.

Reality and I exist simultaneously at this present moment. That's the most important thing.

But now I can't sleep anymore. When I stopped sleeping, I stopped keeping a diary.

I REMEMBER with perfect clarity that first night I lost the ability to sleep. I was having a repulsive dream—a dark, slimy dream. I don't remember what it was about, but I do remember how it felt: ominous and terrifying. I woke at the climactic moment—came fully awake with a start, as if something had dragged me back at the last moment from a fatal turning point. Had I remained immersed in the dream for another second, I would have been lost forever. After I awoke, my breath came in painful gasps for a time. My arms and legs felt paralyzed. I lay there immobilized, listening to my own labored breathing, as if I were stretched out full-length on the floor of a huge cavern.

"It was a dream," I told myself, and I waited for my breathing to calm down. Lying stiff on my back, I felt my heart working violently, my lungs hurrying the blood to it with big, slow, bellowslike contractions. I began to wonder what time it could be. I wanted to look at the clock by my pillow, but I couldn't turn my head far enough. Just then, I seemed to catch a glimpse of something at the foot of the bed, something like a vague, black shadow. I caught my breath. My heart, my lungs, everything inside me, seemed to freeze in that instant. I strained to see the black shadow.

The moment I tried to focus on it, the shadow began to assume a definite shape, as if it had been waiting for me to notice it. Its outline became distinct, and began to be filled with substance, and then with details. It was a gaunt old man wearing a skintight black shirt. His hair was gray and short, his cheeks sunken. He stood at my feet, perfectly still. He said nothing, but his piercing eyes stared at me. They were huge eyes, and I could see the red network of veins in them. The old man's face wore no expression at all. It told me nothing. It was like an opening in the darkness.

This was no longer the dream, I knew. From that I had already awakened. And not just by drifting awake, but by having my eyes ripped open. No, this was no dream. This was reality. And in reality an old man I had never seen before was standing at the foot of my bed. I had to do something—turn on the light, wake my husband, scream. I tried to move. I fought to make my limbs work, but it did no good. I couldn't move a finger. When it became clear to me that I would never be able to move, I was filled with a hopeless terror, a primal fear such as I had never experienced before, like a chill that rises silently from the bottomless well of memory. I tried to scream, but I was incapable of producing a sound or even moving my tongue. All I could do was look at the old man.

Now I saw that he was holding something—a tall, narrow, rounded thing that shone white. As I stared at this object, wondering what it could be, it began to take on a definite shape, just as the shadow had earlier. It was a pitcher, an old-fashioned porcelain pitcher. After some time, the man raised the pitcher and began pouring water from it onto my feet. I could not feel the water. I could see it and hear it splashing down onto my feet, but I couldn't feel a thing.

The old man went on and on pouring water over my feet. Strange—no matter how much he poured, the pitcher never ran dry. I began to worry that my feet would eventually rot and melt away. Yes, of course they would rot. What else could they do with so much water pouring over them? When it occurred to me that my feet were going to rot and melt away, I couldn't take it any longer.

I closed my eyes and let out a scream so loud it took every ounce of strength I had. But it never left my body. It reverberated soundlessly inside, tearing through me, shutting down my heart. Everything inside my head turned white for a moment as the scream penetrated my every cell. Something inside me died. Something melted away, leaving only a shuddering vacuum. An explosive flash incinerated everything my existence depended on.

When I opened my eyes, the old man was gone. The pitcher was gone. The bedspread was dry, and there was no indication that anything near my feet had been wet. My body, though, was soaked with sweat, a horrifying volume of sweat, more sweat than I ever imagined a human being could produce. And yet, undeniably, it was sweat that had come from me.

I moved one finger. Then another, and another, and the rest. Next, I bent my arms and then my legs. I rotated my feet and bent my knees. Nothing moved quite as it should have, but at least it did move. After carefully checking to see that all my body parts were working, I eased myself into a sitting position. In the dim light filtering in from the streetlamp, I scanned the entire room from corner to corner. The old man was definitely not there.

The clock by my pillow said 12:30. I had been sleeping for only an hour and a half. My husband was sound asleep in his bed. Even his breathing was inaudible. He always sleeps like that, as if all mental activity in him had been obliterated. Almost nothing can wake him.

I got out of bed and went into the bathroom. I threw my sweat-soaked nightgown into the washing machine and took a shower. After putting on a fresh pair of pajamas, I went to the living room, switched on the floor lamp beside the sofa, and sat there drinking a full glass of brandy. I almost never drink. Not that I have a physical incompatibility with alcohol, as my husband does. In fact, I used to drink quite a lot, but after marrying him I simply stopped. Sometimes when I had trouble sleeping I would take a sip of brandy, but that night I felt I wanted a whole glass to quiet my overwrought nerves.

The only alcohol in the house was a bottle of Rémy Martin we kept in the sideboard. It had been a gift. I don't even remember who gave it to us, it was so long ago. The bottle wore a thin layer of dust. We had no real brandy glasses, so I just poured it into a regular tumbler and sipped it slowly.

I must have been in a trance, I thought. I had never experienced such a thing, but I had heard about trances from a college friend who had been through one. Everything was incredibly clear, she had said. You can't believe it's a dream. "I didn't believe it was a dream when it was happening, and now I still don't believe it was a dream." Which is exactly how I felt. Of course it had to be a dream—a kind of dream that doesn't feel like a dream.

Though the terror was leaving me, the trembling of my body would not stop. It was in my skin, like the circular ripples on water after an earthquake. I could see the slight quivering. The scream had done it. That scream that had never found a voice was still locked up in my body, making it tremble.

I closed my eyes and swallowed another mouthful of brandy. The warmth spread from my throat to my stomach. The sensation felt tremendously *real*.

With a start, I thought of my son. Again my heart began pounding. I hurried from the sofa to his room. He was sound asleep, one hand across his mouth, the other thrust out to the side, looking just as secure and peaceful in sleep as my husband. I straightened his blanket. Whatever it was that had so violently shattered my sleep, it had attacked only me. Neither of them had felt a thing.

I returned to the living room and wandered about there. I was not the least bit sleepy.

I considered drinking another glass of brandy. In fact, I wanted to drink even more alcohol than that. I wanted to warm my body more, to calm my nerves down more, and to feel that strong, penetrating bouquet in my mouth again. After some hesitation, I decided against it. I didn't want to start the new day drunk. I put the brandy back in the sideboard, brought the glass to the kitchen sink and washed it. I found some strawberries in the refrigerator and ate them.

I realized that the trembling in my skin was almost gone.

What was that old man in black? I asked myself. I had never seen him before in my life. That black clothing of his was so strange, like a tight-fitting sweat suit, and yet, at the same time, old-fashioned. I had never seen anything like it. And those eyes—bloodshot, and never blinking. Who was he? Why did he pour water onto my feet? Why did he have to do such a thing?

I had only questions, no answers.

The time my friend went into a trance, she was spending the night at her fiancé's house. As she lay in bed asleep, an angry-looking man in his early fifties approached and ordered her out of the house. While that was happening, she couldn't move a muscle. And, like me, she became soaked with sweat. She was certain it must be the ghost of her fiancé's father, who was telling her to get out of his house. But when she asked to see a photograph of the father the next day, it turned out to be an entirely different man. "I must have been feeling tense," she concluded. "That's what caused it."

But *I'm* not tense. And this is my own house. There shouldn't be anything here to threaten me. Why did *I* have to go into a trance?

I shook my head. Stop thinking, I told myself. It won't do any good. I had a realistic dream, nothing more. I've probably been building up some kind of fatigue. The tennis I played the day before yesterday must have done it. I met a friend at the club after my swim and she invited me to play tennis and I overdid it a little, that's all. Sure—my arms and legs felt tired and heavy for a while afterward.

When I finished my strawberries, I stretched out on the sofa and tried closing my eyes.

I wasn't sleepy at all. Oh, great, I thought. I really don't feel like sleeping.

I thought I'd read a book until I got tired again. I went to the bedroom and picked a novel from the bookcase. My husband didn't even twitch when I turned on the light to hunt for it. I chose *Anna Karenina*. I was in the mood for a long Russian novel, and I had read *Anna Karenina* only once, long ago, probably in high school. I remembered just a few things about it: the first line, "All happy families resemble one another; every unhappy family is unhappy in its own way," and the heroine's throwing herself under a train at the end. And that early on there was a hint of the final suicide. Wasn't there a scene at a racetrack? Or was that in another novel?

Whatever. I went back to the sofa and opened the book. How many years had it been since I'd sat down and relaxed like this with a book? True, I often spent half an hour or an hour of my private time in the afternoon with a book open. But you couldn't really call that reading. I'd always find myself thinking about other things—my son, or shopping, or the freezer's needing to be fixed, or my having to find something to wear to a relative's wedding, or the stomach operation my father had last month. That kind of stuff would drift into my mind, and then it would grow and take off in a million different directions. After a while I'd notice that the only thing that had gone by was the time, and I had hardly turned any pages.

Without noticing it, I had become accustomed in this way to a life without books. How strange, now that I think of it. Reading had been the center of my life when I was young. I had read every book in the grade-school library, and almost my entire allowance would go for books. I'd even scrimp on lunches to buy books I wanted to read. And this went on into junior high and high school. Nobody read as much as I did. I was the third of five children, and both my parents worked, so nobody paid much attention to me. I could read alone as much as I liked. I'd always enter the essay contests on books so that I could win a gift certificate for more books. And I usually won. In college, I majored in English literature and got good grades. My graduation thesis on Katherine Mansfield won top honors, and my thesis adviser urged me to apply to graduate school. I wanted to go out into the world, though, and I knew that I was no scholar. I just enjoyed reading books. And even if I had wanted to go on studying, my family didn't have the financial wherewithal to send me to graduate school. We weren't poor by any means, but there were two sisters coming along after me, so once I graduated from college I simply had to begin supporting myself.

When had I really read a book last? And what had it been? I couldn't recall anything. Why did a person's life have to change so completely? Where had the old me gone, the one who used to read a book as if possessed by it? What had those days—and that almost abnormally intense passion—meant to me?

THAT NIGHT, I found myself capable of reading *Anna Karenina* with unbroken concentration. I went on turning pages without another thought in mind. In one sitting, I read as far as the scene where Anna and Vronsky first see each other in the Moscow train station. At that point, I stuck my bookmark in and poured myself another glass of brandy.

Though it hadn't occurred to me before, I couldn't help thinking what an odd novel this was. You don't see the heroine, Anna, until Chapter 18. I wondered if it didn't seem unusual to readers in Tolstoy's day. What did they do when the book went on and on with a detailed description of the life of a minor character named Oblonsky—just sit there, waiting for the beautiful heroine to appear? Maybe that was it. Maybe people in those days had lots of time to kill—at least the part of society that read novels.

Then I noticed how late it was. Three in the morning! And still I wasn't sleepy.

What should I do? I don't feel sleepy at all, I thought. I could just keep on reading. I'd love to find out what happens in the story. But I have to sleep.

I remembered my ordeal with insomnia and how I had gone through each day back then, wrapped in a cloud. No, never again. I was still a student in those days. It was still possible for me to get away with something like that. But not now, I thought. Now I'm a wife. A mother. I have responsibilities. I have to make my husband's lunches and take care of my son.

But even if I get into bed now, I know I won't be able to sleep a wink.

I shook my head.

Let's face it, I'm just not sleepy, I told myself. And I want to read the rest of the book.

I sighed and stole a glance at the big volume lying on the table. And that was that. I plunged into *Anna Karenina* and kept reading until the sun came up. Anna and Vronsky stared at each other at the ball and fell into their doomed love. Anna went to pieces when Vronsky's horse fell at the racetrack (so there *was* a racetrack scene, after all!) and confessed her infidelity to her husband. I was there with Vronsky when he spurred his horse over the obstacles. I heard the crowd cheering him on. And I was there in the stands watching his horse go down. When the window brightened with the morning light, I laid down the book and went to the kitchen for a cup of coffee. My mind was filled with scenes from the novel and with a tremendous hunger obliterating any other thoughts. I cut two slices of bread, spread them with butter and mustard, and had a cheese sandwich. My hunger pangs were almost unbearable. It was rare for me to feel that hungry. I had trouble breathing, I was so hungry. One sandwich did hardly anything for me, so I made another one and had another cup of coffee with it.

TO MY HUSBAND I said nothing about either my trance or my night without sleep. Not that I was hiding them from him. It just seemed to me that there was no point in telling him. What good would it have done? And besides, I had simply missed a night's sleep. That much happens to everyone now and then.

I made my husband his usual cup of coffee and gave my son a glass of warm milk. My husband ate toast, and my son ate a bowl of cornflakes. My husband skimmed the morning paper, and my son hummed a new song he had learned in school. The two of them got into the Sentra and left. "Be careful," I said to my husband. "Don't worry," he answered. The two of them waved. A typical morning.

After they were gone, I sat on the sofa and thought about how to spend the rest of the day. What should I do? What did I have to do? I went to the kitchen to inspect the contents of the refrigerator. I could get by without shopping. We had bread, milk, and eggs, and there was meat in the freezer. Plenty of vegetables, too. Everything I'd need through tomorrow's lunch.

I had business at the bank, but it was nothing I absolutely had to take care of immediately. Letting it go a day longer wouldn't hurt.

I went back to the sofa and started reading the rest of *Anna Karenina*. Until that reading, I hadn't realized how little I remembered of what goes on in the book. I recognized virtually nothing—the characters, the scenes, nothing. I might as well have been reading a whole new book. How strange. I must have been deeply moved at the time I first read it, but now there was nothing left. Without my noticing, the memories of all the shuddering, soaring emotions had slipped away and vanished.

What, then, of the enormous fund of time I had consumed back then reading books? What had all that meant?

I stopped reading and thought about that for a while. None of it made sense to me, though, and soon I even lost track of what I was thinking about. I caught myself staring at the tree that stood outside the window. I shook my head and went back to the book.

Just after the middle of Volume 3, I found a few crumbling flakes of chocolate stuck between the pages. I must have been eating chocolate as I read the novel when I was in high school. I used to like to eat and read. Come to think of it, I hadn't touched chocolate since my marriage. My husband doesn't like me to eat sweets, and we almost never give them to our son. We don't usually keep that kind of thing around the house.

As I looked at the whitened flakes of chocolate from over a decade ago, I felt a tremendous urge to have the real thing. I wanted to eat chocolate while reading *Anna Karenina,* the way I did back then. I couldn't bear to be denied it for another moment. Every cell in my body seemed to be panting with this hunger for chocolate.

I slipped a cardigan over my shoulders and took the elevator down. I walked straight to the neighborhood candy shop and bought two of the sweetest-looking milk-chocolate bars they had. As soon as I left the shop, I tore one open and started eating it while walking home. The luscious taste of milk chocolate spread through my mouth. I could feel the sweetness being absorbed directly into every part of my body. I continued eating in the elevator, steeping myself in the wonderful aroma that filled the tiny space.

Heading straight for the sofa, I started reading *Anna Karenina* and eating my chocolate. I wasn't the least bit sleepy. I felt no physical fatigue, either. I could have gone on reading forever. When I finished the first chocolate bar, I opened the second and ate half of that. About two thirds of the way through Volume 3, I looked at my watch. Eleven-forty.

Eleven-forty!

My husband would be home soon. I closed the book and hurried to the kitchen. I put water in a pot and turned on the gas. Then I minced some scallions and took out a handful of buckwheat noodles for boiling. While the water was heating, I soaked some dried seaweed, cut it up, and topped it with a vinegar dressing. I took a block of tofu from the refrigerator and cut it into cubes. Finally, I went into the bathroom and brushed my teeth to get rid of the chocolate smell.

At almost the exact moment the water came to a boil, my husband walked in. He had finished work a little earlier than usual, he said.

Together, we ate the buckwheat noodles. My husband talked about a new piece of dental equipment he was considering bringing into the office, a machine that would remove plaque from patients' teeth far more thoroughly than anything he had used before, and in less time. Like all such equipment, it was quite expensive, but it would pay for itself soon enough. More and more patients were coming in just for a cleaning these days.

"What do you think?" he asked me.

I didn't want to think about plaque on people's teeth, and I especially didn't want to hear or think about it while I was eating. My mind was filled with hazy images of Vronsky falling off his horse. But of course I couldn't tell my husband that. He was deadly serious about the equipment. I asked him the price and pretended to think about it. "Why not buy it if you need it?" I said. "The money will work out one way or another. You wouldn't be spending it for fun, after all."

"That's true," he said. "I wouldn't be spending it for fun." Then he continued eating his noodles in silence.

Perched on a branch of the tree outside the window, a pair of large birds was chirping. I watched them half-consciously. I wasn't sleepy. I wasn't the least bit sleepy. Why not?

While I cleared the table, my husband sat on the sofa reading the paper. *Anna Karenina* lay there beside him, but he didn't seem to notice. He had no interest in whether I read books.

After I finished washing the dishes, my husband said, "I've got a nice surprise today. What do you think it is?"

"I don't know," I said.

"My first afternoon patient has canceled. I don't have to be back in the office until one-thirty." He smiled.

I couldn't figure out why this was supposed to be such a nice surprise. I wonder why I couldn't.

It was only after my husband stood up and drew me toward the bedroom that I realized what he had in mind. I wasn't in the mood for it at all. I didn't understand why I should have sex then. All I wanted was to get back to my book. I wanted to stretch out alone on the sofa and munch on chocolate while I turned the pages of *Anna Karenina*. All the time I had been washing the dishes, my only thoughts had been of Vronsky and of how an author like Tolstoy managed to control his characters so skillfully. He described them with wonderful precision. But that very precision somehow denied them a kind of salvation. And this finally—

I closed my eyes and pressed my fingertips to my temple.

"I'm sorry, I've had a kind of headache all day. What awful timing."

I had often had some truly terrible headaches, so he accepted my explanation without a murmur.

"You'd better lie down and get some rest," he said. "You've been working too hard."

"It's really not that bad," I said.

He relaxed on the sofa until one o'clock, listening to music and reading the paper. And he talked about dental equipment again. You bought the latest high-tech stuff and it was obsolete in two or three years. . . . So then you had to keep replacing everything. . . . The only ones who made any money were the equipment manufacturers—that kind of talk. I offered a few clucks, but I was hardly listening.

After my husband went back to the office, I folded the paper and pounded the sofa cushions until they were puffed up again. Then I leaned on the windowsill, surveying the room. I couldn't figure out what was happening. Why wasn't I sleepy? In the old days, I had done all-nighters any number of times, but I had never stayed awake this long. Ordinarily, I would have been sound asleep after so many hours or, if not asleep, impossibly tired. But I wasn't the least bit sleepy. My mind was perfectly clear.

I went into the kitchen and warmed up some coffee. I thought, Now what should I do? Of course, I wanted to read the rest of *Anna Karenina,* but I also wanted to go to the pool for my swim. I decided to go swimming. I don't know how to explain this, but I wanted to purge my body of something by exercising it to the limit. Purge it—of what? I spent some time wondering about that. Purge it of what?

I didn't know.

But this thing, whatever it was, this mistlike something, hung there inside my body like a certain kind of potential. I wanted to give it a name, but the word refused to come to mind. I'm terrible at finding the right words for things. I'm sure Tolstoy would have been able to come up with exactly the right word.

Anyhow, I put my swimsuit in my bag and, as always, drove my Civic to the athletic club. There were only two other people in the pool—a young man and a middle-aged woman—and I didn't know either of them. A bored-looking lifeguard was on duty.

I changed into my bathing suit, put on my goggles, and swam my usual thirty minutes. But thirty minutes wasn't enough. I swam another fifteen minutes, ending with a crawl at maximum speed for two full lengths. I was out of breath, but I still felt nothing but energy welling up inside my body. The others were staring at me when I left the pool.

It was still a little before three o'clock, so I drove to the bank and finished my business there. I considered doing some shopping at the supermarket, but I decided instead to head straight for home. There, I picked up *Anna Karenina* where I had left off, eating what was left of the chocolate. When my son came home at four o'clock, I gave him a glass of juice and some fruit gelatin that I had made. Then I started on dinner. I defrosted some meat from the freezer and cut up some vegetables in preparation for stir-frying. I made miso soup and cooked the rice. All of these tasks I took care of with tremendous mechanical efficiency.

I went back to *Anna Karenina*.

I was not tired.

AT TEN O'CLOCK, I got into my bed, pretending that I would be sleeping there near my husband. He fell asleep right away, practically the moment the light went out, as if there were some cord connecting the lamp with his brain.

Amazing. People like that are rare. There are far more people who have trouble falling asleep. My father was one of those. He'd always complain about how shallow his sleep was. Not only did he find it hard to get to sleep, but the slightest sound or movement would wake him up for the rest of the night.

Not my husband, though. Once he was asleep, nothing could wake him until morning. We were still newlyweds when it struck me how odd this was. I even experimented to see what it would take to wake him. I sprinkled water on his face and tickled his nose with a brush—that kind of thing. I never once got him to wake up. If I kept at it, I could get him to groan once, but that was all. And he never dreamed. At least he never remembered what his dreams were about. Needless to say, he never went into any paralytic trances. He slept. He slept like a turtle buried in mud.

Amazing. But it helped with what quickly became my nightly routine.

After ten minutes of lying near him, I would get out of bed. I would go to the living room, turn on the floor lamp, and pour myself a glass of brandy. Then I would sit on the sofa and read my book, taking tiny sips of brandy and letting the smooth liquid glide over my tongue. Whenever I felt like it, I would eat a cookie or a piece of chocolate that I had hidden in the sideboard. After a while, morning would come. When that happened, I would close my book and make myself a cup of coffee. Then I would make a sandwich and eat it.

My days became just as regulated.

I would hurry through my housework and spend the rest of the morning reading. Just before noon, I would put my book down and fix my husband's lunch. When he left, before one, I'd drive to the club and have my swim. I would swim for a full hour. Once I stopped sleeping, thirty minutes was never enough. While I was in the water, I concentrated my entire mind on swimming. I thought about nothing but how to move my body most effectively, and I inhaled and exhaled with perfect regularity. If I met someone I knew, I hardly said a word—just the basic civilities. I refused all invitations. "Sorry," I'd say. "I'm going straight home today. There's something I have to do." I didn't want to get involved with anybody. I didn't want to have to waste time on endless gossiping. When I was through swimming as hard as I could, all I wanted was to hurry home and read.

I went through the motions—shopping, cooking, playing

with my son, having sex with my husband. It was easy once I got the hang of it. All I had to do was break the connection between my mind and my body. While my body went about its business, my mind floated in its own inner space. I ran the house without a thought in my head, feeding snacks to my son, chatting with my husband.

After I gave up sleeping, it occurred to me what a simple thing reality is, how easy it is to make it work. It's just reality. Just housework. Just a home. Like running a simple machine. Once you learn to run it, it's just a matter of repetition. You push this button and pull that lever. You adjust a gauge, put on the lid, set the timer. The same thing, over and over.

Of course, there were variations now and then. My mother-in-law had dinner with us. On Sunday, the three of us went to the zoo. My son had a terrible case of diarrhea.

But none of these events had any effect on my being. They swept past me like a silent breeze. I chatted with my mother-in-law, made dinner for four, took a picture in front of the bear cage, put a hot-water bottle on my son's stomach and gave him his medicine.

No one noticed that I had changed—that I had given up sleeping entirely, that I was spending all my time reading, that my mind was someplace a hundred years—and hundreds of miles—from reality. No matter how mechanically I worked, no matter how little love or emotion I invested in my handling of reality, my husband and my son and my mother-in-law went on relating to me as they always had. If anything, they seemed more at ease with me than before.

And so a week went by.

Once my constant wakefulness entered its second week, though, it started to worry me. It was simply not normal. People are supposed to sleep. All people sleep. Once, some years ago, I had read about a form of torture in which the victim is prevented from sleeping. Something the Nazis did, I think. They'd lock the person in a tiny room, fasten his eyelids open, and keep shining lights in his face and making loud noises without a break. Eventually, the person would go mad and die.

I couldn't recall how long the article said it took for the madness to set in, but it couldn't have been much more than three or four days. In my case, a whole week had gone by. This was simply too much. Still, my health was not suffering. Far from it. I had more energy than ever.

One day, after showering, I stood naked in front of the mirror. I was amazed to discover that my body appeared to be almost bursting with vitality. I studied every inch of myself, head to toe, but I could find not the slightest hint of excess flesh, not one wrinkle. I no longer had the body of a young girl, of course, but my skin had far more glow, far more tautness, than it had before. I took a pinch of flesh near my waist and found it almost hard, with a wonderful elasticity.

It dawned on me that I was prettier than I had realized. I looked so much younger than before that it was almost shocking. I could probably pass for twenty-four. My skin was smooth. My eyes were bright, lips moist. The shadowed area beneath my protruding cheekbones (the one feature I really hated about myself) was no longer noticeable—at all. I sat down and looked at my face in the mirror for a good thirty minutes. I studied it from all angles, objectively. No, I had not been mistaken: I was really pretty.

What was happening to me?

I thought about seeing a doctor.

I had a doctor who had been taking care of me since I was a child and to whom I felt close, but the more I thought about how he might react to my story the less inclined I felt to tell it to him. Would he take me at my word? He'd probably think I was crazy if I said I hadn't slept in a week. Or he might dismiss it as a kind of neurotic insomnia. But if he did believe I was telling the truth, he might send me to some big research hospital for testing.

And *then* what would happen?

I'd be locked up and sent from one lab to another to be experimented on. They'd do EEGs and EKGs and urinalyses and blood tests and psychological screening and who knows what else.

I couldn't take that. I just wanted to stay by myself and quietly read my book. I wanted to have my hour of swimming every day. I wanted my freedom: That's what I wanted more than anything. I didn't want to go to any hospitals. And, even if they *did* get me into a hospital, what would they find? They'd do a mountain of tests and formulate a mountain of hypotheses, and that would be the end of it. I didn't want to be locked up in a place like that.

One afternoon, I went to the library and read some books on sleep. The few books I could find didn't tell me much. In fact, they all had only one thing to say: that sleep is rest. Like turning off a car engine. If you keep a motor running constantly, sooner or later it will break down. A running engine must produce heat, and the accumulated heat fatigues the machinery itself. Which is why you have to let the engine rest. Cool down. Turning off the engine—that, finally, is what sleep is. In a human being, sleep provides rest for both the flesh and the spirit. When a person lies down and rests her muscles, she simultaneously closes her eyes and cuts off the thought process. And excess thoughts release an electrical discharge in the form of dreams.

One book did have a fascinating point to make. The author maintained that human beings, by their very nature, are incapable of escaping from certain fixed idiosyncratic tendencies, both in their thought processes and in their physical movements. People unconsciously fashion their own action- and thought-tendencies, which under normal circumstances never disappear. In other words, people live in the prison cells of their own tendencies. What modulates these tendencies and keeps them in check—so the organism doesn't wear down as the heel of a shoe does, at a particular angle, as the author puts it—is nothing other than sleep. Sleep therapeutically counteracts the tendencies. In sleep, people naturally relax muscles that have been consistently used in only one direction; sleep both calms and provides a discharge for thought circuits that have likewise been used in only one direction. This is how people are cooled down. Sleeping is an act that has been programmed, with karmic inevitability, into the human system, and no one can diverge from it. If a person *were* to diverge from it, the person's very "ground of being" would be threatened.

"Tendencies?" I asked myself.

The only "tendency" of mine that I could think of was housework—those chores I perform day after day like an unfeeling machine. Cooking and shopping and laundry and mothering: What were they if not "tendencies"? I could do them with my eyes closed. Push the buttons. Pull the levers. Pretty soon, reality just flows off and away. The same physical movements over and over. Tendencies. They were consuming me, wearing me down on one side like the heel of a shoe. I needed sleep every day to adjust them and cool me down.

Was that it?

I read the passage once more, with intense concentration. And I nodded. Yes, almost certainly, that *was* it.

So, then, what was this life of mine? I was being consumed by my tendencies and then sleeping to repair the damage. My life was nothing but a repetition of this cycle. It was going nowhere.

Sitting at the library table, I shook my head.

I'm through with sleep! So what if I go mad? So what if I lose my "ground of being"? I will not be consumed by my "tendencies." If sleep is nothing more than a periodic repairing of the parts of me that are being worn away, I don't want it anymore. I don't need it anymore. My flesh may have to be consumed, but my mind belongs to me. I'm keeping it for myself. I will not hand it over to anyone. I don't want to be "repaired." I will not sleep.

I left the library filled with a new determination.

NOW MY INABILITY to sleep ceased to frighten me. What was there to be afraid of? Think of the advantages! Now the hours from ten at night to six in the morning belonged to me alone. Until now, a third of every day had been used up by sleep. But no more. No more. Now it was mine, just mine, nobody else's, all mine. I could use this time in any way I liked. No one would get in my way. No one would make demands on me. Yes, that was it. I had expanded my life. I had increased it by a third.

You are probably going to tell me that this is biologically abnormal. And you may be right. And maybe someday in the future I'll have to pay back the debt I'm building up by continuing to do this biologically abnormal thing. Maybe life will try to collect on the expanded part—this "advance" it is paying me now. This is a groundless hypothesis, but there is no ground for negating it, and it feels right to me somehow. Which means that in the end, the balance sheet of borrowed time will even out.

Honestly, though, I didn't give a damn, even if I had to die young. The best thing to do with a hypothesis is to let it run any course it pleases. Now, at least, I was expanding my life, and it was wonderful. My hands weren't empty anymore. Here I was—alive, and I could feel it. It was real. I wasn't being consumed any longer. Or at least there was a part of me in existence that was not being consumed, and that was what gave me this intensely real feeling of being alive. A life without that feeling might go on forever, but it would have no meaning at all. I saw that with absolute clarity now.

After checking to see that my husband was asleep, I would go sit on the living-room sofa, drink brandy by myself, and open my book. I read *Anna Karenina* three times. Each time, I made new discoveries. This enormous novel was full of revelations and riddles. Like a Chinese box, the world of the novel contained smaller worlds, and inside those were yet smaller worlds. Together, these worlds made up a single universe, and the universe waited there in the book to be discovered by the reader. The old me had been able to understand only the tiniest fragment of it, but the gaze of this new me could penetrate to the core with perfect understanding. I knew exactly what the great Tolstoy wanted to say, what he wanted the reader to get from his book; I could see how his message had organically crystallized as a novel, and what in that novel had surpassed the author himself.

No matter how hard I concentrated, I never tired. After reading *Anna Karenina* as many times as I could, I read Dostoyevski. I could read book after book with utter concentration and never tire. I could understand the most difficult passages without effort. And I responded with deep emotion.

I felt that I had always been meant to be like this. By abandoning sleep I had expanded myself. The power to concentrate was the most important thing. Living without this power would be like opening one's eyes without seeing anything.

Eventually, my bottle of brandy ran out. I had drunk almost all of it by myself. I went to the gourmet department of a big store for another bottle of Rémy Martin. As long as I was there, I figured, I might as well buy a bottle of red wine, too. And a fine crystal brandy glass. And chocolate and cookies.

Sometimes while reading I would become overexcited. When that happened, I would put my book down and exercise—do calisthenics or just walk around the room. Depending on my mood, I might go out for a nighttime drive. I'd change clothes, get into my Civic, and drive aimlessly around the neighborhood. Sometimes I'd drop into an all-night fast-food place for a cup of coffee, but it was such a bother to have to deal with other people that I'd usually stay in the car. I'd stop in some safe-looking spot and just let my mind wander. Or I'd go all the way to the harbor and watch the boats.

One time, though, I was questioned by a policeman. It was two-thirty in the morning, and I was parked under a streetlamp near the pier, listening to the car stereo and watching the lights of the ships passing by. He knocked on my window. I lowered the glass. He was young and handsome, and very polite. I explained to him that I couldn't sleep. He asked for my license and studied it for a while. "There was a murder here last month," he said. "Three young men attacked a couple. They killed the man and raped the woman." I remembered having read about the incident. I nodded. "If you don't have any business here, ma'am, you'd better not hang around here at night." I thanked him and said I would leave. He gave me my license back. I drove away.

That was the only time anyone talked to me. Usually, I would drift through the streets at night for an hour or more and no one would bother me. Then I would park in our underground garage. Right next to my husband's white Sentra; he was upstairs sleeping soundly in the darkness. I'd listen to the crackle of the hot engine cooling down, and when the sound died I'd go upstairs.

The first thing I would do when I got inside was check to make sure my husband was asleep. And he always was. Then I'd check my son, who was always sound asleep, too. They didn't know a thing. They believed that the world was as it had always been, unchanging. But they were wrong. It was changing in ways they could never guess. Changing a lot. Changing fast. It would never be the same again.

One time, I stood and stared at my sleeping husband's face. I had heard a thump in the bedroom and rushed in. The alarm clock was on the floor. He had probably knocked it down in his sleep. But he was sleeping as soundly as ever, completely unaware of what he had done. What would it take to wake this man? I picked up the clock and put it back on the night table. Then I folded my arms and stared at my husband. How long had it been—years?—since the last time I had studied his face as he slept?

I had done it a lot when we were first married. That was all it took to relax me and put me in a peaceful mood. I'll be safe as long as he goes on sleeping peacefully like this, I'd tell myself. Which is why I spent a lot of time watching him in his sleep.

But, somewhere along the way, I had given up the habit. When had that been? I tried to remember. It had probably happened back when my mother-in-law and I were sort of quarreling over what name to give my son. She was big on some religious cult kind of thing, and had asked her priest to "bestow" a name on the baby. I don't remember exactly the name she was given, but I had no intention of letting some priest "bestow" a name on my child. We had some pretty violent arguments at the time, but my husband couldn't say a thing to either of us. He stood by and tried to calm us.

After that, I lost the feeling that my husband was my protector. The one thing I thought I wanted from him he had failed to give me. All he had managed to do was make me furious. This happened a long time ago, of course. My mother-in-law and I have long since made up. I gave my son the name I wanted to give him. My husband and I made up right away, too.

I'm pretty sure that was the end, though, of my watching him in his sleep.

So there I stood, looking at him sleeping as soundly as always. One bare foot stuck out from under the covers at a strange angle—so strange that the foot could have belonged to someone else. It was a big, chunky foot. My husband's mouth hung open, the lower lip drooping. Every once in a while, his nostrils would twitch. There was a mole under his eye that bothered me. It was so big and vulgar-looking. There was something vulgar about the way his eyes were closed, the lids slack, covers made of faded human flesh. He looked like an absolute fool. This was what they mean by "dead to the world." How incredibly ugly! He sleeps with such an ugly face! It's just too gruesome, I thought. He couldn't have been like this in the old days. I'm sure he must have had a better face when we were first married, one that was taut and alert. Even sound asleep, he couldn't have been such a blob.

I tried to remember what his sleeping face had looked like back then, but I couldn't do it, though I tried hard enough. All I could be sure of was that he *couldn't* have had such a terrible face. Or was I just deceiving myself? Maybe he had always looked like this in his sleep and I had been indulging in some kind of emotional projection. I'm sure that's what my mother would say. That sort of thinking was a specialty of hers. "All that lovey-dovey stuff lasts two years—three years tops," she always used to insist. "You were a new bride," I'm sure she would tell me now. "Of *course,* your little hubby looked like a darling in his sleep."

I'm sure she would say something like that, but I'm just as sure she'd be wrong. He *had* grown ugly over the years. The firmness had gone out of his face. That's what growing old is all about. He was old now, and tired. Worn out. He'd get even uglier in the years ahead, that much was certain. And I had no choice but to go along with it, put up with it, resign myself to it.

I let out a sigh as I stood there watching him. It was a deep sigh, a noisy one as sighs go, but of course he didn't move a muscle. The loudest sigh in the world would never wake him up.

I left the bedroom and went back to the living room. I poured myself a brandy and started reading. But something wouldn't let me concentrate. I put the book down and went to my son's room. Opening the door, I stared at his face in the light spilling in from the hallway. He was sleeping just as soundly as my husband was. As he always did. I watched him in his sleep, looked at his smooth, nearly featureless face. It was very different from my husband's: It was still a child's face, after all. The skin still glowed; it still had nothing vulgar about it.

And yet, something about my son's face annoyed me. I had never felt anything like this about him before. What could be making me feel this way? I stood there, looking, with my arms folded. Yes, of course I loved my son, loved him tremendously. But still, undeniably, that something was bothering me, getting on my nerves.

I shook my head.

I closed my eyes and kept them shut. Then I opened them and looked at my son's face again. And then it hit me. What bothered me about my son's sleeping face was that it looked exactly like my husband's. And exactly like my mother-in-law's. Stubborn. Self-satisfied. It was in their blood—a kind of arrogance I hated in my husband's family. True, my husband is good to me. He's sweet and gentle and he's careful to take my feelings into account. He's never fooled around with other women, and he works hard. He's serious, and he's kind to everybody. My friends all tell me how lucky I am to have him. And I can't fault him, either. Which is exactly what galls me sometimes. His very absence of faults makes for a strange rigidity that excludes imagination. That's what grates on me so.

And that was exactly the kind of expression my son had on his face as he slept.

I shook my head again. This little boy is a stranger to me, finally. Even after he grows up, he'll never be able to understand me, just as my husband can hardly understand what I feel now.

I love my son, no question. But I sensed that someday I would no longer be able to love this boy with the same intensity. Not a very maternal thought. Most mothers never have thoughts like that. But as I stood there looking at him asleep, I knew with absolute certainty that one day I would come to despise him.

The thought made me terribly sad. I closed his door and turned out the hall light. I went to the living-room sofa, sat down, and opened my book. After reading a few pages, I closed it again. I looked at the clock. A little before three.

I wondered how many days it had been since I stopped sleeping. The sleeplessness started the Tuesday before last. Which made this the seventeenth day. Not one wink of sleep in seventeen days. Seventeen days and seventeen nights. A long, long time. I couldn't even recall what sleep was like.

I closed my eyes and tried to recall the sensation of sleeping, but all that existed for me inside was a wakeful darkness. A wakeful darkness: What it called to mind was death.

Was I about to die?

And if I died now, what would my life have amounted to?

There was no way I could answer that.

All right, then, what *was* death?

Until now, I had conceived of sleep as a kind of model for death. I had imagined death as an extension of sleep. A far deeper sleep than ordinary sleep. A sleep devoid of all consciousness. Eternal rest. A total blackout.

But now I wondered if I had been wrong. Perhaps death was a state entirely unlike sleep, something that belonged to a different category altogether—like the deep, endless, wakeful darkness I was seeing now.

No, that would be too terrible. If the state of death was not to be a rest for us, then what was going to redeem this imperfect life of ours, so fraught with exhaustion? Finally, though, no one knows what death is. Who has ever truly seen it? No one. Except the ones who are dead. No one living knows what death is like. They can only guess. And the best guess is still a guess. Maybe death *is* a kind of rest, but reasoning can't tell us that. The only way to find out what death is is to die. *Death can be anything at all.*

An intense terror overwhelmed me at the thought. A stiffening chill ran down my spine. My eyes were still shut tight. I had lost the power to open them. I stared at the thick darkness that stood planted in front of me, a darkness as deep and hopeless as the universe itself. I was all alone. My mind was in deep concentration, and expanding. If I had wanted to, I could have seen into the uttermost depths of the universe. But I decided not to look. It was too soon for that.

If death was like this, if to die meant being eternally awake and staring into the darkness like this, what should I do?

At last, I managed to open my eyes. I gulped down the brandy that was left in my glass.

I'M TAKING OFF my pajamas and putting on jeans, a T-shirt, and a windbreaker. I tie my hair back in a tight ponytail, tuck it under the windbreaker, and put on a baseball cap of my husband's. In the mirror, I look like a boy. Good. I put on sneakers and go down to the garage.

I slip in behind the steering wheel, turn the key, and listen to the engine hum. It sounds normal. Hands on the wheel, I take a few deep breaths. Then I shift into gear and drive out of the building. The car is running better than usual. It seems to be gliding across a sheet of ice. I ease it into higher gear, move out of the neighborhood, and enter the highway to Yokohama.

It's only three in the morning, but the number of cars on the road is by no means small. Huge semis roll past, shaking the ground as they head east. Those guys don't sleep at night. They sleep in the daytime and work at night for greater efficiency.

What a waste. I could work day *and* night. I don't have to sleep.

This is biologically unnatural, I suppose, but who really knows what is natural? They just infer it inductively. I'm beyond that. A priori. An evolutionary leap. A woman who never sleeps. An expansion of consciousness.

I have to smile. A priori. An evolutionary leap.

Listening to the car radio, I drive to the harbor. I want classical music, but I can't find a station that broadcasts it at night. Stupid Japanese rock music. Love songs sweet enough to rot your teeth. I give up searching and listen to those. They make me feel I'm in a far-off place, far away from Mozart and Haydn.

I pull into one of the white-outlined spaces in the big parking lot at the waterfront park and cut my engine. This is the brightest area of the lot, under a lamp, and wide open all around. Only one car is parked here—an old white two-door coupe of the kind that young people like to drive. Probably a couple in there now, making love—no money for a hotel room. To avoid trouble, I pull my hat low, trying not to look like a woman. I check to see that my doors are locked.

Half-consciously, I let my eyes wander through the surrounding darkness, when all of a sudden I remember a drive I took with my boyfriend the year I was a college freshman. We parked and got into some heavy petting. He couldn't stop, he said, and he begged me to let him put it in. But I refused. Hands on the steering wheel, listening to the music, I try to bring back the scene, but I can't recall his face. It seems to have happened such an incredibly long time ago.

All the memories I have from the time before I stopped sleeping seem to be moving away with accelerating speed. It feels so strange, as if the me who used to go to sleep every night is not the real me, and the memories from back then are not really mine. This is how people change. But nobody realizes it. Nobody notices. Only *I* know what happens. I could try to tell them, but they wouldn't understand. They wouldn't believe me. Or if they did believe me, they would have absolutely no idea what I'm feeling. They would only see me as a threat to their inductive worldview.

I am changing, though. *Really* changing.

How long have I been sitting here? Hands on the wheel. Eyes closed. Staring into the sleepless darkness.

Suddenly I'm aware of a human presence, and I come to myself again. There's somebody out there. I open my eyes and look around. Someone is outside the car. Trying to open the door. But the doors are locked. Dark shadows on either side of the car, one at each door. Can't see their faces. Can't make out their clothing. Just two dark shadows, standing there.

Sandwiched between them, my Civic feels tiny—like a little pastry box. It's being rocked from side to side. A fist is pounding on the right-hand window. I know it's not a policeman. A policeman would never pound on the glass like this and would never shake my car. I hold my breath. What should I do? I can't think straight. My underarms are soaked. I've got to get out of here. The key. Turn the key. I reach out for it and turn it to the right. The starter grinds.

The engine doesn't catch. My hand is shaking. I close my eyes and turn the key again. No good. A sound like fingernails clawing a giant wall. The motor turns and turns. The men—the dark shadows—keep shaking my car. The swings get bigger and bigger. They're going to tip me over!

There's something wrong. Just calm down and think, then

everything will be okay. Think. Just think. Slowly. Carefully. Something is wrong.

Something is wrong.

But what? I can't tell. My mind is crammed full of thick darkness. It's not taking me anywhere. My hands are shaking. I try pulling out the key and putting it back in again. But my shaking hand can't find the hole. I try again and drop the key. I curl over and try to pick it up. But I can't get hold of it. The car is rocking back and forth. My forehead slams against the steering wheel.

I'll never get the key. I fall back against the seat, cover my face with my hands. I'm crying. All I can do is cry. The tears keep pouring out. Locked inside this little box, I can't go anywhere. It's the middle of the night. The men keep rocking the car back and forth. They're going to turn it over.

—translated by Jay Rubin

THE FALL

OF THE

ROMAN

EMPIRE,

THE 1881

INDIAN

UPRISING,

HITLER'S

INVASION

OF POLAND,

AND THE REALM

OF RAGING

WINDS

1

THE FALL
OF THE
ROMAN EMPIRE

I FIRST NOTICED the wind had begun to blow in the afternoon on Sunday. Or more precisely, at seven past two in the afternoon.

At the time, just like always—just like I always do on Sunday afternoons, that is—I was sitting at the kitchen table, listening to some innocuous music while catching up on a week's worth of entries in my diary. I make a practice of jotting down each day's events throughout the week, then writing them up on Sunday.

I'd just finished with the three days up through Tuesday when I became aware of the strong winds droning past my window. I canned the diary entries, capped my pen, and went out to the veranda to take in the laundry. The things on the line were all aflutter, whipping out loud, dry cracks, streaming their crazed comet tails off into space.

When I least suspected it, the wind seemed to have picked up out of nowhere. Hanging out the laundry on the veranda in the morning—at eighteen past ten in the morning, to be exact—there hadn't been the slightest whisper of a breeze. About that my memory is as airtight as the lid on a blast furnace. Because for a second there I'd even thought: No need for clothespins on such a calm day.

There honest to goodness hadn't been a puff of air moving anywhere.

Swiftly gathering up the laundry, I then went around shutting all the windows in the apartment. Once the windows were closed, I could hardly hear the wind at all. Outside in the absence of sound, the trees—Himalayan cedars and chestnuts, mostly—squirmed like dogs with an uncontrollable itch. Swatches of cloud cover slipped across the sky and out of sight like shifty-eyed secret agents, while on the veranda of an apartment across the way several shirts had wrapped themselves around a plastic clothesline and were clinging frantically, like abandoned orphans.

It's really blowing up a gale, I thought.

Upon opening the newspaper and checking out the weather map, however, I didn't find any sign of a typhoon. The probability of rainfall was listed at 0%. A peaceful Sunday afternoon like the heyday of the Roman Empire, it was supposed to have been.

I let out a slight, maybe 30% sigh and folded up the newspaper, tidied the laundry away in the chest of drawers, made coffee while listening to more of the same innocuous music, then carried on with my diary keeping over a hot cup.

Thursday, I slept with my girlfriend. She likes to wear a blindfold during sex. She always carries around a piece of cloth in her airline overnight bag just for that purpose.

Not my thing, really, but she looks so cute blindfolded like that, I can't very well object. We're all human, after all, and everybody's got something a little off somewhere.

That's pretty much what I wrote for the Thursday entry in my diary. Eighty percent facts, 20% short comments, that's my diary policy.

Friday, I ran into an old friend in a Ginza bookstore. He was wearing a tie with the most ungodly pattern. Telephone numbers, a whole slew of them, on a striped background—I'd gotten that far when the telephone rang.

2.

THE 1881
INDIAN
UPRISING

IT WAS THIRTY-SIX past two by the clock when the telephone rang. Probably her—my girlfriend with the thing about blindfolds, that is—or so I thought. She'd planned on coming over on Sunday anyway, and she always makes a point of ringing up beforehand. It was her job to buy groceries for dinner. We'd decided on oyster hot pot for that evening.

Anyway, it was two-thirty-six in the afternoon when the telephone rang. I have the alarm clock sitting right next to the telephone. That way I always see the clock when I go for the telephone, so I recall that much perfectly.

Yet when I picked up the receiver, all I could hear was this fierce wind blowing. A *rummmmmble* full of fury, like the Indians all rising on the warpath in 1881, right there in the receiver. They were burning pioneer cabins, cutting telegraph lines, raping Candice Bergen.

"Hello?" I ventured, but my lone voice got sucked under the overwhelming tumult of history.

"Hello? Hello?" I shouted out loud, again to no avail.

Straining my ears, I could just barely make out the faintest catches of what might have been a woman's voice through the wind. Or then again, maybe I was hearing things. Whatever, the wind was too strong to be sure. And I guess too many buffalo had already bitten the dust.

I couldn't say a word. I just stood there with the receiver to my ear. Hard and fast, I had the thing practically glued to my ear. I almost thought it wasn't going to come off. But then, after fifteen or twenty seconds like that, the telephone cut off. It was as if a lifeline had snapped in a seizure. After which a vast and empty silence, warmthless as overbleached underwear, was all that remained.

3.

HITLER'S

INVASION

OF POLAND

That does it. I let out another sigh. And I continued with my diary, thinking I'd better just finish logging it in.

Saturday, Hitler's armored divisions invaded Poland. Dive bombers over Warsaw—

No, that's not right. That's not what happened. Hitler's invasion of Poland was on September 1, 1939. Not yesterday. After dinner yesterday, I went to the movies and saw Meryl Streep in *Sophie's Choice*. Hitler's invasion of Poland only figured in the film.

In the film, Meryl Streep divorces Dustin Hoffman, but then in a commuter train she meets this civil engineer played by Robert De Niro, and remarries. A pretty all-right movie.

Sitting next to me was a high-school couple, and they kept touching each other on the tummy the whole time. Not bad at all, your high-school student's tummy. Even me, time was I used to have a high-school student's tummy.

4 .

AND THE

REALM OF

RAGING

WINDS

ONCE I'D SQUARED away the previous week's worth in my diary, I sat myself down in front of the record rack and picked out some music for a windy Sunday afternoon's listening. I settled on a Shostakovich cello concerto and a Sly and the Family Stone album, selections that seemed suitable enough for high winds, and I listened to these two records one after the other.

Every so often, things would strafe past the window. A white sheet flying east to west like some sorcerer brewing an elixir of roots and herbs. A long, flimsy tin sign arching its sickly spine like an anal-sex enthusiast.

I was taking in the scene outside to the strains of the Shostakovich cello concerto when again the telephone rang. The alarm clock beside the telephone read 3:48.

I picked up the receiver fully expecting that Boeing 747 jet-engine roar, but this time there was no wind to be heard.

"Hello," she said.

"Hello," I said, too.

"I was just thinking about heading over with the fixings for the oyster hot pot, okay?" said my girlfriend. She'll be on her way with groceries and a blindfold.

"Fine by me, but—"

"You have a casserole?"

"Yes, but," I say, "what gives? I don't hear that wind any-more."

"Yeah, the wind's stopped. Here in Nakano it let up at three twenty-five. So I don't imagine it'll be long before it lets up over there."

"Maybe so," I said as I hung up the telephone, then took down the casserole from the above-closet storage compartment and washed it in the sink.

Just as she had predicted, the winds stopped, at 4:05 on the dot. I opened the windows and looked around outside. Directly below, a black dog was intently sniffing around at the ground. For fifteen or twenty minutes, the dog kept at it tirelessly. I couldn't imagine why the dog felt so compelled.

Other than that, though, the appearances and workings of the world remained unchanged from before the winds had started. The Himalayan cedars and chestnuts stood their open ground, aloof as if nothing had transpired. Laundry hung limply from plastic clotheslines. Atop the telephone poles, crows gave a flap or two of their wings, their beaks shiny as credit cards.

Meanwhile during all of this, my girlfriend had shown up and began to prepare the hot pot. She stood there in the kitchen cleaning the oysters, briskly chopping Chinese cabbage, arrang-ing blocks of tofu just so, simmering broth.

I asked her whether she hadn't tried telephoning at 2:36.

"I called, all right," she answered while rinsing rice in a col-ander.

"I couldn't hear a thing," I said.

"Yeah, right, the wind was tremendous," she said matter-of-factly.

I got a beer out of the refrigerator and sat down on the edge of the table to drink it.

"But, really, why all of a sudden this fury of wind, then, again, just like that, nothing?" I asked her.

"You got me," she said, her back turned toward me as she shelled shrimps with her fingernails. "There's lots we don't know about the wind. Same as there's lots we don't know about ancient history or cancer or the ocean floor or outer space or sex."

"Hmm," I said. That was no answer. Still, it didn't look like there was much chance of furthering this line of conversation with her, so I just gave up and watched the oyster hot pot's progress.

"Say, can I touch your tummy?" I asked her.

"Later," she said.

So until the hot pot was ready, I decided to pull together a few brief notes on the day's events so I could write them up in my diary next week. This is what I jotted down:

- Fall of Roman Empire
- 1881 Indian Uprising
- Hitler's Invasion of Poland

Just this, and even next week I'd be able to reconstruct what went on today. Precisely because of this meticulous system of mine, I have managed to keep a diary for twenty-two years without missing a day. To every meaningful act, its own system. Whether the wind blows or not, that's the way I live.

—*translated by Alfred Birnbaum*

LederHOSEN

"**MOTHER DUMPED MY FATHER,**" a friend of my wife's was saying one day, "all because of a pair of shorts."

I've got to ask. "A pair of shorts?"

"I know it sounds strange," she says, "because it is a strange story."

A LARGE WOMAN, her height and build are almost the same as mine. She tutors electric organ, but most of her free time she divides among swimming and skiing and tennis, so she's trim and always tanned. You might call her a sports fanatic. On days off, she puts in a morning run before heading to the local pool to do laps; then at two or three in the afternoon it's tennis, followed by aerobics. Now, I like my sports, but I'm nowhere near her league.

I don't mean to suggest she's aggressive or obsessive about things. Quite the contrary, she's really rather retiring; she'd never dream of putting emotional pressure on anyone.

Only, she's driven; her body—and very likely the spirit attached to that body—craves after vigorous activity, relentless as a comet.

Which may have something to do with why she's unmarried. Oh, she's had affairs—the woman may be a little on the large side, but she is beautiful; she's been proposed to, even agreed to take the plunge. But inevitably, whenever it's gotten to the wedding stage, some problem has come up and everything falls through.

Like my wife says, "She's just unlucky."

"Well, I guess," I sympathize.

I'm not in total agreement with my wife on this. True, luck may rule over parts of a person's life and luck may cast patches of shadow across the ground of our being, but where there's a will—much less a strong will to swim thirty laps or run twenty kilometers—there's a way to overcome most any trouble with whatever stepladders you have around. No, her heart was never set on marrying, is how I see it. Marriage just doesn't fall within the sweep of her comet, at least not entirely.

And so she keeps on tutoring electric organ, devoting every free moment to sports, falling regularly in and out of unlucky love.

IT'S A RAINY SUNDAY afternoon and she's come two hours earlier than expected, while my wife is still out shopping.

"Forgive me," she apologizes. "I took a rain check on today's tennis, which left me two hours to spare. I'd have been bored out of my mind being alone at home, so I just thought . . . Am I interrupting anything?"

Not at all, I say. I didn't feel quite in the mood to work and was just sitting around, cat on my lap, watching a video. I show her in, go to the kitchen and make coffee. Two cups, for watching the last twenty minutes of Jaws. Of course, we've both seen the movie before—probably more than once—so neither of us is particularly riveted to the tube. But anyway, we're watching it because it's there in front of our eyes.

It's *The End*. The credits roll up. No sign of my wife. So we chat a bit. Sharks, seaside, swimming . . . still no wife. We go on talking. Now, I suppose I like the woman well enough, but after an hour of this our lack of things in common becomes obvious. In a word, she's my wife's friend, not mine.

Short of what else to do, I'm already thinking about popping in the next video when she suddenly brings up the story of her parents' divorce. I can't fathom the connection—at least to my mind, there's no link between swimming and her folks splitting up—but I guess a reason is where you find it.

"THEY WEREN'T REALLY SHORTS," she says. "They were lederhosen."

"You mean those hiking pants the Germans wear? The ones with the shoulder straps?"

"You got it. Father wanted a pair of lederhosen as a souvenir gift. Well, Father's pretty tall for his generation. He might even look good in them, which could be why he wanted them. But can you picture a Japanese wearing lederhosen? I guess it takes all kinds."

I'm still not any closer to the story. I have to ask, what were the circumstances behind her father's request—and of whom?—for these souvenir lederhosen?

"Oh, I'm sorry. I'm always telling things out of order. Stop me if things don't make sense," she says.

Okay, I say.

"Mother's sister was living in Germany and she invited Mother for a visit. Something she'd always been meaning to do. Of course, Mother can't speak German, she'd never even been abroad, but having been an English teacher for so long she'd had that overseas bee in her bonnet. It'd been ages since she'd seen my aunt. So Mother approached Father, How about taking ten days off and going to Germany, the two of us? Father's work couldn't allow it, and Mother ended up going alone."

"That's when your father asked for the lederhosen, I take it?"

"Right," she says. "Mother asked what he wanted her to bring back, and Father said lederhosen."

"Okay so far."

Her parents were reasonably close. They didn't argue until all hours of the night; her father didn't storm out of the house and not come home for days on end. At least not then, though apparently there had been rows more than once over him and other women.

"Not a bad man, a hard worker, but kind of a skirt chaser," she tosses off matter-of-factly. No relation of hers, the way she's talking. For a second, I almost think her father is deceased. But no, I'm told, he's alive and well.

"Father was already up there in years, and by then those troubles were all behind them. They seemed to be getting along just fine."

Things, however, didn't go without incident. Her mother extended the ten days in Germany to nearly a month and a half, with hardly a word back to Tokyo, and when she finally did return to Japan she stayed with another sister of hers in Osaka. She never did come back home.

Neither she—the daughter—nor her father could understand what was going on. Until then, when there'd been marital difficulties, her mother had always been the patient one—so ploddingly patient, in fact, that she sometimes wondered if the woman had no imagination; family always came first, and the mother was selflessly devoted to her daughter. So when the mother didn't come around, didn't even make the effort to call, it was beyond their comprehension. They made phone calls to the aunt's house in Osaka, repeatedly, but they could hardly get her to come to the phone, much less admit what her intentions were.

In mid-September, two months after returning to Japan, her mother made her intentions known. One day, out of the blue, she called home and told her husband, "You will be receiving the necessary papers for divorce. Please sign, seal, and send back to me." Would she care to explain, her husband asked, what was the reason? "I've lost all love for you—in any way, shape, or form." Oh? said her husband. Was there no room for discussion? "Sorry, none, absolutely none."

Telephone negotiations dragged on for the next two or three months, but her mother did not back down an inch, and finally her father consented to the divorce. He was in no position to force the issue, his own track record being what it was, and anyway, he always tended to give in.

"All this came as a big shock," she tells me. "But it wasn't just the divorce. I'd imagined my parents splitting up many times, so I was already prepared for it psychologically. If the two of them had just plain divorced without all that funny business, I wouldn't have gotten so upset. The problem wasn't Mother dumping Father; Mother was dumping me, too. That's what hurt."

I nod.

"Up to that point, I'd always taken Mother's side, and Mother would always stand by me. And yet here was Mother throwing me out with Father, like so much garbage, and not a word of explanation. It hit me so hard, I wasn't able to forgive Mother for the longest time. I wrote her who knows how many letters asking her to set things straight, but she never answered my questions, never even said she wanted to see me."

It wasn't until three years later that she actually saw her mother. At a family funeral, of all places. By then, the daughter was living on her own—she'd moved out in her sophomore year, when her parents divorced—and now she had graduated and was tutoring electric organ. Meanwhile, her mother was teaching English at a prep school.

Her mother confessed that she hadn't been able to talk to her own daughter because she hadn't known what to say. "I myself couldn't tell where things were going," the mother said, "but the whole thing started over that pair of shorts."

"Shorts?" She'd been as startled as I was. She'd never wanted to speak to her mother ever again, but curiosity got the better of her. In their mourning dress, mother and daughter went into a nearby coffee shop and ordered iced tea. She had to hear this—pardon the expression—this short story.

THE SHOP THAT SOLD the lederhosen was in a small town an hour away by train from Hamburg. Her mother's sister looked it up for her.

"All the Germans I know say if you're going to buy lederhosen, this is the place. The craftsmanship is good, and the prices aren't so expensive," said her sister.

So the mother boarded a train to buy her husband his souvenir lederhosen. In her train compartment sat a middle-aged German couple, who conversed with her in halting English. "I go now to buy lederhosen for souvenir," the mother said. "Vat shop you go to?" the couple asked. The mother named the name of the shop, and the middle-aged German couple chimed in together, "Zat is ze place, *jah*. It is ze best." Hearing this, the mother felt very confident.

It was a delightful early-summer afternoon and a quaint old-fashioned town. Through the middle of the town flowed a babbling brook, its banks lush and green. Cobblestone streets led in all directions, and cats were everywhere. The mother stepped into a café for a bite of *Käsekuchen* and coffee.

She was on her last sip of coffee and playing with the shop cat when the owner came over to ask what brought her to their little town. She said lederhosen, whereupon the owner pulled out a pad of paper and drew a map to the shop.

"Thank you very much," the mother said.

How wonderful it was to travel by oneself, she thought as she walked along the cobblestones. In fact, this was the first time in her fifty-five years that she had traveled alone. During the whole trip, she had not once been lonely or afraid or bored. Every scene that met her eyes was fresh and new; everyone she met was friendly. Each experience called forth emotions that had been slumbering in her, untouched and unused. What she had held near and dear until then—husband and home and daughter—was on the other side of the earth. She felt no need to trouble herself over them.

She found the lederhosen shop without problem. It was a tiny old guild shop. It didn't have a big sign for tourists, but inside she could see scores of lederhosen. She opened the door and walked in.

Two old men worked in the shop. They spoke in a whisper as they took down measurements and scribbled them into a notebook. Behind a curtain divider was a larger work space; the monotone of sewing machines could be heard.

"*Darf ich Ihnen helfen, Madame?*" the larger of the two old men addressed the mother.

"I want to buy lederhosen," she responded in English.

"Ziss make problem." The old man chose his words with care. "Ve do not make article for customer who not exist."

"My husband exist," the mother said with confidence.

"*Jah, jah,* your husband exist, of course, of course," the old man responded hastily. "Excuse my not good English. Vat I vant say, if your husband not exist here, ve cannot sell ze lederhosen."

"Why?" the mother asked, perplexed.

"Is store policy. *Ist unser Prinzip.* Ve must see ze lederhosen how it fit customer, ve alter very nice, only zen ve sell. Over one hundred years ve are in business, ve build reputation on ziss policy."

"But I spend half day to come from Hamburg to buy your lederhosen."

"Very sorry, madame," said the old man, looking very sorry indeed. "Ve make no exception. Ziss vorld is very uncertain vorld. Trust is difficult sink to earn but easy sink to lose."

The mother sighed and stood in the doorway. She racked her brain for some way to break the impasse. The larger old man explained the situation to the smaller old man, who nodded sadly, *jah, jah.* Despite their great difference in size, the two old men wore identical expressions.

"Well, perhaps, can we do this?" the mother proposed. "I find man just like my husband and bring him here. That man puts on lederhosen, you alter very nice, you sell lederhosen to me."

The first old man looked her in the face, aghast.

"But, madame, zat is against rule. Is not same man who tries ze lederhosen on, your husband. And ve know ziss. Ve cannot do ziss."

"Pretend you do not know. You sell lederhosen to that man and that man sell lederhosen to me. That way, there is no shame to your policy. Please, I beg you. I may never come back to Germany. If I do not buy lederhosen now, I will never buy lederhosen."

"Hmph," the old man pouted. He thought for a few seconds, then turned to the other old man and spoke a stream of German. They spoke back and forth several times. Then, finally, the large man turned back to the mother and said, "Very well, madame. As exception—very exception, you please understand—ve vill know nossink of ziss matter. Not so many come from Yapan to buy lederhosen, and ve Germans not so slow in ze head. Please find man very like your husband. My brother he says ziss."

"Thank you," she said. Then she managed to thank the other brother in German: *"Das ist so nett von Ihnen."*

SHE—THE DAUGHTER who's telling me this story—folds her hands on the table and sighs. I drink the last of my coffee, long since cold. The rain keeps coming down. Still no sign of my wife. Who'd have ever thought the conversation would take this turn?

"So then?" I interject, eager to hear the conclusion. "Did your mother end up finding someone with the same build as your father?"

"Yes," she says, utterly without expression. "Mother sat on a bench looking for someone who matched Father's size. And along came a man who fit the part. Without asking his permission—it seems the man couldn't speak a word of English—she dragged him to the lederhosen shop."

"The hands-on approach," I joke.

"I don't know. At home, Mother was always a normal sensible-shoes woman," she said with another sigh. "The shopkeepers explained the situation to the man, and the man gladly consented to stand in for Father. He puts the lederhosen on, and they're pulling here and tucking there, the three of them chortling away in German. In thirty minutes the job was done, during which time Mother made up her mind to divorce Father."

"Wait," I say, "I don't get it! Did something happen during those thirty minutes?"

"Nothing at all. Only those three German men *ha-ha-ha*-ing like bellows."

"But what made your mother do it?"

"That's something even Mother herself didn't understand at the time. It made her defensive and confused. All she knew was, looking at that man in the lederhosen, she felt an unbearable disgust rising in her. Directed toward Father. And she could not hold it back. Mother's lederhosen man, apart from the color of his skin, was exactly like Father, the shape of the legs, the belly, the thinning hair. The way he was so happy trying on those new lederhosen, all prancy and cocky like a little boy. As Mother stood there looking at this man, so many things she'd been uncertain of about herself slowly shifted together into something very clear. That's when she realized she hated Father."

MY WIFE GETS HOME from shopping, and the two of them commence their woman talk, but I'm still thinking about the lederhosen. The three of us eat an early dinner and have a few drinks; I keep turning the story over in my mind.

"So, you don't hate your mother anymore?" I ask when my wife leaves the room.

"No, not really. We're not close at all, but I don't hold anything against her."

"Because she told you about the lederhosen?"

"I think so. After she explained things to me, I couldn't go on hating her. I can't say why it makes any difference, I certainly don't know how to explain it, but it may have something to do with us being women."

"Still, if you leave the lederhosen out of it, supposing it was just the story of a woman taking a trip and finding herself, would you have been able to forgive her?"

"Of course not," she says without hesitation. "The whole point is the lederhosen, right?"

A proxy pair of lederhosen, I'm thinking, that her father never even received.

—*translated by Alfred Birnbaum*

Barn

Burning

I MET HER AT the wedding party of an acquaintance and we got friendly. This was three years ago. We were nearly a whole generation apart in age—she twenty, myself thirty-one—but that hardly got in the way. I had plenty of other things to worry my head about at the time, and to be perfectly honest, I didn't have a spare moment to think about age difference. And our ages never bothered her from the very beginning. I was married, but that didn't matter, either. She seemed to consider things like age and family and income to be of the same a priori order as shoe size and vocal pitch and the shape of one's fingernails. The sort of thing that thinking about won't change one bit. And that much said, well, she had a point.

She was working as an advertising model to earn a living while studying pantomime under somebody-or-other, a famous teacher, apparently. Though the work end of things was a drag and she was always turning down jobs her agent lined up, so her money situation was really rather precarious. But whatever she lacked in take-home pay she probably made up for on the goodwill of a number of boyfriends. Naturally, I don't know this for certain; it's just what I pieced together from snippets of her conversation.

Still, I'm not suggesting there was even a glimmer of a hint that she was sleeping with guys for money. Though perhaps she did come close to that on occasion. Yet even if she did, that was not an essential issue; the essentials were surely far more simple. And the long and short of it was, this guileless simplicity is what attracted a particular kind of person. The kind of men who had only to set eyes on this simplicity of hers before they'd be dressing it up with whatever feelings they held inside. Not exactly the best explanation, but even she'd have to admit it was this simplicity that supported her.

Of course, this sort of thing couldn't go on forever. (If it could, we'd have to turn the entire workings of the universe upside down.) The possibility did exist, but only under specific circumstances, for a specific period. Just like with "peeling mandarin oranges."

"Peeling mandarin oranges?" you say?

When we first met, she told me she was studying pantomime.

Oh, really, I'd said, not altogether surprised. Young women are all into *something* these days. Plus, she didn't look like your die-cast polish-your-skills-in-dead-earnest type.

Then she "peeled a mandarin orange." Literally, that's what she did: She had a glass bowl of oranges to her left and another bowl for the peels to her right—so went the setup—in fact, there was nothing there. She proceeded to pick up one imaginary orange, then slowly peel it, pop pieces into her mouth, and spit out the pulp one section at a time, finally disposing of the skin-wrapped residue into the right-hand bowl when she'd eaten the entire fruit. She repeated this maneuver again and again. In so many words, it doesn't sound like much, but I swear, just watching her do this for ten or twenty minutes—she and I kept up a running conversation at the counter of this bar, her "peeling mandarin oranges" the whole while, almost without a second thought—I felt the reality of everything around me being siphoned away. Unnerving, to say the least. Back when Eichmann stood trial in Israel, there was talk that the most fitting sentence would be to lock him in a cell and gradually remove all the air. I don't really know how he did meet his end, but that's what came to mind.

"Seems you're quite talented," I said.

"Oh, this is nothing. Talent's not involved. It's not a question of making yourself believe there *is* an orange there, you have to forget there *isn't* one. That's all."

"Practically Zen."

That's when I took a liking to her.

We generally didn't see all that much of each other. Maybe once a month, twice at the most. I'd ring her up and invite her out somewhere. We'd eat out or go to a bar. We talked intensely; she'd hear me out and I'd listen to whatever she had to say. We hardly had any common topics between us, but so what? We became, well, pals. Of course, I was the one who paid the bill for all the food and drinks. Sometimes she'd call me, typically when she was broke and needed a meal. And then it was unbelievable the amount of food she could put away.

When the two of us were together, I could truly relax. I'd forget all about work I didn't want to do and trivial things that'd never be settled anyway and the crazy mixed-up ideas that crazy mixed-up people had taken into their heads. It was some kind of power she had. Not that there was any great meaning to her words. And if I did catch myself interjecting polite nothings without really tuning in what she was saying, there still was something soothing to my ears about her voice, like watching clouds drift across the far horizon.

I did my share of talking, too. Everything from personal matters to sweeping generalities, I told her my honest thoughts. I guess she also let some of my verbiage go by, likewise with minimum comment. Which was fine by me. It was a mood I was after, not understanding or sympathy.

Then two years ago in the spring, her father died of a heart ailment, and she came into a small sum of money. At least, that's how she described it. With the money, she said, she wanted to travel to North Africa. Why North Africa, I didn't know, but I happened to know someone working at the Algerian embassy, so I introduced her. Thus she decided to go to Algeria. And as things took their course, I ended up seeing her off at the airport. All she carried was a ratty old Boston bag stuffed with a couple of changes of clothes. By the look of her as she went through the baggage check, you'd almost think she was returning from North Africa, not going there.

"You really going to come back to Japan in one piece?" I joked.

"Sure thing. 'I shall return,'" she mocked.

Three months later, she did. Three kilos lighter than when she left and tanned about six shades darker. With her was her new guy, whom she presented as someone she met at a restaurant in Algiers. Japanese in Algeria were all too few, so the two of them easily fell in together and eventually became intimate. As far I know, this guy was her first real regular lover.

He was in his late twenties, tall, with a decent build, and rather polite in his speech. A little lean on looks, perhaps, though I suppose you could put him in the handsome category. Anyway, he struck me as nice enough; he had big hands and long fingers.

The reason I know so much about the guy is that I went to meet her when she arrived. A sudden telegram from Beirut had given a date and a flight number. Nothing else. Seemed she wanted me to come to the airport. When the plane got in— actually, it was four hours late due to bad weather, during which time I read three magazines cover to cover in a coffee lounge— the two of them came through the gate arm in arm. They looked like a happy young married couple. When she introduced us, he shook my hand, virtually in reflex. The healthy handshake of those who've been living a long time overseas. After that, we went into a restaurant. She was dying to have a bowl of tempura and rice, she said; meanwhile, he and I both had beer.

He told me he worked in trading but didn't offer any more details. I couldn't tell whether he simply didn't want to talk business or was thoughtfully sparing me a boring exposition. Nor, in truth, did I especially want to hear about trading, so I didn't press him. With little else to discuss, the conversation meandered between safety on the streets of Beirut and water supplies in Tunis. He proved to be quite well informed about affairs over the whole of North Africa and the Middle East.

By now she'd finished her tempura and announced with a big yawn that she was feeling sleepy. I half expected her to doze off on the spot. She was precisely the type who could fall asleep anywhere. The guy said he'd see her home by taxi, and I said I'd take the train as it was faster. Just why she had me come all the way out to the airport was beyond me.

"Glad I got to meet you," he told me, as if to acknowledge the inconvenience.

"Same here," I said.

THEREAFTER I met up with the guy a number of times. Whenever I ran into her, he was always by her side. I'd make a date with her, and he'd drive up in a spotless silver-gray German sports car to let her off. I know next to nothing about automobiles, but it reminded me of those jaunty coupes you see in old black-and-white Fellini films. Definitely not the sort of car your ordinary salaryman owns.

"The guy's got to be loaded," I ventured to comment to her once.

"Yeah," she said without much interest, "I guess."

"Can you really make that much in trading?"

"Trading?"

"That's what he said. He works in trading."

"Okay, then, I imagine so. . . . But hey, what do I know?
He doesn't seem to do much work at all, as far as I can see. He
does his share of seeing people and talking on the phone, I'll say
that, though."

The young man and his money remained a mystery.

THEN ONE SUNDAY afternoon in October, she rang up.
My wife had gone off to see some relatives that morning and left
me alone at home. A pleasant day, bright and clear, it found me
idly gazing at the camphor tree outside and enjoying the new
autumn apples. I must have eaten a good seven of them that
day—it was either a pathological craving or some kind of pre-
monition.

"Listen," she said right off, "just happened to be heading in
your direction. Would it be all right if we popped over?"

"We?" I threw back the question.

"Me and him," came her self-evident reply.

"Sure," I had to say, "by all means."

"Okay, we'll be there in thirty minutes," she said, then
hung up.

I lay there on the sofa awhile longer before taking a shower
and shaving. As I toweled myself dry, I wondered whether to
tidy up around the house but canned the idea. There wasn't
time. And despite the piles of books and magazines and letters
and records, the occasional pencil here or sweater there, the
place didn't seem particularly dirty. I sat back down on the sofa,
looked at the camphor tree, and ate another apple.

They showed up a little past two. I heard a car stop in front
of the house, and went to the front door to see her leaning out
the window of the silver-gray coupe, waving. I directed them to
the parking space around back.

"We're here," she beamed, all smiles. She wore a sheer
blouse that showed her nipples, and an olive-green miniskirt.
He sported a navy blazer, but there was something else slightly
different about him; maybe it was the two-day growth of beard.

Not at all slovenly looking, it even brought out his features a shade. As he stepped from the car, he removed his sunglasses and shoved them into his breast pocket.

"Terribly sorry to be dropping in on you like this on your day off," he apologized.

"Not at all, don't mind a bit. Every day might as well be a day off with me, and I was getting kind of bored here on my own," I allowed.

"We brought some food," she said, lifting a large white paper bag from the backseat of the car.

"Food?"

"Nothing extraordinary," he spoke up. "It's just that, a sudden visit on a Sunday, I thought, why not take along something to eat?"

"Very kind of you. Especially since I haven't had anything but apples all morning."

We went inside and set the groceries out on the table. It turned out to make quite a spread: roast beef sandwiches, salad, smoked salmon, blueberry ice cream—and good quantities at that. While she transferred the food to plates, I grabbed a bottle of white wine from the refrigerator. It was like an impromptu party.

"Well, let's dig in. I'm starved," pronounced her usual ravenous self.

Midway through the feast, having polished off the wine, we tapped into my stock of beer. I can usually hold my own, but this guy could drink; no matter how many beers he downed, his expression never altered in the slightest. Together with her contribution of a couple of cans, we had in the space of a little under an hour racked up a whole tableful of empties. Not bad. Meanwhile, she was pulling records from my shelf and loading the player. The first selection to come on was Miles Davis's "Airegin."

"A Garrard autochanger like that's a rare find these days," he observed. Which launched us into audiophilia, me going on

about the various components of my stereo system, him inserting appropriate comments, polite as ever.

The conversation had reached a momentary lull when the
guy said, "I've got some grass. Care to smoke?"

I hesitated, for no other reason than I'd only just quit smoking the month before and I wasn't sure what effect it would have.
But in the end, I decided to take a toke or two. Whereupon he
fished a foil packet from the bottom of the paper bag and rolled
a joint. He lit up and took a few puffs to get it started, then
passed it to me. It was prime stuff. For the next few minutes we
didn't say a word as we each took hits in turn. Miles Davis had
finished, and we were now into an album of Strauss waltzes.
Curious combination, but what the hell.

After one joint, she was already beat, pleading grass on top
of three beers and lack of sleep. I ferried her upstairs and helped
her onto the bed. She asked to borrow a T-shirt. No sooner had
I handed it to her than she'd stripped to her panties, pulled on
the T-shirt, and stretched flat out. By the time I got around to
asking if she was going to be warm enough, she had already
snoozed off. I went downstairs, shaking my head.

Back in the living room, her guy was busy rolling another
joint. Plays hard, this dude. Me, I would have just as soon snug-
gled into bed next to her and conked right out. Fat chance. We
settled down to smoke the second joint, Strauss still waltzing
away. Somehow, I was reminded of an elementary-school play.
I had the part of the old glove maker. A fox cub comes with
money to buy gloves, but the glove maker says it's not enough
for a pair.

"'Tain't gonna buy no gloves," I say. Guess I'm something of a
villain.

"But Mother's so very c-c-cold. She'll get chapped p-p-paws.
P-p-please," says the fox cub.

"Uh-uh, nothing doing. Save your money and come back. Otherwise—"

"Sometimes I burn barns," the guy was saying.

"Excuse me?" I asked. Had I misheard him?

"Sometimes I burn barns," the guy repeated.

I looked at him. His fingertips traced the pattern on his lighter. Then he took a deep draw on the joint and held it in for a good ten seconds before slowly exhaling. The smoke came streaming out of his mouth and into the air like ectoplasm. He passed me the roach.

"Quality product, eh?" he said.

I nodded.

"I brought it from India. Top of the line, the best I could find. Smoke this and, it's strange, I recall all kinds of things. Lights and smells and like that. The quality of memory . . ." He paused and snapped his fingers a few times, as if searching for the right words. ". . . completely changes. Don't you think?"

That it did, I concurred. I really was back in the school play, reexperiencing the commotion on stage, the smell of the paint on the cardboard backdrop.

"I'd like to hear about this barn thing," I said.

He looked at me. His face wore no more expression than ever.

"May I talk about it?" he asked.

"Why not?" I said.

"Pretty simple, really. I pour gasoline and throw a lighted match. _Flick,_ and that's it. Doesn't take fifteen minutes for the whole thing to burn to the ground."

"So tell me," I began, then fell silent. I was having trouble finding the right words, too. "Why is it you burn barns?"

"Is it so strange?"

"Who knows? You burn barns. I don't burn barns. There's this glaring difference, and to me, rather than say which of us is strange, first of all I'd like to clear up just what that difference is. Anyway, it was you who brought up this barn thing to begin with."

"Got me there," he admitted. "You tell it like it is. Say, would you have any Ravi Shankar records?"

No, I didn't, I told him.

The guy spaced out awhile. I could practically see his mind kneading like Silly Putty. Or maybe it was *my* mind that was squirming around.

"I burn maybe one barn every two months," he came back. Then he snapped his fingers again. "Seems to me that's just about the right pace. For me, that is."

I nodded vaguely. Pace?

"Just out of interest, is it your own barns you burn?" I thought to ask.

The guy looked at me uncomprehendingly. "Why have I got to burn my own barns? What makes you think I'd have this surplus of barns, myself?"

"Which means," I continued, "you burn other people's barns, right?"

"Correct," he said. "Obviously. Other people's barns. Which makes it, as it were, a criminal act. Same as you and me smoking this grass here right now. A clear-cut criminal act."

I shut up, elbows on the arms of my chair.

"In other words, I wantonly ignite barns that belong to other people. Naturally, I choose ones that won't cause major fires. All I want to do is simply burn barns."

I nodded and ground out what was left of the roach. "But, if you get caught, you'll be in trouble. Whatever, it's arson, and you might get prison."

"Nobody's going to get caught." He laughed at the very idea. "Pour the gas, light the match, and run. Then I watch the whole thing from a distance through binoculars, nice and easy. Nobody catches me. Really, burn one shitty little barn and the cops hardly even budge."

Come to think of it, they probably wouldn't. On top of which, who'd suspect a well-dressed young man driving a foreign car?

"And does she know about this?" I asked, pointing upstairs.

"Not a thing. Fact is, I've never told anyone else about this but you. I'm not the sort to go spouting off to just anyone."

"So why me?"

The guy extended his fingers of his left hand and stroked his cheek. The growth of beard made a dry, rasping sound. Like a bug walking over a thin, taut sheet of paper. "You're someone who writes novels, so I thought, Wouldn't he be interested in patterns of human behavior and all that? And the way I see it, with novelists, before even passing judgment on something, aren't they the kind who are supposed to appreciate its form? And even if they can't *appreciate* it, they should at least accept it at face value, no? That's why I told you. I wanted to tell you, from my side."

I nodded. Just how was I to accept this at *face value*? From my side, I honestly didn't know.

"This might be a strange way to put it," he took off again, spreading both hands, then bringing them slowly together before his eyes. "But there's a lot of barns in this world, and I've got this feeling that they're all just waiting to be burned. Barns built way off by the seaside, barns built in the middle of rice fields . . . well, anyway, all kinds of barns. But nothing that fifteen minutes wouldn't burn down, nice and neat. It's like that's why they were put there from the very beginning. No grief to anyone. They just . . . vanish. One, two, *poof!*"

"But you're judging that they're not needed."

"I'm not judging anything. They're *waiting* to be burned. I'm simply obliging. You get it? I'm just taking on what's there. Just like the rain. The rain falls. Streams swell. Things get swept along. Does the rain judge anything? Well, all right, does this make me immoral? In my own way, I'd like to believe I've got my own morals. And that's an extremely important force in human existence. A person can't exist without morals. I wouldn't doubt if morals weren't the very balance to my simultaneity."

"Simultaneity?"

"Right, I'm here, and I'm there. I'm in Tokyo, and at the same time I'm in Tunis. I'm the one to blame, and I'm also the one to forgive. Just as a for instance. It's that level of balance. Without such balance, I don't think we could go on living. It's like the linchpin to everything. Lose it and we'd literally go to pieces. But for the very reason that I've got it, simultaneity becomes possible for me."

"So what you're saying is, the act of burning barns is in keeping with these morals of yours?"

"Not exactly. It's an act by which to maintain those morals. But maybe we better just forget the morality. It's not essential. What I want to say is, the world is full of these barns. Me, I got my barns, and you got your barns. It's the truth. I've been almost everywhere in the world. Experienced everything. Came close to dying more than once. Not that I'm proud of it or anything. But okay, let's drop it. My fault for being the quiet type all the time. I talk too much when I do grass."

We fell silent, burned out. I had no idea what to say or how. I was sitting tight in my mental passenger seat, just watching one weird scene after the next slip past the car window. My body was so loose I couldn't get a good grasp on what the different parts were doing. Yet I was still in touch with the idea of my bodily existence. Simultaneity, if ever there was such a thing: Here I had me thinking, and here I had me observing myself think. Time ticked on in impossibly minute polyrhythms.

"Care for a beer?" I asked a little later.

"Thank you. I would."

I went to the kitchen, brought out four cans and some Camembert, and we helped ourselves.

"When was the last time you burned a barn?" I had to ask.

"Let's see, now." He strained to remember, beer can in hand. "Summer, the end of August."

"And the next time, when'll that be?"

"Don't know. It's not like I work out a schedule or mark dates in my calendar. When I get the urge, I go burn one."

"But, say. When you get this urge, some likely barn doesn't just happen to be lying around, does it?"

"Of course not," he said quietly. "That's why I scout out ones ripe for burning in advance."

"To lay in stock."

"Exactly."

"Can I ask you one more question?"

"Sure."

"Have you already decided on the next barn to burn?"

This caused him to furrow up wrinkles between his eyes; then he inhaled audibly through his nose. "Well, yes. As a matter of fact, I have."

I sipped the last of my beer and said nothing.

"A great barn. The first barn really worth burning in ages. Fact is, I went and checked it out only today."

"Which means, it must be nearby."

"Very near," he confirmed.

So ended our barn talk.

At five o'clock, he roused his girlfriend, and then apologized to me again for the sudden visit. He was completely sober, despite the quantities of beer I'd seen him drink. Then he fetched the sports car from around back.

"I'll keep an eye out for that barn," I told him.

"You do that," he answered. "Like I said, it's right near here."

"What's this about a barn?" she broke in.

"Man talk," he said.

"Oh, great," she fawned.

And at that, the two of them were gone.

I returned to the living room and lay down on the sofa. The table was littered with all manner of debris. I picked up my duffle coat off the floor, pulled it over my head, and conked out.

Bluish gloom and a pungent marijuana odor covered everything. Oddly uneven, that darkness. Lying on the sofa, I tried to remember what came next in the elementary-school play, but it was long since irretrievable. Did the fox cub ever get the gloves?

I got up from the sofa, opened a window to air the place, went to the kitchen, and made myself some coffee.

THE FOLLOWING DAY, I went to a bookstore and bought a map of the area where I live. Scaled 20,000:1 and detailed down to the smallest lanes. Then I walked around with the map, penciling in X's wherever there was a barn or shed. For the next three days, I covered four kilometers in all four directions. Living toward the outskirts of town, there are still a good many farmers in the vicinity. So it came to a considerable number of barns—sixteen altogether.

I carefully checked the condition of each of these, and from the sixteen I eliminated all those where there were houses in the immediate proximity or greenhouses alongside. I also eliminated those in which there were farm implements or chemicals or signs that they were still in active use. I didn't imagine he'd want to burn tools or fertilizer.

That left five barns. Five barns worth burning. Or, rather, five barns unobjectionable if burned. The kind of barn it'd take fifteen minutes to reduce to ashes, then no one would miss it. Yet I couldn't decide which would be the one he'd be most likely to torch. The rest was a matter of taste. I was beside myself for wanting to know which of the five barns he'd chosen.

I unfolded my map and erased all but those five X's. I got myself a right angle and a French curve and dividers, and tried to establish the shortest course leaving from my house, going around the five barns, and coming back home again. Which proved to be a laborious operation, what with the roads winding about hills and streams. The result: a course of 7.2 kilometers. I measured it several times, so I couldn't have been too far off.

The following morning at six, I put on my training wear and jogging shoes and ran the course. I run six kilometers every morning anyway, so adding an extra kilometer wouldn't kill me. There were two railroad crossings along the way, but they rarely held you up. And otherwise, the scenery wouldn't be bad.

First thing out of the house, I did a quick circuit around the playing field of the local college, then turned down an unpaved road that ran along a stream for three kilometers. Passing the first barn midway, a path took me through woods. A slight uphill grade, then another barn. A little beyond that were racehorse stables. The Thoroughbreds would be alarmed to see flames—but that'd be it. No real damage.

The third and fourth barns resembled each other like ugly twins. Set not two hundred meters apart, both were weather-beaten and dirty. You might as well torch the both of them together.

The last barn stood beside a railroad crossing. Roughly the six-kilometer mark. Utterly abandoned, the barn had a tin Pepsi-Cola billboard nailed to the side facing the tracks. The structure—if you could call it that—was such a shambles, I could see it, as he would say, just waiting to be burned.

I paused before this last barn, took a few deep breaths, cut over the crossing, and headed home. Running time: thirty-one minutes thirty seconds. I showered, ate breakfast, stretched out on the sofa to listen to one record, then got down to work.

For one month, I ran the same course each morning. But— no barns burned.

Sometimes, I could swear he was trying to get me to burn a barn. That is, to plant in my head the image of burning barns, so that it would swell up like a bicycle tire pumped with air. I'll grant you, there were times that, well, as long as I was waiting around for him to do the deed, I half considered striking the match myself. It would have been a lot faster. And anyhow, they were only run-down old barns. . . .

Although on second thought, no, let's not get carried away. You won't see me torch any barn. No matter how inflated the image of burning barns grew in my head, I'm really not the type. Me, burn barns? Never. Then what about him? He'd probably just switched prospects. Or else he was too busy and simply hadn't found the time to burn a barn. In any case, there was no word from her.

December came and went, and the morning air pierced the skin. The barns stood their ground, their roofs white with frost. Wintering birds sent the echo of flapping wings through the frozen woods. The world kept in motion unchanged.

* * *

THE NEXT TIME I met the guy was in the middle of December last year. It was Christmas carols everywhere you went. I had gone into town to buy presents for different people, and while walking around Nogizaka I spotted his car. No mistake, his silver-gray sports car. Shinagawa license plate, small dent next to the left headlight. It was parked in the lot of a café, looking less sparkling than when I last saw it, the silver-gray a hint duller. Though maybe that was a mistaken impression on my part: I have this convenient tendency to rework my memories. I dashed into the café without a moment's hesitation.

The place was dark and thick with the strong aroma of coffee. There weren't many voices to be heard, only atmospheric baroque music. I recognized him immediately. He was sitting alone by the window, drinking a café au lait. And though it was warm enough in there to steam up my glasses, he was wearing a black cashmere coat, with his muffler still wrapped around his neck.

I hedged a second, but then figured I might as well approach the guy. I decided not to say I'd seen his car outside; I'd just happened to step in, and by chance there he was.

"Mind if I sit down?" I asked.

"Please, not at all," he replied.

We talked a bit. It wasn't a particularly lively conversation. Clearly, we didn't have much in the way of common topics; moreover, his mind seemed to be on something else. Still, he didn't show any sign of being put out by my presence. At one point, he mentioned a seaport in Tunisia, then he started describing the shrimp they caught there. He wasn't just talking for my sake: He really was serious about these shrimp. All the same, like water to the desert, the story didn't go anywhere before it dissipated.

He signaled to the waiter and ordered a second café au lait.

"Say, by the way, how's your barn doing?" I braved the question.

The trace of a smile came to his lips. "Oh, you still remember?" he said, removing a handkerchief from his pocket to wipe his mouth. "Why, sure, I burned it. Burned it nice and clean. Just as promised."

"One right near my house?"

"Yeah. Really, right by there."

"When?"

"Last—when was it? Maybe ten days after I visited your place."

I told him about how I plotted the barns on my map and ran my daily circuit. "So there's no way I could have *not* seen it," I insisted.

"Very thorough," he gibed, obviously having his fun. "Thorough and logical. All I can say is, you must have missed it. Does happen, you know. Things so close up, they don't even register."

"It just doesn't make sense."

He adjusted his tie, then glanced at his watch. "So very, very close," he underscored. "But if you'll excuse me, I've got to be going. Let's talk about it next time, shall we? Can't keep a person waiting. Sorry."

I had no plausible reason to detain the guy any further.

He stood up, pocketed his cigarettes and lighter, and then remarked, "Oh, by the way, have you seen her lately?"

"No, not at all. Haven't you?"

"Me, neither. I've been trying to get in touch, but she's never in her apartment and she doesn't answer the phone and she hasn't been to her pantomime class the whole while."

"She must have taken off somewhere. She's been known to do that."

The guy stared down at the table, hands buried in his pockets. "With no money, for a month and a half? As far as making her own way, she hardly has a clue."

He was snapping his fingers in his coat pocket.

"I think I know that girl pretty well, and she absolutely hasn't got yen one. No real friends to speak of. An address book full of names, but that's all they are. She hasn't got anyone she can depend on. No, I take that back, she did trust you. And I'm not saying this out of courtesy. I do believe you're someone special to her. Really, it's enough to make me kind of jealous. And I'm someone who's never ever been jealous at all." He gave a little sigh, then eyed his watch again. "But I really must go. Be seeing you."

Right, I nodded, but no words came. The same as always, whenever I was thrown together with this guy, I became altogether inarticulate.

I tried calling her any number of times after that, but her line had apparently been disconnected. Which somehow bothered me, so I went to her apartment and encountered a locked door, her mailbox stuffed with fliers. The superintendent was nowhere to be found, so I had no way to know if she was even living there anymore. I ripped a page from my appointment book, jotted down "Please contact," wrote my name, and shoved it into the mailbox.

Not a word.

The next time I passed by, the apartment bore the nameplate of another resident. I actually knocked, but no one was in. And like before, no superintendent in sight.

At that, I gave up. This was one year ago.

She'd disappeared.

EVERY MORNING, I still run past those five barns. Not one of them has yet burned down. Nor do I hear of any barn fires. Come December, the birds strafe overhead. And I keep getting older.

Although just now and then, in the depths of the night, I'll think about barns burning to the ground.

—*translated by Alfred Birnbaum*

THE
LITTLE
GREEN
MONSTER

MY HUSBAND LEFT for work as usual, and I couldn't think of anything to do. I sat alone in the chair by the window, staring out at the garden through the gap between the curtains. Not that I had any reason to be looking at the garden: There was nothing else for me to do. And I thought that sooner or later, if I sat there looking, I might think of something. Of all the many things in the garden, the one I looked at most was the oak tree. It was my special favorite. I had planted it when I was a little girl, and watched it grow. I thought of it as my old friend. I talked to it all the time in my head.

That day, too, I was probably talking to the oak tree—I don't remember what about. And I don't know how long I was sitting there. The time slips by when I'm looking at the garden. It was dark before I knew it: I must have been there quite a while. Then, all at once, I heard a sound. It came from some-where far away—a funny, muffled sort of rubbing sort of sound. At first I thought it was coming from a place deep inside me, that I was hearing things—a warning from the dark cocoon my body was spinning within. I held my breath and listened. Yes. No doubt about it. Little by little, the sound was moving closer to me. What was it? I had no idea. But it made my flesh creep.

The ground near the base of the tree began to bulge upward as if some thick, heavy liquid were rising to the surface. Again I caught my breath. Then the ground broke open and the mounded earth crumbled away to reveal a set of sharp claws. My eyes locked onto them, and my hands turned into clenched fists. Something's going to happen, I said to myself. It's starting now. The claws scraped hard at the soil, and soon the break in the earth was an open hole, from which there crawled a little green monster.

Its body was covered with shining green scales. As soon as it emerged from the hole, it shook itself until the bits of soil clinging to it dropped away. It had a long, funny nose, the green of which gradually deepened toward the tip. The very end was narrow and pointed as a whip, but the beast's eyes were exactly like a human's. The sight of them sent a shiver through me. They showed feelings, just like your eyes or mine.

Without hesitation, but moving slowly and deliberately, the monster approached my front door, on which it began to knock with the slender tip of its nose. The dry, rapping sound echoed through the house. I tiptoed to the back room, hoping the beast would not realize I was there. I couldn't scream. Ours is the only house in the area, and my husband wouldn't be coming back from work until late at night. I couldn't run out the back door, either, since my house has only the one door, the very one on which a horrible green monster was now knocking. I breathed as quietly as I could, pretending not to be there, hoping the thing would give up and go away. But it didn't give up. Its nose went from knocking to groping at the lock. It seemed to have no trouble at all clicking the lock open, and then the door itself opened a crack. Around the edge of the door crept the nose, and then it stopped. For a long time it stayed still, like a snake with its head raised, checking conditions in the house. If I had known this was going to happen, I could have stayed by the door and cut the nose off, I told myself: The kitchen had plenty of sharp knives. No sooner had the thought occurred to me than the creature moved past the edge of the door, smiling, as if it had read my mind. Then it spoke, not with a stutter, but repeating certain words as if it were still trying to learn them. It wouldn't have done you any good, any good, the little green monster said. My nose is like a lizard's tail. It always grows back—stronger and longer, stronger and longer. You'd get just the opposite of what what you want want. Then it spun its eyes for a long time, like two weird tops.

Oh, no, I thought to myself. Can it read people's minds? I hate to have anyone know what I'm thinking—especially when that someone is a horrid and inscrutable little creature like this. I broke out in a cold sweat from head to foot. What was this thing going to do to me? Eat me? Take me down into the earth? Oh, well, at least it wasn't so ugly that I couldn't stand looking at it. That was good. It had slender, pink little arms and legs jutting out from its green-scaled body and long claws at the ends of its hands and feet. They were almost darling, the more I looked at them. And I could see, too, that the creature meant me no harm.

Of course not, it said to me, cocking its head. Its scales clicked against one another when it moved—like crammed-together coffee cups rattling on a table when you nudge it. What a terrible thought, madam: Of course I wouldn't eat you. No no no. I mean you no harm, no harm, no harm. So I was right: It knew exactly what I was thinking.

Madam madam madam, don't you see? Don't you see? I've come here to propose to you. From deep deep deep down deep down deep. I had to crawl all the way up here up here up. Awful, it was awful, I had to dig and dig and dig. Look at how it ruined my claws! I could never have done this if I meant you any harm, any harm, any harm. I love you. I love you so much I couldn't stand it anymore down deep down deep. I crawled my way up to you, I had to, I had to. They all tried to stop me, but

I couldn't stand it anymore. And think of the courage that it took, please, took. What if you thought it was rude and presumptuous, rude and presumptuous, for a creature like me to propose to you?

But it *is* rude and presumptuous, I said in my mind. What a rude little creature you are to come seeking my love!

A look of sadness came over the monster's face as soon as I thought this, and its scales took on a purple tinge, as if to express what it was feeling. Its entire body seemed to shrink a little, too. I folded my arms to watch these changes occurring. Maybe something like this would happen whenever its feelings altered. And maybe its awful-looking exterior masked a heart that was as soft and vulnerable as a brand-new marshmallow. If so, I knew I could win. I decided to give it a try. You *are* an ugly little monster, you know, I shouted in my mind's loudest voice—so loud it made my heart reverberate. You *are* an ugly little monster! The purple of the scales grew deeper, and the thing's eyes began to bulge as if they were sucking in all the hatred I was sending them. They protruded from the creature's face like ripe green figs, and tears like red juice ran down from them, splattering on the floor.

I wasn't afraid of the monster anymore. I painted pictures in my mind of all the cruel things I wanted to do to it. I tied it down to a heavy chair with thick wires, and with a needle-nose pliers I began ripping out its scales at the roots, one by one. I heated the point of a sharp knife, and with it I cut deep grooves in the soft pink flesh of its calves. Over and over, I stabbed a hot soldering iron into the bulging figs of its eyes. With each new torture I imagined for it, the monster would lurch and writhe and wail in agony as if those things were actually happening to it. It wept its colored tears and oozed thick gobs of liquid onto the floor, emitting a gray vapor from its ears that had the fragrance of roses. Its eyes sent an unnerving glare of reproach at me. Please, madam, oh please, I beg of you, don't think such terrible thoughts! it cried. I have no evil thoughts for you. I would never harm you. All I feel for you is love, is love. But I refused to listen. In my mind, I said, Don't be ridiculous! You crawled out of my garden. You unlocked my door without permission. You came inside my house. I never asked you here. I have the right to think anything I want to. And I continued to do exactly that—thinking at the creature increasingly terrible thoughts. I cut and tormented its flesh with every machine and tool I could think of, overlooking no method that might exist to torture a living being and make it writhe in pain. See, then, you little monster, you have no idea what a woman is. There's no end to the number of things I can think of to do to you. But soon the monster's outlines began to fade, and even its strong green nose shriveled up until it was no bigger than a worm. Writhing on the floor, the monster tried to move its mouth and speak to me, struggling to open its lips as if it wanted to leave me some final message, to convey some ancient wisdom, some crucial bit of knowledge that it had forgotten to impart to me. Before that could happen, the mouth attained a painful stillness, and soon it went out of focus and disappeared. The monster now looked like nothing more than a pale evening shadow. All that remained, suspended in the air, were its mournful, bloated eyes. That won't do any good, I thought to it. You can look all you want, but you can't say a thing. You can't do a thing. Your existence is over, finished, done. Soon the eyes dissolved into emptiness, and the room filled with the darkness of night.

—translated by Jay Rubin

FAMILY
AFFAIR

IT PROBABLY HAPPENS all the time, but I disliked my kid sister's fiancé right from the start. And the less I liked him, the more doubts I had about her. I was disappointed in her for the choice she had made.

Maybe I'm just narrow-minded.

My sister certainly seemed to think so. We didn't talk about my feelings, but she knew I didn't like her fiancé, and she let her annoyance show.

"You've got such a narrow view of things," she said.

At the time, we were talking about spaghetti. She was telling me that I had a narrow view of spaghetti.

This was not all she had in mind, of course. Her fiancé was lurking somewhere just beyond the spaghetti, and she was really talking about him. We were fighting over him by proxy.

It all started one Sunday afternoon when she suggested we go out for Italian food. "Fine," I said, since I just happened to be in the mood for that. We went to a cute little spaghetti house that had recently opened up across from the station. I ordered spaghetti with eggplant and garlic, and she asked for pesto sauce. While we waited, I had a beer. So far, so good. It was May, a Sunday, and the weather was beautiful.

The problem started with the spaghetti itself, which was a disaster. The surface of the pasta had an unpleasant, floury texture. The center was still hard and uncooked. Even a dog would have turned its nose up at the butter they had used. I couldn't eat more than half of what was on my plate, and I asked the waitress to take the rest away.

My sister glanced at me once or twice but didn't say anything at first. Instead, she took her time, eating everything they had served her, down to the last thread. I sat there, looking out the window and drinking another beer.

"You didn't have to make such a show of leaving your food," she said when the waitress had taken her plate.

"Yuck."

"It wasn't that bad. You could have forced yourself."

"Why should I? It's *my* stomach, not yours."

"It's a brand-new restaurant. The cook's probably not used to the kitchen. It wouldn't have killed you to give him the benefit of the doubt," she said, and took a sip of the thin, tasteless-looking coffee they had brought her.

"You may be right," I said, "but it only makes sense for a discriminating individual to leave food he doesn't like."

"Well, excuse *me*, Mr. Know-it-all."

"What's *your* problem? That time of the month again?"

"Oh, shut up. I deserve better than that from you."

"Take it easy," I said. "You're talking to a guy who knows exactly when your periods started. You were so late, Mom took you to see a doctor."

"You're going to get my pocketbook right between the eyes . . ."

She was turning serious, so I shut up.

"The trouble with you is, you're so narrow-minded about everything," she said as she added cream to her coffee (meaning it *was* tasteless, after all). "You only see the negative things. You don't even *try* to look at the good points. If something doesn't measure up to your standards, you won't touch it. It's so annoying."

"Maybe so. But it's my life, not yours."

"And you don't care how much you hurt people. You just let them clean up your mess. Even when you masturbate."

"What the hell are you talking about?"

"I remember when you were in high school you used to do it in your sheets. The women of the family had to clean up after you. The least you could do is masturbate without getting it all over your sheets."

"I'll be more careful from now on," I said. "Now, forgive me for repeating myself, but it just so happens that I have my own life. I know what I like and I know what I don't like. It's as simple as that."

"Okay, but you don't have to hurt people. Why don't you try a little harder? Why don't you look at the good side? Why don't you at least show some restraint? Why don't you grow up?"

Now she had touched a sore spot. "I am grown up. I can show restraint. And I can look at the good side, too. I'm just not looking at the same things you are."

"That's what I mean. You're so arrogant. That's why you haven't got a steady girlfriend. I mean, you're twenty-seven years old."

"Of course I have a girlfriend."

"You mean a body to sleep with. You know I'm right. Do you enjoy changing partners every year? How about love and understanding and compassion? Without those, what's the point? You might as well be masturbating."

"I don't change partners *every* year, do I?"

"Pretty much. You ought to think about your life more seriously, act more like a grownup."

That marked the end of our conversation. She just tuned out.

Why had her attitude toward me changed so much over the past year? Until then, she had seemed to enjoy being partners with me in my resolutely aimless life-style, and—if I'm not mistaken—she even looked up to me to some extent. She had become gradually more critical of me in the months since she had begun seeing her fiancé.

This, to me, seemed tremendously unfair. She had been seeing him for a few months, but she and I had been "seeing" each other for twenty-three years. We had always gotten along well, practically never had a fight. I didn't know a brother and sister who could talk so honestly and openly with each other, and not only about masturbation and periods: She knew when I first bought condoms (I was seventeen), and I knew when she first bought lace underwear (she was nineteen).

I had dated her friends (but not slept with them, of course), and she had dated mine (but not slept with them, of course—I think). That's just how we were brought up. This excellent relationship of ours turned sour in less than a year. The more I thought about it, the angrier it made me.

She had to buy a pair of shoes at the department store near the station, she said. I left her outside the restaurant and went back to our apartment alone. I gave my girlfriend a call, but she wasn't in. Which wasn't surprising. Two o'clock on a Sunday afternoon was not the best time to ask a girl for a date. I flipped the pages of my address book and tried another girl—a student I had met at some disco. She answered the phone.

"Like to go out for a drink?"

"You're kidding. It's two o'clock in the afternoon."

"So what? We'll drink till the sun goes down. I know the perfect bar for watching the sunset. You can't get good seats if you're not there by three."

"Are you some kind of connoisseur of sunsets?"

But still she accepted, probably out of kindness. I picked her up, and we drove out along the shore just beyond Yokohama to a bar with a view of the ocean. I drank four glasses of I. W. Harper on the rocks, and she had two banana daiquiris (can you believe it?). And we watched the sun go down.

"Are you going to be okay driving with that much to drink?" she asked.

"No problem. Where alcohol is concerned, I'm under par."

" 'Under par'?"

"Four drinks are just enough to bring me up to normal. You haven't got a thing to worry about. Not a thing."

"If you say so . . ."

We drove back to Yokohama, ate, and enjoyed a few kisses in the car. I suggested we go to a hotel, but she didn't want to.

"I'm wearing a tampon."

"So take it out."

"Yeah, right. It's my second day."

And what a day it was. At this rate, I should have just had a date with my girlfriend. But no, this was going to be the day I spent a nice, leisurely Sunday with my sister, something we hadn't done for a long time. So much for *that* plan.

"Sorry," said the girl. "I'm telling you the truth."

"Never mind. It's not your fault. I'm to blame."

"You're to blame for my period?" she asked with an odd look.

"No, it's just the way things worked out." What a stupid question.

I drove her to her house in Setagaya. On the way, the clutch started making funny rattling noises. I'd probably have to bring it into the garage soon, I thought with a sigh. It was one of those classic days, when one thing goes wrong and then everything goes with it.

"Can I invite you out again soon?" I asked.

"On a date? Or to a hotel?"

"Both," I said with a smile. "The two go together. You know. Like a toothbrush and toothpaste."

"Maybe. I'll think about it."

"You do that. Thinking is good for you. It keeps you from getting senile."

"Where do you live? Can I come and visit?"

"Sorry. I live with my sister. We've got rules. I don't bring women home, and she doesn't bring men."

"Yeah, like she's really your sister."

"It's true. Next time I'll bring a copy of our lease. Sunday okay?"

She laughed. "Okay."

I watched her go in through her gate. Then I started my engine and drove home, listening for those clutch noises.

The apartment was pitch-black. I turned on the light and called my sister's name, but she wasn't there. What the hell was she doing out at ten o'clock at night? I looked for the evening paper but couldn't find it. Of course. It was Sunday.

I got a beer from the refrigerator and carried it and a glass into the living room. I switched on the stereo and dropped a new Herbie Hancock record on the turntable. Waiting for the music to start, I took a long swallow of beer. But nothing came from the speakers. Then I remembered. The stereo had gone on the blink three days earlier. The amp had power, but there was no sound.

This also made it impossible to watch TV. I have one of those monitors without any sound circuitry of its own. You have to use it with the stereo.

I stared at my silent TV screen and drank my beer. They were showing an old war movie. Rommel's Afrika Korps tanks were fighting in the desert. Their cannons shot silent shells, their machine guns shot silent bullets, and people died silently, one after another.

I sighed for what must have been the sixteenth time that day.

I HAD STARTED living with my sister five years earlier, in the spring, when I was twenty-two and she was eighteen. I had just graduated from college and taken my first job, and she had just graduated from high school and entered college. Our parents had allowed her to go to school in Tokyo on the condition that she live with me, a condition we were both glad to accept. They found us a nice, big two-bedroom apartment, and I paid half the rent.

The thought of living with my sister was an almost painless proposition. Not only did we get along well, as I mentioned earlier, but our schedules matched well, too. Working for the PR section of an appliance manufacturer, I would leave the house fairly late in the morning and come back late at night. She used to go out early and come home as the sun was going down. In other words, she was usually gone when I woke up and asleep by the time I came back. And since my weekends were mostly taken up with dates, I didn't really talk to my sister more than once or twice a week. We wouldn't have had time to fight even if we had wanted to, and we didn't invade each other's privacy.

I assumed she had her own things going, but I felt it was not my place to say anything. She was eighteen, after all. What business was it of mine who she slept with?

One time, though, I held her hand for a couple of hours— from one to three in the morning, to be exact. I found her at the kitchen table, crying, when I got home from work. Narrow-minded and selfish as I am, I was smart enough to realize that if she was crying at the kitchen table and not in her room she wanted some comforting from me.

So I sat next to her and held her hand—probably for the first time since elementary school, when we went out hunting dragonflies. Her hand was much bigger and stronger than I remembered. Obviously.

She cried for two hours straight, never moving. I could hardly believe the body was capable of producing such quantities of tears. Two minutes of crying was all it took to dry me out.

By the time 3:00 a.m. rolled around, though, I had had it. I couldn't keep my eyes open. Now it was my turn, as the elder brother, to say something, though giving advice was definitely not my line.

"I don't want to interfere with the way you live your life," I began. "It's your life, and you should live it as you please."

She nodded.

"But I do want to give you one word of advice. Don't carry condoms in your purse. They'll think you're a whore."

When she heard that, she grabbed the telephone book that was sitting on the table and heaved it at me with all her might.

"What are you doing snooping in my bag!"

She always threw things when she got mad. Which is why I didn't go on to tell her that I had never looked in her bag.

In any case, it worked. She stopped crying, and I was able to get some sleep.

Our life-style stayed exactly the same, even after she graduated from college and took a job with a travel agency. She worked a standard nine-to-five day, while my schedule became, if anything, looser. I'd show up at the office some time before noon, read the newspaper at my desk, eat lunch, and finally get serious about doing a little something around two in the afternoon. Later, I'd make arrangements with the guys from the ad agency, and we'd go out drinking till after midnight.

For her first summer vacation, my sister went to California with a couple of friends on a package tour put together by her agency. One of the members of the tour group was a computer engineer a year her senior, and she started dating him when they came back to Japan. This kind of thing happens all the time, but it's not for me. First of all, I hate package tours, and the thought of getting serious about somebody you meet in a group like that makes me sick.

After she started seeing this computer engineer, though, my sister began to glow. She paid a lot more attention to appearances, both the apartment's and her own. Until then, she had gone just about everywhere in a work shirt and faded jeans and sneakers. Thanks to her new interest in clothing, the front closet filled up with her shoes, and all the other closets were overflowing with wire hangers from the cleaner's. She was constantly doing laundry and ironing clothes (instead of leaving them to pile up in the bathroom like an Amazonian ants' nest), always cooking and cleaning. These were dangerous symptoms, I seemed to recall from my own experience. When a woman starts acting like this, a man has only one choice: to clear out fast or marry her.

Then she showed me his picture. She had never done anything like that before. Another dangerous symptom.

Actually, she showed me two pictures. One had been taken on Fisherman's Wharf in San Francisco. It showed my sister and the computer engineer standing in front of a swordfish and wearing big smiles on their faces.

"Nice swordfish," I said.

"Stop joking. I'm serious."

"So what should I say?"

"Don't say anything. This is him."

I took the photo again and studied his face. If there was one single type of face in the world designed to arouse instant dislike in me, this was it. Worse, something about him reminded me of a particular upperclassman in a high-school club of mine, a guy I hated—not a bad-looking type, but absolutely empty-headed and a real whiner. He had a memory like an elephant; once he had some picky thing on you, he'd never let go. He made up for lack of brains with this phenomenal memory.

"How many times have you done it with him?" I asked.

"Don't be stupid," she said, blushing. "You don't have to judge the whole world by your own standards. Not everybody is like you, you know."

The second photo had been taken after the trip. It showed the computer engineer by himself. He wore a leather jacket and was leaning against a big motorcycle, his helmet perched on the saddle. His face had exactly the same expression as in San Francisco. Maybe he didn't *have* any other expressions.

"He likes motorcycles," she said.

"No kidding. I didn't think he put on the leather jacket just to have his picture taken."

Maybe it was another example of my narrow-minded personality, but I could never like motorcycle freaks—the way they swagger around, so pleased with themselves. I kept my mouth shut and handed the picture back.

"Well, then," I said.

"Well, then, what?"

"Well, then, what comes next?"

"I don't know. We might get married."

"Has he proposed?"

"Sort of. But I haven't given him my answer."

"I see."

"Actually, I'm not sure I want to get married. I've just started working, and I think I'd like to take it easy, play around a little more. Not go crazy like you, of course . . ."

"That's probably a healthy attitude," I offered.

"But I don't know, he's really nice. Sometimes I think I'd like to marry him. It's hard."

I picked up the photos again and looked at them. I kept my sigh to myself.

This conversation happened before Christmas. One morning after New Year's, my mother called me at nine o'clock. I was brushing my teeth to Bruce Springsteen's "Born in the U.S.A."

She asked if I knew the man my sister was seeing.

I said I didn't.

She said she had gotten a letter from my sister asking if she could bring him home two weeks from Saturday.

"I suppose she wants to marry him," I said.

"That's why I'm trying to find out from you what kind of man he is. I'd like to learn something about him before I actually meet him."

"Well, I've never met the guy. He's a year older than she is and he's a computer engineer. Works at one of those three-letter places—IBM or NEC or TNT, I don't know. I've seen his picture. A nothing kind of face. Not my taste, but then I don't have to marry him."

"Where did he graduate from? Does he have a house?"

"How should I know?"

"Well, would you please meet him and find out about these things?"

"No way. I'm busy. Ask him yourself when you meet him in two weeks."

Finally, though, I had no choice but to meet my sister's computer engineer. She was going to pay a formal visit to his family's home the following Sunday, and she wanted me to come with her. I put on a white shirt and a tie and my most conservative suit. They lived in an imposing house in the middle of a nice residential neighborhood in Meguro. The 500cc Honda I had seen in the photo was parked in front of the garage.

"Nice swordfish."

"*Please,*" she said, "none of your stupid jokes. All I'm asking is that you restrain yourself for one day."

"Yes, ma'am."

His parents were fine people, very proper—maybe a little too proper. The father was an oil-company executive. Since my father owned a chain of gas stations in Shizuoka, this was by no means an unthinkable match. The mother served us tea on an elegant tray.

I offered the father my calling card, and he gave me his. Then I managed to dredge up all the proper phrases to explain that I was here to represent my parents, who were unfortunately unable to attend, owing to a previous engagement; we hoped that on some future date acceptable to both parties they might be allowed to pay their formal respects.

He replied that his son had told him much about my sister and that, meeting her now, he saw that she was far lovelier than his son deserved. He knew we came from an upstanding family, and as far as he and his wife were concerned they had no objection to the "present discussions." I imagined he must have had our family background thoroughly investigated, but he couldn't possibly have found out that my sister had not had her first period until she was sixteen and that she was chronically constipated.

Once the formalities ended without mishap, the father poured me a brandy—pretty decent stuff. As we drank, we talked about jobs of various kinds. My sister poked me now and then with the toe of her slipper, warning me not to drink too much.

The computer engineer, meanwhile, said nothing, but sat next to his father all the while with a tense expression on his face. You could see right away that he was under his father's thumb, at least while he remained in this house. It figured. The sweater he was wearing had a strange pattern of a kind I had never seen before, and its color clashed with his shirt. Why couldn't she have found somebody a little sharper?

The conversation reached a lull around four o'clock, and we stood up to leave. The computer engineer saw us as far as the station. "How about a cup of tea?" he urged. I didn't want tea and I certainly didn't want to sit at the same table with a guy wearing such a weird sweater, but it would have been awkward for me to refuse, so the three of us went into a nearby coffeehouse.

They ordered coffee and I ordered beer, but the place didn't serve beer so I ordered coffee, too.

"Thanks so much for coming today," he said. "I appreciate your help."

"Just doing what's expected of me," I said simply. "No thanks necessary." I had lost the energy to make wisecracks.

"She's told me so much about you—Brother."

Brother!?

I scratched an earlobe with the handle of my coffee spoon and returned it to the saucer. My sister gave me another healthy kick, but its meaning seemed lost on the computer engineer. Maybe he only got jokes in binary notation.

"I envy the two of you being so close," he said.

"We kick each other in the leg when we're happy," I said.

He took this with a puzzled expression.

"It's supposed to be a joke," grumbled my sister. "He likes to say things like that."

"Just a joke," I concurred. "We share the housework. She does the laundry and I do the jokes."

The computer engineer—his name was Noboru Watanabe—gave a little laugh, as though this had solved a problem for him.

"You two are so bright and cheery," he said. "That's the kind of household I want to have. Bright and cheery is best."

"See?" I said to my sister. "Bright and cheery is best. You're too uptight."

"Not if the jokes are funny," she said.

"If possible, we'd like to marry in the autumn," said Noboru Watanabe.

"Autumn *is* the best time for a wedding," I said. "You can still invite the squirrels and bears."

He laughed. She didn't. She was starting to look seriously angry. I excused myself and left.

Back at the apartment, I phoned my mother and summed up the afternoon for her.

"He's not such a bad guy," I said, scratching my ear.

"What do you mean by that?" she asked.

"He's a serious individual. At least, more serious than I am."

"But you're not serious at all."

"I'm glad to hear that. Thanks," I said, looking at the ceiling.

"So, where did he graduate from?"

"Graduate?"

"Where did he go to college?"

"Ask him yourself," I said, and hung up. I was sick of all this. I took a beer from the refrigerator and drank it alone.

THE DAY AFTER the spaghetti argument with my sister, I woke up at eight-thirty. It was another beautiful, cloudless day, just like yesterday. In fact, it was like a continuation of yesterday, and my life seemed to be starting up again, too, after a halftime break.

I threw my sweat-dampened pajamas into the hamper, took a shower, and shaved. While shaving, I thought about the girl I hadn't quite been able to get last night. Ah, well, it just wasn't in the cards. I did my best. I'll have plenty more opportunities. Like next Sunday.

I toasted two slices of bread and warmed up some coffee. I wanted to listen to an FM station but remembered the stereo was broken. Instead, I read book reviews in the paper and ate my toast. Not one of the books reviewed was something I thought I'd want to read: a novel on "the sex life of an old Jewish man, mingling fantasy and reality," a historical study of treatments for schizophrenia, a complete exposé of the 1907 Ashio Copper Mine pollution incident. It'd be a lot more fun to sleep with the captain of a girls' softball team. The newspaper probably chose books like this just to annoy us.

Munching on my toast, I laid the paper on the table; then I noticed a memo under the jam jar. In my sister's tiny handwriting, it said that she had invited Noboru Watanabe for dinner this Sunday and she expected me to be there.

I finished eating, brushed the crumbs off my shirt, and put the dishes in the sink. Then I called the travel agency. My sister took the phone and said, "I can't talk right now. I'll call you back in ten minutes."

The call came twenty minutes later. In the meantime, I had done forty-three push-ups, trimmed all twenty finger- and toe-nails, picked out my shirt, necktie, jacket, and pants for the day, brushed my teeth, combed my hair, and yawned twice.

"Did you see my note?" she asked.

"Yup. Sorry, but I've got a date this Sunday. Made it a long time ago. If I had known, I would have left the day open. Too bad."

"You expect me to believe that? I know what you're going to do: go somewhere and do something with some girl whose name you hardly know. Well, you can do that on Saturday."

"Saturday I have to be in the studio all day with an electric-blanket commercial. We're busy these days."

"So cancel your date."

"I can't. She'll charge me a cancellation fee. And things are at a pretty delicate stage with her."

"Meaning things are not so delicate in my case?"

"No, I don't mean that at all," I said, holding the necktie I had chosen next to the shirt hanging on a chairback. "But don't forget: We've got this rule not to trespass on each other's lives. You eat dinner with your fiancé and I'll have a date with my girlfriend. What's wrong with that?"

"You know what's wrong with that. Look how long it's been since you've seen him. You met him once, and that was four months ago. It's just not right. Every time I arrange something, you run away. Don't you see how rude you're being? He's your sister's fiancé. It wouldn't kill you to have dinner with him once."

She had a point there, so I kept quiet. In fact, I had been trying to avoid crossing paths with him, but to me it seemed the most natural thing in the world to do. We had nothing in common to talk about, and it was exhausting to tell jokes using my sister as a simultaneous interpreter.

"Will you *please* just join us this once? If you'll do that much for me, I promise I won't interfere with your sex life till the end of the summer."

"My sex life is pretty feeble at the moment. It might not make it through the summer."

"You *will* be home for dinner this Sunday, though, won't you?"

"How can I say no?"

"He'll probably fix the stereo for us. He's good at that."

"Good with his hands, huh?"

"You and your dirty mind," she said, and hung up.

I put on my necktie and went to work.

The weather was clear all that week. Each day was like a continuation of the previous one. Wednesday night, I called my girlfriend to say we couldn't get together on the weekend. She was understandably annoyed: We hadn't seen each other for three weeks. Receiver still in hand, I dialed the college girl I had made a date with for Sunday, but she was out. She was out again on Thursday and on Friday.

My sister woke me up at eight o'clock on Sunday morning. "Get out of bed, will you? I have to wash the sheets."

She stripped the sheets and pillowcase and ordered me out of my pajamas. My only refuge was the bathroom, where I showered and shaved. She was getting to be more and more like our mother. Women are like salmon: In the end, they all swim back to the same place.

After the shower, I put on a pair of shorts and a faded T-shirt, and with long, long yawns I drank a glass of orange juice. My veins still carried some of last night's alcohol; opening the Sunday paper would have been too much for me. I nibbled a few soda crackers from the box on the kitchen table and decided that that was all the breakfast I needed.

My sister threw the sheets into the washing machine and cleaned our two rooms. Next, she put some soap and water in a bucket and washed down the walls and floors of the living room and kitchen. I sprawled on the sofa all this time, looking at the nude photos in a copy of *Hustler* that a friend of mine in the States had gotten past the postal censors. Amazing, the variety in shape and size of the female sex organ. They can be as different as people's heights or IQs.

"Stop hanging around and do some shopping for me, will you?" She handed me a list crammed full of things to buy. "And please hide that magazine. He's very proper."

I laid the magazine down and studied the list. Lettuce, tomatoes, celery, French dressing, smoked salmon, mustard, onions, soup stock, potatoes, parsley, three steaks . . .

"Steaks? I just had steak last night. Why don't you make croquettes?"

"Maybe *you* had steak last night, but we didn't. Don't be so selfish. You can't serve croquettes when you have a guest for dinner."

"If some girl invited me to her house and fed me fresh-fried croquettes, I'd be deeply moved. With a nice pile of julienned white cabbage, a bowl of miso clam soup . . . that's real life."

"Maybe so, but I have decided on steak. Next time I'll feed you croquettes till you drop, but today you'll have to make do with steak. Please."

"That'll be fine," I told her reassuringly. I can be a pain in the neck, but finally I'm a kind, understanding human being.

I went to the neighborhood supermarket and bought everything on the list. On the way home, I stopped off at a liquor store and bought a 4,500-yen bottle of Chablis—my gift to the young couple. Only a kind, understanding human being would think of something like that.

At home, I found a blue Ralph Lauren polo shirt and a spotless pair of cotton pants neatly folded on the bed.

"Change into those," she said.

With another silent sigh, I did as I was told. I couldn't have said anything to her that would have brought me back my pleasantly messy, peaceful Sunday.

NOBORU WATANABE came riding up at three. Astride his trusty cycle, he arrived with the gentle zephyrs of springtime. I caught the ominous put-put of his 500cc Honda from a quarter mile away. I stuck my head out over the edge of the balcony to see him parking next to the entrance of our apartment house and taking off his helmet. Fortunately, once he removed that white dome with its STP sticker, his outfit today approached that of a normal human being: overstarched button-down check shirt, baggy white pants, and brown loafers with tassels—though the color of the shoes and belt didn't match.

"I think your friend from Fisherman's Wharf is here," I said to my sister, who was peeling potatoes at the kitchen sink.

"Keep him company for a while, will you? I'll finish up here."

"Bad idea. I don't know what to talk to him about. You talk to him—I'll do this."

"Don't be silly. It wouldn't look right for me to leave you in the kitchen. You talk to him."

The bell rang, and I opened the door to find Noboru Watanabe standing there. I showed him into the living room and settled him onto the couch. His gift for the evening was a selection of Baskin-Robbins's thirty-one flavors, but cramming it into our tiny, already-stuffed freezer took a major effort on my part. What a pain. Of all the things he could have brought, why did he have to pick ice cream?

"How about a beer?"

"No thanks. I think I'm allergic to alcohol. One glass is enough to make me sick."

"I once drank a whole washbasinful of beer on a bet with some college friends."

"What did it do to you?"

"My pee stank beer for two whole days. And I kept burping up this—"

"Why don't you have Noboru look at the stereo set?" interjected my sister, who had come along in the nick of time, as if she had smelled smoke, with two glasses of orange juice.

"Good idea," said Noboru.

"I hear you're good with your hands," I said.

"It's true," he confessed unabashedly. "I always used to enjoy making plastic models and radio kits. Anytime something broke in the house, I'd fix it. What's wrong with the stereo?"

"No sound," I said. I turned on the amp and put on a record to show him.

He crouched down in front of the stereo like a mongoose ready to spring. After fiddling with all the switches, he announced, "It's definitely in the amplifier system, but it's not internal."

"How can you tell?"

"By the inductive method."

Oh, sure, the inductive method.

He pulled out the mini-preamp and the power amplifier, removed all the cords connecting them, and began to examine each one. While he was busy with this, I took a can of Budweiser from the refrigerator and drank it alone.

"It must be fun to be able to drink alcohol," he said as he poked at a plug with a mechanical pencil.

"I wonder," I said. "I've been doing it so long I wouldn't have anything to compare it with."

"I've been practicing a little."

"Practicing drinking?"

"Yes. Is there something odd about that?"

"No, not at all. You should start with white wine. Put some in a big glass with ice, cut it with Perrier and a squeeze of lemon juice. That's what I drink instead of fruit juice."

"I'll give it a try," he said. "Aha! I thought so!"

"What's that?"

"The connecting cords between the preamp and the power amp. The connection's been broken at the plugs on both channels. This kind of pin plug can't take much movement. In addition to which, they're cheaply made. I'll bet somebody moved the amplifier recently."

"I did the other day, when I was cleaning," said my sister.

"That's it."

She looked at me. "We got this thing from *your* company. It's their fault for using such weak parts."

"Well, *I* didn't make it," I muttered. "I just do the commercials."

"Don't worry," said Noboru Watanabe. "I can fix it right away if you've got a soldering iron."

"A soldering iron? Not in this house."

"Never mind. I'll zip out and buy one. You really ought to have a soldering iron in the house. They come in handy."

"Yeah, I'll bet. But I don't know where there's a hardware store."

"I do. I passed one on the way."

I stuck my head out over the balcony again and watched Noboru Watanabe strap on his helmet, mount his bike, and disappear around a corner.

"He's so nice," sighed my sister.

"Yeah, a real honey."

NOBORU WATANABE finished repairing the pin plugs before five o'clock. He asked to hear some easy-listening vocals, so my sister put on a Julio Iglesias record. Since when did we have crap like that in the house?

Noboru asked me, "What kind of music do you like?"

"Oh, I just *love* stuff like this," I blurted out. "You know: Bruce Springsteen, Jeff Beck, the Doors."

"Funny, I've never heard of any of those. Are they like Julio?"

"Yeah, a lot like Julio."

He talked about the new computer system that his project team was currently developing. It was designed to generate an instantaneous diagram showing the most effective method for returning trains to the depot after an accident. In fact, it sounded like a great idea, but the principle made about as much sense to me as Finnish verb conjugations. While he raved on and on, I nodded at appropriate times and thought about women—like who I should take where to drink what on my next day off, including where we would eat and the hotel we'd use. I must have an inborn liking for such things. Just as there are those who like to make plastic models and draw train diagrams, I like to get drunk with women and sleep with them. It was a matter of Destiny, something that surpassed all human understanding.

Around the time I was finishing my fourth beer, dinner was ready: smoked salmon, vichyssoise, steak, salad, and fried potatoes. As always, my sister's cooking was pretty good. I opened the Chablis and drank it alone.

As he sliced his tenderloin, Noboru Watanabe asked me,

"Why did you take a job with an appliance manufacturer? I gather you're not particularly interested in electrical devices."

My sister answered for me. "He's not particularly interested in anything that's of benefit to society. He would have taken a job anywhere. It just so happened he had an in with that particular company."

"I couldn't have said it any better myself," I chimed in.

"All he thinks about is having fun. It never occurs to him to concentrate on anything seriously, to make himself a better person."

"Yours truly, the summer grasshopper."

"He gets a kick out of smirking at those who *do* choose to live seriously."

"Now, there you're wrong," I interjected. "What I do has nothing to do with what anybody else does. I just go along burning my own calories in accordance with my own ideas about things. What other people do doesn't concern me. I don't smirk at them; I don't even look at them. I may be a good-for-nothing, but at least I don't get in the way of other people."

"That's not true!" cried Noboru Watanabe in something like a reflex action. "You're not a good-for-nothing!" He must have been brought up well.

"Thank you," I said, raising my wineglass to him. "And by the way, congratulations on your engagement. Sorry to be the only one drinking."

"We're planning to have the ceremony in October," he said. "Probably too late to invite the squirrels and bears."

"Not to worry," I said. Incredible, he was making jokes!

"So, where will you go on your honeymoon? I suppose you can get discount fares?"

"Hawaii," my sister answered curtly.

We talked for a while about airplanes. Having just read several books on the crash in the Andes, I brought up that topic.

"When they ate human flesh, they would roast it in the sun on pieces of aluminum from the airplane."

My sister stopped eating and glared at me. "Why do you have to talk about such awful things at the dinner table? Do you say things like that when you're eating with girls you're trying to seduce?"

Like a guest invited to dinner by a feuding married couple, Noboru Watanabe tried to come between us by asking me, "Have you ever thought of marrying?"

"Never had the chance," I said as I was about to put a chunk of fried potato in my mouth. "I had to raise my little sister without any help, and then came the long years of war . . ."

"War? What war?"

"It's just another one of his stupid jokes," said my sister, shaking the bottle of salad dressing.

"Just another one of my stupid jokes," I added. "But the part about not having had the chance is true. I've always been a narrow-minded guy, and I never used to wash my socks, so I was never able to find a nice girl who wanted to spend her life with me. Unlike you."

"Was there something wrong with your socks?" asked Noboru Watanabe.

"That's a joke, too," my sister explained wearily. "I wash his socks, at least, every day."

Noboru Watanabe nodded and laughed for one and a half seconds. I was determined to make him laugh for three seconds next time.

"But *she's* been spending her life with you, hasn't she?" he said, gesturing toward my sister.

"Well, after all, she's my sister."

"And we've stayed together because you do anything you please and I don't say a thing. But that's not a *real* life. In a real, grown-up, *adult* life, people confront each other honestly. I'm not saying the past five years with you haven't been fun. It's been a free and easy time for me. But lately, I've come to see that it's not a real life. It hasn't got—oh, I don't know—the *feel* of what real life is all about. All you think about is yourself, and if somebody tries to have a serious conversation with you, you make fun of them."

"Deep down, I'm really a shy person."

"No, you're just plain arrogant."

"I'm shy and arrogant," I explained to Noboru Watanabe as I poured myself more wine. "I have this shy, arrogant way of returning trains to the depot after an accident."

"I think I see what you mean," he said, nodding. "But do you know what I think? I think that after you're alone—I mean, after she and I get married—that you are going to start wanting to get married, too."

"You may be right," I said.

"Really?" my sister piped up. "If you're really thinking about getting married, I've got a good friend, a nice girl, I'd be glad to introduce you."

"Sure. When the time comes," I said. "Too dangerous now."

WHEN DINNER WAS OVER, we moved to the living room for coffee. This time my sister put on a Willie Nelson record—maybe one small step up from Julio Iglesias.

My sister was in the kitchen, cleaning up, when Noboru Watanabe said to me with an air of confidentiality, "To tell you the truth, I wanted to stay single until I was closer to thirty, like you. But when I met her, all I could think of was getting married."

"She's a good kid," I said. "She can be stubborn and a little constipated, but I really think you've made the right choice."

"Still, the idea of getting married is kind of frightening, don't you think?"

"Well, if you make an effort to always look at the good side, always think about the good things, there's nothing to be afraid of. If something bad comes up, you can think again at that point."

"You may be right."

"I'm good at giving advice to others."

I went to the kitchen and told my sister I would be going

out for a walk. "I won't come back before ten o'clock, so the two of you can relax and enjoy yourselves. The sheets are fresh."

"Is that all you think about?" she said with an air of disgust, but she didn't try to stop me from going out.

I went back to the living room and told Noboru Watanabe that I had an errand to run and might be late getting back.

"I'm glad we had a chance to talk," he said. "Please be sure to visit us often after we're married."

"Thanks," I said, momentarily shutting down my imagination.

"Don't you dare drive," my sister called out to me as I was leaving. "You've had too much to drink."

"Don't worry. I'll walk."

It was a little before eight when I entered a neighborhood bar. I sat at the counter, drinking an I. W. Harper on the rocks. The TV behind the bar was tuned to a Giants–Swallows game. The sound was off, and instead they had a Cyndi Lauper record going. The pitchers were Nishimoto and Obana, and the Swallows were ahead, 3–2. There was something to be said for watching TV with the sound off.

I had three whiskeys while I watched the ball game. It was the bottom of the seventh, score tied 3–3, when the broadcast ended at nine o'clock and the set was switched off. Two seats away from me was a girl around twenty I had seen there a few times. She had been watching the game, too, so I started talking to her about baseball.

"I'm a Giants fan," she said. "Which team do *you* like?"

"They're all the same to me. I just like to watch them play."

"What's the fun of that? How can you get excited about the game?"

"I don't have to get excited. *I'm* not playing. *They* are."

I had two more whiskeys on the rocks and treated her to two daiquiris. She was a major in commercial design at Tokyo University of the Arts, so we talked about art in advertising. At ten, we moved on to a bar with more comfortable seats, where I had a whiskey and she had a grasshopper. She was pretty drunk by this time, and so was I. At eleven, I accompanied her to her apartment, where we had sex as a matter of course, the way they give you a cushion and a cup of tea at an inn.

"Put the light out," she said, so I did. From her window you could see a big Nikon ad tower. A TV next door was blasting the day's pro-baseball results. What with the darkness and my drunkenness, I hardly knew what I was doing. You couldn't call it sex. I just moved my penis and discharged some semen.

As soon as the moderately abbreviated act was finished, she went to sleep as if she couldn't wait any longer to be unconscious. Without even bothering to wipe up properly, I got dressed and left. The hardest thing was picking out my polo shirt and underpants from among her stuff in the dark.

Outside, my alcoholic high tore through me like a midnight freight. I felt like shit. My joints creaked like the Tin Woodman's in *The Wizard of Oz*. I bought a can of juice from a vending machine to sober me up, but the second I drank it down I vomited the entire contents of my stomach onto the road—the corpses of my steak and smoked salmon and lettuce and tomatoes.

How many years had it been since I last vomited from drinking? What the hell was I doing these days? The same thing over and over. But each repetition was worse than the one before.

Then, with no connection at all, I thought about Noboru Watanabe and the soldering iron he had bought me. "You really ought to have a soldering iron in the house. They come in handy," he had said.

What a wholesome idea, I said to him mentally as I wiped my lips with a handkerchief. Now, thanks to you, my house is equipped with a soldering iron. But because of that damned soldering iron, my house doesn't feel like my house any longer.

That's probably because I have such a narrow personality.

IT WAS AFTER midnight by the time I got home. The motorcycle was, of course, no longer parked by the front entrance. I took the elevator to the fourth floor, unlocked the apartment door, and went in. Everything was pitch-black except for a small fluorescent light above the sink. My sister had probably gotten fed up and gone to bed. I couldn't blame her.

I poured myself a glass of orange juice and emptied it in one gulp. I used lots of soap in the shower to wash the foul-smelling sweat from my body, and then I did a thorough job of brushing my teeth. My face in the bathroom mirror was enough to give me chills. I looked like one of those middle-aged men you see on the last trains from downtown, sprawling drunk on the seats and fouling themselves with their own vomit. My skin was rough, my eyes looked sunken, and my hair had lost its sheen.

I shook my head and turned out the bathroom light. With nothing on but a towel wrapped around my waist, I went to the kitchen and drank some tap water. Something will work out tomorrow, I thought. And if not, then tomorrow I'll do some thinking. Ob-la-di, ob-la-da, life goes on.

"You were so late tonight," came my sister's voice out of the gloom. She was sitting on the living-room couch, drinking a beer alone.

"I was drinking," I said.

"You drink too much."

"I know."

I got a beer from the refrigerator and sat down across from her.

For a while, neither of us said anything. We sat there, occasionally tipping back our beer cans. The leaves of the potted plants on the balcony fluttered in the breeze, and beyond them floated the misty semicircle of the moon.

"Just to let you know, we didn't do it," she said.

"Do what?"

"Do anything. Something got on my nerves. I just couldn't do it."

"Oh." I seem to lose the power of speech on half-moon nights.

"Aren't you going to ask what got on my nerves?"

"What got on your nerves?"

"This room! This place! I just couldn't do it here."

"Oh."

"Hey, is something wrong with you? Are you feeling sick?"

"I'm tired. Even I get tired sometimes."

She looked at me without a word. I drained the last sip of my beer and rested my head on the seat back, eyes closed.

"Was it our fault? Did we make you tired?"

"No way," I said with my eyes still closed.

"Are you too tired to talk?" she asked in a tiny voice.

I straightened up and looked at her. Then I shook my head.

"I'm worried. Did I say something terrible to you today? Something about you yourself, or about the way you live?"

"Not at all," I said.

"Really?"

"Everything you've said lately has been right on the mark. So don't worry. But what's bothering you now, all of a sudden?"

"I don't know, it just sort of popped into my mind after he left, while I was waiting for you. I wondered if I hadn't gone too far."

I got two cans of beer from the refrigerator, switched on the stereo, and put on the Richie Beirach Trio at very low volume. It was the record I listened to whenever I came home drunk in the middle of the night.

"I'm sure you're a little confused," I said. "These changes in life are like changes in the barometric pressure. I'm kind of confused, too, in my own way."

She nodded.

"Am I being hard on you?" she asked.

"Everybody's hard on somebody," I said. "But if I'm the one you chose to be hard on, you made the right choice. So don't let it worry you."

"Sometimes, I don't know, it scares me. The future."

"You have to make an effort to always look at the good side, always think about the good things. Then you've got nothing to be afraid of. If something bad comes up, you do more thinking at that point." I gave her the same speech I had given Noboru Watanabe.

"But what if things don't work out the way you want them to?"

"If they don't work out, that's when you think again."

She gave a little laugh. "You're as strange as ever."

"Say, can I ask you one question?" I yanked open another can of beer.

"Sure."

"How many men did you sleep with before him?"

She hesitated a moment before holding up two fingers. "Two."

"And one was your age, and the other was an older man?"

"How did you know?"

"It's a pattern." I took another swig of beer. "I haven't been fooling around for nothing all these years. I've learned that much."

"So, I'm typical."

"Let's just say 'healthy.' "

"How many girls have you slept with?"

"Twenty-six. I counted them up the other day. There were twenty-six I could remember. There might be another ten or so I can't remember. I'm not keeping a diary or anything."

"Why do you sleep with so many girls?"

"I don't know," I answered honestly. "I guess I'll have to stop at some point, but I can't seem to figure out how."

We remained silent for a while, alone with our own thoughts. From the distance came the sound of a motorcycle's exhaust, but it couldn't have been Noboru Watanabe's. Not at one o'clock in the morning.

"Tell me," she said, "what do you really think of him?"

"Noboru Watanabe?"

"Uh-huh."

"He's not a bad guy, I guess. Just not my type. Funny taste in clothes, for one thing." I thought about it some more and said, "There's nothing wrong in having one guy like him in every family."

"That's what I think. And then there's you: this person I call my brother. I'm very fond of you, but if everybody were like you the world would probably be a terrible place!"

"You may be right."

We drank what was left of the beer and withdrew to our separate rooms. My sheets were new and clean and tight. I stretched out on top of them and looked through the curtain at the moon. Where were we headed? I wondered. But I was far too tired to think very deeply about such things. When I closed my eyes, sleep floated down on me like a dark, silent net.

—*translated by Jay Rubin*

A WINDOW

GREETINGS,

The winter cold diminishes with each passing day, and now the sunlight hints at the subtle scent of springtime. I trust that you are well.

Your recent letter was a pleasure to read. The passage on the relationship between hamburger steak and nutmeg was especially well written, I felt: so rich with the genuine sense of daily living. How vividly it conveyed the warm aromas of the kitchen, the lively tapping of the knife against the cutting board as it sliced through the onion!

In the course of my reading, your letter filled me with such an irrepressible desire for hamburger steak that I had to go to a nearby restaurant and have one that very night. In fact, the particular neighborhood establishment in question offers eight different varieties of hamburger steak; Texas-style, Hawaiian-style, Japanese-style, and the like. Texas-style is big. Period. It would no doubt come as a shock to any Texans who might find their way to this part of Tokyo. Hawaiian-style is garnished with a slice of pineapple. California-style . . . I don't remember. Japanese-style is smothered with grated daikon. The place is smartly decorated, and the waitresses are all pretty, with extremely short skirts.

Not that I had made my way there for the express purpose of studying the restaurant's interior décor or the waitresses' legs. I was there for one reason only, and that was to eat hamburger steak—not Texas-style or California-style or any other style, but plain, simple hamburger steak.

Which is what I told the waitress. "I'm sorry," she replied, "but such-and-such-style hamburger steak is the only kind we have here."

I couldn't blame the waitress, of course. *She* hadn't set the menu. *She* hadn't chosen to wear this uniform that revealed so much thigh each time she cleared a dish from a table. I smiled at her and ordered a Hawaiian-style hamburger steak. As she pointed out, I merely had to set the pineapple aside when I ate the steak.

What a strange world we live in! All I want is a perfectly ordinary hamburger steak, and the only way I can have it at this particular point in time is Hawaiian-style without pineapple.

Your own hamburger steak, I gather, is the normal kind. Thanks to your letter, what I wanted most of all was an utterly normal hamburger steak made by you.

By contrast, the passage on the National Railways' automatic ticket machines struck me as a bit superficial. Your angle on the problem is a good one, to be sure, but the reader can't vividly grasp the scene. Don't try so hard to be the penetrating observer. Writing is, after all, a makeshift thing.

Your overall score on this newest letter is 70. Your style is improving slowly but surely. Don't be impatient. Just keep working as hard as you have been all along. I look forward to your next letter. Won't it be nice when spring really comes?

P.S. Thank you for the box of assorted cookies. They are delicious. The Society's rules, however, strictly forbid personal contact beyond the exchange of letters. I must ask you to restrain your kindness in the future.

Nevertheless, thank you once again.

I KEPT THIS part-time job going for a year. I was twenty-two at the time.

I ground out thirty or more letters like this every month at two thousand yen per letter for a strange little company in the Iidabashi district that called itself "The Pen Society."

"You, too, can learn to write captivating letters," boasted the company's advertisements. New "members" paid an initiation fee and monthly dues, in return for which they could write four letters a month to The Pen Society. We "Pen Masters" would answer their letters with letters of our own, such as the one quoted above, containing corrections, comments, and guidance for future improvement. I had gone for a job interview after seeing an ad posted in the student office of the literature department. At the time, certain events had led me to delay my graduation for a year, and my parents had informed me that they would consequently be decreasing my monthly support. For the first time in my life, I was faced with having to make a living. In addition to the interview, I was asked to write several compositions, and a week later I was hired. Then came a week of training in how to make corrections, offer guidance, and other tricks of the trade, none of which was very difficult.

All Society members are assigned to Pen Masters of the opposite sex. I had a total of twenty-four members, ranging in age from fourteen to fifty-three, the majority in the twenty-five-to-thirty-five range. Which is to say, most of them were older than I was. The first month, I panicked: The women were far better writers than I was, and they had a lot more experience as correspondents. I had hardly written a serious letter in my life, after all. I'm not quite sure how I made it through that first month. I was in a constant cold sweat, convinced that most of the members in my charge would demand a new Pen Master—a privilege touted in the Society's rules.

The month went by, and not one member raised a complaint about my writing. Far from it. The owner said I was very popular. Two more months went by, and it even began to seem that my charges were improving thanks to my "guidance." It was weird. These women looked up to me as their teacher with complete trust. When I realized this, it enabled me to dash off my critiques to them with far less effort and anxiety.

I didn't realize it at the time, but these women were lonely (as were the male members of the Society). They wanted to write but they had no one to write to. They weren't the type to send fan letters to a deejay. They wanted something more personal —even if it had to come in the form of corrections and critiques.

And so it happened that I spent a part of my early twenties like a crippled walrus in a warmish harem of letters.

And what amazingly varied letters they were! Boring letters, funny letters, sad letters. Unfortunately, I couldn't keep any of them (the rules required us to return all letters to the company), and this happened so long ago that I can't recall them in detail, but I do remember them as filled to overflowing with life in all its aspects, from the largest of questions to the tiniest of trivia. And the messages they were sending seemed to me— to me, a twenty-two-year-old college student—strangely divorced from reality, seemed at times to be utterly meaningless. Nor was this due solely to my own lack of life experience. I realize now that the reality of things is not something you convey to people but something you make. It is this that gives birth to meaning. I didn't know it then, of course, and neither did the women. This was surely one of the reasons that everything in their letters struck me as oddly two-dimensional.

When it came time for me to leave the job, all the members in my care expressed their regret. And though, quite frankly, I was beginning to feel that I had had enough of this endless job of letter writing, I felt sorry, too, in a way. I knew that I would never again have so many people opening themselves to me with such simple honesty.

•   •   •

HAMBURGER STEAK. I did actually have the opportunity to eat a hamburger steak made by the woman to whom the earlier-quoted letter was addressed.

She was thirty-two, no children, husband worked for a company that was generally considered the fifth-best-known in the country. When I informed her in my last letter that I would have to be leaving the job at the end of the month, she invited me to lunch. "I'll fix you a perfectly normal hamburger steak," she wrote. In spite of the Society's rules, I decided to take her up on it. The curiosity of a young man of twenty-two was not to be denied.

Her apartment faced the tracks of the Odakyu Line. The rooms had an orderliness befitting a childless couple. Neither the furniture nor the lighting fixtures nor the woman's sweater was of an especially costly sort, but they were nice enough. We began with mutual surprise—mine at her youthful appearance, hers at my actual age. She had imagined me as older than herself. The Society did not reveal the ages of its Pen Masters.

Once we had finished surprising each other, the usual tension of a first meeting was gone. We ate our hamburger steak and drank coffee, feeling much like two would-be passengers who had missed the same train. And speaking of trains, from the window of her third-floor apartment one could see the electric train line below. The weather was lovely that day, and over the railings of the building's verandas hung a colorful assortment of sheets and futons drying in the sun. Every now and then came the slap of a bamboo whisk fluffing out a futon. I can bring the sound back even now. It was strangely devoid of any sense of distance.

The hamburger steak was perfect—the flavor exactly right, the outer surface grilled to a crisp dark brown, the inside full of juice, the sauce ideal. Although I could not honestly claim that I had never eaten such a delicious hamburger in my life, it was certainly the best I had had in a very long time. I told her so, and she was pleased.

After the coffee, we told each other our life stories while a

Burt Bacharach record played. Since I didn't really have a life story as yet, she did most of the talking. In college she had wanted to be a writer, she said. She talked about Françoise Sagan, one of her favorites. She especially liked *Aimez-vous Brahms?* I myself did not dislike Sagan. At least, I didn't find her as cheap as everyone said. There's no law requiring everybody to write novels like Henry Miller or Jean Genet.

"I can't write, though," she said.

"It's never too late to start," I said.

"No, I know I can't write. You were the one who informed me of that." She smiled. "Writing letters to you, I finally realized it. I just don't have the talent."

I turned bright red. It's something I almost never do now, but when I was twenty-two I blushed all the time. "Really, though, your writing had something honest about it."

Instead of answering, she smiled—a tiny smile.

"At least one letter made me go out for a hamburger steak."

"You must have been hungry at the time."

And indeed, maybe I had been.

A train passed below the window with a dry clatter.

WHEN THE CLOCK struck five, I said I would be leaving. "I'm sure you have to make dinner for your husband."

"He comes home very late," she said, her cheek against her hand. "He won't be back before midnight."

"He must be a very busy man."

"I suppose so," she said, pausing momentarily. "I think I once wrote to you about my problem. There are certain things I can't really talk with him about. My feelings don't get through to him. A lot of the time, I feel we're speaking two different languages."

I didn't know what to say to her. I couldn't understand how one could go on living with someone to whom it was impossible to convey one's feelings.

"But it's all right," she said softly, and she made it sound as if it really were all right. "Thanks for writing letters to me all these months. I enjoyed them. Truly. And writing back to you was my salvation."

"I enjoyed your letters, too," I said, though in fact I could hardly remember anything she had written.

For a while, without speaking, she looked at the clock on the wall. She seemed almost to be examining the flow of time.

"What are you going to do after graduation?" she asked.

I hadn't decided, I told her. I had no idea what to do. When I said this, she smiled again. "Maybe you ought to do some kind of work that involves writing," she said. "Your critiques were beautifully written. I used to look forward to them. I really did. No flattery intended. For all I know, you were just writing them to fulfill a quota, but they had real feeling. I've kept them all. I take them out every once in a while and reread them."

"Thank you," I said. "And thanks for the hamburger."

TEN YEARS have gone by, but whenever I pass her neighborhood on the Odakyu Line I think of her and of her crisply grilled hamburger steak. I look out at the buildings ranged along the tracks and ask myself which window could be hers. I think about the view from that window and try to figure out where it could have been. But I can never remember.

Perhaps she doesn't live there anymore. But if she does, she is probably still listening to that same Burt Bacharach record on the other side of her window.

Should I have slept with her?

That's the central question of this piece.

The answer is beyond me. Even now, I have no idea. There are lots of things we never understand, no matter how many years we put on, no matter how much experience we accumulate. All I can do is look up from the train at the windows in the buildings that might be hers. Every one of them could be her window, it sometimes seems to me, and at other times I think that none of them could be hers. There are simply too many of them.

—*translated by Jay Rubin*

TV

PEOPLE

IT WAS SUNDAY evening when the TV People showed up. The season, spring. At least, I think it was spring. In any case, it wasn't particularly hot as seasons go, not particularly chilly.

To be honest, the season's not so important. What matters is that it's a Sunday evening.

I don't like Sunday evenings. Or, rather, I don't like everything that goes with them—that Sunday-evening state of affairs. Without fail, come Sunday evening my head starts to ache. In varying intensity each time. Maybe a third to a half of an inch into my temples, the soft flesh throbs—as if invisible threads lead out and someone far off is yanking at the other ends. Not that it hurts so much. It ought to hurt, but strangely, it doesn't—it's like long needles probing anesthetized areas.

And I hear things. Not sounds, but thick slabs of silence being dragged through the dark. *KRZSHAAAL KKRZSHAAAAAL KKKKRMMMS.* Those are the initial indications. First, the aching. Then, a slight distortion of my vision. Tides of confusion wash through, premonitions tugging at memories, memories tugging at premonitions. A finely honed razor moon floats white in the sky, roots of doubt burrow into the earth. People walk extra loud down the hall just to get me. *KRRSPUMK DUWB KRRSPUMK DUWB KRRSPUMK DUWB.*

All the more reason for the TV People to single out Sunday evening as the time to come around. Like melancholy moods, or the secretive, quiet fall of rain, they steal into the gloom of that appointed time.

LET ME EXPLAIN how the TV People look.

The TV People are slightly smaller than you or me. Not obviously smaller—*slightly* smaller. About, say, 20 or 30%. Every part of their bodies is uniformly smaller. So rather than "small," the more terminologically correct expression might be "reduced."

In fact, if you see TV People somewhere, you might not notice at first that they're small. But even if you don't, they'll probably strike you as somehow strange. Unsettling, maybe. You're sure to think something's odd, and then you'll take another look. There's nothing unnatural about them at first glance, but that's what's so unnatural. Their smallness is completely different from that of children and dwarfs. When we see children, we *feel* they're small, but this sense of recognition comes mostly from the misproportioned awkwardness of their bodies. They are small, granted, but not uniformly so. The hands are small, but the head is big. Typically, that is. No, the smallness of TV People is something else entirely. TV People look as if they were reduced by photocopy, everything mechanically calibrated. Say their height has been reduced by a factor of 0.7, then their shoulder width is also in 0.7 reduction; ditto (0.7 reduction) for the feet, head, ears, and fingers. Like plastic models, only a little smaller than the real thing.

Or like perspective demos. Figures that look far away even

close up. Something out of a trompe-l'oeil painting where the surface warps and buckles. An illusion where the hand fails to touch objects close by, yet brushes what is out of reach.

That's TV People.

That's TV People.

That's TV People.

THERE WERE THREE of them altogether.

They don't knock or ring the doorbell. Don't say hello. They just sneak right in. I don't even hear a footstep. One opens the door, the other two carry in a TV. Not a very big TV. Your ordinary Sony color TV. The door was locked, I think, but I can't be certain. Maybe I forgot to lock it. It really wasn't foremost in my thoughts at the time, so who knows? Still, I think the door was locked.

When they come in, I'm lying on the sofa, gazing up at the ceiling. Nobody at home but me. That afternoon, the wife has gone out with the girls—some close friends from her high-school days—getting together to talk, then eating dinner out. "Can you grab your own supper?" the wife said before leaving. "There's vegetables in the fridge and all sorts of frozen foods. That much you can handle for yourself, can't you? And before the sun goes down, remember to take in the laundry, okay?"

"Sure thing," I said. Doesn't faze me a bit. Rice, right? Laundry, right? Nothing to it. Take care of it, simple as *SLUPPP KRRRTZ!*

"Did you say something, dear?" she asked.

"No, nothing," I said.

All afternoon I take it easy and loll around on the sofa. I have nothing better to do. I read a bit—that new novel by García Márquez—and listen to some music. I have myself a beer. Still, I'm unable to give my mind to any of this. I consider going back to bed, but I can't even pull myself together enough to do that. So I wind up lying on the sofa, staring at the ceiling.

The way my Sunday afternoons go, I end up doing a little bit of various things, none very well. It's a struggle to concentrate on any one thing. This particular day, everything seems to be going right. I think, Today I'll read this book, listen to these records, answer these letters. Today, for sure, I'll clean out my desk drawers, run errands, wash the car for once. But two o'clock rolls around, three o'clock rolls around, gradually dusk comes on, and all my plans are blown. I haven't done a thing; I've been lying around on the sofa the whole day, same as always. The clock ticks in my ears. *TRPP Q SCHAOUS TRPP Q SCHAOUS*. The sound erodes everything around me, little by little, like dripping rain. *TRPP Q SCHAOUS TRPP Q SCHAOUS*. Little by little, Sunday afternoon wears down, shrinking in scale. Just like the TV People themselves.

THE TV PEOPLE ignore me from the very outset. All three of them have this look that says the likes of me don't exist. They open the door and carry in their TV. The two put the set on the sideboard, the other one plugs it in. There's a mantel clock and a stack of magazines on the sideboard. The clock was a wedding gift, big and heavy—big and heavy as time itself—with a loud sound, too. *TRPP Q SCHAOUS TRPP Q SCHAOUS*. All through the house you can hear it. The TV People move it off the sideboard, down onto the floor. The wife's going to raise hell, I think. She hates it when things get randomly shifted about. If everything isn't in its proper place, she gets really sore. What's worse, with the clock there on the floor, I'm bound to trip over it in the middle of the night. I'm forever getting up to go to the toilet at two in the morning, bleary-eyed and stumbling over something.

Next, the TV People move the magazines to the table. All of them women's magazines. (I hardly ever read magazines; I read books—personally, I wouldn't mind if every last magazine in the world went out of business.) *Elle* and *Marie Claire* and *Home Ideas,* magazines of that ilk. Neatly stacked on the sideboard. The wife doesn't like me touching her magazines— change the order of the stack, and I never hear the end of it—so I don't go near them. Never once flipped through them. But the

TV People couldn't care less: They move them right out of the way, they show no concern, they sweep the whole lot off the sideboard, they mix up the order. *Marie Claire* is on top of *Croissant*; *Home Ideas* is underneath *An-An*. Unforgivable. And worse, they're scattering the bookmarks onto the floor. They've lost her place, pages with important information. I have no idea what information or how important—might have been for work, might have been personal—but whatever, it was important to the wife, and she'll let me know about it. "What's the meaning of this? I go out for a nice time with friends, and when I come back, the house is a shambles!" I can just hear it, line for line. Oh, great, I think, shaking my head.

EVERYTHING GETS REMOVED from the sideboard to make room for the television. The TV People plug it into a wall socket, then switch it on. Then there is a tinkling noise, and the screen lights up. A moment later, the picture floats into view. They change the channels by remote control. But all the channels are blank—probably, I think, because they haven't connected the set to an antenna. There has to be an antenna outlet somewhere in the apartment. I seem to remember the superintendent telling us where it was when we moved into this condominium. All you had to do was connect it. But I can't remember where it is. We don't own a television, so I've completely forgotten.

Yet somehow the TV People don't seem bothered that they aren't picking up any broadcast. They give no sign of looking for the antenna outlet. Blank screen, no image—makes no difference to them. Having pushed the button and had the power come on, they've completed what they came to do.

The TV is brand-new. It's not in its box, but one look tells you it's new. The instruction manual and guarantee are in a plastic bag taped to the side; the power cable shines, sleek as a freshly caught fish.

All three TV People look at the blank screen from here and there around the room. One of them comes over next to me and verifies that you can see the TV screen from where I'm sitting. The TV is facing straight toward me, at an optimum viewing distance. They seem satisfied. One operation down, says their air of accomplishment. One of the TV People (the one who'd come over next to me) places the remote control on the table.

The TV People speak not a word. Their movements come off in perfect order, hence they don't need to speak. Each of the three executes his prescribed function with maximum efficiency. A professional job. Neat and clean. Their work is done in no time. As an afterthought, one of the TV People picks the clock up from the floor and casts a quick glance around the room to see if there isn't a more appropriate place to put it, but he doesn't find any and sets it back down. *TRPP Q SCHAOUS TRPP Q SCHAOUS.* It goes on ticking weightily on the floor. Our apartment is rather small, and a lot of floor space tends to be taken up with my books and the wife's reference materials. I am bound to trip on that clock. I heave a sigh. No mistake, stub my toes for sure. You can bet on it.

All three TV People wear dark-blue jackets. Of who-knows-what fabric, but slick. Under them, they wear jeans and tennis shoes. Clothes and shoes all proportionately reduced in size. I watch their activities for the longest time, until I start to think maybe it's *my* proportions that are off. Almost as if I were riding backward on a roller coaster, wearing strong prescription glasses. The view is dizzying, the scale all screwed up. I'm thrown off balance, my customary world is no longer absolute. That's the way the TV People make you feel.

Up to the very last, the TV People don't say a word. The three of them check the screen one more time, confirm that there are no problems, then switch it off by remote control. The glow contracts to a point and flickers off with a tinkling noise. The screen returns to its expressionless, gray, natural state. The world outside is getting dark. I hear someone calling out to someone else. Anonymous footsteps pass by down the hall, intentionally loud as ever. *KRRSPUMK DUWB KRRSPUMK DUWB.* A Sunday evening.

The TV People give the room another whirlwind inspection, open the door, and leave. Once again, they pay no attention to me whatsoever. They act as if I don't exist.

FROM THE TIME the TV People come into the apartment to the moment they leave, I don't budge. Don't say a word. I remain motionless, stretched out on the sofa, surveying the whole operation. I know what you're going to say: That's unnatural. Total strangers—not one but three—walk unannounced right into your apartment, plunk down a TV set, and you just sit there staring at them, dumbfounded. Kind of odd, don't you think?

I know, I know. But for whatever reason, I don't speak up, I simply observe the proceedings. Because they ignore me so totally. And if you were in my position, I imagine you'd do the same. Not to excuse myself, but *you* have people right in front of you denying your very presence like that, then see if you don't doubt whether you actually exist. I look at my hands half expecting to see clear through them. I'm devastated, powerless, in a trance. My body, my mind are vanishing fast. I can't bring myself to move. It's all I can do to watch the three TV People deposit their television in my apartment and leave. I can't open my mouth for fear of what my voice might sound like.

The TV People exit and leave me alone. My sense of reality comes back to me. These hands are once again my hands. It's only then I notice that the dusk has been swallowed by darkness. I turn on the light. Then I close my eyes. Yes, that's a TV set sitting there. Meanwhile, the clock keeps ticking away the minutes. *TRPP Q SCHAOUS TRPP Q SCHAOUS.*

CURIOUSLY, THE WIFE makes no mention of the appearance of the television set in the apartment. No reaction at all. Zero. It's as if she doesn't even see it. Creepy. Because, as I said before, she's extremely fussy about the order and arrangement of furniture and other things. If someone dares to move anything in the apartment, even by a hair, she'll jump on it in an instant. That's her ascendancy. She knits her brows, then gets things back the way they were.

Not me. If an issue of *Home Ideas* gets put under an *An-An*, or a ballpoint pen finds its way into the pencil stand, you don't see me go to pieces. I don't even notice. This is her problem; I'd wear myself out living like her. Sometimes she flies into a rage. She tells me she can't abide my carelessness. Yes, I say, and sometimes I can't stand carelessness about universal gravitation and π and $E = mc^2$, either. I mean it. But when I say things like this, she clams up, taking them as a personal insult. I never mean it that way; I just say what I feel.

That night, when she comes home, first thing she does is look around the apartment. I've readied a full explanation— how the TV People came and mixed everything up. It'll be difficult to convince her, but I intend to tell her the whole truth.

She doesn't say a thing, just gives the place the once-over. There's a TV on the sideboard, the magazines are out of order on the table, the mantel clock is on the floor, and the wife doesn't even comment. There's nothing for me to explain.

"You get your own supper okay?" she asks me, undressing.

"No, I didn't eat," I tell her.

"Why not?"

"I wasn't really hungry," I say.

The wife pauses, half-undressed, and thinks this over. She gives me a long look. Should she press the subject or not? The clock breaks up the protracted, ponderous silence. *TRPP Q SCHAOUS TRPP Q SCHAOUS.* I pretend not to hear; I won't let it in my ears. But the sound is simply too heavy, too loud to shut out. She, too, seems to be listening to it. Then she shakes her head and says, "Shall I whip up something quick?"

"Well, maybe," I say. I don't really feel much like eating, but I won't turn down the offer.

The wife changes into around-the-house wear and goes to the kitchen to fix zosui and tamago-yaki while filling me in on her friends. Who'd done what, who'd said what, who'd changed her hairstyle and looked so much younger, who'd broken up with her boyfriend. I know most of her friends, so I pour myself a beer and follow along, inserting attentive uh-huhs at proper intervals. Though, in fact, I hardly hear a thing she says. I'm thinking about the TV People. That, and why she didn't remark on the sudden appearance of the television. No way she couldn't have noticed. Very odd. Weird, even. Something is wrong here. But what to do about it?

The food is ready, so I sit at the dining-room table and eat. Rice, egg, salt plum. When I've finished, the wife clears away the dishes. I have another beer, and she has a beer, too. I glance at the sideboard, and there's the TV set, with the power off, the remote-control unit sitting on the table. I get up from the table, reach for the remote control, and switch it on. The screen glows and I hear it tinkling. Still no picture. Only the same blank tube. I press the button to raise the volume, but all that does is increase the white-noise roar. I watch the snowstorm for twenty, thirty seconds, then switch it off. Light and sound vanish in an instant. Meanwhile, the wife has seated herself on the carpet and is flipping through *Elle,* oblivious of the fact that the TV has just been turned on and off.

I replace the remote control on the table and sit down on the sofa again, thinking I'll go on reading that long García Márquez novel. I always read after dinner. I might set the book down after thirty minutes, or I might read for two hours, but the thing is to read every day. Today, though, I can't get myself to read more than a page and a half. I can't concentrate; my thoughts keep returning to the TV set. I look up and see it, right in front of me.

I ᴡᴀᴋᴇ ᴀᴛ ʜᴀʟꜰ ᴘᴀsᴛ ᴛᴡᴏ in the morning to find the TV still there. I get out of bed half hoping the thing has disappeared. No such luck. I go to the toilet, then plop down on the sofa and put my feet up on the table. I take the remote control in hand and try turning on the TV. No new developments in that department, either; only a rerun of the same glow and noise. Nothing else. I look at it awhile, then switch it off.

I go back to bed and try to sleep. I'm dead tired, but sleep isn't coming. I shut my eyes and I see them. The TV People carrying the TV set, the TV People moving the clock out of the way, the TV People transferring magazines to the table, the TV People plugging the power cable into the wall socket, the TV People checking the screen, the TV People opening the door and silently exiting. They've stayed on in my head. They're in there walking around. I get back out of bed, go to the kitchen, and pour a double brandy into a coffee cup. I down the brandy and head over to the sofa for another session with Márquez. I open the pages, yet somehow the words won't sink in. The writing is opaque.

Very well, then, I throw García Márquez aside and pick up *Elle*. Reading *Elle* from time to time can't hurt anyone. But there isn't anything in *Elle* that catches my fancy. New hairstyles and elegant white silk blouses and eateries that serve good beef stew and what to wear to the opera, articles like that. Do I care? I throw *Elle* aside. Which leaves me the television on the sideboard to look at.

I end up staying awake until dawn, not doing a thing. At six o'clock, I make myself some coffee. I don't have anything else to do, so I go ahead and fix ham sandwiches before the wife gets up.

"You're up awful early," she says drowsily.

"Mmm," I mumble.

After a nearly wordless breakfast, we leave home together and go our separate ways to our respective offices. The wife works at a small publishing house. Edits a natural-food and life-style magazine. "Shiitake Mushrooms Prevent Gout," "The Future of Organic Farming," you know the kind of magazine. Never sells very well, but hardly costs anything to produce; kept afloat by a handful of zealots. Me, I work in the advertising department of an electrical-appliance manufacturer. I dream up ads for toasters and washing machines and microwave ovens.

• • •

IN MY OFFICE BUILDING, I pass one of the TV People on the stairs. If I'm not mistaken, it's one of the three who brought the TV the day before—probably the one who first opened the door, who didn't actually carry the set. Their singular lack of distinguishing features makes it next to impossible to tell them apart, so I can't swear to it, but I'd say I'm eight to nine out of ten on the mark. He's wearing the same blue jacket he had on the previous day, and he's not carrying anything in his hands. He's merely walking down the stairs. I'm walking up. I dislike elevators, so I generally take the stairs. My office is on the ninth floor, so this is no mean feat. When I'm in a rush, I get all sweaty by the time I reach the top. Even so, getting sweaty has got to be better than taking the elevator, as far as I'm concerned. Everyone jokes about it: doesn't own a TV or a VCR, doesn't take elevators, must be a modern-day Luddite. Maybe a childhood trauma leading to arrested development. Let them think what they like. They're the ones who are screwed up, if you ask me.

In any case, there I am, climbing the stairs as always; I'm the only one on the stairs—almost nobody else uses them—when between the fourth and fifth floors I pass one of the TV People coming down. It happens so suddenly I don't know what to do. Maybe I should say something?

But I don't say anything. I don't know what to say, and he's unapproachable. He leaves no opening; he descends the stairs so functionally, at one set tempo, with such regulated precision. Plus, he utterly ignores my presence, same as the day before. I don't even enter his field of vision. He slips by before I can think what to do. In that instant, the field of gravity warps.

At work, the day is solid with meetings from the morning on. Important meetings on sales campaigns for a new product line. Several employees read reports. Blackboards fill with figures, bar graphs proliferate on computer screens. Heated discussions. I participate, although my contribution to the meetings is not that critical because I'm not directly involved with the project. So between meetings I keep puzzling things over. I voice an opinion only once. Isn't much of an opinion, either—something perfectly obvious to any observer—but I couldn't very well go without saying anything, after all. I may not be terribly ambitious when it comes to work, but so long as I'm receiving a salary I have to demonstrate responsibility. I summarize the various opinions up to that point and even make a joke to lighten the atmosphere. Half covering for my daydreaming about the TV People. Several people laugh. After that one utterance, however, I only pretend to review the materials; I'm thinking about the TV People. If they talk up a name for the new microwave oven, I certainly am not aware of it. My mind is all TV People. What the hell was the meaning of that TV set? And why haul the TV all the way to my apartment in the first place? Why hasn't the wife remarked on its appearance? Why have the TV People made inroads into my company?

The meetings are endless. At noon, there's a short break for lunch. Too short to go out and eat. Instead, everyone gets sandwiches and coffee. The conference room is a haze of cigarette smoke, so I eat at my own desk. While I'm eating, the section chief comes around. To be perfectly frank, I don't like the guy. For no reason I can put my finger on: There's nothing you can fault him on, no single target for attack. He has an air of breeding. Moreover, he's not stupid. He has good taste in neckties, he doesn't wave his own flag or lord it over his inferiors. He even looks out for me, invites me out for the occasional meal. But there's just something about the guy that doesn't sit well with me. Maybe it's his habit of coming into body contact with people he's talking to. Men or women, at some point in the course of the conversation he'll reach out a hand and touch. Not in any suggestive way, mind you. No, his manner is brisk, his bearing perfectly casual. I wouldn't be surprised if some people don't even notice, it's so natural. Still—I don't know why—it does bother me. So whenever I see him, almost instinctively I brace myself. Call it petty, it gets to me.

He leans over, placing a hand on my shoulder. "About your

statement at the meeting just now. Very nice," says the section chief warmly. "Very simply put, very pivotal. I was impressed. Points well taken. The whole room buzzed at that statement of yours. The timing was perfect, too. Yessir, you keep 'em coming like that."

And he glides off. Probably to lunch. I thank him straight out, but the honest truth is I'm taken aback. I mean, I don't remember a thing of what I said at the meeting. Why does the section chief have to come all the way over to my desk to praise me for *that*? There have to be more brilliant examples of *Homo loquens* around here. Strange. I go on eating my lunch, uncomprehending. Then I think about the wife. Wonder what she's up to right now. Out to lunch? Maybe I ought to give her a call, exchange a few words, anything. I dial the first three digits, have second thoughts, hang up. I have no reason to be calling her. My world may be crumbling, out of balance, but is that a reason to ring up her office? What can I say about all this, anyway? Besides, I hate calling her at work. I set down the receiver, let out a sigh, and finish off my coffee. Then I toss the Styrofoam cup into the wastebasket.

AT ONE OF THE AFTERNOON MEETINGS, I see TV People again. This time, their number has increased by two. Just as on the previous day, they come traipsing across the conference room, carrying a Sony color TV. A model one size bigger. Uh-oh. Sony's the rival camp. If, for whatever reason, any competitor's product gets brought into our offices, there's hell to pay, barring when other manufacturers' products are brought in for test comparisons, of course. But then we take pains to remove the company logo—just to make sure no outside eyes happen upon it. Little do the TV People care: The Sony mark is emblazoned for all to see. They open the door and march right into the conference room, flashing it in our direction. Then they parade the thing around the room, scanning the place for somewhere to set it down, until at last, not finding any location, they carry it backward out the door. The others in the room show no reaction to the TV People. And they can't have missed them. No, they've definitely seen them. And the proof is they even got out of the way, clearing a path for the TV People to carry their television through. Still, that's as far as it went: a reaction no more alarmed than when the nearby coffee shop delivered. They'd made it a ground rule not to acknowledge the presence of the TV People. The others all knew they were there; they just acted as if they weren't.

None of it makes any sense. Does everybody know about the TV People? Am I alone in the dark? Maybe the wife knew about the TV People all along, too. Probably. I'll bet that's why she wasn't surprised by the television and why she didn't mention it. That's the only possible explanation. Yet this confuses me even more. Who or what, then, are the TV People? And why are they always carrying around TV sets?

One colleague leaves his seat to go to the toilet, and I get up to follow. This is a guy who entered the company around the same time I did. We're on good terms. Sometimes we go out for a drink together after work. I don't do that with most people. I'm standing next to him at the urinals. He's the first to complain. "Oh, joy! Looks like we're in for more of the same, straight through to evening. I swear! Meetings, meetings, meetings, going to drag on forever."

"You can say that again," I say. We wash our hands. He compliments me on the morning meeting's statement. I thank him.

"Oh, by the way, those guys who came in with the TV just now . . ." I launch forth, then cut off.

He doesn't say anything. He turns off the faucet, pulls two paper towels from the dispenser, and wipes his hands. He doesn't even shoot a glance in my direction. How long can he keep drying his hands? Eventually, he crumples up his towels and throws them away. Maybe he didn't hear me. Or maybe he's pretending not to hear. I can't tell. But from the sudden strain in the atmosphere, I know enough not to ask. I shut up, wipe my hands, and walk down the corridor to the conference room. The rest of the afternoon's meetings, he avoids my eyes.

WHEN I GET HOME from work, the apartment is dark. Outside, dark clouds have swept in. It's beginning to rain. The apartment smells like rain. Night is coming on. No sign of the wife. I loosen my tie, smooth out the wrinkles, and hang it up. I brush off my suit. I toss my shirt into the washing machine. My hair smells like cigarette smoke, so I take a shower and shave. Story of my life: I go to endless meetings, get smoked to death, then the wife gets on my case about it. The very first thing she did after we were married was make me stop smoking. Four years ago, that was.

Out of the shower, I sit on the sofa with a beer, drying my hair with a towel. The TV People's television is still sitting on the sideboard. I pick up the remote control from the table and push the "on" switch. Again and again I press, but nothing happens. The screen stays dark. I check the plug; it's in the socket, all right. I unplug it, then plug it back in. Still no go. No matter how often I press the "on" switch, the screen does not glow. Just to be sure, I pry open the back cover of the remote-control unit, remove the batteries, and check them with my handy electrical-contact tester. The batteries are fine. At this point, I give up, throw the remote control aside, and slosh down more beer.

Why should it upset me? Supposing the TV did come on, what then? It would glow and crackle with white noise. Who cares, if that's all that'd come on?

I care. Last night it worked. And I haven't laid a finger on it since. Doesn't make sense.

I try the remote control one more time. I press slowly with my finger. But the result is the same. No response whatsoever. The screen is dead. Cold.

Dead cold.

I pull another beer out of the fridge and eat some potato salad from a plastic tub. It's past six o'clock. I read the whole evening paper. If anything, it's more boring than usual. Almost no article worth reading, nothing but inconsequential news items. But I keep reading, for lack of anything better to do. Until I finish the paper. What next? To avoid pursuing that thought any further, I dally over the newspaper. Hmm, how about answering letters? A cousin of mine has sent us a wedding invitation, which I have to turn down. The day of the wedding, the wife and I are going to be off on a trip. To Okinawa. We've been planning it for ages; we're both taking time off from work. We can't very well go changing our plans now. God only knows when we'll get the next chance to spend a long holiday together. And to clinch it all, I'm not even that close to my cousin; haven't seen her in almost ten years. Still, I can't leave replying to the last minute. She has to know how many people are coming, how many settings to plan for the banquet. Oh, forget it. I can't bring myself to write, not now. My heart isn't in it.

I pick up the newspaper again and read the same articles over again. Maybe I ought to start preparing dinner. But the wife might be working late and could come home having eaten. Which would mean wasting one portion. And if I am going to eat alone, I can make do with leftovers; no reason to make something up special. If she hasn't eaten, we can go out and eat together.

Odd, though. Whenever either of us knows he or she is going to be later than six, we always call in. That's the rule. Leave a message on the answering machine if necessary. That way, the other can coordinate: go ahead and eat alone, or set something out for the late arriver, or hit the sack. The nature of my work sometimes keeps me out late, and she often has meetings, or proofs to dispatch, before coming home. Neither of us has a regular nine-to-five job. When both of us are busy, we can go three days without a word to each other. Those are the breaks—just one of those things that nobody planned. Hence we always keep certain rules, so as not to place unrealistic burdens on each other. If it looks as though we're going to be late, we call in and let the other one know. I sometimes forget, but she, never once.

Still, there's no message on the answering machine.

I toss the newspaper, stretch out on the sofa, and shut my eyes.

I DREAM ABOUT a meeting. I'm standing up, delivering a statement I myself don't understand. I open my mouth and talk. If I don't, I'm a dead man. I have to keep talking. Have to keep coming out with endless blah-blah-blah. Everyone around me is dead. Dead and turned to stone. A roomful of stone statues. A wind is blowing. The windows are all broken; gusts of air are coming in. And the TV People are here. Three of them. Like the first time. They're carrying a Sony color TV. And on the screen are the TV People. I'm running out of words; little by little I can feel my fingertips growing stiffer. Gradually turning to stone.

I open my eyes to find the room aglow. The color of corridors at the Aquarium. The television is on. Outside, everything is dark. The TV screen is flickering in the gloom, static crackling. I sit up on the sofa, and press my temples with my fingertips. The flesh of my fingers is still soft; my mouth tastes like beer. I swallow. I'm dried out; the saliva catches in my throat. As always, the waking world pales after an all-too-real dream. But no, this is real. Nobody's turned to stone. What time is it getting to be? I look for the clock on the floor. *TRPP Q SCHAOUS TRPP Q SCHAOUS*. A little before eight.

Yet, just as in the dream, one of the TV People is on the television screen. The same guy I passed on the stairs to the office. No mistake. The one who first opened the door to the apartment. I'm 100% sure. He stands there—against a bright, fluorescent white background, the tail end of a dream infiltrating my conscious reality—staring at me. I shut, then reopen my eyes, hoping he'll have slipped back to never-never land. But he doesn't disappear. Far from it. He gets bigger. His face fills the whole screen, getting closer and closer.

The next thing I know, he's stepping through the screen. Hands gripping the frame, lifting himself up and over, one foot after the other, like climbing out of a window, leaving a white TV screen glowing behind him.

He rubs his left hand in the palm of his right, slowly acclimating himself to the world outside the television. On and on, reduced right-hand fingers rubbing reduced left-hand fingers, no hurry. He has that all-the-time-in-the-world nonchalance. Like a veteran TV-show host. Then he looks me in the face.

"We're making an airplane," says my TV People visitant. His voice has no perspective to it. A curious, paper-thin voice.

He speaks, and the screen is all machinery. Very professional fade-in. Just like on the news. First, there's an opening shot of a large factory interior, then it cuts to a close-up of the work space, camera center. Two TV People are hard at work on some machine, tightening bolts with wrenches, adjusting gauges. The picture of concentration. The machine, however, is unlike anything I've ever seen: an upright cylinder except that it narrows toward the top, with streamlined protrusions along its surface. Looks more like some kind of gigantic orange juicer than an airplane. No wings, no seats.

"Doesn't look like an airplane," I say. Doesn't sound like my voice, either. Strangely brittle, as if the nutrients had been strained out through a thick filter. Have I grown so old all of a sudden?

"That's probably because we haven't painted it yet," he says. "Tomorrow we'll have it the right color. Then you'll see it's an airplane."

"The color's not the problem. It's the shape. That's not an airplane."

"Well, if it's not an airplane, what is it?" he asks me. If he doesn't know, and I don't know, then what *is* it? "So, that's why it's got to be the color." The TV People rep puts it to me gently. "Paint it the right color, and it'll be an airplane."

I don't feel like arguing. What difference does it make? Orange juicer or airplane—flying orange juicer?—what do I care? Still, where's the wife while all this is happening? Why doesn't she come home? I massage my temples again. The clock ticks on. *TRPP Q SCHAOUS TRPP Q SCHAOUS.* The remote control lies on the table, and next to it the stack of women's magazines. The telephone is silent, the room illuminated by the dim glow of the television.

The two TV People on the screen keep working away. The image is much clearer than before. You can read the numbers on the dials, hear the faint rumble of machinery. *TAABZHRAYBGG TAABZHRAYBGG ARP ARRP TAABZHRAYBGG.* This bass line is punctuated periodically by a sharp, metallic grating. *AREEEENBT AREEEENBT.* And various other noises are interspersed through the remaining aural space; I can't hear anything clearly over them. Still, the two TV People labor on for all they're worth. That, apparently, is the subject of this program. I go on watching the two of them as they work on and on. Their colleague outside the TV set also looks on in silence. At them. At that *thing*—for the life of me, it does not look like an airplane—that insane machine all black and grimy, floating in a field of white light.

The TV People rep speaks up. "Shame about your wife."

I look him in the face. Maybe I didn't hear him right. Staring at him is like peering into the glowing tube itself.

"Shame about your wife," the TV People rep repeats in exactly the same absent tone.

"How's that?" I ask.

"How's that? It's gone too far," says the TV People rep in a voice like a plastic-card hotel key. Flat, uninflected, it slices into me as if it were sliding through a thin slit. "It's gone too far: She's out there."

"*It's gone too far: She's out there,*" I repeat in my head. Very plain, and without reality. I can't grasp the context. Cause has effect by the tail and is about to swallow it whole. I get up and go to the kitchen. I open the refrigerator, take a deep breath, reach for a can of beer, and go back to the sofa. The TV People rep stands in place in front of the television, right elbow resting on the set, and watches me extract the pull-tab. I don't really want to drink beer at this moment; I just need to do something.

I drink one sip, but the beer doesn't taste good. I hold the can in my hand dumbly until it becomes so heavy I have to set it down on the table.

Then I think about the TV People rep's revelation, about the wife's failure to materialize. He's saying she's gone. That she isn't coming home. I can't bring myself to believe it's over. Sure, we're not the perfect couple. In four years, we've had our spats; we have our little problems. But we always talk them out. There are things we've resolved and things we haven't. Most of what we couldn't resolve we let ride. Okay, so we have our ups and downs as a couple. I admit it. But is this cause for despair? C'mon, show me a couple who don't have problems. Besides, it's only a little past eight. There must be some reason she can't get to a phone. Any number of possible reasons. For instance . . . I can't think of a single one. I'm hopelessly confused.

I fall back deep into the sofa.

How on earth is that airplane—if it is an airplane—supposed to fly? What propels it? Where are the windows? Which is the front, which is the back?

I'm dead tired. Exhausted. I still have to write that letter, though, to beg off from my cousin's invitation. My work schedule does not afford me the pleasure of attending. Regrettable. Congratulations, all the same.

The two TV People in the television continue building their airplane, oblivious of me. They toil away; they don't stop for anything. They have an infinite amount of work to get through before the machine is complete. No sooner have they finished one operation than they're busy with another. They have no assembly instructions, no plans, but they know precisely what to do and what comes next. The camera ably follows their deft motions. Clear-cut, easy-to-follow camera work. Highly credible, convincing images. No doubt other TV People (Nos. 4 and 5?) are manning the camera and control panel.

Strange as it may sound, the more I watch the flawless form of the TV People as they go about their work, the more the thing starts to look like an airplane. At least, it'd no longer surprise me if it actually flew. What does it matter which is front or back? With all the exacting detail work they're putting in, it *has* to be an airplane. Even if it doesn't appear so—to them, it's an airplane. Just as the little guy said, "If it's not an airplane, then what is it?"

The TV People rep hasn't so much as twitched in all this time. Right elbow still propped up on the TV set, he's watching me. I'm being watched. The TV People factory crew keeps working. Busy, busy, busy. The clock ticks on. *TRPP Q SCHAOUS TRPP Q SCHAOUS*. The room has grown dark, stifling. Someone's footsteps echo down the hall.

Well, it suddenly occurs to me, maybe so. Maybe the wife *is* out there. She's gone somewhere far away. By whatever means of transport, she's gone somewhere far out of my reach. Maybe our relationship has suffered irreversible damage. Maybe it's a total loss. Only I haven't noticed. All sorts of thoughts unravel inside me, then the frayed ends come together again. "Maybe so," I say out loud. My voice echoes, hollow.

"Tomorrow, when we paint it, you'll see better," he resumes. "All it needs is a touch of color to make it an airplane."

I look at the palms of my hands. They have shrunk slightly. Ever so slightly. Power of suggestion? Maybe the light's playing tricks on me. Maybe my sense of perspective has been thrown off. Yet, my palms really do look shriveled. Hey now, wait just a minute! Let me speak. There's something I should say. I must say. I'll dry up and turn to stone if I don't. Like the others.

"The phone will ring soon," the TV People rep says. Then, after a measured pause, he adds, "In another five minutes."

I look at the telephone; I think about the telephone cord. Endless lengths of phone cable linking one telephone to another. Maybe somewhere, at some terminal of that awesome megacircuit, is my wife. Far, far away, out of my reach. I can feel her pulse. Another five minutes, I tell myself. *Which way is front, which way is back?* I stand up and try to say something, but no sooner have I got to my feet than the words slip away.

—*translated by Alfred Birnbaum*

A
sLOW
BOAT
TO
cHINA

When did I meet my first Chinese?

Just like that, my archaeologist begins sifting through the tell of my own past. Labeling all the artifacts, categorizing, analyzing.

And so, when *was* that first encounter? As near as I can figure, it was 1959 or 1960. Whichever, whatever, what's the difference? Precisely nothing. The years '59 and '60 stand there like gawky twins in matching nerd suits. Even if I hopped a time machine back to the period, I doubt I could tell the two apart.

In spite of which, I persist with my labors. Doggedly expanding the dig, filling out the picture with every least new find. Shards of memory.

Okay, I'm sure it was the year Johnson and Patterson fought for the world heavyweight title. Which means, all I have to do is go search through the sports section in old copies of *The Year in News*. That would settle everything.

In the morning, I'm off on my bike to the local library. Next to the main entrance, for who knows what reason, there's a tiny henhouse, in which five chickens are enjoying what is either a late breakfast or an early lunch. It's a bright, clear day, so before going inside I sit down on the pavement next to the chickens and light up a cigarette. I watch the chickens pecking at their feedbox busily. Frenetically, in fact, so that they look like one of those old newsreels with too few frames per second.

After my cigarette, something's changed in me. Again, who knows why? But for what it's worth, the new me—five chickens and a smoke away from what I was—now poses myself two questions:

First, *Who could possibly have any interest in the exact date when I met my first Chinese?*

And second, *What exactly is there to be gained by spreading out those* Year In News*es on a sunny reference-room desk?*

Good questions. I smoke another cigarette, then get back onto my bike and bid farewell to fowl and file copies. If birds in flight go unburdened by names, let my memories be free of dates.

Granted, most of my memories don't bear dates anyway. My recall is a damn sight short of total. It's so unreliable that I sometimes think I'm trying to prove something by it. But what would I be proving? Especially since inexactness is not exactly the sort of thing you can prove with any accuracy.

Anyway—or rather, that being the case—my memory can be impressively iffy. I get things the wrong way around, fabrication filters into fact, sometimes my own eyewitness account interchanges with somebody else's. At which point, can you even call it memory anymore? Witness the sum of what I'm capable of dredging up from primary school (those pathetic six years of sunsets in the heyday of postwar democracy). Two events: this Chinese story, for one, and for another, a baseball game one afternoon during summer vacation. In that game, I was playing center field, and I blacked out in the bottom of the third. I mean, I didn't just collapse out of nowhere. The reason I blacked out that day was that we were allowed only one small corner of the nearby high school's athletic field, and so when I was running full speed after a pop fly I smashed head-on into the post of the backboard of the basketball court next to where we were playing.

WHEN I CAME TO, I was lying on a bench under an arbor, it was late in the day, and the first things I noticed were the wet-and-dry smell of water that had been sprinkled over the baked earth and the musk of my brand-new leather glove, which they'd put under my head for a pillow. Then there was this dull pain in my temple. I guess I must have said something. I don't really remember. Only later did a buddy of mine who'd been looking after me get around to telling. That what I apparently said was, *That's okay, brush off the dirt and you can still eat it.*

Now, where did that come from? To this day, I have no idea. I guess I was dreaming, probably about lunch. But two decades later the phrase is still there, kicking around in my head.

That's okay, brush off the dirt and you can still eat it.

With these words, I find myself thinking about my ongoing existence as a human being and the path that lies ahead of me. Though of course these thoughts lead to but one place—death. Imagining death is, at least for me, an awfully hazy proposition. And death, for some reason, reminds me of the Chinese.

2 .

THERE WAS AN ELEMENTARY school for Chinese up the hill from the harbor (forgive me, I've completely forgotten the name of the school, so I'll just call it "the Chinese elementary school"), and I had to go there to take a standard aptitude test.

Out of several test locations, the Chinese elementary school was the farthest away, and I was the only one in my class assigned there. A clerical mix-up, maybe? Everybody else was sent somewhere closer.

Chinese elementary school?

I asked everyone I knew if they knew anything about this Chinese elementary school. No one knew a thing, except that it was half an hour away by train. Now, back then I didn't do much in the way of exploring, hardly ever rode around to places by myself, so for me this might as well have been the end of the earth.

The Chinese elementary school at the edge of the world.

S U N D A Y   M O R N I N G two weeks later found me in a dark funk as I sharpened a dozen pencils, then packed my lunch and classroom slippers into my plastic schoolbag, as prescribed. It was a sunny day, maybe a little too warm for autumn, but my mother made me wear a sweater anyway. I boarded the train all by myself and stood by the door the whole way, looking out the window. I didn't want to miss the stop.

I spotted the Chinese elementary school even without looking at the map printed on the back of the registration form. All I had to do was follow a flock of kids with slippers and lunch boxes stuffed into their schoolbags. There were tens, maybe hundreds, of kids filing up the steep grade. A pretty remarkable sight. No one was kicking a ball, no one was pulling at a younger kid's cap; everyone was just walking quietly. Like a demonstration of indeterminate perpetual motion. Climbing the hill, I started sweating under my heavy sweater.

C O N T R A R Y   T O   W H A T E V E R vague expectations I may have had, the Chinese elementary school did not look much different from my own school. In fact, it was cleaner. The long, dark corridors, the musty air. . . . All the images that had filled my head for two weeks proved totally unfounded. Passing through the fancy iron gates, I followed the gentle arc of a stone path between plantings to the main entrance, where a clear pond sparkled in the 9:00 A.M. sun. Along the façade stood a row of trees, each with a plaque identifying the tree in Chinese. Some characters I could read, some I couldn't. The entrance opened onto an enclosed courtyard, in the corners of which were a bronze bust of somebody, a small white rain gage, and an exercise bar.

I removed my shoes at the entrance as instructed, then went to the classroom assigned to me. It was bright, with forty fold-top desks neatly arranged in rows, each place affixed with a registration tag. My seat was in the very front row by the window; I guess I had the lowest number.

The blackboard was a pristine deep green; the teacher's place was set with a box of chalk and a vase bearing a single white chrysanthemum. Everything was spotless, a flawless picture of order. There were no drawings or compositions tacked up willy-nilly on the bulletin board. Maybe they'd been taken down so as not to distract us during the test. I took my seat, set out my pencil case and writing pad, propped up my chin, and closed my eyes.

It was nearly fifteen minutes later when the proctor of the test came in, carrying the stack of exams under his arm. He didn't look anything over forty, but he walked with a cane and dragged his left foot in a slight limp. The cane was made of cherry wood, sort of crudely, the kind of thing they sell as souvenirs at the summit of a hiking trail. The proctor's limp was unaffected, so you noticed the cheap cane more. Forty pairs of eyes focused on this guy, or, rather, on the exams, and all was resounding silence.

The proctor mounted the stand in front of the class, placed the exams on his desk, then plunked his cane down on the side. He checked that all the seats were filled, coughed, and glanced at his watch. Then, clamping both hands on the edges of the desk as if to hold himself down, he lifted his gaze straight to a corner of the ceiling.

Silence.

Fifteen seconds and not a sound. The kids all tensed and held their breath, staring at the stack of exams; the lame-legged proctor stared at the ceiling. He was wearing a light-gray suit with a white shirt and a tie of eminently forgettable color and pattern. He took off his glasses, wiped the lenses with a handkerchief, very deliberately, and put them back on.

"I shall be acting as your test proctor," the man finally spoke. *Shall.* "As soon as you receive your exam booklet, place it facedown on your desk. Do not turn it over. Keep both hands flat on your lap. When I say 'Begin,' you may turn it faceup and begin. When there are ten minutes remaining before the end of the test period, I shall say to you, 'Ten minutes left.' At that time, check your work to see that you have not made any minor errors. When I say 'Stop,' that is the end of the test period. Turn your examination booklet facedown and place your hands on your lap. Is that understood?"

Silence.

He looked at his watch again.

"Well, as I see that we have ten minutes before the beginning of the test, I'd like to have a little talk with you. Please relax."

Phew, phew. There were several sighs.

"I am Chinese and I teach at this school."

MY FIRST CHINESE!

He didn't *look* Chinese. But what did I expect? What was a Chinese supposed to look like?

"In this classroom," he continued, "Chinese students the same age as yourselves all study as hard as you do. . . . Now, as you all know, China and Japan are neighboring countries. In order for everyone to enjoy happy lives, neighbors must make friends. Isn't that right?"

Silence.

"Of course, some things about our two countries are very similar and some things are very different. Some things we understand about each other and some things we do not. But isn't that the same with you and your friends? Even if they are your friends, some things they cannot understand. But if you make an effort, you can still become close. That is what I believe. But in order to do that, we must begin with respect for each other. . . . That is the first step."

Silence.

"For instance. Suppose many, many Chinese children went to your school to take a test. Just as you yourselves are doing now, sitting at Chinese children's desks. Think about this, please."

Hmm.

"Suppose that on Monday morning, all of you go back to your school. You go to your desks. And what do you see? You see that there are doodles and marks all over your desks, chewing gum stuck under the seat, one of your classroom slippers is missing. How would you feel?"

Silence.

"For instance, you," he said, turning to point right at me, me with the lowest registration number, "would you be happy?"

Everyone looked at me.

I blushed bright red and shook my head.

"So you see," he said, turning back to the class again, as everyone's eyes shifted back to the front of the room, "you must not mark up the desks or stick gum under the seats or go fooling around with what's inside the desks. Is that understood?"

Silence.

"Chinese children speak up louder when they answer."

Yes, came forty replies. Or, rather, thirty-nine. My mouth wouldn't open.

"Well, then, heads up, chests out."

We looked up and swelled to attention.

"And be proud."

•   •   •

SOME TWENTY YEARS ON, I've completely forgotten the results of the test. All I remember is the school kids walking quietly up the hill and the Chinese teacher. That, and how to hold my head up with pride.

3.

THE TOWN WHERE I WENT to high school was a port town, so there were quite a few Chinese around. Not that they seemed any different from the rest of us. Nor did they have any special traits. They were as different from each other as could be, and in that way they were the same as us. When I think about it, the curious thing about individuals is that their singularity always goes beyond any category or generalization in the book.

There were several Chinese kids in my class. Some got good grades, others didn't. There was the cheerful type and the dead-quiet character. One who lived in an almost palatial spread, another in a sunless one-room-kitchenette walk-up. Really, all sorts. Though I never did get especially close to any of them. I wasn't your let's-make-friends sort of guy. Japanese or Chinese or anything else, made no difference.

I did, however, meet up with one of them ten years later, though I probably shouldn't get into that just yet.

Meanwhile, the scene shifts to Tokyo.

MY NEXT CHINESE—that is, not counting those high-school Chinese classmates whom I didn't especially speak to—was a shy girl I got to know at a part-time job during the spring of my sophomore year. She was nineteen, like me, and petite, and pretty. We worked together for three weeks during the break.

She was exceedingly diligent about work. I did my part, working as hard as I could, I suppose, but whenever I peeked over at her plugging away it was pretty obvious that her idea and my idea of applying oneself weren't the same animal. I mean, compared to my "If you're going to do something, it's worth doing it well," her inner drive cut closer to the root of humanity. Not that it's much of an explanation, but this drive of hers had the disturbing urgency of someone whose whole worldly existence was barely held together by that one thread. Most people couldn't possibly keep up with the pace she maintained; sooner or later they would throw up their hands in frustration. The only one who managed to stick it out to the very end working with her was me.

Even so, we hardly spoke a word at first. I tried a couple of times to strike up a conversation, but she didn't seem particularly interested in speaking, so I backed off. The first time we actually sat down and talked was two weeks after we started working together. That morning, for half an hour, she'd been thrown into something of a panic. It was unprecedented for her. The cause of it all was a slight oversight, one small operation out of order. Sure, it was her fault, her responsibility, if it came to that, but from where I stood it seemed like a common enough mishap. A momentary lapse and—*glitch!* Could have happened to anyone. But not to her. A tiny crack in her head widened into a fissure, eventually becoming a gaping chasm. She wouldn't, she couldn't, take another step. At a total loss for words, she froze in place. She was a sorry sight, a ship sinking slowly in the night sea.

I cut short what I was doing, sat her down in a chair, pried loose her clenched fingers one by one, made her drink some hot coffee. Then I told her, It's all right, there's nothing to worry about, nothing's too late to remedy, you just redo that part again from the beginning and you won't be so far behind in your work. And even if you are a little behind, it won't kill you. Her eyes were glazed, but she nodded silently. With some coffee in her, she began to calm down.

"I'm sorry," she whispered.

That lunch break, we talked about this and that. And that was when she told me she was Chinese.

WHERE WE WORKED was a tiny, dark, small-time publisher's warehouse in Bunkyo Ward, downtown Tokyo. A dirty little open sewer of a stream ran right beside it. The work was easy, boring, busy. I got order slips, which told us how many copies of what books to haul out to the entrance. She would bind these up with cord and check them off against the inventory record. That was the whole job. There was no heating in the place, so we had to hustle our buns off to keep from freezing to death. Sometimes it was so cold I thought we wouldn't be any better off shoveling snow at the airport in Anchorage.

At lunchtime, we'd head out for something hot to eat, warming ourselves for the hour until our break was up. More than anything, the main objective was to thaw out. But from the time she had her panic, little by little we found ourselves on speaking terms. Her words came in bits and pieces, but after a while I got the picture. Her father ran a small import business in Yokohama, most of the merchandise he handled being bargain clothing from Hong Kong. Although Chinese, she herself was Japanese-born and had never once been to China or Hong Kong or Taiwan. Plus, she'd gone to Japanese schools, not Chinese. Hardly spoke a word of Chinese, but was strong in English. She was attending a private women's university in the city and hoped to become an interpreter. Meanwhile, she was sharing her brother's apartment in Komagome, or, to borrow her turn of phrase, she'd fallen in with him. Seemed she didn't get along well with her father. And that's the sum total of what I found out about her.

Those two weeks in March passed along with the sleet of the season. On the evening of our last day of work, after picking up my pay from accounting and after some hesitation, I decided to ask my Chinese co-worker out to a discotheque in Shinjuku. Not that I had any intention of making a pass at her. I already had a steady girlfriend since high school, though if the truth be told we were beginning to go our separate ways.

The Chinese girl thought it over a few seconds, then said, "But I've never been dancing."

"There's nothing to it," I said. "It's not ballroom dancing. All you have to do is move to the beat. Anyone can do it."

FIRST, WE WENT and had some beer and pizza. No more work. No more freezing warehouse. What a liberating feeling! I was more jovial than may have been usual; she laughed more, too. Then we went to the disco and danced for two whole hours. The place was nice and warm, swimming with mirror balls and incense. A Filipino band was pounding out Santana covers. We'd work up a sweat dancing, then go sit out a number over a beer, then, when the sweat subsided, we'd get up and dance again. In the colored strobe lights, she looked like a different person from the shy warehouse stock girl I knew. And once she got the hang of dancing, she actually seemed to enjoy it.

When we'd finally danced ourselves out, we left the club. The March night was brisk, but there was a hint of spring in the air. We were overheated from all that exercise, so we just walked, aimlessly, hands in our pockets. We stopped into an arcade, got a cup of coffee, kept walking. We still had half the school break ahead of us. We were nineteen. If someone had told us to, we would have walked clear out to the Tama River.

At ten-twenty, she said she had to go. "I have to be home by eleven." She was almost apologetic.

"That's pretty strict," I said.

"My brother thinks he's my guardian protector. But I guess I can't complain, since he's giving me a roof over my head." From the way she spoke, I could tell she really liked her brother.

"Just don't forget your slipper," I said with a wink.

"My slipper?" Five, six steps later, she burst out laughing. "Oh, you mean like Cinderella? Don't worry, I won't forget."

We climbed the steps in Shinjuku Station and sat down on a platform bench.

"You know," I said, "do you think I could have your phone number? Maybe we can go out and have some fun again sometime."

She bit her lip, nodded, then gave me her number. I scribbled it down on a matchbook from the disco. The train came in and I put her on board and said good night. Thanks, it was fun, see you. The doors closed, the train pulled out, and I crossed over to the next track to wait for my train bound for Ikebukuro. Leaning back on a column, I lit up a cigarette and thought about the evening. From the restaurant to the disco to the walk. Not bad. It'd been ages since I'd been out on a date. I'd had a good time and I knew she had a good time, too. We could be friends. Maybe she was a little shy, maybe she had her nervous side. Still, I liked her.

I put my cigarette out under my heel and lit another one. The sounds of the city blurred lazily into the dark. I shut my eyes and took a deep breath. Nothing was amiss, but I couldn't shake this nagging feeling. Something wasn't right. What was it? What had I done?

Then it hit me, right when I got off the train at Mejiro. *I'd put her on the Yamanote Loop Line going the wrong way.*

My dormitory was in Mejiro, four stops before hers. So she could have taken the same train as me. It would have been all so simple. Why had I taken it upon myself to see that she got on a train going the opposite way around? Did I have that much to drink? Was I thinking too much, or only, about myself? The station clock read 10:45. She'd never make her curfew. I hoped she'd realized my mistake and switched to a train going the right way. But I doubted she would have. She wasn't that type. No, she was the type to keep riding the train the wrong way around. But shouldn't she have known about this mistake from the start? She had to know she was being put on the wrong train. Great, I thought. Just great.

· · ·

IT WAS TEN AFTER ELEVEN when she finally got off at Komagome Station. When she saw me standing by the stairs, she stopped in her tracks with this expression, like she didn't know whether to laugh or fume. It was all I could do to take her by the arm and sit her down on a bench. She put her bag in her lap and clutched the strap with both hands. She placed her feet straight out in front of her and stared at the toes of her white pumps.

I apologized to her. I told her I didn't know why I'd made that stupid mistake. My mind must have been elsewhere.

"You *honestly* made a mistake?" she asked.

"Of course. If not, why would I have done such a thing?"

"I thought you did it on purpose."

"On purpose?"

"Because I thought you were angry."

"Angry?" What was she talking about?

"Yeah."

"What makes you think I'd be angry?"

"I don't know," she said in a shrinking voice.

Two tears spilled from her eyes and fell audibly onto her bag.

What was I to do? I just sat there, not saying a word. Trains pulled in, discharged passengers, and pulled out. People disappeared down the stairs, and it was quiet again.

"Please. Just leave me alone." She smiled, parting her bangs to the side. "At first, I thought it was a mistake, too. So I thought, Why not just go on riding the opposite way? But by the time I passed Tokyo Station, I thought otherwise. Everything was wrong. I don't ever want to be in a position like that again."

I wanted to say something, but the words wouldn't come. Wind blew stray pieces of newspaper to the far end of the platform.

"It's okay." She smiled weakly. "This was never any place I was meant to be. This isn't a place for me."

This place Japan? This lump of stone spinning around in the blackness of space? Silently I took her hand and placed it on my lap, resting my hand lightly on hers. Her palm was wet.

I forced words out: "There are some things about myself I can't explain to anyone. There are some things I don't understand at all. I can't tell what I think about things or what I'm after. I don't know what my strengths are or what I'm supposed to do about them. But if I start thinking about these things in too much detail, the whole thing gets scary. And if I get scared, I can only think about myself. I become really self-centered, and without meaning to, I hurt people. So I'm not such a wonderful human being."

I didn't know what else to say. And she said nothing. She seemed to wait for me to continue. She kept staring at the toe of her shoes. Far away, there was an ambulance siren. A station attendant was sweeping the platform. He didn't even look at us. It was getting late, so the trains were few.

"I enjoyed myself with you," I said. "It's true, really. I don't know how to put this, but you strike me as a *real* person. I don't know why. Just being with you and talking, you know."

She looked up and stared at me.

"I didn't put you on the wrong train on purpose," I said. "I just wasn't thinking."

She nodded.

"I'll call you tomorrow," I said. "We can go somewhere and talk."

She wiped away the traces of her tears and slipped her hands in her pockets. "Thank you. I'm sorry for everything."

"You shouldn't apologize. It was my mistake."

We parted. I stayed on the bench and smoked my last cigarette, then threw the empty pack in the trash. It was close to midnight.

Nine hours later, I realized my second error of the evening. A fatal miss. I'm so stupid. Together with the cigarette pack, I'd thrown away the disco matches with her phone number on them. I checked everywhere. I went to the warehouse, but they didn't have her number. I tried the telephone directory. I even tried the student union at her school. No luck.

I never saw her again, my second Chinese.

4 .

NOW THE STORY of my third Chinese.

An acquaintance from high school, whom I mentioned earlier. A friend of a friend, whom I'd spoken to maybe a few times.

This happened when I'd just turned twenty-eight. Six years after I got married. Six years during which time I'd laid three cats to rest. Burned how many aspirations, bundled up how much suffering in thick sweaters, and buried them in the ground. All in this fathomlessly huge city Tokyo.

It was a chilly December afternoon. There was no wind; the air was so cold that what little light filtered through the clouds did nothing to clear away the gray of the city. I was heading home from the bank and stepped into a glass-fronted café on Aoyama Boulevard for a cup of coffee. I was flipping through the novel I'd just bought, looking up now and then, watching the passing cars.

Then I noticed the guy standing in front of me. He was addressing me by name.

"That is you, isn't it?" he was saying.

I was taken aback. I answered in the affirmative, but I couldn't place the guy. He seemed to be about my age, and wore a well-tailored navy blazer and a suitably colored rep tie. Something about the guy made him seem a little worn down. His clothes weren't old, and he didn't look exhausted. Nothing like that. It had more to do with his face. Which, although presentable, gave me the feeling that his every expression had been thrown together on the spur of the moment. Like mismatched dishes set out in make-do fashion on a party table.

"Mind if I sit down?" he said, taking the seat opposite me. He fished a pack of cigarettes and a gold lighter from his pocket. He didn't light up, though; he merely put them on the table. "Well, remember me?"

"Afraid not," I confessed. "I'm sorry, I'm terrible about these things. I'm terrible with people's faces."

"Or maybe you'd just rather forget the past. Subliminally, that is."

"Maybe so," I said. What if I did?

The waitress brought over a glass of water for him, and he ordered an American coffee. Water it down, please, he told her.

"I got a bad stomach. I really ought to quit smoking, too," he said, fiddling with his cigarettes. He had that look that people with stomach troubles get when they talk about their stomach. "Anyway, like I was saying myself, for the same reason as you, I remember absolutely every last detail about the old days. It's weird, I tell you. Because believe me, some things I'd like to forget. But the more I try to wipe them away, the more they pop into my mind. You know what it's like when you're trying to fall asleep and it only makes you more wide awake? It's the same thing. I can't figure it out. I remember things I couldn't possibly have known. Sometimes it worries me, remembering the past in so much detail—how am I supposed to have room for what's to come? My memory's so sharp, it's a nuisance."

I set my book facedown on the table and sipped my coffee.

"Everything is vivid. The weather that day, the temperature, the smells. Just like now. It gets confusing, like where am I? Makes me wonder if things are only memories. Ever get that feeling?"

I shook my head absently.

"I remember you very well. I was walking by and saw you through the glass and I knew you right away. Did I bother you coming in here like this?"

"No," I said. "Still, you have to forgive me. I really don't remember you."

"Nothing to forgive. I'm the one who barged in on you. If the time comes to remember, you'll remember. That's how it goes. Memory works in different ways for everybody. Different capacities, different directions, too. Sometimes memory helps you think, sometimes it impedes. Doesn't mean it's good or bad. Probably means it's no big deal."

"Do you suppose you could tell me your name? It's simply not coming to me, and if I don't remember it's going to drive me crazy," I said.

"What's a name, really?" he answered. "So if it comes, okay; if it doesn't, that's okay, too. Either way, no big deal, like I said. But if not remembering my name bugs you that much, pretend we've just met for the first time. No mental block that way."

His coffee arrived and he drank it slowly. I couldn't get a handle at all on anything he was saying.

"*A lot of water has gone under the bridge.* That phrase was in our high-school English textbook. Remember?"

High school? Did I know this guy in high school?

"I'm sure that's how it went. The other day, I was standing on a bridge looking down, and suddenly that English phrase popped into my head. Clear as a bell. Like, sure, here's how time passes."

He folded his arms and sat back deep in his chair, looking inscrutable. If that expression was meant to convey a particular meaning, it was lost on me. The guy's expression-forming genes must have worn through in places.

"Are you married?" he asked, out of nowhere.

I nodded.

"Kids?"

"No."

"I've got a son," he said. "He's four now and goes to nursery school."

End of conversation about children. We sat there, silent. I put a cigarette to my lips and he offered his lighter. A natural gesture. I generally don't like other people lighting my cigarettes or pouring my drinks, but this time I hardly paid any mind. In fact, it was a while before I even realized he'd lit my cigarette.

"What line of work you in?"

"Business," I said.

His mouth fell open and the word formed a second or two later. "Business?"

"Yeah. Nothing much to speak of." I let it slide.

He nodded and left it at that. It wasn't that I didn't want to talk about work. I just didn't feel like starting in on what promised to be another escapade. I was tired, and I didn't even know the guy's name.

"That surprises me. You in business. I wouldn't have figured you for a businessman."

I smiled.

"Used to be that all you did was read books," he went on, with a bit of mystery.

"Well, I still read a lot." I forced a laugh.

"Encyclopedias?"

"Encyclopedias?"

"Sure, you got an encyclopedia?"

"No." I shook my head, not comprehending.

"You don't read encyclopedias?"

"Maybe if there's one around," I said. Of course, in the place I was living there wouldn't be any room to have one around.

"Actually, I sell encyclopedias," he said.

Oh, boy, an encyclopedia salesman. Half my curiosity about the guy immediately drained away. I took a sip of my now-lukewarm coffee and quietly set the cup back on its saucer.

"You know, I wouldn't mind having a set," I said, "but unfortunately, I don't have the money. No money at all. I'm only just now beginning to pay off my loans."

"Whoa there!" he said, shaking his head. "I'm not trying to sell you any encyclopedia or anything. Me, I may be broke, but I'm not that hard up. And anyway, the truth is, I don't have to try to sell to Japanese. It's part of the deal I have."

"Don't have to sell to Japanese?"

"Right, I specialize in Chinese. I only sell encyclopedias to Chinese. I go through the Tokyo directory picking out Chinese names. I make a list, then go through the list one by one. I don't know who dreamed this scam up, but why not? Seems to work, saleswise. I ring the doorbell, I say, *Ni hao,* I hand them my card. After that, I'm in."

Suddenly there was a click in my head. This guy was that Chinese boy I'd known in high school.

"Strange, huh, how someone ends up walking around selling encyclopedias to Chinese? I don't understand it," the guy said, seeming to distance himself from the whole thing. "Sure, I can remember each of the little circumstances leading up to it, but the big picture, you know, how it all comes together moving in this one direction, escapes me. I just looked up one day and here I was."

This guy and I had never been in the same class, nor, as I said, had we been on such close personal terms. But as near as I could place him, he hadn't been your encyclopedia-salesman type, either. He seemed well bred, got better grades than I did. Girls liked him.

"Things happen, eh? It's a long, dark, dumb story. Nothing you'd want to hear," he said.

The line didn't seem to demand a response, so I let it drop.

"It's not all my doing," he picked up. "All sorts of things just piled on. But in the end, it's nobody's fault but mine."

I was thinking back to high school with this guy, but all I came up with was vague scenes. I seemed to recall sitting around a table at someone's house, drinking beer and talking about music. Probably on a summer afternoon, but more like in a dream.

"Wonder what made me want to say hello?" he asked, half to me, twirling the lighter around on the table. "Guess I kind of bothered you. Sorry about that."

"No bother at all," I said. Honestly, it wasn't.

We both fell silent for a minute. Neither of us had anything to say. I finished my cigarette, he finished his coffee.

"Well, guess I'll be going," he said, pocketing his cigarettes and lighter. Then he slid back his chair a bit. "Can't be spending the whole day talking. Not when there's things to sell, eh?"

"You have a pamphlet?" I asked.

"A pamphlet?"

"About the encyclopedia."

"Oh, right," he mumbled. "Not on me. You want to see one?"

"Sure, just out of curiosity."

"I'll send you one. Give me your address."

I tore out a page of my Filofax, wrote down my address, and handed it to him. He looked it over, folded it in quarters, and slipped it into his business-card case.

"It's a good encyclopedia, you know. I'm not just saying that because I sell them. Really, it's well done. Lots of color photos. Very handy. Sometimes I'll thumb through the thing myself, and I never get bored."

"Someday, when my ship comes in, maybe I'll buy one."

"That'd be nice," he said, an election-poster smile returning to his face. "But by then, I'll probably have done my time with encyclopedias. I mean, there's only so many Chinese families to visit. Maybe I'll have moved on to insurance for Chinese. Or funeral plots. What's it really matter?"

I wanted to say something. I would never see this guy again in my life. I wanted to say something to him about the Chinese, but what? Nothing came. So we parted with your usual good-byes.

Even now, I still can't think of anything to say.

5

SUPPOSING I FOUND myself chasing another fly ball and ran head-on into a basketball backboard, supposing I woke up once again lying under an arbor with a baseball glove under my head, what words of wisdom could this man of thirty-odd years bring himself to utter? Maybe something like: *This is no place for me.*

This occurs to me while I'm riding the Yamanote Line. I'm standing by the door, holding on to my ticket so I won't lose it, gazing out the window at the buildings we pass. Our city, these streets, I don't know why it makes me so depressed. That old familiar gloom that befalls the city dweller, regular as due dates, cloudy as mental Jell-O. The dirty façades, the nameless crowds, the unremitting noise, the packed rush-hour trains, the gray skies, the billboards on every square centimeter of available space, the hopes and resignation, irritation and excitement. And everywhere, infinite options, infinite possibilities. An infinity, and at the same time, zero. We try to scoop it all up in our hands, and what we get is a handful of zero. That's the city. That's when I remember what that Chinese girl said.

This was never any place I was meant to be.

I LOOK AT TOKYO and I think China.

That's how I've met my share of Chinese. I've read dozens of books on China, everything from the *Annals* to *Red Star over China*. I've wanted to find out as much about China as I could. But that China is only my China. Not any China I can read about. It's the China that sends messages just to me. It's not the big yellow expanse on the globe, it's another China. Another hypothesis, another supposition. In a sense, it's a part of myself that's been cut off by the word *China.*

I wander through China. Without ever having boarded a plane. My travels take place here in the Tokyo subways, in the backseat of a taxi. My adventures take me to the waiting room of the nearby dentist, to the bank teller's window. I can go everywhere and I don't go anywhere.

Tokyo—one day, as I ride the Yamanote Loop, all of a sudden this city will start to go. In a flash, the buildings will crumble. And I'll be holding my ticket, watching it all. Over the Tokyo streets will fall my China, like ash, leaching into everything it touches. Slowly, gradually, until nothing remains. No, this isn't a place for me. That is how we will lose our speech, how our dreams will turn to mist. The way our adolescence, so tedious we worried it would last forever, evaporated.

Misdiagnosis, as a psychiatrist might say, as it was with that Chinese girl. Maybe, in the end, our hopes were the wrong way around. But what am I, what are you, if not a misdiagnosis? And if so, is there a way out?

Even so, I have packed into a trunk my faithful little outfielder's pride. I sit on the stone steps by the harbor, and I wait for that slow boat to China. It is due to appear on the blank horizon. I am thinking about China, the shining roofs, the verdant fields.

Let loss and destruction come my way. They are nothing to me. I am not afraid. Any more than the clean-up batter fears the inside fastball, any more than the committed revolutionary fears the garrote. If only, if only . . .

Oh, friends, my friends, China is so far away.

—translated by Alfred Birnbaum

THE

DANCING

DWARF

A DWARF CAME INTO my dream and asked me to dance.

I knew this was a dream, but I was just as tired in my dream as in real life at the time. So, very politely, I declined. The dwarf was not offended but danced alone instead.

He set a portable record player on the ground and danced to the music. Records were spread all around the player. I picked up a few from different spots in the pile. They comprised a genuine musical miscellany, as if the dwarf had chosen them with his eyes closed, grabbing whatever his hand happened to touch. And none of the records was in the right jacket. The dwarf would take half-played records off the turntable, throw them onto the pile without returning them to their jackets, lose track of which went with which, and afterward put records in jackets at random. There would be a Rolling Stones record in a Glenn Miller jacket, a recording of the Mitch Miller chorus in the jacket for Ravel's *Daphnis and Chloé*.

But none of this confusion seemed to matter to the dwarf.

As long as he could dance to whatever was playing, he was satisfied. At the moment, he was dancing to a Charlie Parker record that had been in a jacket labeled *Great Selections for the Classical Guitar*. His body whirled like a tornado, sucking up the wild flurry of notes that poured from Charlie Parker's saxophone. Eating grapes, I watched him dance.

The sweat poured out of him. Each swing of his head sent drops of sweat flying from his face; each wave of an arm shot streams of sweat from his fingertips. But nothing could stop him. When a record ended, I would set my bowl of grapes down and put on a new one. And on he would go.

"You're a great dancer," I cried out to him. "You're music itself."

"Thank you," he answered with a hint of affectation.

"Do you always go at it like this?"

"Pretty much," he said.

Then the dwarf did a beautiful twirl on tiptoe, his soft, wavy hair flowing in the wind. I applauded. I had never seen such accomplished dancing in my life. The dwarf gave a respectful bow as the song ended. He stopped dancing and toweled himself down. The needle was clicking in the inner groove of the record. I lifted the tonearm and turned the player off. I put the record into the first empty jacket that came to hand.

"I guess you haven't got time to hear my story," said the dwarf, glancing at me. "It's a long one."

Unsure how to answer, I took another grape. Time was no problem for me, but I wasn't that eager to hear the long life story of a dwarf. And besides, this was a dream. It could evaporate at any moment.

Rather than wait for me to answer, the dwarf snapped his fingers and started to speak. "I'm from the north country," he said. "Up north, they don't dance. Nobody knows how. They don't even realize that it's something you can do. But I wanted to dance. I wanted to stamp my feet and wave my arms, shake my head and spin around. Like this."

The dwarf stamped his feet, waved his arms, shook his head,

and spun around. Each movement was simple enough in itself, but in combination the four produced an almost incredible beauty of motion, erupting from the dwarf's body all at once, as when a globe of light bursts open.

"I wanted to dance like this. And so I came south. I danced in the taverns. I became famous, and danced in the presence of the king. That was before the revolution, of course. Once the revolution broke out, the king passed away, as you know, and I was banished from the town to live in the forest."

The dwarf went to the middle of the clearing and began to dance again. I put a record on. It was an old Frank Sinatra record. The dwarf danced, singing "Night and Day" along with Sinatra. I pictured him dancing before the throne. Glittering chandeliers and beautiful ladies-in-waiting, exotic fruits and the long spears of the royal guard, portly eunuchs, the young king in jewel-bedecked robes, the dwarf drenched in sweat but dancing with unbroken concentration: As I imagined the gorgeous scene, I felt that at any moment the roar of the revolution's cannon would echo from the distance.

The dwarf went on dancing, and I ate my grapes. The sun set, covering the earth in the shadows of the forest. A huge black butterfly the size of a bird cut across the clearing and vanished into the depths of the forest. I felt the chill of the evening air. It was time for my dream to melt away, I knew.

"I guess I have to go now," I said to the dwarf.

He stopped dancing and nodded in silence.

"I enjoyed watching you dance," I said. "Thanks a lot."

"Anytime," said the dwarf.

"We may never meet again," I said. "Take care of yourself."

"Don't worry," said the dwarf. "We will meet again."

"Are you sure?"

"Oh, yes. You'll be coming back here," he said with a snap of his fingers. "You'll live in the forest. And every day you'll dance with me. You'll become a really good dancer yourself before long."

"How do you know?" I asked, taken aback.

"It's been decided," he answered. "No one has the power to change what has been decided. I know that you and I will meet again soon enough."

The dwarf looked right up at me as he spoke. The deepening darkness had turned him the deep blue of water at night.

"Well, then," he said. "Be seeing you."

He turned his back to me and began dancing again, alone.

I WOKE UP ALONE. Facedown in bed, I was drenched in sweat. There was a bird outside my window. It seemed different from the bird I was used to seeing there.

I washed my face with great care, shaved, put some bread in the toaster, and boiled water for coffee. I fed the cat, changed its litter, put on a necktie, and tied my shoes. Then I took a bus to the elephant factory.

Needless to say, the manufacture of elephants is no easy matter. They're big, first of all, and very complex. It's not like making hairpins or colored pencils. The factory covers a huge area, and it consists of several buildings. Each building is big, too, and the sections are color-coded. Assigned to the ear section that month, I worked in the building with the yellow ceiling and posts. My helmet and pants were also yellow. All I did there was make ears. The month before, I had been assigned to the green building, where I wore a green helmet and pants and made heads. We moved from section to section each month, like Gypsies. It was company policy. That way, we could all form a complete picture of what an elephant looked like. No one was permitted to spend his whole life making just ears, say, or just toenails. The executives put together the chart that controlled our movements, and we followed the chart.

Making elephant heads is tremendously rewarding work. It requires enormous attention to detail, and at the end of the day you're so tired you don't want to talk to anybody. I've lost as much as six pounds working there for a month, but it does give me a great sense of accomplishment. By comparison, making ears is a breeze. You just make these big, flat, thin things, put a few wrinkles in them, and you're done. We call working in the ear section "taking an ear break." After a monthlong ear break, I go to the trunk section, where the work is again very demanding. A trunk has to be flexible, and its nostrils must be unobstructed for its entire length. Otherwise, the finished elephant will go on a rampage. Which is why making the trunk is nerveracking work from beginning to end.

We don't make elephants from nothing, of course. Properly speaking, we reconstitute them. First we saw a single elephant into six distinct parts: ears, trunk, head, abdomen, legs, and tail. These we then recombine to make five elephants, which means that each new elephant is in fact only one-fifth genuine and fourfifths imitation. This is not obvious to the naked eye, nor is the elephant itself aware of it. We're that good.

Why must we artificially manufacture—or, should I say, reconstitute—elephants? It is because we are far less patient than they are. Left to their own devices, elephants would give birth to no more than one baby in four or five years. And because we love elephants, of course, it makes us terribly impatient to see this custom—or habitual behavior—of theirs. This is what led us to begin reconstituting them ourselves.

To protect the newly reconstituted elephants against improper use, they are initially purchased by the Elephant Supply Corporation, a publicly owned monopoly, which keeps them for two weeks and subjects them to a battery of highly exacting tests, after which the sole of one foot is stamped with the corporation's logo before the elephant is released into the jungle. We make fifteen elephants in a normal week. Though in the pre-Christmas season we can increase that to as many as twenty-five by running the machinery at full speed, I think that fifteen is just about right.

As I mentioned earlier, the ear section is the easiest single phase in the elephant-manufacturing process. It demands little physical exertion on the part of workers, it requires no close concentration, and it employs no complex machinery. The number of actual operations involved is limited, as well. Workers can either work at a relaxed pace all day or exert themselves to meet their quota in the morning so as to have the afternoon free.

My partner and I in the ear shop liked the second approach. We'd finish up in the morning and spend the afternoon talking or reading or amusing ourselves separately. The afternoon following my dream of the dancing dwarf, all we had to do was hang ten freshly wrinkled ears on the wall, after which we sat on the floor enjoying the sunshine.

I told my partner about the dwarf. I remembered the dream in vivid detail and described everything about it to him, no matter how trivial. Where description was difficult, I demonstrated by shaking my head or swinging my arms or stamping my feet. He listened with frequent grunts of interest, sipping his tea. He was five years my senior, a strongly built fellow with a dark beard and a penchant for silence. He had this habit of thinking with his arms folded. Judging by the expression on his face, you would guess that he was a serious thinker, looking at things from all angles, but usually he'd just come up straight after a while and say, "That's a tough one." Nothing more.

He sat there thinking for a long time after I told him about my dream—so long that I started polishing the control panel of the electric bellows to kill time. Finally, he came up straight, as always, and said, "That's a tough one. Hmmm. A dancing dwarf. That's a tough one."

This came as no great disappointment to me. I hadn't been expecting him to say any more than he usually did. I had just wanted to tell someone about it. I put the electric bellows back and drank my now-lukewarm tea.

He went on thinking, though, for a much longer time than he normally devoted to such matters.

"What gives?" I asked.

"I'm pretty sure I once heard about that dwarf."

This caught me off guard.

"I just can't remember who told me."

"Please try," I urged him.

"Sure," he said, and gave it another go.

He finally managed to recall what he knew about the dwarf three hours later, as the sun was going down near quitting time.

"That's it!" he exclaimed. "The old guy in Stage Six! You know, the one who plants hairs. C'mon, you know: long white hair down to his shoulders, hardly any teeth. Been working here since before the revolution."

"Oh," I said. "Him." I had seen him in the tavern any number of times.

"Yeah. He told me about the dwarf way back when. Said it was a good dancer. I didn't pay much attention to him, figured he was senile. But now I don't know. Maybe he wasn't crazy after all."

"So, what did he tell you?"

"Gee, I'm not so sure. It was a long time ago." He folded his arms and fell to thinking again. But it was hopeless. After a while, he straightened up and said, "Can't remember. Go ask him yourself."

As soon as the bell rang at quitting time, I went to the Stage 6 area, but there was no sign of the old man. I found only two young girls sweeping the floor. The thin girl told me he had probably gone to the tavern, "the older one." Which is exactly where I found him, sitting very erect at the bar, drinking, with his lunch box beside him.

The tavern was an old, old place. It had been there since long before I was born, before the revolution. For generations now, the elephant craftsmen had been coming here to drink, play cards, and sing. The walls were lined with photographs of the old days at the elephant factory. There was a picture of the first president of the company inspecting a tusk, a photo of an old-time movie queen visiting the factory, shots taken at summer dances, that kind of thing. The revolutionary guards had burned all pictures of the king and the royal family and anything else that was deemed to be royalist. There were pictures of the revolution, of course: the revolutionary guards occupying the

factory and the revolutionary guards stringing up the plant superintendent.

I found the old fellow drinking Mecatol beneath an old, discolored photo labeled THREE FACTORY BOYS POLISHING TUSKS.
When I took the stool next to him, the old man pointed to the
photo and said, "This one is me."

I squinted hard at the photo. The young boy on the right,
maybe twelve or thirteen years old, did appear to be this old
man in his youth. You would never notice the resemblance on
your own, but once it had been pointed out to you, you could
see that both had the same sharp nose and flat lips. Apparently,
the old guy always sat here, and whenever he noticed an unfa-
miliar customer come in he'd say, "This one is me."

"Looks like a real old picture," I said, hoping to draw him
out.

"'Fore the revolution," he said matter-of-factly. "Even an
old guy like me was still a kid back then. We all get old, though.
You'll look like me before too long. Just you wait, sonny boy!"

He let out a great cackle, spraying spit from a wide-open
mouth missing half its teeth.

Then he launched into stories about the revolution. Obviously, he hated both the king and the revolutionary guards. I
let him talk all he wanted, bought him another glass of Mecatol,
and when the time was right asked him if, by any chance, he
happened to know about a dancing dwarf.

"Dancing dwarf?" he said. "You wanna hear about the dancing dwarf?"

"I'd like to."

His eyes glared into mine. "What the hell for?" he asked.

"I don't know," I lied. "Somebody told me about him.
Sounded interesting."

He continued to look hard at me until his eyes reverted to
the special mushy look that drunks have. "Awright," he said.
"Why not? Ya bought me a drink. But just one thing," he said,
holding a finger in my face, "don't tell anybody. The revolution
was a hell of a long time ago, but you're still not supposed to

talk about the dancing dwarf. So, whatever I tell you, keep it to yourself. And don't mention my name. Okay?"

"Okay."

"Now, order me another drink and let's go to a booth."

I ordered two Mecatols and brought them to the booth, away from the bartender. The table had a green lamp in the shape of an elephant.

"It was before the revolution," said the old man. "The dwarf came from the north country. What a great dancer he was! Nah, he wasn't just great *at* dancing. He *was* dancing. Nob'dy could touch 'im. Wind and light and fragrance and shadow: It was all there bursting inside him. That dwarf could do that, y'know. It was somethin' to see."

He clicked his glass against his few remaining teeth.

"Did you actually see him dance?" I asked.

"Did I see him?" The old fellow stared at me, spreading the fingers of both hands out atop the table. "Of *course* I saw him. Every day. Right here."

"Here?"

"You heard me. Right here. He used to dance here every day. Before the revolution."

THE OLD MAN WENT ON to tell me how the dwarf had arrived from the north country without a penny in his pocket. He holed up in this tavern, where the elephant-factory workers gathered, doing odd jobs until the manager realized what a good dancer he was and hired him to dance full-time. At first, the workers grumbled because they wanted to have a dancing girl, but that didn't last long. With their drinks in their hands, they were practically hypnotized watching him dance. And he danced like nobody else. He could draw feelings out of his audience, feelings they hardly ever used or didn't even know they had. He'd bare these feelings to the light of day the way you'd pull out a fish's guts.

The dwarf danced at this tavern for close to half a year. The place overflowed with customers who wanted to see him dance.

And as they watched him, they would steep themselves in boundless happiness or be overcome with boundless grief. Soon, the dwarf had the power to manipulate people's emotions with a mere choice of dance step.

Talk of the dancing dwarf eventually reached the ears of the chief of the council of nobles, a man who had deep ties with the elephant factory and whose fief lay nearby. From this nobleman—who, as it turned out, would be captured by the revolutionary guard and flung, still living, into a boiling pot of glue—word of the dwarf reached the young king. A lover of music, the king was determined to see the dwarf dance. He dispatched the vertical-induction ship with the royal crest to the tavern, and the royal guards carried the dwarf to the palace with the utmost respect. The owner of the tavern was compensated for his loss, almost too generously. The customers grumbled over *their* loss, but they knew better than to grumble to the king. Resigned, they drank their beer and Mecatol and went back to watching the dances of young girls.

Meanwhile, the dwarf was given a room in the palace, where the ladies-in-waiting washed him and dressed him in silk and taught him the proper etiquette for appearing before the king. The next night, he was taken to the great hall, where the king's orchestra, upon cue, performed a polka that the king had composed. The dwarf danced to the polka, sedately at first, as if allowing his body to absorb the music, then gradually increasing the speed of his dance until he was whirling with the force of a tornado. People watched him, breathless. No one could speak. Several of the noble ladies fainted to the floor, and from the king's own hand fell a crystal goblet containing gold-dust wine, but not a single person noticed the sound of it shattering.

AT THIS POINT in his story, the old man set his glass on the table and wiped his mouth with the back of his hand, then reached out for the elephant-shaped lamp and began to fiddle with it. I waited for him to continue, but he remained silent for several minutes. I called to the bartender and ordered more beer and Mecatol. The tavern was slowly filling up, and onstage a young woman singer was tuning her guitar.

"Then what happened?" I asked.

"Then?" he said. "Then the revolution started. The king was killed, and the dwarf ran away."

I set my elbows on the table and, cradling my mug, took a long swallow of beer. I looked at the old man and asked, "You mean the revolution occurred just after the dwarf entered the palace?"

"Not long after. 'Bout a year, I'd say." The old man let out a huge burp.

"I don't get it," I said. "Before, you said that you weren't supposed to talk about the dwarf. Why is that? Is there some connection between the dwarf and the revolution?"

"Ya got me there. One thing's sure, though. The revolutionary guard wanted to bring that dwarf in somethin' terrible. Still do. The revolution's an old story already, but they're still lookin' for the dancing dwarf. Even so, I don't know what the connection is between the dwarf and the revolution. All you hear is rumors."

"What kind of rumors?"

I could see that he was having trouble deciding whether to tell me any more. "Rumors are just rumors," he said finally. "You never know what's true. But some folks say the dwarf used a kind of evil power on the palace, and that's what caused the revolution. Anyhow, that's all I know about the dwarf. Nothin' else."

The old man let out one long hiss of a sigh, and then he drained his glass in a single gulp. The pink liquid oozed out at the corners of his mouth, dripping down into the sagging collar of his undershirt.

I DIDN'T DREAM about the dwarf again. I went to the elephant factory every day as usual and continued making ears, first softening an ear with steam, then flattening it with a press hammer, cutting out five ear shapes, adding the ingredients to make five full-size ears, drying them, and finally, adding wrinkles. At noon, my partner and I would break to eat our pack lunches and talk about the new girl in Stage 8.

There were lots of girls working at the elephant factory, most of them assigned to splicing nervous systems or machine stitching or cleanup. We'd talk about them whenever we had free time. And whenever they had free time, they'd talk about us.

"Great-looking girl," my partner said. "All the guys've got their eye on her. But nobody's nailed her yet."

"Can she really be that good-looking?" I asked. I had my doubts. Any number of times I had made a point of going to see the latest "knockout," who turned out to be nothing much. This was one kind of rumor you could never trust.

"No lie," he said. "Check her out yourself. If you don't think she's a beauty, go to Stage Six and get a new pair of eyes. Wish I didn't have a wife. I'd get her. Or die tryin'."

Lunch break was almost over, but as usual my section had almost no work left for the afternoon so I cooked up an excuse to go to Stage 8. To get there, you had to go through a long underground tunnel. There was a guard at the tunnel entrance, but he knew me from way back, so I had no trouble getting in.

The far end of the tunnel opened on a riverbank, and the Stage 8 building was a little ways downstream. Both the roof and the smokestack were pink. Stage 8 made elephant legs. Having worked there just four months earlier, I knew the layout well. The young guard at the entrance was a newcomer I had never seen before, though.

"What's your business?" he demanded. In his crisp uniform, he looked like a typical new-broom type, determined to enforce the rules.

"We ran out of nerve cable," I said, clearing my throat. "I'm here to borrow some."

"That's weird," he said, glaring at my uniform. "You're in the ear section. Cable from the ear and leg sections shouldn't be interchangeable."

"Well, let me try to make a long story short. I was originally planning to borrow cable from the trunk section, but they didn't have any extra. And *they* were out of leg cable, so they said if I could get them a reel of that, they'd let me have a reel of the fine stuff. When I called here, they said they have extra leg cable, so that's why I'm here."

The guard flipped through the pages of his clipboard. "I haven't heard anything about this," he said. "These things are supposed to be arranged beforehand."

"That's strange. It has been. Somebody goofed. I'll tell the guys inside to straighten it out."

The guard just stood there whining. I warned him that he was slowing down production and that I would hold him responsible if somebody from upstairs got on my back. Finally, still grumbling, he let me in.

Stage 8—the leg shop—was housed in a low-set, spacious building, a long, narrow place with a partially sunken sandy floor. Inside, your eyes were at ground level, and narrow glass windows were the only source of illumination. Suspended from the ceiling were movable rails from which hung dozens of elephant legs. If you squinted up at them, it looked as if a huge herd of elephants was winging down from the sky.

The whole shop had no more than thirty workers altogether, both men and women. Everybody had on hats and masks and goggles, so in the gloom it was impossible to tell which one was the new girl. I recognized one guy I used to work with and asked him where I could find her.

"She's the girl at Bench Fifteen attaching toenails," he said. "But if you're planning to put the make on her, forget it. She's hard as nails. You haven't got a chance."

"Thanks for the advice," I said.

The girl at Bench 15 was a slim little thing. She looked like a boy in a medieval painting.

"Excuse me," I said. She looked at me, at my uniform, at my shoes, and then up again. Then she took her hat off, and her goggles. She was incredibly beautiful. Her hair was long and curly; her eyes were as deep as the ocean.

"Yes?"

"I was wondering if you'd like to go out dancing with me tomorrow night. Saturday. If you're free."

"Well, I *am* free tomorrow night, and I *am* going to go dancing, but not with you."

"Have you got a date with someone else?"

"Not at all," she said. Then she put her goggles and hat back on, picked up an elephant toenail from her bench, and held it against a foot, checking the fit. The nail was just a little too wide, so she filed it down with a few quick strokes.

"C'mon," I said. "If you haven't got a date, go with me. It's more fun than going alone. And I know a good restaurant we could go to."

"That's all right. I want to dance by myself. If you want to dance, too, there's nothing stopping you from coming."

"I will," I said.

"It's up to you," she said.

Ignoring me, she continued to work. Now she pressed the filed nail into the hollow at the front of the foot. This time, it fit perfectly.

"Pretty good for a beginner," I said.

She didn't answer me.

THAT NIGHT, the dwarf came into my dream again, and again I knew it was a dream. He was sitting on a log in the middle of the clearing in the forest, smoking a cigarette. This time he had neither record player nor records. There were signs of weariness in his face that made him look a little more advanced in years than he had when I first saw him—though in no way could he be taken for someone who had been born before the revolution. He looked perhaps two or three years older than me, but it was hard to tell. That's the way it is with dwarfs.

For lack of anything better to do, I strolled around the

dwarf, looked up at the sky, and finally sat down beside him. The sky was gray and overcast, and black clouds were drifting westward. It might have begun to rain at any time. The dwarf had probably put away the records and player to keep them from being rained on.

"Hi," I said to the dwarf.

"Hi," he answered.

"Not dancing today?" I asked.

"No, not today," he said.

When he wasn't dancing, the dwarf was a feeble, sad-looking creature. You would never guess that he had once been a proud figure of authority in the royal palace.

"You look a little sick," I said.

"I am," he replied. "It can be very cold in the forest. When you live alone for a long time, different things start to affect your health."

"That's terrible," I said.

"I need energy. I need a new source of energy flowing in my veins—energy that will enable me to dance and dance, to get wet in the rain without catching cold, to run through the fields and hills. That's what I need."

"Gosh," I said.

We sat on the log for a long time, saying nothing. From far overhead, I heard the wind in the branches. Flitting among the trunks of the trees, a huge butterfly would appear and disappear.

"Anyhow," he said, "you wanted me to do something for you."

"I did?" I had no idea what he was talking about.

The dwarf picked up a branch and drew a star on the ground. "The girl," he said. "You want the girl, don't you?"

He meant the pretty new girl in Stage 8. I was amazed that he knew so much. Of course, this was a dream, so anything could happen.

"Sure, I want her. But I can't ask you to help me get her. I'll have to do it myself."

"You can't."

"What makes you so sure?"

"I know," he said. "Go ahead and get angry, but the fact is you can't do it yourself."

He might be right, I thought. I was so ordinary. I had nothing to be proud of—no money, no good looks, no special way with words, even—nothing special at all. True, I wasn't a bad guy, and I worked hard. The people at the factory liked me. I was strong and healthy. But I wasn't the type that girls go crazy over at first sight. How could a guy like me ever hope to get his hands on a beauty like that?

"You know," the dwarf whispered, "if you let me help you, it just might work out."

"Help me? How?" He had aroused my curiosity.

"By dancing. She likes dancing. Show her you're a good dancer and she's yours. Then you just stand beneath the tree and wait for the fruit to fall into your hands."

"You mean you'll teach me to dance?"

"I don't mind," he said. "But a day or two of practice won't do you any good. It takes six months at least, and then only if you work at it all day, every day. That's what it takes to capture someone's heart by dancing."

I shook my head. "It's no use, then," I said. "If I have to wait six months, some other guy will get her for sure."

"When do you go dancing?"

"Tomorrow night. Saturday. She'll be going to the dance hall, and I will, too. I'll ask her to dance with me."

The dwarf used the branch to draw a number of vertical lines in the dirt. Then he bridged them with a horizontal line to make a strange diagram. Silent, I followed the movement of his hand. The dwarf spit the butt of his cigarette on the ground and crushed it with his foot.

"There's a way to do it—if you really want her," he said. "You want her, don't you?"

"Sure I do."

"Want me to tell you how it can be done?"

"Please. I'd like to know."

"It's simple, really. I just get inside you. I use your body to dance. You're healthy and strong: You should be able to manage a little dancing."

"I *am* in good shape. Nobody better," I said. "But can you really do such a thing—get inside me and dance?"

"Absolutely. And then she's yours. I guarantee it. And not just her. You can have any girl."

I licked my lips. It sounded too good to be true. If I let the dwarf get inside me, he might never come out. My body could be taken over by this dwarf. As much as I wanted the girl, I was not willing to let that happen.

"You're scared," he said, as if reading my mind. "You think I'll take possession of your body."

"I've heard things about you," I said.

"Bad things, I suppose."

"Yes, bad things."

He gave me a sly smile. "Don't worry. I may have power, but I can't just take over a person's body once and for all. An agreement is required for that. I can't do it unless both parties agree. *You* don't want your body permanently taken over, do you?"

"No, of course not," I said with a shiver.

"And *I* don't want to help you get your girl without any kind of compensation." The dwarf raised a finger. "But I'll do it on one condition. It's not such a difficult condition, but it is a condition nonetheless."

"What is it?"

"I get into your body. We go to the dance hall. You ask her to join you and you captivate her with your dancing. Then you take her. But you're not allowed to say a word from beginning to end. You can't make a sound until you've gone all the way with her. That's the one condition."

"How am I supposed to seduce her if I can't say a word to her?" I protested.

"Don't worry," said the dwarf, shaking his head. "As long as you have me dancing for you, you can get any woman without opening your mouth. So, from the time you set foot in the dance hall to the moment you make her yours, you are absolutely forbidden to use your voice."

"And if I do?"

"Then your body is mine," he said, as if stating the obvious.

"And if I do the whole thing without making a sound?"

"Then the girl is yours, and I leave your body and go back to the forest."

I released a deep, deep sigh. What was I to do? While I wrestled with the question, the dwarf scratched another strange diagram into the earth. A butterfly came and rested on it, exactly in the center. I confess I was afraid. I could not say for certain that I would be able to keep silent from beginning to end. But I knew it was the only way for me to hold that gorgeous girl in my arms. I pictured her in Stage 8, filing the elephant toenail. I had to have her.

"All right," I said. "I'll do it."

"That's it," said the dwarf. "We've got our agreement."

THE DANCE HALL STOOD by the main factory gate, its floor always packed on a Saturday night with the young men and women who worked at the elephant factory. Virtually all of us unattached workers, both male and female, would come here every week to dance and drink and talk with our friends. Couples would eventually slip out to make love in the woods.

How I've missed this! the dwarf sighed within me. *This is what dancing is all about—the crowd, the drinks, the lights, the smell of sweat, the girls' perfume. Oh, it takes me back!*

I cut through the crowd, searching for her. Friends who noticed me would clap me on the shoulder and call out to me. I responded to each with a big, friendly smile but said nothing. Before long, the band started playing, but still there was no sign of her.

Take it slow, said the dwarf. *The night is young. You've got plenty to look forward to.*

The dance floor was a large, motorized circle that rotated

very slowly. Chairs and tables were set in rows around its outer edge. Over it, a large chandelier hung from the high ceiling, the immaculately polished wood of the floor reflecting its brilliance like a sheet of ice. Beyond the circle rose the bandstand, like bleachers in an arena. On it were arranged two full orchestras that would alternate playing every thirty minutes, providing lush dance music all evening without a break. The one on the right featured two complete drum sets, and all the musicians wore the same red elephant logo on their blazers. The main attraction of the left-hand orchestra was a ten-member trombone section, and this troupe wore green elephant masks.

I found a seat and ordered a beer, loosening my tie and lighting a cigarette. The dance-hall girls, who danced for a fee, would approach my table now and then and invite me to dance, but I ignored them. Chin in hand, and taking an occasional sip of beer, I waited for the girl to come.

An hour went by, and still she failed to show. A parade of songs crossed the dance floor—waltzes, fox-trots, a battle of the drummers, high trumpet solos—all wasted. I began to feel that she might have been toying with me, that she had never intended to come here to dance.

Don't worry, whispered the dwarf. *She'll be here. Just relax.*

The hands of the clock had moved past nine before she showed herself in the dance-hall door. She wore a tight, shimmering one-piece dress and black high heels. The entire dance hall seemed ready to vanish in a white blur, she was so sparkling and sexy. First one man, then another and another, spotted her and approached to offer himself as an escort, but a single wave of the hand sent each of them back into the crowd.

I followed her movements as I sipped my beer. She sat at a table directly across the dance floor from me, ordered a red-colored cocktail, and lit a long cigarette. She hardly touched the drink, and when she finished the cigarette she crushed it out without lighting another. Then she stood and proceeded toward the dance floor, slowly, with the readiness of a diver approaching the high platform.

She danced alone. The orchestra played a tango. She moved to the music with mesmerizing grace. Whenever she bent low, her long, black, curly hair swept past the floor like the wind, and her slender fingers stroked the strings of an invisible harp that floated in the air. Utterly unrestrained, she danced by herself, for herself. I couldn't take my eyes off her. It felt like the continuation of my dream. I grew confused. If I was using one dream to create another, where was the real me in all this?

She's a great dancer, said the dwarf. *It's worth doing it with somebody like her. Let's go.*

Hardly conscious of my movements, I stood and left my table for the dance floor. Shoving my way past a number of men, I came up beside her and clicked my heels to signal to the others that I intended to dance. She cast a glance at me as she whirled, and I flashed her a smile to which she did not respond. Instead, she went on dancing alone.

I started dancing, slowly at first, but gradually faster and faster until I was dancing like a whirlwind. My body no longer belonged to me. My arms, my legs, my head, all moved wildly over the dance floor unconnected to my thoughts. I gave myself to the dance, and all the while I could hear distinctly the transit of the stars, the shifting of the tides, the racing of the wind. This was truly what it meant to dance. I stamped my feet, swung my arms, tossed my head, and whirled. A globe of white light burst open inside my head as I spun round and round.

Again she glanced at me, and then she was whirling and stamping with me. The light was exploding inside her, too, I knew. I was happy. I had never been so happy.

This is a lot more fun than working in some elephant factory, isn't it? said the dwarf.

I said nothing in return. My mouth was so dry, I couldn't have spoken if I had tried to.

We went on dancing, hour after hour. I led, she followed. Time seemed to have given way to eternity. Eventually, she stopped dancing, looking utterly drained. She took my arm, and I—or, should I say, the dwarf—stopped dancing, too.

Standing in the very center of the dance floor, we gazed into each other's eyes. She bent over to remove her high heels, and with them dangling from her hand, she looked at me again.

WE LEFT THE DANCE HALL and walked along the river. I had no car, so we just kept walking and walking. Soon the road began its gradual climb into the hills. The air became filled with the perfume of white night-blooming flowers. I turned to see the dark shapes of the factory spread out below. From the dance hall, yellow light spilled out onto its immediate surroundings like so much pollen, and one of the orchestras was playing a jump tune. The wind was soft, and the moonlight seemed to drench her hair.

Neither of us spoke. After such dancing, there was no need to say anything. She clung to my arm like a blind person being led along the road.

Topping the hill, the road led into an open field surrounded by pine woods. The broad expanse looked like a calm lake. Evenly covered in waist-high grass, the field seemed to dance in the night wind. Here and there a shining flower poked its head into the moonlight, calling out to insects.

Putting my arm around her shoulders, I led her to the middle of the grassy field, where, without a word, I lowered her to the ground. "You're not much of a talker," she said with a smile. She tossed her shoes away and wrapped her arms around my neck. I kissed her on the lips and drew back from her, looking at her face once again. She was beautiful, as beautiful as a dream. I still could not believe I had her in my arms like this. She closed her eyes, waiting for me to kiss her again.

That was when her face began to change. A fleshy white thing crept out of one nostril. It was a maggot, an enormous maggot, larger than any I had ever seen before. Then came another and another, emerging from both her nostrils, and suddenly the stench of death was all around us. Maggots were falling from her mouth to her throat, crawling across her eyes and burrowing into her hair. The skin of her nose slipped away, the flesh beneath melting until only two dark holes were left. From these, still more maggots struggled to emerge, their pale white bodies smeared with the rotting flesh that surrounded them.

Pus began to pour from her eyes, the sheer force of it causing her eyeballs to twitch, then fall and dangle to either side of her face. In the gaping cavern behind the sockets, a clot of maggots like a ball of white string swarmed in her rotting brain. Her tongue dangled from her mouth like a huge slug, then festered and fell away. Her gums dissolved, the white teeth dropping out one by one, and soon the mouth itself was gone. Blood spurted from the roots of her hair, and then each hair fell out. From beneath the slimy scalp, more maggots ate their way through to the surface. Arms locked around me, the girl never loosened her grip. I struggled vainly to free myself, to avert my face, to close my eyes. A hardened lump in my stomach rose to my throat, but I could not disgorge it. I felt as if the skin of my body had turned inside out. By my ear resounded the laughter of the dwarf.

The girl's face continued to melt until suddenly the jaw popped open, as if from a sudden twisting of the muscles, and clots of liquefied flesh and pus and maggots sprang in all directions.

I sucked my breath in to let out a scream. I wanted someone—anyone—to drag me away from this unbearable hell. In the end, however, I did not scream. This can't be happening, I said to myself. This can't be real, I knew almost intuitively. The dwarf is doing this. He's trying to trick me. He's trying to make me use my voice. One sound, and my body will be his forever. That is exactly what he wants.

Now I knew what I had to do. I closed my eyes—this time without the least resistance—and I could hear the wind moving across the grassy field. The girl's fingers were digging into my back. Now I wrapped my arms around her and drew her to me with all my strength, planting a kiss upon the suppurating flesh where it seemed to me her mouth had once been. Against my face I could feel the slippery flesh and the maggoty lumps; my nostrils filled with a putrid smell. But this lasted only a moment. When I opened my eyes, I found myself kissing the beautiful girl I had come here with. Her pink cheeks glowed in the soft moonlight. And I knew that I had defeated the dwarf. I had done it all without making a sound.

You win, said the dwarf in a voice drained of energy. *She's yours. I'm leaving your body now.* And he did.

"But you haven't seen the last of me," he went on. "You can win as often as you like. But you can only lose once. Then it's the end for you. And you *will* lose. The day is bound to come. I'll be waiting, no matter how long it takes."

"Why does it have to be me?" I shouted back. "Why can't it be someone else?"

But the dwarf said nothing. He only laughed. The sound of his laughter floated in the air until the wind swept it away.

IN THE END, the dwarf was right. Every policeman in the country is out looking for me now. Someone who saw me dancing—maybe the old man—reported to the authorities that the dwarf had danced in my body. The police started watching me, and everyone who knew me was called in for questioning. My partner testified that I had once told him about the dancing dwarf. A warrant went out for my arrest. The police surrounded the factory. The beautiful girl from Stage 8 came secretly to warn me. I ran from the shop and dove into the pool where the finished elephants are stockpiled. Clinging to the back of one, I fled into the forest, crushing several policemen on the way.

For almost a month now, I've been running from forest to forest, mountain to mountain, eating berries and bugs, drinking water from the river to keep myself alive. But there are too many policemen. They're bound to catch me sooner or later. And when they do, they'll strap me to the winch and tear me to pieces. Or so I'm told.

The dwarf comes into my dreams every night and orders me to let him inside me.

"At least that way, you won't be arrested and dismembered by the police," he says.

"No, but then I'll have to dance in the forest forever."

"True," says the dwarf, "but you're the one who has to make that choice."

He chuckles when he says this, but I can't make the choice.

I hear the dogs howling now. They're almost here.

—translated by Jay Rubin

The Last Lawn of The afternoON

I MUST HAVE BEEN eighteen or nineteen when I mowed lawns, a good fourteen or fifteen years ago. Ancient history.

Sometimes, though, fourteen or fifteen years doesn't seem *so* long ago. I'll think, that's when Jim Morrison was singing "Light My Fire," or Paul McCartney "The Long and Winding Road"—maybe I'm scrambling my years a bit, but anyway, about that time—it somehow never quite hits that it was really all that long ago. I mean, I don't think I myself have changed so much since those days.

No, I take that back. I'm sure I must have changed a lot. There'd be too many things I couldn't explain if I hadn't.

Okay, I've changed. And these things happened all of fourteen, fifteen years back.

In my neighborhood—I'd just recently moved there—we had a public junior high school, and whenever I went out to run shopping errands or take a walk I'd pass right by it. So I'd find myself looking at the junior-high kids exercising or drawing pictures or just goofing off. Not that I especially enjoyed looking at them; there wasn't anything else to look at. I could just as well have looked at the line of cherry trees off to the right, but the junior-high kids were more interesting.

So as things went, looking at these junior-high-school kids every day, one day it struck me. *They were all just fourteen or fifteen years old*. It was a minor discovery for me, something of a shock. Fourteen or fifteen years ago, they weren't even born; or if they were, they were little more than semiconscious blobs of pink flesh. And here they were now, already wearing brassieres, masturbating, sending stupid little postcards to disc jockeys, smoking out in back of the gym, writing FUCK on somebody's fence with red spray paint, reading—maybe—*War and Peace*. *Phew,* glad that's done with.

I really meant it. *Phew.*

Me, back fourteen or fifteen years ago, I was mowing lawns.

MEMORY IS LIKE FICTION: or else it's fiction that's like memory. This really came home to me once I started writing fiction, that memory seemed a kind of fiction, or vice versa. Either way, no matter how hard you try to put everything neatly into shape, the context wanders this way and that, until finally the context isn't even there anymore. You're left with this pile of kittens lolling all over one another. Warm with life, hopelessly unstable. And then to put these things out as saleable items, you call them finished products—at times it's downright embarrassing just to think of it. Honestly, it can make me blush. And if *my* face turns that shade, you can be sure everyone's blushing.

Still, you grasp human existence in terms of these rather absurd activities resting on relatively straightforward motives, and questions of right and wrong pretty much drop out of the picture. That's where memory takes over and fiction is born. From that point on, it's a perpetual-motion machine no one can stop.

Tottering its way throughout the world, trailing a single unbroken thread over the ground.

Here goes nothing. Hope all goes well, you say. But it never has. Never will. It just doesn't go that way.

So where does that leave you? What do you do?

What is there to do? I just go back to gathering kittens and piling them up again. Exhausted kittens, all limp and played out. But even if they woke to discover themselves stacked like kindling for a campfire, what would the kittens think? Well, it might scarcely raise a "Hey, what gives?" out of them. In which case—if there was nothing to particularly get upset about—it would make my work a little easier. That's the way I see it.

AT EIGHTEEN OR NINETEEN I mowed lawns, so we're talking ancient history. Around that time I had a girlfriend the same age, but a simple turn of events had taken her to live in a town way out of the way. Out of a whole year we could get together maybe two weeks total. In that short time we'd have sex, go to the movies, wine and dine at some pretty fancy places, tell each other things nonstop, one thing after the next. And in the end we'd always cap it off with one hell of a fight, then make up, and have sex again. In other words, we'd be doing what most any couple does, only in a condensed version, like a short feature.

At this point in time, I don't actually know if I really and truly loved her or not. Oh, I can bring her to mind, all right, but I just don't know. These things, they happen. I liked eating out with her, liked watching her take off her clothes one piece at a time, liked how soft it felt inside her vagina. And after sex, I liked just looking at her with her head on my chest, talking softly until she'd fall asleep. But that's all. Beyond that, I'm not sure of one single thing.

Save for that two-week period I was seeing her, my life was excruciatingly monotonous. I'd go to the university whenever I had classes and got more or less average marks. Maybe go to the movies alone, or stroll the streets for no special reason, or take some girl I got along with out on a date—no sex. Never much for loud get-togethers, I was always said to be on the quiet side. When I was by myself, I'd listen to rock 'n' roll, nothing else. Happy enough, I guess, though probably not so very happy. But at the time, that was about what you'd expect.

One summer morning, the beginning of July, I got this long letter from my girlfriend, and in it she'd written that she wanted to break up with me. I've always felt close to you, and I still like you even now, and I'm sure that from here on I'll continue to . . . et cetera, et cetera. In short, she was wanting to break it off. She had found herself a new boyfriend. I hung my head and smoked six cigarettes, went outside and drank a can of beer, came back in and smoked another cigarette. Then I took three HB pencils I had on my desk and snapped them in half. It wasn't that I was angry, really. I just didn't know what to do. In the end, I merely changed clothes and headed off to work. And for a while there, everyone within shouting distance was commenting on my suddenly "outgoing disposition." What is it about life?

That year I had a part-time job for a lawn-care service near Kyodo Station on the Odakyu Line, doing a fairly good business. Most people, when they built houses in the area, put in lawns. That, or they kept dogs. The two things seemed mirror alternatives. (Although there *were* folks who did both.) Each had its own advantages: A green lawn is a thing of beauty; a dog is cute. But half a year passes, and things start to drag on everyone. The lawn needs mowing, and you have to walk the dog. Not quite what they bargained for.

Well, as it ended up, we mowed lawns for these people. The summer before, I'd found the job through the student union at the university. Besides me, a whole slew of others had come in at the same time, but they all quit soon thereafter; only I stayed on. It was demeaning work, but the pay wasn't bad. What's more, you could get by pretty much without talking to anyone.

Just made for me. Since joining on there, I'd managed to save up a tidy little sum. Enough for my girlfriend and me to take a trip somewhere that summer. But now that she'd called the whole thing off, what difference did it make? For a week or so after I got her good-bye letter, I tried thinking up all sorts of ways to use the money. Or rather, I didn't have anything better to think about than how to spend the money. A lost week it was. My penis looked like any other guy's penis. But somebody—a somebody I didn't know—was nibbling at her little nipples. Strange sensation. What was wrong with me?

I was hard-pressed to come up with some way of spending the money. There was a deal to buy someone's used car—a 1000cc Subaru—not bad condition and the right price, but somehow I just didn't feel like it. I also thought of buying new speakers, but in my tiny apartment with its wood-and-plasterboard walls, what would have been the point? I guess I could have moved, but I didn't really have any reason to. And even if I did up and move out of my apartment, there wouldn't have been enough money left over to buy the speakers.

There just wasn't any way to spend the money. I bought myself a polo shirt and a few records, and the whole rest of the lump remained. So then I bought a really good Sony transistor radio—big speakers, clear FM reception, the works.

The whole week went past before it struck me. The fact of the matter was that if I had no way of spending the money, there was no point in my earning it.

So one morning I broached the matter to the head of the lawn-mowing company, told him I'd like to quit. It was getting on time when I had to begin studying for exams, and before that I'd been thinking about taking a trip. I wasn't about to say that I didn't want the money anymore.

"Well, now, sorry to hear that," said the head exec (I guess you'd call him that, although he seemed more like your neighborhood gardening man). Then he let out a sigh and sat down in his chair to take a puff of his cigarette. He looked up at the ceiling and craned his neck stiffly from side to side. "You really and truly do fine work. You're the heart of the operation, the best of my part-timers. Got a good reputation with the customers, too. What can I say? You've done a tremendous job for someone so young."

Thanks, I told him. Actually, I did have a good reputation. That's because I did meticulous work. Most part-timers give the grass a thorough once-over with a big electric lawn mower and do only a mediocre job on the remaining areas. That way, they get done quickly without wearing themselves out. My method was exactly the opposite. I'd rough in with the mower, then put time into the hand trimming. So naturally, the finished product looked nice. The only thing was that the take was small, seeing as the pay was calculated at so much per job. The price went by the approximate area of the yard. And what with all that bending and stooping, my back would get plenty sore. It's the sort of thing you have to be in the business to really understand. So much so that until you get used to it, you have trouble going up and down stairs.

Now, I didn't do such meticulous work especially to build a reputation. You probably won't believe me, but I simply enjoy mowing lawns. Every morning, I'd hone the grass clippers, head out to the customers in a minivan loaded with a lawn mower, and cut the grass. There's all kinds of yards, all kinds of turf, all kinds of housewives. Quiet, thoughtful housewives and ones who shoot off their mouths. There were even your housewives who'd crouch down right in front of me in loose T-shirts and no bra so that I could see all the way to their nipples.

No matter, I kept on mowing the lawn. Generally, the grass in the yard would be pretty high. Overgrown like a thicket. The taller the grass, the more rewarding I'd find the job. When the job was finished, the yard would yield an entirely different impression. Gives you a really great feeling. It's as if a thick bank of clouds has suddenly lifted, letting in the sun all around.

One time and one time only—*after* I'd done my work—did I ever sleep with one of these housewives. Thirty-one, maybe thirty-two she was, petite, with small, firm breasts. She closed all the shutters, turned out the lights, and we made it in the pitch-blackness. Even so, she kept on her dress, merely slipping off her underwear. She got on top of me, but wouldn't let me touch her anywhere below her breasts. And her body was incredibly cold; only her vagina was warm. She hardly spoke a word. I, too, kept silent. There was just the rustling of her dress, now slower, now faster. The telephone rang midway. The ringing went on for a while, then stopped.

Later, I wondered if my girlfriend and I breaking up mightn't have been on account of that interlude. Not that there was any particular reason to think so. It somehow just occurred to me. Probably because of the phone call that went unanswered. Well, whatever, it's all over and done with.

"This really leaves me in a fix, you know," said my boss. "If you pull out now, I won't be able to stir up business. And it's peak season, too."

The rainy season really made lawns grow like crazy.

"What do you say? How about one more week? Give me a week. I'll be able to find some new hands, and everything'll be okay. If you'd just do that for me, I'll give you a bonus."

Fine, I told him. I didn't especially have any other plans for the time being, and above all, I had no objections to the work itself. All the same, I couldn't help thinking what an odd turn of events this was: The minute I decide I don't need money, the dough starts pouring in.

Clear weather three days in a row, then one day of rain, then three more days of clear weather. So went my last week on the job. It was summer, though nothing special as summers go. Clouds drifted across the sky like distant memories. The sun broiled my skin. My back peeled three times, and by then I was tanned dark all over. Even behind my ears.

The morning of my last day of work found me in my usual gear—T-shirt and shorts, tennis shoes, sunglasses—only now as I climbed into the minivan, I was heading out for what would be my last lawn. The car radio was on the blink, so I brought along my transistor radio from home for some driving music. Creedence, Grand Funk, your regular AM rock. Everything revolved around the summer sun. I whistled along with snatches of the music, and smoked when not whistling. An FEN newscaster was stumbling over a rapid-fire list of the most impossible-to-pronounce Vietnamese place-names.

My last job was near Yomiuri Land Amusement Park. Fine by me. Don't ask why someone living over the line in Kanagawa Prefecture felt compelled to call a Setagaya Ward lawn-mowing service. I had no right to complain, though. I mean, I myself chose that job. Go into the office first thing in the morning, and all the day's jobs would be written up on a blackboard; each person then signed up for the places he wanted to work. Most of the crew generally chose places nearby. Less time back and forth, so they could squeeze in more jobs. Me, on the other hand, I chose jobs as far away as I could. Always. And that always puzzled everyone. But like I said before, I was the lead guy among the part-timers, so I got first choice of any jobs I wanted.

No reason for choosing what I did, really. I just liked mowing lawns farther away. I enjoyed the time on the road, enjoyed a longer look at the scenery on the way. I wasn't about to tell anyone that—who would've understood?

I drove with all the windows open. The wind grew brisk as I headed out of the city, the surroundings greener. The simmering heat of the lawns and the smell of dry dirt came on stronger; the clouds were outlined sharp against the sky. Fantastic weather. Perfect for taking a little summer day trip with a girl somewhere. I thought about the cool sea and the hot sands. And then I thought of a cozy air-conditioned room with crisp blue sheets on the bed. That's all. Aside from that, I didn't think about a thing. My head was all beach and blue sheets.

I went on thinking about these very things while getting the tank filled at a gas station. I stretched out on a nearby patch of grass and casually watched the attendant check the oil and wipe the windows. Putting my ear to the ground, I could hear all kinds of things. I could even hear what sounded like distant waves, though of course it wasn't. Only the rumble of all the different sounds the earth sucked in. Right in front of my eyes, a bug was inching along a blade of grass. A tiny green bug with wings. The bug paused when it reached the end of the grass blade, thought things over awhile, then decided to go back the same way it came. Didn't look all that particularly upset.

Wonder if the heat gets to bugs, too?

Who knows?

In ten minutes, the tank was full, and the attendant honked the horn to let me know.

My destination address turned out to be up in the hills. Gentle, stately hills, rolling down to rows of zelkova trees on either flank. In one yard, two small boys in their birthday suits showering each other with a hose. The spray made a strange little two-foot rainbow in the air. From an open window came the sound of someone practicing the piano. Quite beautifully, too; you could almost mistake it for a record.

I pulled the van to a stop in front of the appointed house, got out, and rang the doorbell. No answer. Everything was dead quiet. Not a soul in sight, kind of like siesta time in a Latin country. I rang the doorbell one more time. Then I just kept on waiting.

It seemed a nice enough little house: cream-colored plaster walls with a square chimney of the same color sticking up from right in the middle of the roof. White curtains hung in the windows, which were framed in gray, though both were sun-bleached beyond belief. It was an old house, a house all the more becoming for its age. The sort of house you often find at summer resorts, occupied half the year and left empty the other half. You know the type. There was a lived-in air to the house that gave it its charm.

The yard was enclosed by a waist-high French-brick wall topped by a rosebush hedge. The roses had completely fallen off, leaving only the green leaves to take in the glaring summer sun. I hadn't really taken a look at the lawn yet, but the yard seemed fairly large, and there was a big camphor tree that cast a cool shadow over the cream-colored house.

It took a third ring before the front door slowly opened and a middle-aged woman emerged. A huge woman. Now, I'm not so small myself, but she must have been a good inch and a half taller than me. And broad at the shoulders, too. She looked like she was plenty angry at something. She was around fifty, I'd say. No beauty certainly, but a presentable face. Although, of course, by "presentable" I don't mean to suggest that hers was the most likable face. Rather thick eyebrows and a squarish jaw attested to a stubborn, never-go-back-on-your-word temperament.

Through sleep-dulled eyes she gave me the most bothered look. A slightly graying shock of stiff frizzy hair rippled across the crown of her head; her two thick arms drooped out of the shoulders of a frumpy brown cotton dress. Her limbs were utterly pale. "What is it?" she said.

"I've come to mow the lawn," I said, taking off my sunglasses.

"The lawn?" She twisted her neck. "You mow lawns?"

"That's right, and since you called—"

"Oh, I guess I did. The lawn. What's the date today?"

"The fourteenth."

To which she yawned, "The fourteenth, eh?" Then she yawned again. "Say, you wouldn't have a cigarette, would you?"

Taking a pack of Hope regulars out of my pocket, I offered her one and lit it with a match. Whereupon she exhaled a long, leisurely puff of smoke up into the open air.

"Of all the . . ." she began. "What's it gonna take?"

"Timewise?"

She thrust out her jaw and nodded.

"Depends on the size and how much work it needs. May I take a look?"

"Go ahead. Seeing's how you gotta size it up first."

There were some hydrangea bushes and that camphor tree and the rest was lawn. Two empty birdcages were set out beneath a window. The yard looked well tended, the grass was fairly short—hardly in need of mowing. I was kind of disappointed.

"This here's still okay for another two weeks. No reason to mow now."

"That's for me to decide, am I right?"

I gave her a quick look. Well, she did have me there.

"I want it shorter. That's what I'm paying you money for. Fair enough?"

I nodded. "I'll be done in four hours."

"Awful slow, don't you think?"

"I like to work slow."

"Well, suit yourself."

I went to the van, took out the electric lawn mower, grass clippers, rake, garbage bag, my thermos of iced coffee, and my transistor radio, and brought them into the yard. The sun was climbing steadily toward the center of the sky. The temperature was also rising steadily. Meanwhile, as I was hauling out my equipment, the woman had lined up ten pairs of shoes by the front door and began dusting them with a rag. All of them women's shoes, but of two different sizes, small and extra-large.

"Would it be all right if I put on some music while I work?" I asked.

The woman looked up from where she crouched. "Fine by me. I like music myself."

Immediately I set about picking up whatever stones lay around the yard, and only then started up the lawn mower. Stones can really damage the blades. The mower was fitted with a plastic receptacle to collect all the clippings. I'd remove this receptacle whenever it got too full and empty the clippings into the garbage bag. With two thousand square feet to mow, even a short growth can amount to a lot of clippings. The sun kept broiling down on me. I stripped off my sweat-soaked T-shirt and kept working. In my shorts, I must have looked dressed down for some barbecue. I was all sweat. At this rate, I could have kept drinking water and drinking water and still not pissed a drop.

After about an hour of mowing, I took a break and sat myself down under the camphor tree to drink some iced coffee. I could feel my entire body just drinking up the sugar. Cicadas were droning overhead. I turned on the radio and poked around the dial for a decent disc jockey. I stopped when I came to a station playing Three Dog Night's "Mama Told Me Not to Come," lay down on my back, and just looked up through my shades at the sun filtering between the branches.

The woman came and planted herself by my head. Viewed from below, she resembled the camphor tree. Her right hand held a glass, and in it whiskey and ice were aswirl in the summer light.

"Hot, eh?" she said.

"You said it," I replied.

"So what's a guy like you do for lunch?"

I looked at my watch. It was 11:20.

"When noon rolls around, I'll go get myself something to eat somewhere. I think there's a hamburger stand nearby."

"No need to go out of your way. I'll fix you a sandwich or something."

"Really, it's all right. I always go off to get a bite."

She raised the glass of whiskey to her mouth and downed half of it in one swallow. Then she pursed her lips and let out a sigh. "No bother to me. I was going to make something for myself anyway. C'mon, let me get you something."

"Well, then, all right. Much obliged."

"That's okay," she said, and trudged back into the house, slowly swaying at the shoulders.

I worked with the grass clippers until twelve. First, I went over the uneven spots in my mowing job; then, after raking up the clippings, I proceeded to trim where the mower hadn't reached. Real time-consuming work. If I'd wanted to do just an adequate job, I could have done only so much and no more; if I wanted to do it right, I could do it right. But just because I'd get down to details didn't necessarily mean my labors were always appreciated. Some folks would call it tedious nit-picking. Still, as I said before, I'm one for doing my best. It's just my nature. And even more, it's a matter of pride.

A noon whistle went off somewhere, and the woman took me into the kitchen for sandwiches. The kitchen wasn't big, but it was clean and tidy. And except for the humming of the huge refrigerator, all was quiet. The plates and silverware were practically antiques. She offered me a beer, which I declined, seeing as I was "still on the job." So she served me some orange juice instead. She herself, however, had a beer. A half-empty bottle of White Horse stood prominently on the table, and the sink was filled with all kinds of empty bottles.

I enjoyed the sandwich. Ham, lettuce, and cucumber, with a tang of mustard. Excellent sandwich, I told her. Sandwiches were the only things she was good at, she said. She didn't eat a bite, though—just nibbled at a pickle, and devoted the rest of her attention to her beer. She wasn't especially talkative, nor did I have anything worth bringing up.

At twelve-thirty, I returned to the lawn. My last afternoon lawn.

I listened to rock music on FEN while I gave one last touch-up trim, then raked the lawn repeatedly and checked from several angles for any overlooked places, just like barbers do. By one-thirty, I was two-thirds done. Time and again, sweat would get into my eyes, and I would go douse my face at the outdoor faucet. A couple of times I got a hard-on, then it would go away. Pretty ridiculous, getting a hard-on just mowing a lawn.

I finished working by two-twenty. I turned off the radio, took off my shoes, and walked all over the lawn in my bare feet: nothing left untrimmed, no uneven patches. Smooth as a carpet.

"Even now, I still like you," she had written in her last letter. "You're kind, and one of the finest people I know. But somehow, that just wasn't enough. I don't know why I feel that way, I just do. It's a terrible thing to say, I know, and it probably won't amount to much of an explanation. Nineteen is an awful age to be. Maybe in a few years I'll be able to explain things better, but after a few years it probably won't matter anymore, will it?"

I washed my face at the faucet, then loaded my equipment back into the van and changed into a new T-shirt. Having done that, I went to the front door of the house to announce that I'd finished.

"How about a beer?" the woman asked.

"Don't mind if I do," I said. What could be the harm of one beer, after all?

Standing side by side at the edge of the yard, we surveyed the lawn, I with my beer, she with a long vodka tonic, no lemon. Her tall glass was the kind they give away at liquor stores. The cicadas were still chirping the whole while. The woman didn't look a bit drunk; only her breathing seemed a little unnatural, drawn slow between her teeth with a slight wheeze.

"You do good work," she said. "I've called in a lot of lawn-maintenance people before, but you're the first to do this good a job."

"You're very kind," I said.

"My late husband was fussy about the lawn, you know. Always did a crack job himself. Very much like the way you work."

I took out my cigarettes and offered her one. As we stood there smoking, I noticed how big her hands were compared to mine. Big enough to dwarf both the glass in her right hand and the Hope regular in her left. Her fingers were stubby—no rings—and several of the nails had strong vertical lines running through them.

"Whenever my husband got any time off, he'd always be mowing the lawn. But mind you, he was no oddball."

I tried to conjure up an image of the woman's husband, but I couldn't quite picture the guy. Any more than I could imagine a camphor-tree husband and wife.

The woman wheezed again. "Ever since my husband passed

away," she said, "I've had to call in professionals. I can't stand too much sun, you know, and my daughter, she doesn't like getting tanned. Other than to get a tan, no real reason for a young girl to be mowing lawns anyway, right?"

I nodded.

"My, but I do like the way you work, though. That's the way lawns ought to be mowed."

I looked the lawn over one more time. The woman belched.

"Come again next month, okay?"

"Next month's no good," I said.

"How's that?" she said.

"This job here today's my last," I said. "If I don't get myself back on the ball with my studies, my grade point average is going to be in real trouble."

The woman looked me hard in the face, then glanced at my feet, then looked back at my face.

"A student, eh?"

"Yeah," I said.

"What school?"

The name of the university made no visible impression on her. It wasn't a very impressive university. She just scratched behind her ear with her index finger.

"So you're giving up this line of work, then?"

"Yeah, for this summer at least," I said. No more mowing lawns for me this summer. Nor next summer, nor the next.

The woman filled her cheeks with vodka tonic as if she were going to gargle, then gulped down her precious mouthwash half a swallow at a time. Her whole forehead beaded up with sweat, like it was crawling with tiny bugs.

"Come inside," the woman said. "It's too hot outdoors."

I looked at my watch. Two thirty-five. Getting late? Still early? I couldn't make up my mind. I'd already finished with all my work. From tomorrow, I wouldn't have to mow another inch of grass. I had really mixed feelings.

"You in a hurry?" she asked.

I shook my head.

"So why don't you just come in and have something cool to drink before you get on your way? Won't take much time. And besides, I've got something I want you to see."

Something she wants me to see?

Still, there was no hesitating, one way or another. She had already started to shuffle off ahead of me. She didn't even bother to look back in my direction. I had no choice but to follow her. I felt kind of light-headed from the heat.

The interior of the house was just as deathly quiet as before. Ducking in from the flood of summer afternoon light so suddenly, I felt my eyes tingle from deep behind my pupils. Darkness—in a dim, somehow dilute solution—washed through the place, a darkness that seemed to have settled in decades ago. The air was chilly, but not with the chill of air-conditioning. It was the fluid chill of air in motion: Somewhere a breeze was getting in, somewhere it was leaking out.

"This way," the woman said, traipsing off down a long, straight hallway. There were several windows along the passage, but the stone wall of a neighboring house and an overgrowth of zelkova trees still managed to block out the light. All sorts of smells drifted the length of the hallway, each recalling something different. Time-worn smells, built up over time, only to dissipate in time. The smell of old clothes and old furniture, old books, old lives. At the end of the hallway was a staircase. The woman turned around to make sure I was following, then headed up the stairs. The old boards creaked with every step.

At the top of the stairs, some light finally shone into the house. The window on the landing had no curtain, and the summer sun pooled on the floor. There were only two rooms upstairs, one a storage room, the other a regular bedroom. The smoky-green door had a small frosted-glass portal. The green paint had begun to chip slightly, and the brass doorknob was patinaed white on the handgrip.

The woman pursed her lips and blew out a slow stream of air, set her empty vodka-tonic glass on the windowsill, fished a key ring out of her dress pocket, and noisily unlocked the door.

"Go on in," she said. We stepped into the room. Inside, it was pitch-black and stuffy, full of hot, still air. Only the thinnest silver-foil sheets of light sliced into the room from the cracks between the tightly closed shutters. I couldn't make out a thing, just flickering specks of airborne dust. The woman drew back the curtains, opened the windows, and slid back shutters that rattled in their tracks. Instantly, the room was swept with brilliant sunlight and a cool southerly breeze.

The bedroom was your typical teenage girl's room. Study desk by the window, small wood-framed bed over on the other side of the room. The bed was dressed in coral-blue sheets—not a wrinkle on them—and pillowcases of the same color. There was also a blanket folded at the foot of the bed. Next to the bed stood a wardrobe and a dresser on which were arranged a few toiletries. A hairbrush and a small pair of scissors, a lipstick, a compact, and whatnot. She didn't seem all that much of a makeup enthusiast.

Stacked on the desk were notebooks and two dictionaries, French and English. Both looked well used. Literally so; not ill-treated but handled with some care. An assortment of pens and pencils were neatly laid out in a small tray, along with an eraser worn round on one side only. Then there was an alarm clock, a desk lamp, and a glass paperweight. All quite plain. On the wood-paneled wall hung five full-color bird pictures and a calendar with only dates. A finger run over the desktop became white with dust, a whole month's worth. The calendar still read June.

Overall, though, I had to say the room was refreshingly uncluttered for a girl these days. No stuffed toys, no photos of rock stars. No frilly decorations or flower-print wastepaper bin. Just a built-in bookcase lined with anthologies, volumes of poetry, movie magazines, painting-exhibition catalogs. There were even some English paperbacks. I tried to form an image of the girl whose room this was, but the only face that came to mind was that of my ex-girlfriend.

The woman sat her middle-aged bulk down on the bed and

looked at me. She had been following my line of vision all along but seemed to be thinking of something entirely different. Her eyes were turned in my direction, all right, yet she wasn't actually seeing anything. I plunked myself down in the chair by the desk and gazed at the plaster wall behind the woman. Nothing hung there; it was a blank wall. Stare at it long enough, though, and the top began to tilt in toward me. It seemed sure to topple over onto her head any minute. But of course, it wouldn't; the light just made it look that way.

"Won't you have something to drink?" she asked. I told her no

"Really now, don't stand on ceremony. It's not like you're going to kick yourself afterward for having something."

So I said okay, I'd have the same, pointing to her vodka tonic, only watered down a bit, please. Five minutes later, she returned with two vodka tonics and an ashtray. I took a sip of my vodka tonic. It wasn't watered at all. I decided to smoke a cigarette and wait for the ice to melt.

"You've got a healthy body," she said. "You won't get drunk."

I nodded vaguely. My father was that way, too. Still, there hasn't been a human being yet won out in a match against alcohol. The only stories you hear are about people who never catch on to things until they've sunk past their noses. My father died when I was sixteen. A real fine-line case, his was. So fine I can hardly recall if he'd even been alive or not.

The woman remained silent all this time. The only sound she made was the tinkling of ice in her glass each time she took a sip. Every so often a cool breeze would blow in through the open window from another hill across the way to the south. A tranquil summer afternoon that seemed destined to put me to sleep. Somewhere, far off, a phone was ringing.

"Have a look inside the wardrobe," the woman prompted. I walked over to the wardrobe and opened the double doors, as I was told. The inside was absolutely packed with hangers and hangers of clothes. Half dresses, the other half skirts and blouses and jackets, all of them summer clothes. Some things looked pretty old, others as if they'd scarcely even been tried on. All the skirts were minis. Everything was nice enough, I suppose. The taste, the material, nothing that would catch your eye, but not bad.

With this many clothes, a girl could wear a different outfit each date for an entire summer. I looked at the rack of clothes awhile longer, then shut the door.

"Nice stuff," I said.

"Have a look in the drawers," the woman said. I was hesitant, but what could I do? I gave in and pulled open the drawers in the bottom of the wardrobe one by one. Going into a girl's room in her absence and turning it inside out—even with her mother's permission—wasn't my idea of the decent thing to do, but it would have been equally bothersome to refuse. Far be it from me to figure out what goes on in the mind of someone who starts hitting the bottle at eleven in the morning. In the first big drawer on top were sweaters, polo shirts, and T-shirts, washed and neatly folded without a wrinkle. In the second drawer were handbags, belts, handkerchiefs, bracelets, plus a few fabric hats. In the third drawer, underwear, socks, and stockings. Everything was clean and neat. Somehow, it made me just a little sad, as if something were weighing down on my chest. I shut the last drawer.

The woman was still sitting on the bed, staring out the window at the scenery. The vodka tonic in her right hand was almost empty.

I returned to the chair and lit up a brand-new cigarette. The window looked out on a gentle slope that ran down to where another slope picked up. Greenery as far as the eye could see, hill and dale, with tract-house streets pasted on as an afterthought. Each house having its own yard, each yard its lawn.

"What d'you think?" asked the woman, eyes still fixed on the window. "You know, about the girl . . ."

"How can I say without ever having met her?" I said.

"Most women, you look at their clothes, you know what they're like," she said.

I thought about my girlfriend. Then I tried to remember the sort of clothes she wore. I drew a blank. What I could recall of her was all too vague. No sooner had I begun to see her skirt than I lost sight of her blouse; I'd managed to bring her hat to mind when the face changed into some other girl's. I couldn't remember a single thing from just half a year before. When it came right down to it, what *had* I known about her?

"How can I say?" I repeated.

"General impressions are good enough. Whatever comes to mind. Anything you'd care to say, any little bit at all."

I took a sip of my vodka tonic to gain myself some time. The ice had almost all melted, making the tonic water taste like lemonade. The vodka still packed a punch going down, creating a warm glow in my stomach. A breeze burst through the window and sent white cigarette ash flying all over the desk.

"Seems she's nice—very nice—keeps everything in order," I said. "Not too pushy, though not without character, either. Grades in the upper mid-range of her class. Goes to a women's college or junior college, doesn't have so many friends, but close ones . . . Am I on target?"

"Keep going."

I swirled the glass around in my hand a couple of times, then set it down on the desk. "I don't know what more to say. In the first place, I don't even know if what I've said so far was anywhere close."

"You're pretty much on target," she said blankly, "pretty much on target."

Little by little, I was beginning to get a feel for the girl; her presence hovered over everything in the room like a hazy white shadow. No face, no hands, nothing. Just a barely perceptible disturbance in a sea of light. I took another sip of my vodka tonic.

"She's got a boyfriend," I continued, "or two. I don't know.

I can't tell how close they are. But that's neither here nor there. What matters is . . . she hasn't really taken to anything. Her own body, the things she thinks about, what she's looking for, what others seek in her . . . the whole works."

"Uh-huh," the woman said after a moment's pause. "I see what you're saying."

I didn't. Oh, I knew what the words meant, but to whom were they directed? And from whose point of view? I was exhausted, wanted just to sleep. If only I could get some sleep, a lot of things would surely become clearer. All the same, I couldn't believe that getting things clearer would make them any easier.

At that the woman fell silent for a long time. I also held my tongue. Ten, fifteen minutes like that. Nothing better to do with my hands, I ended up drinking half the vodka tonic. The breeze picked up a bit, and the round leaves of the camphor tree began to sway.

"Sorry, I shouldn't have kept you here," the woman said sometime later. "You did such a beautiful job on the lawn, I was just so pleased."

"Thanks," I said.

"Let me pay you," she said, thrusting her big white hand into her dress pocket. "How much is it?"

"They'll be sending you a regular bill later. You can pay by bank transfer," I said.

"Oh," said the woman.

We went back down the same staircase, through the same hallway, out to the front door. The hallway and entryway were just as chilly as when we came in, chilly and dark. I felt I'd returned to my childhood, back in the summers when I used to wade up this shallow creek and would pass under a big iron bridge. It was exactly the same sensation. Darkness, and suddenly the temperature of the water would drop. And the pebbles would have this funny slime. When I got to the front door and put on my tennis shoes, was I ever relieved! Sunlight all around me, the leaf-scented breeze, a few bees buzzing sleepily about the hedge.

"Really beautifully mowed," said the woman, once again viewing the lawn.

I gave the lawn another look, too. A really beautiful job, to be sure.

The woman reached into her pocket, and started pulling out all kinds of stuff—truly all kinds of junk—from which she picked out a crumpled ten-thousand-yen note. The bill wasn't even that old, just all crumpled up. It could have passed for four-teen, fifteen years old. After a moment's hesitation, I decided I'd better not refuse.

"Thank you," I said.

The woman seemed to have still left something unsaid. As if she didn't quite know how to put it. She stared down at the glass in her right hand, kind of lost. The glass was empty. Then she looked back up at me.

"You decide to start mowing lawns again, be sure to give me a call. Anytime at all."

"Right," I said. "Will do. And say, thanks for the sandwich and the drink."

The woman hemmed and hawed, then promptly turned an about-face and walked back to the front door. I started the engine on the van and turned on the radio. Getting on three o'clock, it was.

I pulled into a drive-in for a little pick-me-up and ordered a Coca-Cola and spaghetti. The spaghetti was so utterly disgusting I could finish only half of it. But if you really want to know, I wasn't hungry anyway. A sickly-looking waitress cleared the table, and I dozed off right there, seated on the vinyl-covered chair. The place was empty, after all, and the air-conditioning just right. It was only a short nap—no dreams. If anything, the nap itself seemed like a dream. Although when I opened my eyes, the sun's rays weren't as intense as they had been. I drank another Coke, then paid the bill with the ten-thousand-yen note I'd just received.

I went out to the parking lot, got in the van, put the keys on the dashboard, and smoked a cigarette. Loads of minuscule aches came over my weary muscles all at once. All things considered, I was worn out. I put aside any notion of driving and just sank into the seat. I smoked another cigarette. Everything seemed so far off, like looking through the wrong end of a pair of binoculars. "I'm sure you must want many things from me," my girlfriend had written, "but I myself just can't conceive that there's anything in me you'd want."

All I wanted, it came to me, was to mow a good lawn. To give it a once-over with the lawn mower, rake up the clippings, and then trim it nice and even with clippers—that's all. And that, I can do. Because that's the way I feel it ought to be done.

Isn't that right? I spoke out loud.

No answer.

Ten minutes later, the manager of the drive-in came out and crouched by the van to inquire if everything was all right.

"I felt a little faint," I said.

"Yes, it's been a scorcher. Shall I bring you some water?"

"Thank you. But really, I'm fine."

I pulled out of the parking lot and started east. On both sides of the road were different homes, different yards, different people all leading different lives. My hands on the wheel, I took in the whole passing panorama, the lawn mower rattling all the while in the compartment behind.

NOT ONCE SINCE then have I mowed a lawn. Someday, though, should I come to live in a house with a lawn, I'll probably be mowing again. That'll be a good while yet, I figure. But when that time comes, I'm sure to do the job just right.

—*translated by Alfred Birnbaum*

THE

silENCE

So I turned to Ozawa and asked him, had he ever punched out a guy in an argument?

"What makes you want to ask something like that?" Ozawa squinted his eyes at me. The look seemed out of character on him. As if there'd been a sudden flash of light only he had witnessed. A flare that just as quickly subsided, returning him to his normal passive expression.

No real reason, I told him, only a passing thought. Hadn't meant anything by it, just asked out of curiosity. Totally uncalled-for, probably.

I proceeded to change the subject, but Ozawa didn't exactly rally to it. He seemed to be somewhere else in his thoughts, holding back or wavering. I gave up trying to engage him in conversation and gazed instead out the window at the rows of silver jets.

I don't know how the subject came up. We'd been killing time waiting for our plane, and he started talking about how he'd been going to a boxing gym ever since he was in junior high school. More than once, he'd been chosen to represent his university in boxing matches. Even today, at age thirty-one, he still went to the gym every week.

I could hardly picture it. Here was this guy I'd done business with a lot; no way did he strike me as your rough-and-tumble boxer of close to twenty years. The guy was a singularly quiet fellow; he hardly ever spoke. Yet you couldn't ask for anyone more clear-cut in his work habits. Faultlessly sincere. Never pushed people too far, never talked about others behind their back, never complained. No matter how overworked he was, he never raised his voice or even arched his brows. In a word, he was the sort of guy you couldn't help but like. Warm, easygoing, a far cry from anything you could call aggressive. Where was the connection between this man and boxing? Why had he taken up the sport in the first place? So I asked that question.

We were drinking coffee in the airport restaurant, waiting for our flight to Niigata. This was the beginning of November; the sky was heavy with clouds. Niigata was snowed in, and planes were running late. The airport was full of people milling about, looking more depressed with each announcement of flight delays. In the restaurant, the heat was too high, and I kept having to wipe off the sweat with my handkerchief.

"Basically, no," Ozawa suddenly spoke up after a lengthy silence. "From the time I started boxing, I never hit anyone. They pound that into you from the moment you start boxing. Anyone who boxes must absolutely never, without gloves, hit anyone outside the ring. An ordinary person could get into trouble if he hit someone and landed a punch in the wrong place. But if a boxer did it, it'd be intentional assault with a deadly weapon."

I nodded.

"To be honest, I did hit someone. Once," Ozawa said. "I was in eighth grade. It was right around the time I was starting to learn how to box. No excuse, but this was before I learned a single boxing technique. I was still on the basic bodybuilding menu. Jumping rope and stretching and running, stuff like that. And the thing is, I didn't even mean to throw the punch. I just got mad, and my hand flew out ahead of me. I couldn't stop it. And before I knew it, I'd decked him. I hit the guy, and still my whole body was trembling with rage."

Ozawa had taken up boxing because his uncle ran a boxing gym. This wasn't just the local sweat room; this was a major establishment that had launched a two-time East Asia welterweight champion. In fact, it'd been Ozawa's parents who suggested he go to the gym to begin with. They were worried about their son, the bookworm, always holed up in his room. At first, the boy wasn't keen on the idea, but he liked his uncle well enough, and, he told himself, if he didn't like the sport, he could always quit. So all very casually, he got in the habit of commuting regularly to his uncle's gym, an hour away by train.

After the first few months, Ozawa's interest in boxing surprised even himself. The biggest reason was that, fundamentally, boxing is a loner's sport, an extremely solitary pursuit. It was something of a discovery for him, a new world. And that world excited him. The sweat flying off the bodies of the older men, the hard, squeaky feel of the gloves, the intense concentration of men with their muscles tuned to lightning-fast efficiency—little by little, it all took hold of his imagination. Spending Saturdays and Sundays at the gym became one of his few indulgences.

"One of the things I like about boxing is the depth. That's what grabbed me. Compared to that, hitting and getting hit is no big deal. That's only the outcome. The same with winning or losing. If you could get to the bottom of the depth, losing doesn't matter—nothing can hurt you. And anyway, nobody can win at everything; somebody's got to lose. The important thing is to get deep down into it. That—at least to me—is boxing. When I'm in a match, I feel like I'm at the bottom of a deep, deep hole. So far inside I can't see anyone else and no one can see me. Way down there in the darkness, doing battle. All alone. But not *sad* alone," said Ozawa. "There's all different kinds of loneliness. There's the tragic loneliness that tears at your nerves with pain. And then there's the loneliness that isn't like that at all—though in order to reach that point, you've got to pare your body down. If you make the effort, you get back what you put in. That's what I learned from boxing."

Ozawa paused a moment.

"Actually, I'd just as soon not talk about it," he said. "I even wish I could wipe the story out of my mind entirely. But of course, you never can. Why is it you can't forget what you really want to forget?" Ozawa broke into a smile. Then he glanced at his watch. We still had plenty of time. He began his deliberation.

The guy Ozawa hit was a classmate. Aoki was his name. Ozawa hated the guy from the very beginning. Why, he couldn't really say. All he knew was that he hated his guts from the moment he set eyes on him. It was the first time in his life he despised anyone.

"But it does happen, right?" he said. "Maybe once, but everyone has that experience. You loathe someone for no reason whatsoever. I'm not the type to have blind hate, but I swear there are people who just set you off. It's not a rational thing. But the problem is, in most cases, the other guy feels the same way toward you.

"This kid Aoki was a model student. He got good grades, sat at the head of the class, teacher's pet, all that. And he was pretty popular, too. Granted, we were an all-boys' school, but everyone liked him. Everyone except me. I couldn't stand him. I couldn't stand his smarts, his calculating ways. Okay, if you asked me what exactly bugged me about him I wouldn't be able to say. The only thing I can tell you is that I *knew* what he was all about. And his pride, that headstrong stink of ego he gave off, I couldn't stand it. Purely physiological, like how someone's body odor will turn you off. But Aoki was a clever guy and knew how to cover his scent. So most of the kids in the class thought he was clean and kind and considerate. Every time I heard how great people thought he was—of course, I wasn't about to go against everyone—it burned me up.

"In almost every way, Aoki and I were polar opposites. I was a quiet kid and didn't stand out in class. I was happy to be left alone. Sure, I had friends, but no real friends for life. In a sense, maybe I was too mature too soon. Instead of hanging around with my classmates, I kept to myself. I read books or listened to my father's classical records or went to the gym to hear the older guys talk. I wasn't much to look at. My grades weren't so bad, but they weren't so hot. Teachers would forget my name. So, you know, I was the type you never got to know. That's how I was, never quite surfacing. I never told anybody about the boxing gym or books or records.

"With Aoki, though, whatever the guy did he was like a white swan in a sea of mud. The star of the class, his opinions valued, always on top of things. Even *I* had to admit that. He was amazingly quick-witted. He could pick up on what others were thinking, and he could redirect his responses to match in no time whatsoever. He had a well-tuned head on his shoulders. No wonder everyone was impressed with Aoki. Everyone but me.

"I figure Aoki had to be aware of what I thought of him. He wasn't dumb. I could tell he wasn't too crazy about me. After all, I wasn't stupid, either. I mean, I read more than anybody else. But you know, when you're young you gotta show it, so I'm sure I came off stuck-up, even condescending. Plus, the way I kept to myself probably didn't help.

"Then once, at the end of the term, I got the highest marks on an English exam. It was a first for me, scoring the highest. But it wasn't an accident. There was something I really wanted—I can't even remember what it was anymore—and I made this deal with my folks that if I got the best grade in the class they'd buy it for me. So of course I studied like mad. I studied anything that could possibly be covered in the exam. If I had a spare moment, I went over verb conjugations. I practically memorized the whole textbook. So when I aced the test, it was no surprise. It was even predictable.

"But everyone else was caught off guard. The teacher, too.

And Aoki, I mean, he was shocked. *He* had always been the best student in English. The teacher even kidded Aoki about it when he announced the test grades. Aoki turned red. Probably thought people were laughing at him.

"A few days later, someone told me Aoki was spreading a rumor about me. That I'd cheated on the exam, how else could I have scored so high? When I heard that, I got really pissed off. What I should have done was laugh and let it go. But a junior-high-school kid doesn't have that kind of cool.

"One noon recess, I confronted Aoki. I said I wanted to talk to him alone, away from everybody else. I said I'd heard this rumor, and what was the meaning of it? But Aoki could only show his contempt. Like, why was I getting all bent out of shape? Like, if by some fluke I happened to get the best score, why was I being so defensive, and what right did I have to act so uppity, anyway? After all, everyone knew what really happened, right? Then he tried to brush me aside, probably thinking that since he was in good shape and taller than me he had to be stronger, too. That's when I hauled off and punched the jerk in the face. It was pure reflex action. I didn't realize I'd slugged him square on the left cheek until a second later when Aoki fell back sideways and hit his head on a wall. With a hard conk. Blood was running out of his nose and onto his white shirt. He lay there, dazed, not knowing what had happened.

"On my part, I regretted hitting him the instant my fist connected with his cheekbone. I shouldn't have done it. I felt miserable. It was a totally useless thing to have done. Like I said, my body was still trembling with rage, but I knew I'd done something stupid.

"I considered apologizing to Aoki. But I didn't. If it had been anybody else but Aoki, I probably would have apologized. I simply couldn't bring myself to apologize to the creep. I was sorry I hit Aoki, but not sorry enough to say I was sorry. I didn't feel one iota of remorse toward the guy. Jerks like him deserved to get punched out. He was a worm, and worms get stepped on. Still, *I shouldn't have hit him.* A truth I knew deep down, only too late. I'd already slugged him. I left Aoki there and walked off.

"That afternoon, Aoki didn't show up in class. Probably went straight home, I thought. But for the rest of the day, a horrible feeling ate at me. It didn't give me a moment's rest. I couldn't listen to music, couldn't read, I couldn't enjoy a thing. I felt this murky substance coagulating in my gut, and it wouldn't let me concentrate. It was like I'd swallowed something slimy. I lay in bed staring at my fist. And it dawned on me, how lonely I was. I hated Aoki even more for making me realize this.

"From the next day on, Aoki ignored me. He acted like I didn't exist. He went on scoring the highest on exams. Me, I never again poured my heart and soul into studying for a test. I couldn't imagine what difference it would make. The idea of competing seriously with anyone bored me. I did enough schoolwork to keep my head above water and did what I wanted to the rest of the time. I kept on going to my uncle's gym. I was getting heavy into my training. For a junior-high student, I was beginning to show results. I could feel my body changing. Shoulders broadening, chest thickening. My arms got firm, my cheeks taut. I thought, This is what it's like to become an adult. I felt great. Every night, I stood naked in front of the big mirror in the bathroom, I was so fascinated with my body.

"The following school year, Aoki and I were in different classes. I was glad not to have to see him every day, and I'm sure the feeling was mutual. So I thought the whole affair would fade away like some bad memory. But it wasn't so simple. Seems Aoki was lying in wait to get his revenge. Waiting for the right moment to cut everything out from under me. The bastard was full of spite.

"Aoki and I advanced together grade by grade. It was the same private junior high and senior high, but every year we were in different classes. Until the very last year—boy, did it feel ugly when we came face-to-face in that classroom. The way he looked at me, it pried open my gut. I could feel that same slime come oozing out again."

Ozawa pursed his lips and stared down at his coffee cup. Then he glanced up at me with a slight smile. From outside the plate-glass windows came the roar of jet engines. A 737 shot straight off like a wedge into the clouds and vanished from sight.

"The first semester passed pretty uneventfully. Aoki hadn't changed a bit since the eighth grade. Some people don't grow, and they don't degenerate; they keep on exactly as they always were. Aoki was still at the top of the class; he was still Mr. Popular. Though to me, he was still a disgusting creep. We did our best not to look at each other. Let me tell you, it's no fun having your own personal demon in the same classroom. But it couldn't be helped. Half the blame was mine, anyway.

"Then summer vacation came around. My last summer vacation as a high-school student. My grades were okay, okay enough to get me into an average university, so I didn't really cram for the entrance exams. My folks didn't raise a fuss, so I just studied as I always did. Saturdays and Sundays, I went to the gym. The rest of the time I read and listened to records.

"Meanwhile, everyone else was going bug-eyed. Our whole school, junior high up through senior high, was a typical cram factory. Who got into what university, what ranking by how many matriculations into where—the teachers couldn't talk about anything else. The same with the students. By senior year, everyone was hot under the collar, and the atmosphere in class was tense. It stank. I didn't like it when I first started school there, and I didn't like it six years later. Plus, to the very end, I didn't make one honest friend. If I hadn't taken up boxing, if I hadn't gone to my uncle's gym, I would have been pretty damn lonely.

"Anyway, during summer vacation a terrible thing happened. One of my classmates, a kid named Matsumoto, committed suicide. He wasn't a particularly outstanding student. To be frank, he made almost no impression at all. When I heard that he died, I could hardly remember what he looked like. He'd been in my class, but I doubt if we ever talked more than two or three times. Kind of gangly, poor complexion—that's about all I could say about him. Matsumoto died a little before August fifteenth, I remember, because his funeral was on Armistice Day. It was a real scorcher. There was this phone call saying that the boy had died and that everyone had to attend the funeral. The whole class. Matsumoto had leapt in front of a subway, for unknown reasons. He left a suicide note, but all it said was that he didn't want to go to school anymore. Nothing else. At least, that's how the story went.

"Naturally, this suicide had the whole school administration scrambling. After the funeral, the seniors were called back to the school and lectured by the headmaster about how we were supposed to mourn Matsumoto's death, how we all had to bear the weight of his death, how we had to work extra hard to overcome our grief. The usual stock sentiments. Then we were asked if we knew anything about the reason Matsumoto committed suicide; if we did, we had to come right out and set the record straight. Nobody said a word.

"I felt sorry for my dead classmate, but somehow it seemed pretty absurd. I mean, did he *have* to jump? If you don't like school, don't go to school. It was only half a year before you wouldn't have to go to that miserable school, anyway. Why kill yourself? It didn't make sense. The guy was probably neurotic, I figured, driven to the brink by all this cramming for entrance exams day and night. Not so surprising, if you think about it. One nut's bound to crack.

"After summer vacation ended and school started up again, I noticed something strange in the air. My classmates seemed to be keeping their distance. I'd ask somebody about something and only get these cold, curt replies. At first I thought it was nerves, since everyone was on edge, right? I didn't think too much about it. But then five days later, out of nowhere, I was told to report to the headmaster. Was it true, he asked me, that I was training at a boxing gym? Yes, I was, but I wasn't breaking any school rules doing it. How long had I been going there?

Since the eighth grade. Was it true I struck Aoki with a clenched fist in junior high school? Yes, it was; I wasn't about to lie. And was that before or after I took up boxing? After, but it was before I was even allowed to put on the gloves, I explained. The headmaster wasn't listening. Very well, he cleared his throat, had I ever hit Matsumoto? I was stunned. I mean, like I was saying, I hardly ever spoke to this Matsumoto—why would I have hit him? Which is what I told the headmaster.

"Matsumoto was always getting beaten up at school, the headmaster informed me. He often went home covered with bruises. His mother complained that someone at school, *at this school*, was rolling him for his pocket money. But Matsumoto never gave his mother any names. He probably thought he'd get beaten up worse if he squealed. And with all this bearing on him, the boy committed suicide. Pitiful, didn't I think, he couldn't turn to anyone. He'd been worked over pretty badly. So the school was looking into the situation. If there was anything I had on my mind, I was to own up. In which case, matters would be settled quietly. If not, the police would take over the investigation. Did I understand?

"Immediately, I knew Aoki was behind this. It was his touch, this using something like Matsumoto's death to his own advantage. I bet he didn't even lie. He didn't need to. He found out that I went to a boxing gym—who knows how?—then when he heard about someone beating up on Matsumoto, the rest was easy. Just put one and one together. Report how I went to a gym and how I'd hit him. It didn't take much more. Oh, I'm sure he added in a few trimmings, like, say, how he was scared of me, so he never told anyone about this before, or how I really bled him. Nothing that could easily be exposed as a lie. He was careful that way. Coloring plain facts just enough, shaping this undeniable atmosphere of implication. It was a skill he practiced.

"The headmaster glared at me: guilty as charged. For him, anyone who went to a boxing gym was already suspected of delinquency. Nor was I exactly the type of student teachers took to. Three days later, the police called me in for questioning. Needless to say, I was in shock.

"They put me through a simple police interrogation. I said how I'd hardly ever spoken to Matsumoto. It was true that I had hit a fellow student named Aoki three years before, but that was a perfectly ordinary, stupid argument, and I hadn't caused any trouble since. That was it. There is a rumor that you were hitting this Matsumoto, said the officer on duty. That's all it is, I told him, a rumor. Someone who has it in for me is spreading it around. There is no truth, no proof, no case.

"Word got around school that the police had questioned me. And the atmosphere in class grew even colder. A police summons was like a verdict—like, they didn't haul people in for no reason, right? Everyone believed I'd been beating up on Matsumoto. I don't know what nonsense Aoki was peddling, but everyone bought it. I didn't even want to know what the story was; I knew it was dirt. No one in the entire school would speak to me. As if by consensus—it had to be—I got the silent treatment. Even urgent requests from me got a deaf ear. I was avoided like the plague. My existence was wiped from their field of vision.

"Even the teachers did their best not to look in my direction. They'd say my name when they took roll, but they never called on me in class. Phys. Ed. was the worst. When the class split into teams, I wouldn't end up on either side. No one would pair up with me, and the gym teacher would pretend it wasn't happening. I went to school in silence, attended classes in silence, went home in silence. Day after day, a vacuum. After two or three weeks of this, I lost my appetite. I lost weight. I couldn't sleep at night. I'd lie there, all worked up, my head filled with this endless succession of ugly images. And when I was awake, my mind was in a fog. I wasn't sure if I was awake or asleep.

"I even laid off boxing practice. My folks got worried and asked me what was wrong. What was I supposed to say? Nothing, I'm just tired. What good would it do to tell them? After school I hid out in my room. There was nothing else for me to do. I'd see these things play out on the ceiling. I imagined all kinds of scenarios. Most often, I saw myself punching Aoki out. I'd catch him alone and I'd pummel him, over and over again. I'd tell him what I thought of him—a piece of trash—and I'd knock the crap out of him. He could scream and cry all he wanted—forgive me, forgive me—but I'd just keep hitting him, beating his face to a pulp. Only after a while, punching away, I'd start to get sick. It was fine at first, it was great, it served the bastard right. Then, slowly, this nausea would creep up in me. But I still wouldn't be able to stop beating Aoki up. I'd look up at the ceiling and Aoki's face would be there and I'd be hitting him. And I wouldn't be able to stop. Before long, he was a bloody mess and I felt like puking.

"I thought about getting up in front of everyone and declaring outright that I was innocent, that I hadn't done anything. But who was going to believe me? And why was it up to me to apologize to that bunch of turkeys who'd maw down anything Aoki said to begin with?

"So I was stuck. I couldn't give Aoki the beating he had coming, and I couldn't explain myself. I had to put up and shut up. It was only another half year. After this semester, school would be finished and I wouldn't have to answer to anyone. One half year more, sparring with the silence. But could I hold out that long? I doubted I could go one month. At home, I ticked off each day on my calendar—one more day down, one more day down. I was getting crushed. Thinking back on it now, I can't believe how close I got to the danger zone.

"My first hint of a reprieve came a month later. By accident, on my way to school, I found myself face-to-face with Aoki on the train. As usual, it was so packed you couldn't move. And there was Aoki, two or three people away, over someone's shoulder, facing me. I must have looked terrible, short on sleep, a neurotic wreck. At first, he gave me this smirk. Like, so how's it going now, eh? Aoki had to know that I knew that he was behind everything. Our eyes locked. We glared at each other.

But as I was staring the guy in the eye, a strange emotion came over me. Sure, I was furious at Aoki. I hated the guy; I wanted to kill him. But suddenly, at the same time, there in the train, I felt something like pity. I mean, was this really the best this joker could do? Was this all it took to give him such airs of superiority? Could he actually be so satisfied, so happy with himself, for *this*? It was pathetic. I was practically moved to grief. To think that this fool would be eternally incapable of knowing true happiness, true pride. That there existed creatures so lacking in human depth. Not that I'm such a deep guy, but at least I know a real human being when I see one. But his kind, no. His life was as flat as a piece of slate. It was all surface, no matter what he did. He was nothing.

"I kept looking him in the face as these emotions went through me, and I didn't feel like punching him out anymore. I couldn't have cared less about him. Honest, I was surprised how little I cared. And then I knew I could put up with another five months of the silence. I still had my pride. I wasn't going to let some slime like Aoki drag me down with him.

"That was the look I gave Aoki. He must have thought it was a stare-down, which he wasn't about to lose, and when the train reached the station we didn't break our gaze. But in the end, it was Aoki who wavered. Just the slightest tremble of his pupils, but I picked up on it. Right away. The look of a boxer whose legs are giving out on him. He's working them, only they're not moving. And the stiff doesn't get it; he thinks they're still pacing. But his legs are dead. They've died in their tracks and now his shoulders won't dance. Which means the power's gone out of his punch. It was that look. Something's wrong, but he can't tell what.

"After that, I was home free. I slept soundly, ate square meals, went to the gym. I wasn't going to be defeated. It wasn't like I had triumphed over Aoki, either. It was a matter of my not losing out on life. It's too easy to let yourself get ground down by those who give you shit. So I held out for five more months. No one said word one to me. I'm not wrong, I kept telling myself, everybody else is. I held my chest up every day I went to school. And after graduating, I went to a university in Kyushu. Far from any of that high-school lot."

At that, Ozawa let out a big sigh. Then he asked if I wanted another cup of coffee. No thanks, I said, I'd already had three.

"People who go through a heavy experience like that are changed men, like it or not," he said. "They change for the better and they change for the worse. On the good side, they become unshakable. Next to that half year, the rest of the suffering I've experienced doesn't even count. I can put up with almost anything. And I also am a lot more sensitive to the pain of people around me. That's on the plus side. It made me capable of making some real friends. But there's also the minus side. I mean, it's impossible, in my own mind, to believe in people. I don't hate people, and I haven't lost my faith in humanity. I've got a wife and kids. We've made a home and we protect each other. Those things you can't do without trust. It's just that, sure, we're living a good life right now, but if something were to happen, if something really were to come along and yank up everything by the roots, even surrounded by a happy family and good friends, I don't know what I'd do. What would happen if one day, for no reason, no one believes a word you say? It happens, you know. Suddenly, one day, out of the blue. I'm always thinking about it. Last time, it was only six months, but the next time? No one can say; there's no guarantee. I don't have confidence in how long I can hold out the next time. When I think of these things, I really get shaken up. I'll dream about it and wake up in the middle of the night. It happens a little too often, in fact. And when it happens, I wake my wife up and I hold on to her and cry. Sometimes for a whole hour, I'm so scared."

He broke off and looked out the window to the clouds. They'd barely moved. A heavy lid, bearing down from the heavens. Absorbing all color from the control tower and airplanes and ground-transport vehicles and tarmac and men in uniform.

"People like Aoki don't scare me. They're all over the place, but I don't trouble myself with them anymore. When I run into them, I don't get involved. I see them coming and I head the other way. I can spot them in an instant. But at the same time, I've got to admire the Aokis of this world. Their ability to lay low until the right moment, their knack for latching on to opportunities, their skill in fucking with people's minds—that's no ordinary talent. I hate their kind so much it makes me want to puke, but it is a talent.

"No, what really scares me is how easily, how uncritically, people will believe the crap that slime like Aoki deal out. How these Aoki types produce nothing themselves, don't have an idea in the world, and talk so nice, how this slime can sway gullible types to any opinion and get them to perform on cue, as a group. And this group never entertains even a sliver of doubt that they could be wrong. They think nothing of hurting someone, senselessly, permanently. They don't take any responsibility for their actions. Them. *They're* the real monsters. *They're* the ones I have nightmares about. In those dreams, there's only the silence. And these faceless people. Their silence seeps into everything like ice water. And then it all goes murky. And I'm dissolving and I'm screaming, but no one hears."

Ozawa just shook his head.

I waited for him to continue, but he was quiet. He folded his hands and lay them on the table.

"We still have time—how about a beer?" he said after a while.

Yeah, let's, I said. We probably both could use one.

—translated by Alfred Birnbaum

THE
elePHANT
VANISHES

W HEN THE ELEPHANT disappeared from our town's elephant house, I read about it in the newspaper. My alarm clock
woke me that day, as always, at 6:13. I went to the kitchen, made
coffee and toast, turned on the radio, spread the paper out on
the kitchen table, and proceeded to munch and read. I'm one of
those people who read the paper from beginning to end, in order, so it took me awhile to get to the article about the vanishing
elephant. The front page was filled with stories of SDI and the
trade friction with America, after which I plowed through the
national news, international politics, economics, letters to the
editor, book reviews, real-estate ads, sports reports, and finally,
the regional news.

The elephant article was the lead story in the regional section. The unusually large headline caught my eye: ELEPHANT
MISSING IN TOKYO SUBURB, and, beneath that, in type one
size smaller, CITIZENS' FEARS MOUNT. SOME CALL FOR PROBE.

There was a photo of policemen inspecting the empty elephant house. Without the elephant, something about the place seemed wrong. It looked bigger than it needed to be, blank and empty like some huge, dehydrated beast from which the innards had been plucked.

Brushing away my toast crumbs, I studied every line of the article. The elephant's absence had first been noticed at two o'clock on the afternoon of May 18—the day before—when men from the school-lunch company delivered their usual truckload of food (the elephant mostly ate leftovers from the lunches of children in the local elementary school). On the ground, still locked, lay the steel shackle that had been fastened to the elephant's hind leg, as though the elephant had slipped out of it. Nor was the elephant the only one missing. Also gone was its keeper, the man who had been in charge of the elephant's care and feeding from the start.

According to the article, the elephant and keeper had last been seen sometime after five o'clock the previous day (May 17) by a few pupils from the elementary school, who were visiting the elephant house, making crayon sketches. These pupils must have been the last to see the elephant, said the paper, since the keeper always closed the gate to the elephant enclosure when the six-o'clock siren blew.

There had been nothing unusual about either the elephant or its keeper at the time, according to the unanimous testimony of the pupils. The elephant had been standing where it always stood, in the middle of the enclosure, occasionally wagging its trunk from side to side or squinting its wrinkly eyes. It was such an awfully old elephant that its every move seemed a tremendous effort—so much so that people seeing it for the first time feared it might collapse at any moment and draw its final breath.

The elephant's age had led to its adoption by our town a year earlier. When financial problems caused the little private zoo on the edge of town to close its doors, a wildlife dealer found places for the other animals in zoos throughout the country. But all the zoos had plenty of elephants, apparently, and not one of them was willing to take in a feeble old thing that looked as if it might die of a heart attack at any moment. And so, after its companions were gone, the elephant stayed alone in the decaying zoo for nearly four months with nothing to do—not that it had had anything to do before.

This caused a lot of difficulty, both for the zoo and for the town. The zoo had sold its land to a developer, who was planning to put up a high-rise condo building, and the town had already issued him a permit. The longer the elephant problem remained unresolved, the more interest the developer had to pay for nothing. Still, simply killing the thing would have been out of the question. If it had been a spider monkey or a bat, they might have been able to get away with it, but the killing of an elephant would have been too hard to cover up, and if it ever came out afterward, the repercussions would have been tremendous. And so the various parties had met to deliberate on the matter, and they formulated an agreement on the disposition of the old elephant:

1. The town would take ownership of the elephant at no cost.

2. The developer would, without compensation, provide land for housing the elephant.

3. The zoo's former owners would be responsible for paying the keeper's wages.

I had had my own private interest in the elephant problem from the very outset, and I kept a scrapbook with every clipping I could find on it. I had even gone to hear the town council's debates on the matter, which is why I am able to give such a full and accurate account of the course of events. And while my account may prove somewhat lengthy, I have chosen to set it down here in case the handling of the elephant problem should bear directly upon the elephant's disappearance.

When the mayor finished negotiating the agreement—with its provision that the town would take charge of the elephant—

a movement opposing the measure boiled up from within the ranks of the opposition party (whose very existence I had never imagined until then). "Why must the town take ownership of the elephant?" they demanded of the mayor, and they raised the following points (sorry for all these lists, but I use them to make things easier to understand):

1. The elephant problem was a question for private enterprise—the zoo and the developer; there was no reason for the town to become involved.

2. Care and feeding costs would be too high.

3. What did the mayor intend to do about the security problem?

4. What merit would there be in the town's having its own elephant?

"The town has any number of responsibilities it should be taking care of before it gets into the business of keeping an elephant—sewer repair, the purchase of a new fire engine, etcetera," the opposition group declared, and while they did not say it in so many words, they hinted at the possibility of some secret deal between the mayor and the developer.

In response, the mayor had this to say:

1. If the town permitted the construction of high-rise condos, its tax revenues would increase so dramatically that the cost of keeping an elephant would be insignificant by comparison; thus it made sense for the town to take on the care of this elephant.

2. The elephant was so old that it neither ate very much nor was likely to pose a danger to anyone.

3. When the elephant died, the town would take full possession of the land donated by the developer.

4. The elephant could become the town's symbol.

The long debate reached the conclusion that the town would take charge of the elephant after all. As an old, well-established residential suburb, the town boasted a relatively affluent citizenry, and its financial footing was sound. The adoption of a homeless elephant was a move that people could look upon favorably. People like old elephants better than sewers and fire engines.

I myself was all in favor of having the town care for the elephant. True, I was getting sick of high-rise condos, but I liked the idea of my town's owning an elephant.

A wooded area was cleared, and the elementary school's aging gym was moved there as an elephant house. The man who had served as the elephant's keeper for many years would come to live in the house with the elephant. The children's lunch scraps would serve as the elephant's feed. Finally, the elephant itself was carted in a trailer to its new home, there to live out its remaining years.

I joined the crowd at the elephant-house dedication ceremonies. Standing before the elephant, the mayor delivered a speech (on the town's development and the enrichment of its cultural facilities); one elementary-school pupil, representing the student body, stood up to read a composition ("Please live a long and healthy life, Mr. Elephant"); there was a sketch contest (sketching the elephant thereafter became an integral component of the pupils' artistic education); and each of two young women in swaying dresses (neither of whom was especially good-looking) fed the elephant a bunch of bananas. The elephant endured these virtually meaningless (for the elephant, entirely meaningless) formalities with hardly a twitch, and it chomped on the bananas with a vacant stare. When it finished eating the bananas, everyone applauded.

On its right rear leg, the elephant wore a solid, heavy-looking steel cuff from which there stretched a thick chain perhaps thirty feet long, and this in turn was securely fastened to a concrete slab. Anyone could see what a sturdy anchor held the beast in place: The elephant could have struggled with all its might for a hundred years and never broken the thing.

I couldn't tell if the elephant was bothered by its shackle. On the surface, at least, it seemed all but unconscious of the enormous chunk of metal wrapped around its leg. It kept its blank gaze fixed on some indeterminate point in space, its ears and a few white hairs on its body waving gently in the breeze.

The elephant's keeper was a small, bony old man. It was hard to guess his age; he could have been in his early sixties or late seventies. He was one of those people whose appearance is no longer influenced by their age after they pass a certain point in life. His skin had the same darkly ruddy, sunburned look both summer and winter, his hair was stiff and short, his eyes were small. His face had no distinguishing characteristics, but his almost perfectly circular ears stuck out on either side with disturbing prominence.

He was not an unfriendly man. If someone spoke to him, he would reply, and he expressed himself clearly. If he wanted to he could be almost charming—though you always knew he was somewhat ill at ease. Generally, he remained a reticent, lonely-looking old man. He seemed to like the children who visited the elephant house, and he worked at being nice to them, but the children never really warmed to him.

The only one who did that was the elephant. The keeper lived in a small prefab room attached to the elephant house, and all day long he stayed with the elephant, attending to its needs. They had been together for more than ten years, and you could sense their closeness in every gesture and look. Whenever the elephant was standing there blankly and the keeper wanted it to move, all he had to do was stand next to the elephant, tap it on a front leg, and whisper something in its ear. Then, swaying its huge bulk, the elephant would go exactly where the keeper had indicated, take up its new position, and continue staring at a point in space.

On weekends, I would drop by the elephant house and study these operations, but I could never figure out the principle on which the keeper-elephant communication was based. Maybe the elephant understood a few simple words (it had certainly been living long enough), or perhaps it received its information through variations in the taps on its leg. Or possibly it had some special power resembling mental telepathy and could read the keeper's mind. I once asked the keeper how he gave his orders to the elephant, but the old man just smiled and said, "We've been together a long time."

AND SO A YEAR went by. Then, without warning, the elephant vanished. One day it was there, and the next it had ceased to be.

I poured myself a second cup of coffee and read the story again from beginning to end. Actually, it was a pretty strange article—the kind that might excite Sherlock Holmes. "Look at this, Watson," he'd say, tapping his pipe. "A very interesting article. Very interesting indeed."

What gave the article its air of strangeness was the obvious confusion and bewilderment of the reporter. And this confusion and bewilderment clearly came from the absurdity of the situation itself. You could see how the reporter had struggled to find clever ways around the absurdity in order to write a "normal" article. But the struggle had only driven his confusion and bewilderment to a hopeless extreme.

For example, the article used such expressions as "the elephant escaped," but if you looked at the entire piece it became obvious that the elephant had in no way "escaped." It had vanished into thin air. The reporter revealed his own conflicted state of mind by saying that a few "details" remained "unclear," but this was not a phenomenon that could be disposed of by using such ordinary terminology as "details" or "unclear," I felt.

First, there was the problem of the steel cuff that had been fastened to the elephant's leg. This had been found *still locked.* The most reasonable explanation for this would be that the keeper had unlocked the ring, removed it from the elephant's leg, *locked the ring again,* and run off with the elephant—a hypothesis to which the paper clung with desperate tenacity despite the fact that the keeper had no key! Only two keys existed, and they, for security's sake, were kept in locked safes, one in police headquarters and the other in the firehouse, both beyond the reach of the keeper—or of anyone else who might attempt to steal them. And even if someone had succeeded in stealing a key, there was no need whatever for that person to make a point of returning the key after using it. Yet the following morning both keys were found in their respective safes at the police and fire stations. Which brings us to the conclusion that the elephant pulled its leg out of that solid steel ring without the aid of a key—an absolute impossibility unless someone had sawed the foot off.

The second problem was the route of escape. The elephant house and grounds were surrounded by a massive fence nearly ten feet high. The question of security had been hotly debated in the town council, and the town had settled upon a system that might be considered somewhat excessive for keeping one old elephant. Heavy iron bars had been anchored in a thick concrete foundation (the cost of the fence was borne by the real-estate company), and there was only a single entrance, which was found locked from the inside. There was no way the elephant could have escaped from this fortresslike enclosure.

The third problem was elephant tracks. Directly behind the elephant enclosure was a steep hill, which the animal could not possibly have climbed, so even if we suppose that the elephant had somehow managed to pull its leg out of the steel ring and leap over the ten-foot-high fence, it would still have had to escape down the path to the front of the enclosure, and there was not a single mark anywhere in the soft earth of that path that could be seen as an elephant's footprint.

Riddled as it was with such perplexities and labored circumlocutions, the newspaper article as a whole left but one possible conclusion: The elephant had not escaped. It had vanished.

Needless to say, however, neither the newspaper nor the police nor the mayor was willing to admit—openly, at least—that the elephant had vanished. The police were continuing to investigate, their spokesman saying only that the elephant either "was taken or was allowed to escape in a clever, deliberately calculated move. Because of the difficulty involved in hiding an elephant, it is only a matter of time till we solve the case." To this optimistic assessment he added that they were planning to search the woods in the area with the aid of local hunters' clubs and sharpshooters from the national Self-Defense Force.

The mayor had held a news conference, in which he apologized for the inadequacy of the town's police resources. At the same time, he declared, "Our elephant-security system is in no way inferior to similar facilities in any zoo in the country. Indeed, it is far stronger and far more fail-safe than the standard cage." He also observed, "This is a dangerous and senseless antisocial act of the most malicious kind, and we cannot allow it to go unpunished."

As they had the year before, the opposition-party members of the town council made accusations. "We intend to look into the political responsibility of the mayor; he has colluded with private enterprise in order to sell the townspeople a bill of goods on the solution of the elephant problem."

One "worried-looking" mother, thirty-seven, was interviewed by the paper. "Now I'm afraid to let my children out to play," she said.

The coverage included a detailed summary of the steps leading to the town's decision to adopt the elephant, an aerial sketch of the elephant house and grounds, and brief histories of both the elephant and the keeper who had vanished with it. The man, Noboru Watanabe, sixty-three, was from Tateyama, in Chiba Prefecture. He had worked for many years as a keeper in the mammalian section of the zoo, and "had the complete trust of the zoo authorities, both for his abundant knowledge of these animals and for his warm sincere personality." The elephant had been sent from East Africa twenty-two years earlier, but little was known about its exact age or its "personality." The report concluded with a request from the police for citizens of the town to come forward with any information they might have regarding the elephant.

I thought about this request for a while as I drank my second cup of coffee, but I decided not to call the police—both because I preferred not to come into contact with them if I could help it and because I felt the police would not believe what I had to tell them. What good would it do to talk to people like that, who would not even consider the possibility that the elephant had simply vanished?

I took my scrapbook down from the shelf, cut out the elephant article, and pasted it in. Then I washed the dishes and left for the office.

I watched the search on the seven-o'clock news. There were hunters carrying large-bore rifles loaded with tranquilizer darts, Self-Defense Force troops, policemen, and firemen combing every square inch of the woods and hills in the immediate area as helicopters hovered overhead. Of course, we're talking about the kind of "woods" and "hills" you find in the suburbs outside Tokyo, so they didn't have an enormous area to cover. With that many people involved, a day should have been more than enough to do the job. And they weren't searching for some tiny homicidal maniac: They were after a huge African elephant. There was a limit to the number of places a thing like that could hide. But still they had not managed to find it. The chief of police appeared on the screen, saying, "We intend to continue the search." And the anchorman concluded the report, "Who released the elephant, and how? Where have they hidden it? What was their motive? Everything remains shrouded in mystery."

The search went on for several days, but the authorities were unable to discover a single clue to the elephant's whereabouts. I studied the newspaper reports, clipped them all, and pasted them in my scrapbook—including editorial cartoons on the subject. The album filled up quickly, and I had to buy another. Despite their enormous volume, the clippings contained not one fact of the kind that I was looking for. The reports were either pointless or off the mark: ELEPHANT STILL MISSING, GLOOM THICK IN SEARCH HQ, MOB BEHIND DISAPPEARANCE? And even articles like this became noticeably scarcer after a week had gone by, until there was virtually nothing. A few of the weekly magazines carried sensational stories—one even hired a psychic—

but they had nothing to substantiate their wild headlines. It seemed that people were beginning to shove the elephant case into the large category of "unsolvable mysteries." The disappearance of one old elephant and one old elephant keeper would have no impact on the course of society. The earth would continue its monotonous rotations, politicians would continue issuing unreliable proclamations, people would continue yawning on their way to the office, children would continue studying for their college-entrance exams. Amid the endless surge and ebb of everyday life, interest in a missing elephant could not last forever. And so a number of unremarkable months went by, like a tired army marching past a window.

Whenever I had a spare moment, I would visit the house where the elephant no longer lived. A thick chain had been wrapped round and round the bars of the yard's iron gate, to keep people out. Peering inside, I could see that the elephant-house door had also been chained and locked, as though the police were trying to make up for having failed to find the elephant by multiplying the layers of security on the now-empty elephant house. The area was deserted, the previous crowds having been replaced by a flock of pigeons resting on the roof. No one took care of the grounds any longer, and thick green summer grass had sprung up there as if it had been waiting for this opportunity. The chain coiled around the door of the elephant house reminded me of a huge snake set to guard a ruined palace in a thick forest. A few short months without its elephant had given the place an air of doom and desolation that hung there like a huge, oppressive rain cloud.

I MET HER NEAR the end of September. It had been raining that day from morning to night—the kind of soft, monotonous, misty rain that often falls at that time of year, washing away bit by bit the memories of summer burned into the earth. Coursing down the gutters, all those memories flowed into the sewers and rivers, to be carried to the deep, dark ocean.

We noticed each other at the party my company threw to

launch its new advertising campaign. I work for the PR section of a major manufacturer of electrical appliances, and at the time I was in charge of publicity for a coordinated line of kitchen equipment, which was scheduled to go on the market in time for the autumn-wedding and winter-bonus seasons. My job was to negotiate with several women's magazines for tie-in articles—not the kind of work that takes a great deal of intelligence, but I had to see to it that the articles they wrote didn't smack of advertising. When magazines gave us publicity, we rewarded them by placing ads in their pages. They scratched our backs, we scratched theirs.

As an editor of a magazine for young housewives, she had come to the party for material for one of these "articles." I happened to be in charge of showing her around, pointing out the features of the colorful refrigerators and coffeemakers and microwave ovens and juicers that a famous Italian designer had done for us.

"The most important point is unity," I explained. "Even the most beautifully designed item dies if it is out of balance with its surroundings. Unity of design, unity of color, unity of function: This is what today's *kit-chin* needs above all else. Research tells us that a housewife spends the largest part of her day in the *kit-chin*. The *kit-chin* is her workplace, her study, her living room. Which is why she does all she can to make the *kit-chin* a pleasant place to be. It has nothing to do with size. Whether it's large or small, one fundamental principle governs every successful *kit-chin,* and that principle is unity. This is the concept underlying the design of our new series. Look at this cooktop, for example. . . ."

She nodded and scribbled things in a small notebook, but it was obvious that she had little interest in the material, nor did I have any personal stake in our new cooktop. Both of us were doing our jobs.

"You know a lot about kitchens," she said when I finished. She used the Japanese word, without picking up on "*kit-chin.*"

"That's what I do for a living," I answered with a professional smile. "Aside from that, though, I do like to cook. Nothing fancy, but I cook for myself every day."

"Still, I wonder if unity is all that necessary for a kitchen."

"We say '*kit-chin*,' " I advised her. "No big deal, but the company wants us to use the English."

"Oh. Sorry. But still, I wonder. Is unity so important for a *kit-chin*? What do *you* think?"

"My personal opinion? That doesn't come out until I take my necktie off," I said with a grin. "But today I'll make an exception. A kitchen probably *does* need a few things more than it needs unity. But those other elements are things you can't sell. And in this pragmatic world of ours, things you can't sell don't count for much."

"*Is* the world such a pragmatic place?"

I took out a cigarette and lit it with my lighter.

"I don't know—the word just popped out," I said. "But it explains a lot. It makes work easier, too. You can play games with it, make up neat expressions: 'essentially pragmatic,' or 'pragmatic in essence.' If you look at things that way, you avoid all kinds of complicated problems."

"What an interesting view!"

"Not really. It's what everybody thinks. Oh, by the way, we've got some pretty good champagne. Care to have some?"

"Thanks. I'd love to."

As we chatted over champagne, we realized we had several mutual acquaintances. Since our part of the business world was not a very big pond, if you tossed in a few pebbles, one or two were bound to hit a mutual acquaintance. In addition, she and my kid sister happened to have graduated from the same university. With markers like this to follow, our conversation went along smoothly.

She was unmarried, and so was I. She was twenty-six, and I was thirty-one. She wore contact lenses, and I wore glasses. She praised my necktie, and I praised her jacket. We compared rents and complained about our jobs and salaries. In other words, we were beginning to like each other. She was an attractive woman, and not at all pushy. I stood there talking with her for a full twenty minutes, unable to discover a single reason not to think well of her.

As the party was breaking up, I invited her to join me in the hotel's cocktail lounge, where we settled in to continue our conversation. A soundless rain went on falling outside the lounge's panoramic window, the lights of the city sending blurry messages through the mist. A damp hush held sway over the nearly empty cocktail lounge. She ordered a frozen daiquiri and I had a scotch on the rocks.

Sipping our drinks, we carried on the kind of conversation that a man and woman have in a bar when they have just met and are beginning to like each other. We talked about our college days, our tastes in music, sports, our daily routines.

Then I told her about the elephant. Exactly how this happened, I can't recall. Maybe we were talking about something having to do with animals, and that was the connection. Or maybe, unconsciously, I had been looking for someone—a good listener—to whom I could present my own, unique view on the elephant's disappearance. Or, then again, it might have been the liquor that got me talking.

In any case, the second the words left my mouth, I knew that I had brought up one of the least suitable topics I could have found for this occasion. No, I should never have mentioned the elephant. The topic was—what?—too complete, too closed.

I tried to hurry on to something else, but as luck would have it she was more interested than most in the case of the vanishing elephant, and once I admitted that I had seen the elephant many times she showered me with questions—what kind of elephant was it, how did I think it had escaped, what did it eat, wasn't it a danger to the community, and so forth.

I told her nothing more than what everybody knew from the news, but she seemed to sense constraint in my tone of voice. I had never been good at telling lies.

As if she had not noticed anything strange about my behavior, she sipped her second daiquiri and asked, "Weren't you shocked when the elephant disappeared? It's not the kind of thing that somebody could have predicted."

"No, probably not," I said. I took a pretzel from the mound in the glass dish on our table, snapped it in two, and ate half. The waiter replaced our ashtray with an empty one.

She looked at me expectantly. I took out another cigarette and lit it. I had quit smoking three years earlier but had begun again when the elephant disappeared.

"Why 'probably not'? You mean you could have predicted it?"

"No, of course I couldn't have predicted it," I said with a smile. "For an elephant to disappear all of a sudden one day—there's no precedent, no need, for such a thing to happen. It doesn't make any logical sense."

"But still, your answer was very strange. When I said, 'It's not the kind of thing that somebody could have predicted,' you said, 'No, probably not.' Most people would have said, 'You're right,' or 'Yeah, it's weird,' or something. See what I mean?"

I sent a vague nod in her direction and raised my hand to call the waiter. A kind of tentative silence took hold as I waited for him to bring me my next scotch.

"I'm finding this a little hard to grasp," she said softly. "You were carrying on a perfectly normal conversation with me until a couple of minutes ago—at least until the subject of the elephant came up. Then something funny happened. I can't understand you anymore. Something's wrong. Is it the elephant? Or are my ears playing tricks on me?"

"There's nothing wrong with your ears," I said.

"So then it's you. The problem's with you."

I stuck my finger in my glass and stirred the ice. I like the sound of ice in a whiskey glass.

"I wouldn't call it a 'problem,' exactly. It's not that big a deal. I'm not hiding anything. I'm just not sure I can talk about it very well, so I'm trying not to say anything at all. But you're right—it's very strange."

"What do you mean?"

It was no use: I'd have to tell her the story. I took one gulp of whiskey and started.

"The thing is, I was probably the last one to see the elephant before it disappeared. I saw it after seven o'clock on the evening of May seventeenth, and they noticed it was gone on the afternoon of the eighteenth. Nobody saw it in between because they lock the elephant house at six."

"I don't get it. If they closed the house at six, how did you see it after seven?"

"There's a kind of cliff behind the elephant house. A steep hill on private property, with no real roads. There's one spot, on the back of the hill, where you can see into the elephant house. I'm probably the only one who knows about it."

I had found the spot purely by chance. Strolling through the area one Sunday afternoon, I had lost my way and come out at the top of the cliff. I found a little flat open patch, just big enough for a person to stretch out in, and when I looked down through the bushes, there was the elephant-house roof. Below the edge of the roof was a fairly large vent opening, and through it I had a clear view of the inside of the elephant house.

I made it a habit after that to visit the place every now and then to look at the elephant when it was inside the house. If anyone had asked me why I bothered doing such a thing, I wouldn't have had a decent answer. I simply enjoyed watching the elephant during its private time. There was nothing more to it than that. I couldn't see the elephant when the house was dark inside, of course, but in the early hours of the evening the keeper would have the lights on the whole time he was taking care of the elephant, which enabled me to study the scene in detail.

What struck me immediately when I saw the elephant and keeper alone together was the obvious liking they had for each other—something they never displayed when they were out before the public. Their affection was evident in every gesture. It almost seemed as if they stored away their emotions during the day, taking care not to let anyone notice them, and took them out at night when they could be alone. Which is not to say that they did anything different when they were by themselves inside. The elephant just stood there, as blank as ever, and the keeper would perform those tasks one would normally expect him to do as a keeper: scrubbing down the elephant with a deck broom, picking up the elephant's enormous droppings, cleaning up after the elephant ate. But there was no way to mistake the special warmth, the sense of trust, between them. While the keeper swept the floor, the elephant would wave its trunk and pat the keeper's back. I liked to watch the elephant doing that.

"Have you always been fond of elephants?" she asked. "I mean, not just that particular elephant?"

"Hmm . . . come to think of it, I do like elephants," I said. "There's something about them that excites me. I guess I've always liked them. I wonder why."

"And that day, too, after the sun went down, I suppose you were up on the hill by yourself, looking at the elephant. May— what day was it?"

"The seventeenth. May seventeenth at seven P.M. The days were already very long by then, and the sky had a reddish glow, but the lights were on in the elephant house."

"And was there anything unusual about the elephant or the keeper?"

"Well, there was and there wasn't. I can't say exactly. It's not as if they were standing right in front of me. I'm probably not the most reliable witness."

"What did happen, exactly?"

I took a swallow of my now somewhat watery scotch. The rain outside the windows was still coming down, no stronger or weaker than before, a static element in a landscape that would never change.

"Nothing happened, really. The elephant and the keeper were doing what they always did—cleaning, eating, playing around with each other in that friendly way of theirs. It wasn't what they *did* that was different. It's the way they looked. Something about the balance between them."

"The balance?"

"In size. Of their bodies. The elephant's and the keeper's. The balance seemed to have changed somewhat. I had the feeling that to some extent the difference between them had shrunk."

She kept her gaze fixed on her daiquiri glass for a time. I could see that the ice had melted and that the water was working its way through the cocktail like a tiny ocean current.

"Meaning that the elephant had gotten smaller?"

"Or the keeper had gotten bigger. Or both simultaneously."

"And you didn't tell this to the police?"

"No, of course not," I said. "I'm sure they wouldn't have believed me. And if I had told them I was watching the elephant from the cliff at a time like that, I'd have ended up as their number one suspect."

"Still, are you *certain* that the balance between them had changed?"

"Probably. I can only say 'probably.' I don't have any proof, and as I keep saying, I was looking at them through the air vent. But I had looked at them like that I don't know how many times before, so it's hard for me to believe that I could make a mistake about something as basic as the relation of their sizes."

In fact, I had wondered at the time whether my eyes were playing tricks on me. I had tried closing and opening them and shaking my head, but the elephant's size remained the same. It definitely looked as if it had shrunk—so much so that at first I thought the town might have got hold of a new, smaller elephant. But I hadn't heard anything to that effect, and I would never have missed any news reports about elephants. If this was not a new elephant, the only possible conclusion was that the old elephant had, for one reason or another, shrunk. As I watched, it became obvious to me that this smaller elephant had all the same gestures as the old one. It would stamp happily on the ground with its right foot while it was being washed, and with its now somewhat narrower trunk it would pat the keeper on the back.

It was a mysterious sight. Looking through the vent, I had the feeling that a different, chilling kind of time was flowing through the elephant house—but nowhere else. And it seemed to me, too, that the elephant and the keeper were gladly giving themselves over to this new order that was trying to envelop them—or that had already partially succeeded in enveloping them.

Altogether, I was probably watching the scene in the elephant house for less than a half hour. The lights went out at seven-thirty—much earlier than usual—and from that point on, everything was wrapped in darkness. I waited in my spot, hoping that the lights would go on again, but they never did. That was the last I saw of the elephant.

"So, then, you believe that the elephant kept shrinking until it was small enough to escape through the bars, or else that it simply dissolved into nothingness. Is that it?"

"I don't know," I said. "All I'm trying to do is recall what I saw with my own eyes, as accurately as possible. I'm hardly thinking about what happened after that. The visual image I have is so strong that, to be honest, it's practically impossible for me to go beyond it."

That was all I could say about the elephant's disappearance. And just as I had feared, the story of the elephant was too particular, too complete in itself, to work as a topic of conversation between a young man and woman who had just met. A silence descended upon us after I had finished my tale. What subject could either of us bring up after a story about an elephant that had vanished—a story that offered virtually no openings for further discussion? She ran her finger around the edge of her cocktail glass, and I sat there reading and rereading the words stamped on my coaster. I never should have told her about the elephant. It was not the kind of story you could tell freely to anyone.

"When I was a little girl, our cat disappeared," she offered after a long silence. "But still, for a cat to disappear and for an elephant to disappear—those are two different stories."

"Yeah, really. There's no comparison. Think of the size difference."

Thirty minutes later, we were saying good-bye outside the hotel. She suddenly remembered that she had left her umbrella in the cocktail lounge, so I went up in the elevator and brought it down to her. It was a brick-red umbrella with a large handle.

"Thanks," she said.

"Good night," I said.

That was the last time I saw her. We talked once on the phone after that, about some details in her tie-in article. While we spoke, I thought seriously about inviting her out for dinner, but I ended up not doing it. It just didn't seem to matter one way or the other.

I felt like this a lot after my experience with the vanishing elephant. I would begin to think I wanted to do something, but then I would become incapable of distinguishing between the probable results of doing it and of not doing it. I often get the feeling that things around me have lost their proper balance, though it could be that my perceptions are playing tricks on me. Some kind of balance inside me has broken down since the elephant affair, and maybe that causes external phenomena to strike my eye in a strange way. It's probably something in me.

I continue to sell refrigerators and toaster ovens and coffee-makers in the pragmatic world, based on afterimages of memories I retain from that world. The more pragmatic I try to become, the more successfully I sell—our campaign has succeeded beyond our most optimistic forecasts—and the more people I succeed in selling myself to. That's probably because people are looking for a kind of unity in this *kit-chin* we know as the world. Unity of design. Unity of color. Unity of function.

The papers print almost nothing about the elephant anymore. People seem to have forgotten that their town once owned an elephant. The grass that took over the elephant enclosure has withered now, and the area has the feel of winter.

The elephant and keeper have vanished completely. They will never be coming back.

—*translated by Jay Rubin*

Also by HARUKI MURAKAMI

"A world-class writer who takes big risks. . . . If Murakami is the voice of a generation . . . then it is the generation of Thomas Pynchon and Don DeLillo."

—*Washington Post Book World*

HARD-BOILED WONDERLAND AND
THE END OF THE WORLD

In this hyperkinetic novel, Japan's most popular fiction writer hurtles into the consciousness of the West, drawing readers into a highly stylized postmodern detective story.

Fiction/Literature/0-679-74346-4

DANCE DANCE DANCE

In search of a former lover who has vanished, the protagonist of this wildly imagined novel turns up clues that draw him deeper into a labyrinth of sexual violence and metaphysical dread.

Fiction/Literature/0-679-75379-6

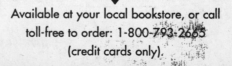

Available at your local bookstore, or call
toll-free to order: 1-800-793-2665
(credit cards only).